FINAL BOARDING

FINAL BOARDING

A NOVEL BY

A.J. MAYERS

www.mascotbooks.com

Final Boarding

For more information, please contact:
Mascot Books
560 Herndon Parkway #120
Herndon, VA 20170
info@mascotbooks.com

Library of Congress Control Number: 2016914105

CPSIA Code: PBANG0916A
ISBN-13: 978-1-63177-916-9

www.aj-mayers.com
www.finalboardingbook.com

Printed in the United States of America

For Mom and Dad, my biggest fans

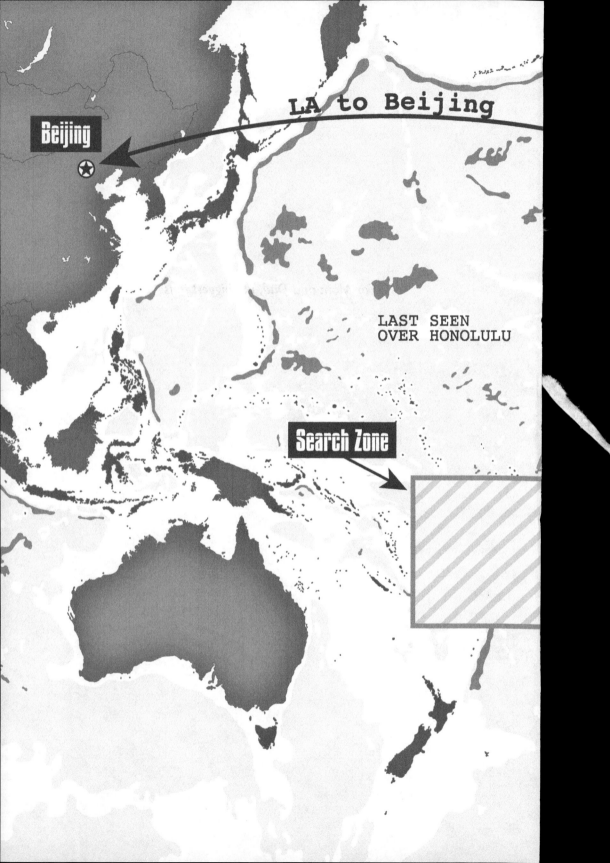

Los Angeles

DIVERTED

Phoenix Airlines

PHOENIX AIRLINES
FLIGHT 619

———————— INTENDED ROUTE

— — — — — — — POSSIBLE ROUTE

Acknowledgements

Taking flight with this book was no easy feat. To my parents, who taught me how to walk and who have been there for me since day one, thank you for believing in me and letting me fly out from the nest while giving me the support and love to push myself harder than I ever have before. Thank you to my friends and mentors who have supported me in my career endeavors. Special thanks to Mary Lou, Susan, Lawrence, Michael, Alexis, Jing, Luke, Kevin, Jessica, and Wanjiru for being an integral part in finessing this story. And to the reader, thank you. You're in for a turbulent ride. Buckle your seat belts and enjoy the flight...

Preface

In Greek mythology, the phoenix was a bird that could regenerate and be reborn. It was associated with our solar system's only star, the sun. When the phoenix's life ended, it would erupt into flames and turn into ashes. From those ashes, it would rise again; thus, a new birth and life were given to the bird. Renewal. Rebirth. Regrowth. It was offered a new opportunity to take flight and continue to write its own story...

The story that will unfold is one of great mystery, scandal, and cover-ups. Mankind has had many mysteries. Some may never be answered, such as where we came from, or whether there really is a God who created us. But there are mysteries in our world that could be easily solved through our advancements in technology and science. For certain questions, we can find proofs to solve them; however, one mystery defied those rules and baffled the world. The disappearance of Phoenix Airlines Flight 619 in the summer of 2016 would go down as one of the greatest mysteries in the history of aviation, right alongside the disappearance of Amelia Earhart's airplane during her world flight in 1937, which, to this day, has never been found.

Professor Patrick Baldwin left behind an account of his journey to solve and find the missing Phoenix Airlines 619, or, as the media called it, PA 619 or Flight 619. What he discovered in his death-defying journey would change the course of history and mankind's quest on Earth forever. There are many powerful people on this planet who do not want you to know the truth, but the story that will unfold here details the biggest cover-up in the history of aviation and the media. What you are about to read is Baldwin's personal journal documenting his involvement with PA 619 and accounts of several others affected by the airliner's disappearance. The journal was found inside his cabin in Montana a few years after the airliner's disappearance. This is his story...

I can clearly remember the first time I ever *heard* real quiet. The irony of this quiet calm was that I was falling from the sky at 12,500 feet, at a rate of 115 miles per hour. It was only for one minute, but it felt like the longest minute of my life. The wind was roaring in my ears. The skin on my face, particularly my cheeks, was being pressed back into my skull. I clenched my teeth closed, so as not to suck in the cold air from my plummet to Earth. The distance between the ground and me was lessening. I was strapped tandem to a man with long gray hair, who signaled a thumbs-up to me before he pulled the cord of our parachute.

There was a sudden jolt, and my body was jerked up opposite to the ground. The sensation was strange, and my adrenaline rush began to subside as the parachute completely expanded. It was the feeling you get when you take your first drop on a rollercoaster ride. You know—the empty feeling in the pit of your stomach when you fall so suddenly at an extreme speed while your metal cart winds left, right, up, and down over metal bars, nuts, and bolts. That was the only other instance that feeling in my stomach had occurred. We were airborne and slowly gliding safely down to the Montana prairie below us.

"What a rush, eh?" my tandem skydiving instructor said while he maneuvered us left and right, with the apparent goal to ensure we landed in a field a few yards away from the skydiving company's building.

I simply nodded and gave him a thumbs-up. I believed my voice had been left behind on the airplane we had just dived out of, and it had not caught up with me to reply with words. It did not matter, though. Being up there in the sky was very calming, even after the adrenaline of the free fall. There was complete silence. I could not hear anything for miles. High up in the air, it was as if sound did not exist. There was not even a hint of wind or any other airplanes in the vicinity. We were still too high up to hear any of the vehicles that were driving on the roads below. In the distance, all I could see were mountains and the outskirts of the city where I attended the university. It felt like I was flying. It did not even faze me that there was another human strapped to me, or the fact that if the ropes of the parachute gave way, we would drop to the ground and die. This man's weight would be my anchor to the soil below.

I could hear silence. It sounds like an oxymoron, but if silence had a sound, then that day, I heard it. It was peaceful. It was at that moment that my true calling came to me. I loved the sky and airplanes. I was a freshman in college at the time, and that skydive had been something on my bucket list that I wanted to cross off before death. The study of aviation became my aspiration. In the weeks that would follow my jump, I would eventually change my major to aerospace engineering. My new bucket list goal was to improve the way people travel in the atmosphere.

The descent back to the ground took probably ten minutes or so. It was therapeutic for me to take in the silence. I closed my eyes and remembered playing with model airplanes as a child. In third grade, I had told my mother my dream to be an astronaut. In fourth grade, I changed my mind, because a space shuttle that was making its way back to Earth after a mission in space had exploded over the United States. That scared me, and my interest in flying to outer space ceased. A decision to stick to something closer to home felt like a safer bet. I had a love for flying. Every time we took a family trip that required air travel, I was thrilled. I would try to meet as many pilots as I could over my years of family air travel. I even dabbled with the idea of becoming a pilot and maneuvering my own aircraft one day.

Yet, there I was, eighteen year-old Patrick Baldwin, slowly descending toward the ground after my first-ever skydiving experience. I was not on a track or training to become a pilot. As I'd matured during my teenage years, my inner child had become more fascinated with building airplanes.

It was not until one fateful morning, on July 14, 2016, that I heard that same silence once again. This time it was not because I was parachuting back to the ground. It was because I had received the most awful and shocking news. It was unnerving. The shock was so sudden. I remember chills running up and down my spine. I began to cry, but the tears were silent. I was not sobbing aloud. For an entire minute, it was as if I were back up in that Montana sky, where everything was calm and peaceful. Presently, there was anything but calm running through the nerves in my system. I could feel the blood pumping through the chambers of my heart. My silence was instantly interrupted by a series of phone calls. People in my life, who cared about me and probably could not believe the news, must have mustered some kind of courage to call my cell phone, even though there was a chance that I was dead or missing. To explain what led up to this nightmare of a news revelation, I need to explain how I was even alive that July morning to write this tale.

July 13, 2016

I was working as an aerospace engineer for a newly established commercial airline company called Phoenix Airlines. I had specialized in aeronautics while in college, so I worked with aircraft that flew in Earth's atmosphere, such as commercial airplanes. A very wealthy entrepreneur by the name of Royce Killington had established Phoenix Airlines in 2014. He was the son of the late Jackson Killington, a billionaire who struck it rich with a real estate business in Texas. Royce Killington became CEO of his company, which quickly rose in popularity because it was affordable to travelers. The airplanes were very sleek, and there was no division of business or economy class. The planes were designed for everyone to be treated equally. Royce invested a large amount of money in Phoenix. He was not out to make a profit—he was an heir to billions. Money was never an issue for him. He wanted to bring the luxury of travel, which he was born into and accustomed, to the masses. Phoenix Airlines grew quickly within a year, and several competing major airlines were at the mercy of its rapid growth. Some companies folded and were eventually acquired by Phoenix.

Phoenix Airlines was the new way to travel. Every seat was spacious, and the food and drinks were five-star quality. The entertainment systems attached to each chair were state-of-the-art, with the latest films, TV shows, and video games. Wireless Internet was free for every passenger, which was a first for the commercial airline business. If they did not own a laptop or smartphone, then they could access the Internet on the entertainment video screens on the seats and surf the web or check email. And if that was not enough to get travelers excited about boarding the new top-of-the-line commercial airplanes, each seat also had access to a phone that was also free to use to make calls to anywhere in the world. Phoenix Airlines' goal was all about luxury, convenience, connectivity, entertainment, and excellent customer service. A one-way ticket domestically was ninety-nine dollars or less. For a domestic round trip, one could expect to pay less than two hundred dollars. And to travel anywhere in the world, the highest priced ticket was five hundred dollars. For the first time in aviation history, traveling and vacationing became affordable to the lower income families of America and other parts of the world. Phoenix Airlines was on the rise and tracking to become profitable since its birth. It soared high above the competition. It made sense that their slogan was "Born to fly."

July 13 was a Wednesday. Wednesday afternoons were reserved for our weekly meetings with Royce Killington. I walked into our conference room where the entire wall was a window that overlooked El Segundo, the area of Los Angeles where several commercial airlines had their corporate offices. We were less than a mile from the Los Angeles International Airport, or as many called it for short, LAX. Upon entering, I immediately noticed that there were only three of my colleagues sitting at a giant roundtable with Royce. There was usually a larger group of engineers in this meeting.

"Where is everyone?" I asked.

Royce smiled at me and replied, "I canceled the weekly meeting so that I can meet with you four."

I looked around at my three colleagues, Jim King, Dylan Sparks, and Charles Rosenberg. They did not seem as surprised by the sudden change in the meeting as I was. Their faces were stoic and calm.

"Take a seat," Dylan requested of me. "We have some business to discuss."

"Okay," I replied, sounding very curious and confused at the same time. I took my seat next to Jim, who was the very first person I had met when I'd started at Phoenix over a year ago.

"You're quite an asset to this company," Royce said cheerfully to me.

I smiled and felt my face turn red. I had to hand it to Royce. For a CEO of a large corporation, he made sure to have plenty of face time with the people who worked for him. I believe that was the first time he had ever complimented me.

"I appreciate that," I replied almost instantaneously. I felt nervous. These types of small meetings where the head of the company was present sometimes meant layoffs. However, Royce looked in good spirits, so I was instantly relieved that I was not sitting in that brightly lit conference room for the last time.

"Patrick," Royce began, "Jim, Dylan, and Charles are our senior engineers, as you know. They have been with the company and me since our launch in the summer of 2014…only two years ago. They are three of the most brilliant minds I have ever had the pleasure of working with. When you joined a year later, you brought so much more to our team of engineers in helping design our planes for the modern and changing world we live in today. You have helped us by making our planes not only safer, but more cost efficient, by utilizing our outsourced tech companies from China. Because you have proved your merit and worth, I wanted to offer you a promotion to join these three men as a senior engineer. Currently you are junior, but your work has gone above and beyond the call of duty. I want to applaud you for such efforts, especially because you power through a typical forty to fifty-hour week between Monday and Thursday, so that you can have Fridays off to teach engineering courses at your alma mater university in Montana…*professor*. You are a model employee, and I want to commend you."

"Well…" I struggled for words. I felt so choked up by Killington's wonderful praise. "I am so overwhelmed with gratitude, Mr. Killington. Thank you so much. I am honored and privileged to work with these fine, intelligent men and to be considered worthy of their ranks."

"You are most certainly welcome," Royce replied. "And please, call me Royce. My father was Mr. Killington." Royce adjusted his tie and winked at me.

"Royce, thank you," I reiterated. Jim, Dylan, and Charles then applauded for me and exchanged several congratulatory comments with me.

"There is a conference on Friday in China with our tech company that manufactures our safety systems on our planes," Royce stated. "I want you to join these three at the conference as your first task at the senior level. I know you have to teach in Montana on Friday, but I'm hoping you can find a substitute or reschedule that class, because this will be an important conference, and it would behoove you to attend."

"Yes, of course," I said instantly. I was too excited about my new promotion to think about an absence from my students at that moment. I wrestled with the idea that I could potentially do a videoconference session for my lesson on Friday. "When do we leave?"

"Tonight," Royce replied. "All four of your itineraries will be emailed to you shortly by my assistant, Natasha. You will be taking a red eye out of LAX to Beijing on one of our largest international airplanes tonight. You'll return Sunday afternoon to Los Angeles. I want to give you all Saturday to explore the city on your day off. Your hotel is booked as well. I'm giving you the rest of the day off—all of you—so that you can go home and pack. A car service will pick you up and take you to the airport. The future of Phoenix Airlines has never looked brighter, and you four are going to help us build models that will be practically crash proof. I have a dream that one day there will be zero flight accidents or crashes. Flying will be even safer. We are on the verge of making history. Affordable flying can be checked off our list, and next is accident-free travel. Even though none of our planes have had any mechanical failures or crashes in the two years we have been in business, I want to make sure that it never happens. We will be the future of travel. Even for the president of the United States! If we can effectively create an airplane that does not crash and has safety systems to get passengers to the ground in a time of crisis without a scratch on them, then we might be building the next Air Force One for President Howard."

"This sounds amazing," I said, still trying to wrap my head around all this new information. "Is it physically possible to create a plane that does not crash? I mean, look what happened to the Titanic. They said it could never sink..."

"Technology has advanced significantly in over a century since the Titanic sank," Jim spoke up. "Don't be silly. We are growing with modern technology, at the brink of systems that will ensure no human ever perishes in the skies again." Dylan patted Jim on the back after his statement.

"Well said," Royce spoke up again. "I have to run to an offsite meeting now, but I will let these three tell you about the plans for the trip, Patrick. Safe travels everyone!" Royce gathered his smartphone and tablet from the table in front of him, and he walked out of the conference room with a quick glance at the clock on the wall.

Charles waited until Royce had shut the conference door before turning to Dylan and Jim. They all nodded in some kind of silent agreement and then faced me. "We want to tell you something."

"What is it?" I asked with intrigue.

Charles lowered his voice to an almost inaudible whisper. I had to lean in closer to hear him. "We are on the verge of something much bigger than the safety systems Killington wants to work on. The three of us have been working on something much greater. It will change the world and the method of travel forever, but Killington must remain oblivious to this. We will attend this conference in China, but we have another more important meeting with an agency and another tech company on Saturday. We are inviting you to join us. Phoenix Airlines is not the future. I mean, it can be, but our discovery will change that significantly. We plan to leave Phoenix by the end of this quarter to pursue our new research and project. The three of us believe you can be an asset to us, and we want you on our team."

I looked at my colleagues with confusion. I was quite shocked, to be honest. I thought I was joining a team to better the company that paid our bills; they'd thrown a curveball at me with a secret plan of their own, and for some reason, they trusted me. I had just been promoted, and my colleagues were planning an exit strategy.

"What is this discovery?" That was the first question that I could think of.

Jim looked at me seriously and whispered, "We will tell you in a very private meeting place on Saturday. We cannot speak of it in this very building, or in this very country, for that matter. You have a choice if you want to join us or not. I think that once you learn about our project, you will be very excited about it. When we get to the meeting in Beijing on Saturday, you will have to sign several non-disclosure forms for legal reasons, because of the amount of confidential information you will be told."

"I don't know what to say," I said honestly. "There's so much to process."

"I know," Charles said. "But you will have a better sense of where you want your future to be on Sunday when we fly back to L.A." Charles gathered some of his notes that were spread over the table in front of him. "I'm going to head home to pack. I will see you all at the international terminal this evening. Our flight leaves at 9:00 PM."

"I'm right behind you," Dylan said, and he put his smartphone in his pocket and followed Charles out of the conference room. He waved goodbye to Jim and me before he closed the door.

"Can you tell me anything?" I asked Jim. I figured he would be able to tell me something, as I had a closer bond with him. Jim seemed to be struggling with a thought. He furrowed his eyebrows and gave me an apologetic look.

"It's confidential until you sign the paperwork on Saturday," he responded. "I promise you, this is all very good stuff. It will be overwhelming, but the future of mankind's quest for travel will be significantly changed and upgraded. That's all I will say. Patrick, Phoenix Airlines is wonderful, don't get me wrong. I'm thankful for what Royce has done for the country and for giving me the ability to provide for my family. I have a wife and two kids, as you know. Royce is not a spoiled rich brat. He's a smart man with a good heart. Phoenix is only becoming profitable because other commercial airlines filed for bankruptcy because of our popularity and low prices. That was not Royce's intention, but it is how our economy works. He wanted middle and lower class customers to enjoy the convenience of cheap, yet luxurious travel. His net worth is so large that even if Phoenix was not making a profit, he could maintain it for several years. He knew it would be successful though, and he took that risk. He's a good man. He donates his Phoenix paycheck to charities because he does not need the extra income."

"And don't you feel guilty about going behind his back with some other plan, after all he has done for us?" I asked. Jim had a look of sadness on his face. I could see his guilt clearly etched on his wrinkled forehead. He was balding, and any hair he had left was silver. Jim was approaching his fifties, but his hard work over the last two years at Phoenix had aged him significantly, and he appeared to be over the age of sixty.

"Royce doesn't have the intelligence that we have," Jim said. "We are scholars. We redesigned what it means to fly commercial. We've built this new line of planes. Royce wanted to do good for mankind. We are going to do better. It's not being selfish. We are doing a service for the future of this country and this world. You will understand in a few days. It is the biggest discovery of the twenty-first century, and you will soon be a part of it. Dragons symbolize power in ancient Chinese folklore. We have the power to change the world for good. Be a dragon like me, and join us in China."

Chills went up and down my arms at Jim's words. I had always looked up to him with admiration. To be considered to join his team on this mysterious and secret project was flattering. These three men were the smartest men I'd ever met, and I was confident that, whatever their project was, it probably would be extraordinary. "I'm with you, Jim," I said. "I look forward to learning about your work."

"Good," he replied with a big grin on his face. He put his hand on my shoulder and squeezed it. "You're a brilliant and good man, *Professor Patrick Baldwin*. I'm ecstatic to have you on board with us on this project. I think you will be a great asset to our team."

"Thank you for including me, Jim," I said. "I hope that my expertise will be of value to you, Dylan, and Charles."

"Great," he replied. "See you tonight, my friend."

He grabbed his workbag and looked at me, then gave me a friendly wave as he made his way to exit the conference room. I waved back. He pulled out his smartphone and glanced at the screen for a few seconds. Then he pulled out a small black flip phone and quickly typed something on it before leaving the room. That would be the last time I would ever see my friend and colleague, Jim King.

2

It was 4:00 PM. I pulled out a bottle of my favorite top shelf vodka from my freezer. I had finished packing for my trip to China at my Westwood condo—an area of the city near the University of California, Los Angeles. The bottle of vodka was cold to the touch and slightly frosted from sitting in my freezer for a week. Since I was going to have to work abroad the next few days, I figured a celebratory drink was in order for my promotion and the prospect of a project that was probably bigger than my own existence. Well, that was my humble way of putting it, at least. I pulled out a glass from the bar in my kitchen. It was short and perfect for a small cocktail. Since I was in my early forties—forty-two, to be exact—I was very conscious of my health. I made sure to exercise several times a week, and I was aware of anything I consumed. Vodka mixed with club soda was my drink of choice, mainly for its low caloric content and my fear of getting the beer belly that my father had. I was also single, mainly by choice and partly by profession. Actually, it was the other way around. I was single mainly by profession and partly by choice.

It had been three years since my last romantic relationship. It ended because I was always working late hours and had to spend my weekends in my home state of Montana, teaching aerospace engineering at the University of Montana. It was the university from which I had obtained my bachelors, masters, and PhD. I taught a five-hour lab every Friday and stayed at a cabin I owned in the country, just a few miles from where I grew up. I loved Montana. It was such a simple place. I had a large painting on the wall of my condo's living room that depicted a mountain terrain and several farm fields. It reminded me of my upbringing.

I focused so much on exercise and remaining fit because I was not getting any younger, and I wanted to marry one day. However, the more I thought about the prospects of my colleagues' project, the more I realized that I might have to marry my work and remain single forever. I had always dreamed of having a son and a daughter, yet my line of work never allowed me the opportunity to settle. I could not even own a dog, because my long work hours would be unfair to the poor creature.

I opened the door to my balcony and sat at my bistro table. It was a gorgeous day. The skies were clear, and the sun was shining. The rays felt warm to the touch on my tanned skin. In a rare break from my work-life, I had been in Mexico the weekend before for the Fourth of July, for a much needed quick vacation with some old college fraternity brothers. The ice in my vodka soda quickly melted, as it was slightly warmer than usual that day. My phone app said that my area of town was in the mid-eighties. I swirled my drink with a straw and took a few sips. I let out a sigh of relief and basked in the glorious shine from the only star in our solar system. I closed my eyes and imagined myself on top of a mountain in Montana. I was even able to fade out the sounds of the L.A. traffic rumbling below me.

When I finished my drink, I went back inside to pour myself another. I decided to bring the entire bottle outside, so that I would not have to get up again from my comfortable outdoor balcony chair. I figured if I flew slightly drunk to China, I would be able to fall asleep at takeoff. I had insomnia. My doctor joked that it was because I was a genius, and was unable to shut my mind off. He was right about not being able to shut my mind off. Whenever I would lie in bed after a long day of work, my mind would buzz with ideas and calculations regarding projects I was working on. Sometimes my mind would race with thoughts of my own and endeavors I wanted to start outside of my day job. It was like a TV that could not be turned off. I felt my whole body go numb as one drink became two, and two became three. I was relaxed. A small alcohol buzz was one of the best ways to shut my mind off and let me relax. It distracted me from thinking of anything intellectual. If it was not alcohol, then it was the Klonopin prescribed to me by my doctor that would help me sleep and reduce my anxiety. And if I did not want to take medication, then I would use something a little more natural, like cannabis; in California, it was legal to use for medical purposes, and insomnia was definitely a medical purpose for me. I wish I could say I never used it recreationally, but I would be lying. It helped open up my mind to several ideas and possibilities in my line of work. I felt that most of history's geniuses experimented with cannabis. I was pretty sure Albert Einstein had. I had a theory that the plant was able to enhance our senses in a way that we normally could not without its effects. It tapped into parts of our brains that were far more complex than we may ever know. I knew that Jim tended to smoke it very often, and he was a world-renowned engineer, author, and all-around scholar. He, in my opinion, was our twenty-first century Albert Einstein. That was why when Jim, Dylan, and Charles told me they were working on something remarkable, I believed them. My predictions for Jim did not center on *if* he would ever discover or invent something that would change our lives, but *when* he would. Whatever this Saturday meeting was going to be, I knew it was something epic. I tossed back my sixth or maybe seventh vodka soda of the evening and slowly fell into a stupor. My mistake was that I had completely forgotten to eat something for dinner. I say *mistake* lightly, because at the end of that day, it was probably the best mistake of my life, and I rarely ever make mistakes that I am proud of. I mean, a mistake is not something that is usually classified as something to be proud of, but on this very day, it would save my life.

There was a buzzing sound coming from my pocket. My phone sounded angry. I pulled it out and saw that I had missed calls from Jim, Charles, and Dylan. I even had several missed calls from an unknown number that was presumably my car service.

"Oh no!" I yelled. It was 7:45 PM. My flight was leaving in an hour and fifteen minutes. Sudden panic hit me like a whip, and then I realized my head was pounding from the drinks I had consumed. I had passed out on my balcony. The sun was beginning to set over the horizon. I called Jim in panic.

"Jim!" I said to him in haste. "I'm so sorry! I, um, overslept. I'm calling a car now."

"Hurry!" Jim said with a worrisome tone. "You still need to get through security."

"We work for Phoenix. We have priority access, remember?" I said, which actually made me feel calm, because going through TSA at LAX was a nightmare for regular travelers. "I'll be quick. I hope the traffic isn't too bad on the 405 right now."

"Please do hurry," Jim urged, and I ended the call.

I rushed to my bedroom and gathered my luggage. I raced out of my condo and habitually patted my pockets to check if my keys, wallet, and phone were in them; they were. I raced to the elevator and impatiently waited for it to arrive. I used an app on my phone to request car service. The app noted that there was a car two minutes away.

"Good," I said to myself. I waved at the concierge of my condo and ran out of the front doors. The car arrived in a timely fashion, and I loaded my bags into the trunk. "To LAX," I told the driver.

It turned out to be hell on the 405, as was the case most of the time if you were driving on it to get to the airport around rush hour. I asked the driver to take an alternate route because I was cutting it very close to my flight.

"Where are you heading to?" the driver asked me.

I replied, "China."

"Aren't you supposed to be at the airport at least two hours before for an international flight?" he asked.

"Yes," I responded. "I overslept." Then I realized that since I unintentionally had gotten a few hours of sleep, I was probably not going to sleep much on the flight.

At 8:35 PM, we finally arrived at the international terminal at LAX. I paid the driver and gave him a generous tip. I wheeled my luggage to the check-in kiosk and printed out my boarding pass. I took off my gold Rolex watch and threw it into my luggage in a secret compartment before checking it in. I did not like to wear jewelry on long flights, as it made me feel constricted. The watch had been a gift from my father for graduation from undergrad. He'd had my initials engraved on the back.

I checked my luggage in with a woman at the counter, who then placed a sticker on my bags to indicate that I had a late check-in, so that it could be quickly delivered to my flight. She gave me a disapproving look as she carried it over to a conveyor belt behind her. I was cutting it close. I popped an ibuprofen to fight the nasty headache and impending hangover that were the results of the vodka. I reached for my cell phone and called Jim.

"I'm going through security!" I told him. He was already in his seat on our airplane.

"See you soon!" Jim said, sounding relieved.

I ran through the priority access lane. Had I not had this wonderful perk from Phoenix Airlines, I would have been stuck in line for half an hour, at least. The line for regular passengers was long. I quickly placed my carry-on bag on the X-ray machine and walked through the metal detector. A TSA officer asked me to step aside. I had brought contact lens solution that was bigger than the allotted size for liquids.

"Toss it," I told the officer. "I'll buy some later."

8:55 PM. In the distance, I could hear a voice calling over the speaker, "Final boarding call for flight number 619 to Beijing." I was racing through the terminal at that point. I looked at my boarding pass. It read "Gate 3 – Phoenix Airlines 619" on the top portion of it. My heart began to pound against my ribcage. I was not paying attention to my surroundings, and I was getting stares from strangers as I sprinted through the terminal as if my life depended on it.

And then it happened. Apparently someone had spilled soda on the ground, and I was too preoccupied with making it to Gate 3 to notice. As soon as my dress shoe made contact with it, I knew it was over. I quickly lost balance and fell backwards, hitting my head with a loud smack onto the floor. My carry-on bag flew out of my hands, and the contents inside spilled onto the ground. I saw my laptop fly out and crash hard. I cursed aloud, and the next thing I remembered was a bunch of random strangers coming to my aid. An airport security officer gave me a hand to get up.

"Are you all right, sir?" he asked me.

I nodded my head to indicate yes, but the pain was probably evident by the look on my face. Hitting your head on the floor when you have a headache is not a good combination. For a second, I felt as if I had lost my intelligence and become instantly dumb. Or maybe I was just numb?

"F-fine," I finally was able to string a word together. "Need to get to my flight. Gate 3."

"I'm sorry, sir," the man said. "It looks like your flight has just left the gate."

"NO!" I yelled. I scrambled for my belongings and pushed through the crowd of random strangers gawking over me. I should have been more polite as they helped me. I finally arrived at Gate 3. I looked out the window and saw Phoenix Airlines 619 taxiing on the runway. The magnificent metallic silver plane, which had a red tail wing with our company logo painted in white, taunted me as it prepared for takeoff. There was also a logo of the phoenix on the nose of the airplane, above the cockpit windows. I once joked with Jim, saying that our airplanes had a phoenix on the aircraft's "forehead." The logo on the nose was a red phoenix bird with its wings outstretched. Looking at it made me feel as though I had let down my team. I was so upset with myself. I was never late to meetings and always on time for everything on my calendar. I cursed under my breath. But this was one appointment I would be thankful I had missed by the next morning.

"And my bags are flying to China without me…" I said to myself and put my forehead against the glass window.

"Were you supposed to be on that flight?" a blond-haired man asked me.

"Yeah," I said with frustration.

"I just sent off my daughter on that flight. She's studying abroad over there."

"Well, she's lucky she didn't miss that flight," I said sarcastically. The man laughed, and I bid him farewell as I walked over to a kiosk to explain my dilemma.

"When is the next flight to Beijing?"

"In the morning," a female attendant replied. She was wearing a red blazer with a white Phoenix logo over a breast pocket. "We can get you on that one, if you would like?"

I did the calculations in my head. I would probably be able to make the Friday meeting, but just barely. I would have to go straight to the meeting from the airport. I would definitely be able to attend the top-secret meeting on Saturday.

"Sure," I replied to the woman. "Can you get me on that flight?"

"All right, Mr. Baldwin," she said after she input my information into the system. "We'll get you on that flight. There's availability."

I checked myself into a hotel near the airport because I wanted to eliminate the possibility of missing the morning flight to Beijing. As soon as I was in my room, I emailed Jim, Dylan, and Charles to explain my situation. I also asked Jim in another email to grab my checked luggage for me. I knew that as soon as they were at 35,000 feet, he would get on his laptop and connect to the Internet and respond. I was thankful Phoenix Airlines had Wi-Fi on board international flights. I waited for a response before bed, but an email reply never came through. Perhaps they went to sleep right away? I thought about emailing Royce, but it was late, and I did not want to stress him out. I decided I would email him before boarding my flight in the morning.

July 14, 2016

I woke up to the sound of my alarm. I dressed quickly, brushed my teeth of the smell of vodka from the night before, and gathered my belongings. As my clothes were on board Flight 619, I was forced to wear the same thing I'd worn the night before.

I arrived at my gate with an hour and a half to spare. The first thing I did, once I had passed through security, was buy a new bottle of contact lens solution. I went to the bathroom and took out my contacts. My eyes were slightly red and felt dry. I pulled out my eyeglasses from my carry-on and put them on. I looked at myself in the reflection of the mirror. I attempted to fix my salt and pepper dark brown hair, as I had not done it at the hotel. My face was stubbly, but my razors were in my luggage. It was 8:05 AM. When I walked out of the bathroom, I checked my work email on my phone. There were still no replies from any of my colleagues. They were still in flight, and had a few hours left until their arrival in Beijing.

A security officer ran by me quickly and nearly knocked me over.

"Sorry!" he yelled, and then continued running to meet up with three other security officers. They had worried looks on their faces and were deep in serious conversation.

"That can't be good," I said to myself, and out of curiosity, I walked over near them to eavesdrop on their conversation.

"...lost contact. The transponder was not operating. It was either shut off intentionally or it lost power. Radar is not picking it up either," one officer was telling his colleagues.

"Do they think it crashed?" another officer asked.

"We don't know," he replied. "The airplane was assigned to a different flight route than the normal L.A. to Beijing path due to weather, which was why it was near Hawaii instead of being much farther north in the Pacific. The last ping identified on radar was when it flew past Hawaii. Then—gone. No more signals. It was scheduled to land two hours from now. They'll need to notify the passengers' next of kin."

My heart sank. I quickly opened my Phoenix Airlines app to check the flight status of Flight 619. The status read "Delayed." My hands started to shake. I refused to believe that something had happened to Flight 619. I walked to my gate and saw that the status of my upcoming flight read "Canceled" on the marquee.

"Excuse me?" I spoke to the flight representative at my gate. "Why has this flight been canceled?"

"I do not have full details yet. I was just told by my supervisor."

I checked my email again. My inbox was empty. There was nothing new. I checked a couple of news websites on my phone, but there was nothing being reported yet. I racked my mind on who I should call. I called Royce's office line. I was pretty sure that the CEO of Phoenix Airlines would have answers. His assistant Natasha answered.

"Hello," she said.

"Hi there, is Mr. Killington available?" I asked.

"May I ask who is calling?" she asked.

"It's Patrick Baldwin. One of his engineers," I told her.

"Hello, Mr. Baldwin," she replied. "He was rushed to an offsite emergency meeting. I'm not sure when he will be back in the office. He's currently in back-to-back meetings. *Wait*—aren't you supposed to be on a flight?"

Something was happening. Or…something had happened. I ended the call with Natasha and decided I would just go into the office. When I arrived at my office, there was nobody around. The halls were empty. I checked my email, and there was a message from corporate urging everyone to meet in our largest conference room for an emergency meeting. Before I left my office, I turned on the TV. It was as if time had stopped. I did not want to believe something had happened, but there it was, flashing on my screen. Every news outlet was finally reporting the same thing. "Phoenix Airlines 619: Missing" or "Phoenix Airlines 619: Crashed or Hijacked?"

I put my hand over my mouth in shock. Instantly, I received a slew of notification alerts and calls. My mother was among them, and hers was the call I took first.

"Oh my God!" She cried with relief when she heard my voice. "I saw the news. It was your plane. How? Where are you? You didn't board the plane, did you?"

"I missed it," I finally broke down. "I'm okay, Mom. I'm at my office. This is so crazy. I was a few minutes late. I could have been on that plane. It doesn't look like anyone knows what happened. It just disappeared."

"Oh my God!" she cried again. "Thank you, Lord!"

I spent a couple of minutes on the phone with my frantic yet relieved mother. I was thankful that I still had the opportunity to talk to her. When I ended her call, I read the other messages from friends and family, who were texting me in hopes that my plane had not crashed and I was still alive. They knew I was supposed to be on that plane because I had checked-in on Facebook right before missing my flight. I spent ten minutes writing back to everyone, saying I missed the flight and that I was alive and well. The shock was beginning to set in. I was so glad that the vodka had prevented me from being on time for my flight.

I quickly ran down the empty hall of the office in the direction of the conference room. I heard a buzz of murmurs through the door. When I opened it, everyone turned and looked at me. They had a look of shock in their eyes, as if they had just seen a ghost. Royce's expression was the most memorable. He looked happy to see me. After the few seconds of shock, people began to cry and rushed over to hug me.

I spent the next hour retelling my story of oversleeping (I did not want my colleagues to know I was actually passed out drunk—or the part where I slipped on a soda spill). I received many handshakes and hugs. However, there was a somber tone, because Jim, Dylan, and Charles were on Phoenix Airlines 619. Royce had briefed the company on the situation, and even though he knew I had missed my flight (since Natasha had informed him of our conversation earlier), he had kept it from the employees to avoid questions he did not have answers to. My dramatic entrance and retelling of my account alleviated that burden.

Royce did not have much information on why the flight went off radar. The strangest part of the mystery was that the transponder on the plane was off. Theories of hijackings were proposed by some of my colleagues. Then there was the possibility that the plane crashed. I found it ironic that we had been going to a meeting about enhancing our plane's safety features when the flight that I would have been on had disappeared. Everything felt surreal. It was as if I'd died and was living as a ghost, yet I was alive. I was physical. This was not a dream, but a nightmare was unfolding.

What was the top secret meeting Jim, Dylan, and Charles had invited me to? What projects were they working on that would change the way mankind travels? Royce had no idea what they were planning, and now it was possible that I would never know. These questions raced through my brain over and over. My head began to hurt again just thinking about them.

Noon rolled around. I found my eyes glued to a live news report broadcasting from Beijing Capital International Airport. Flight PA 619 should have landed already. It never surfaced over the Chinese skies. I was in my office and preparing to go to lunch when my phone rang. It was Royce.

"Can you meet me in my office?" he asked.

"I'll be right down," I told him.

I felt my stomach growl. I was starving. I hoped that whatever Royce wanted to speak to me about would not take long. Maybe he had answers? I got off the elevator on Royce's floor. As I was exiting into the lobby, a tall muscular man entered the elevator. He had on a security uniform and a badge. He had a tattoo sleeve on one arm protruding from underneath his uniform sleeve, which was short and snug around his bicep. He gave me a polite nod right before the doors closed between us.

Natasha was at her desk outside of Royce's office. She was a black woman with curly hair and bright brown eyes. She was dressed in a designer business blazer and skirt. She greeted me with a smile and said, "You're very lucky. I can't believe you missed the flight."

"Me either," I responded. "May I go in?"

"In a moment," she said. "Here's some water, Mr. Baldwin. It's quite delicious. It's spa-like water with cucumber. Would you like to try some while you wait?" She gave me a sweet smile while passing me a glass.

"Sure," I said, and I grabbed it from her and drank the entire contents in a few seconds flat. I set the empty glass down on her desk next to a copy of a work order for an airplane part she was submitting.

"Okay, he's ready." Natasha gestured toward Royce's door.

I walked into his office. He was on his cell phone. It appeared as though he was having a heated conversation. Behind his desk was a large painting of the sun shining over the ocean. There was what looked like a pupil in the center of the sun, staring menacingly back at me. It gave me the creeps. He also had a giant map of the Pacific Ocean sprawled over his desk. When I stepped in, he ended his call and tossed his cell phone aside.

"Patrick!" he said. "Please, have a seat."

I sat down in front of Royce's desk. He moved the map out of the way. Before he rolled it up, I saw a couple of red dots on it and notes scribbled next to them.

"We're trying to locate the plane as soon as possible—or at least any remains of it," Royce said. "I've marked this map to the location of the last ping from the plane before it went off radar."

"Do you have any answers?" I asked.

"No," Royce said. "We don't know what happened. The last message from the pilot came at 5:00 in the morning. There was nothing suspicious. He wished a good morning to air traffic controllers in Hawaii, and they announced themselves. Other than that, we have no idea what the hell happened up there. You must be overwhelmed and thankful for missing that flight. I almost considered going on the trip as well."

"I don't know how I feel," I said honestly. "It's still shocking. Jim was one of my closest friends."

"We've lost three intelligent minds," Royce said sadly.

"We don't know that they've been lost yet," I added. "There's the possibility that they landed the plane. Or, if it was hijacked, maybe they are alive somewhere."

"I don't know," Royce shrugged. "We need to find the plane first and go from there. There really aren't any clues. We are looking at the flight manifest to see if there were any passengers with suspicious backgrounds, to help us clue in on if this was an act of terrorism or not. Two hundred forty-one people were on board, including the crew. It's also the first time we've ever had a tragedy with Phoenix Airlines."

"I emailed the three of them last night, thinking they would get on the Phoenix Wi-Fi, but I never heard back from them," I said.

"The wireless Internet was not in service last night," Royce said. "I looked into it, because I figured if something happened, anyone could have easily made a call or gone online to send a message to someone. But it turns out that, for some unknown reason, the Wi-Fi was down. All communication systems were down. It was as if the plane became invisible in the sky."

I felt my phone vibrate in my pocket. I pulled it out and glanced at the screen. It was more friends checking in to see if I was alive. I turned to Royce and asked, "So, why did you call me in here?"

"Right," he replied. "The reason I asked you to come is because you might be approached by the media regarding the fact that you were supposed to be on the airplane. Your story will probably get out, and there will be a hailstorm of reporters hounding you. I already have a headache from the insane requests from the press. I'm going to have a press conference tomorrow to address this issue, since we'll have more details by then. A search is currently being set up. We are having several surrounding countries search for any trace of the plane or debris. Now, I need to inform you that, as an employee of Phoenix Airlines, you are not permitted to talk to the press or speak on behalf of the company. Our company will be under scrutiny. This will be a PR nightmare, and we all want answers to smooth things over. Just keep your lips sealed. I don't want to draw attention to the fact that you were going on official business for advancement in our aircraft safety systems. That is a confidential project, and if word gets out, our competitors could have the upper hand. Am I clear?"

"I understand," I said. The last thing I wanted was to be in newspapers or on TV or online blogs. "I promise not to speak to the press."

"When they reach out to you," he said, "just say that you are not authorized to speak on behalf of Phoenix Airlines."

"Won't that sound suspicious?" I asked.

"Maybe, but not saying anything is the best defense we have right now. I've spoken to our publicity team, and they feel that the press will eventually give up if you continue to keep quiet."

"Will do, Mr. Killington—Royce. I really hope we find the plane, or at least some answers."

"Me too," Royce said, staring blankly into the distance.

By the time I arrived at my condo, I had already received calls and emails from local news stations and major news networks. The networks were reporting PA 619 as officially lost at 6:00 PM. I did not bother to answer any of them. The phone was ringing off the hook, and around 7:00 PM, I decided to turn it off. I needed to disconnect from the world. The only thing the news stations on TV were discussing was the missing PA 619. I decided I needed a hot shower, so I walked into my bathroom, only to realize that all my toiletries were in my checked bag, which was on the missing plane. Some of my best work clothes and suits, as well as my father's Rolex, were in my bag. As most everything was replaceable, I comforted myself with the thought that I was fortunate enough to not have been on that plane. I felt lucky I did not perish with my belongings.

I ordered Chinese food that night, as I was in no mood to eat out or cook. When it arrived, I turned my TV on to watch a movie on Netflix, avoiding news networks. Eventually I could not handle being away from my phone, so I turned it back on. I had eight voicemails, all from unknown numbers. More news outlets were trying to hassle me. I looked at my recent call log and saw Jim's name. I decided to call his phone, which was what many of my friends had done when they'd believed I was on Flight 619. There was a second of silence before the phone started to ring. My heart was racing.

"Come on, pick up, Jim," I said with hope. "Please. I want to know you are alive. Maybe the plane landed and everyone is alive."

After three or four rings, the phone went to voicemail. I wondered if there was a chance his phone was intact, since it allowed me to connect to it and ring a few times. Some of the news stations eventually disclosed that theory, as many of the passengers' family members had tried to contact their loved ones.

Nonetheless, I absent-mindedly left Jim a voicemail: "Jim, it's Patrick. I hope nothing horrible happened. I pray you get this voicemail. I wish I would have known more about the secret side project." I hung up and immediately regretted leaving that voicemail. I had said the words "secret side project," but if the plane had crashed, his phone would be at the bottom of the Pacific Ocean. I shuddered at the thought.

Against my desire, I decided to watch CNN after I could not decide on a movie to stream. As expected, my name was mentioned. It was reported that I had missed my flight. They ended the report with, "We have yet to reach Mr. Baldwin for comments." Then there were images of families crying at the Beijing airport. There was chaos and angry families placing blame on Phoenix Airlines because of the fact that the plane went off radar and essentially vanished without a trace. I flipped through the channels and found a story highlighting some of the passengers. There was one passenger named Mallory Cooper. She was on the plane, destined to begin her semester abroad in China. A photo of her mother and father was put on the screen. Her father was the man I had spoken to briefly at the terminal the previous night after missing the flight.

"Oh my…" I gasped. I could only imagine how this man must be feeling. I felt so sad because his daughter was only twenty-one years old and had not even finished college. A part of me wished I had been on the plane instead of her. I was twice her age. I had lived and done enough to be proud of.

I dabbled with the thought of flying to Montana early in the morning to teach my class, since I was no longer scheduled to be in China. I called the dean, Dexter Brandon, and asked him if I should come in.

"You could take the day off," Dexter said to me on the phone. "You've had a rough day. It's still unbelievable that you missed the flight."

"I think getting out of L.A. will be good for me," I told him. "It will be nice to stay at my cabin for the weekend."

"If you insist," Dexter replied. "We'll see you soon."

After I got off the phone with Dexter, I pulled out my laptop, which had a large crack in the screen from my fall at the airport the day before. Normally it would upset me to see a valuable piece of technology broken, but considering that the fall saved my life, I was not going to complain. I booked my flight for the earliest departure to Montana and set my alarm. I popped a sleeping pill and slipped into my pajamas.

Sleep was the only escape for me. It was much more of an escape than an actual vacation, because it rejuvenated my body. It was also a challenge for me, because of my insomnia. My mind was difficult to shut down. I sometimes wished I had a function, like a computer, to shut off instantly. The anxiety of the day and the incessant calls from the media had worn me out. I could not stop thinking about PA 619, but the pill was slowly helping to take the edge off my insomnia. I could feel my eyelids getting heavy. My body felt relaxed. I stopped reliving my adventure at LAX the night before and exchanged those thoughts for random dreams and a complete night's sleep.

July 15, 2016

The following morning, I was drinking my coffee in my seat. Phoenix Airlines actually made amazing coffee. My flight attendant was really sweet. She brought me two cups of coffee. A woman in the seat behind me was frantic about flying on Phoenix due to recent events. I had to admit, I was nervous as well.

"I mean…how do you lose an airplane in this day and age?" I heard her asking her husband. "What goes up must come down. Where is it? I was watching the news before we arrived here, and saw that they are searching the Pacific Ocean left and right. It's like finding a needle in the haystack, but you would think there would be some kind of tracking device on the plane. And it's *this* airliner too. Phoenix has the most advanced technology on their jets. How come they can't just track the plane?"

She had a good point. If I was not an engineer who designed these planes, I would have wondered that myself. The truth was, Phoenix Airlines could have had some kind of tracking device, but it would have upped the cost on the production of the planes. A transponder would be enough, but for some reason, the transponder had failed or was intentionally shut off on Flight 619. The same was true for the wireless communication. Only someone with knowledge of the aircraft would know how and where to locate the transponder and shut it off.

The woman's husband spoke up and answered her. "They'll have their answers once they find the black box. The black box data recorder could paint a picture of what happened. I read it in an online article. If the plane crashed into the Pacific, then once the box touches water, it would send out these pings or signals that can be tracked with sonar technology. The battery life is only guaranteed for thirty days. They need to find the plane before that; if not, there might never be any hope of locating it. It's a big ocean out there."

The wife replied, "But still, why is there not some kind of GPS tracking system that can pinpoint where the plane might have ended up? It seems like it would be such an obvious addition to the fleet."

"This all sounds shady to me," the husband said. "There is something suspicious about all this, and I have a feeling we are not being told the truth."

I agreed silently with the man. I had been obsessively following the news on the missing plane for the last twenty-four hours. I had wanted to keep my eyes off the reports, because it pained me to occasionally hear my colleagues' names pop up in the news, but curiosity got the best me. I glanced at my phone and realized that the Phoenix Airlines press conference was going to take place live. I turned on the media center located in front of me, on the back of the seat before mine. I plugged in my headphones and pressed the remote buttons on the side of the screen. I found my preferred news station and saw a ticker headline that read "CEO of Phoenix Airlines to give briefing in five minutes."

Royce walked up to a podium with the red Phoenix logo adorning it. The conference was happening in the largest conference room at our corporate offices. There were several reporters and flashing cameras buzzing as Royce took the stand. He was the main attraction of this briefing, so it made sense that the crowd was going wild over his sudden, yet pristine appearance. Royce cleaned up very well. He looked extremely polished and had a look of concern on his face. He did not seem happy to be there.

"Thank you for joining us today," he began his briefing. "I know many of you have a ton of questions, but let me preface this with letting you know that we have several questions too. It's been a full day since PA 619 was supposed to land in Beijing. It never arrived. Air traffic control realized that the plane went off radar early in the morning of July 14 at around 5:00 AM. My condolences go out to the family members of the passengers and crew on board. There were 241 souls on Flight 619. While we are not sure if this was a mechanical failure or something intentional, I want to assure you that we are working with several countries on a massive search for any debris that could help us find wreckage or clues. The search party is being led by Australia, with help from China and the U.S. Former Australian Air Marshal Ted Holt is heading the search efforts. Phoenix Airlines is dedicated to safety. We have looked into our records, and it shows that Flight 619 was in excellent condition. There was nothing questionable in the maintenance records from the evening of July 13—the evening it took off on its journey over the Pacific—that suggests the plane could have had any mechanical issues. Phoenix has a clean history during the two years we have been up and flying. That being said, we had a few of our employees on board, who were flying on official business. We lost three good men—"

"What about Patrick Baldwin?" a reporter interrupted, and there was a murmur of agreement from other audience members, who began to repeat the question. "Was he supposed to be on the flight? Why has he remained silent?"

"I can answer that," Royce said with poise. "Mr. Baldwin was working on a project that had to do with improving safety on our airplanes. While I cannot go into detail about this, I can confirm that, due to the legal issues and contracts he signed in regard to this project, he cannot speak to the press. He missed the flight. I guess you can see that this was the best luck Mr. Baldwin could have ever had. There really is nothing more to it than that, but he is a private man as well. We ask that you respect his privacy, because he worked closely with the three engineers we lost, and he is dealing with this tragedy."

I had to admit that Royce's media training was impeccable. What he said was perfect, and I hoped that it would keep the media from harassing me for answers and interviews.

Royce continued his press briefing. "We are working hard to search for the plane. We will make sure that the media and families are continually updated. When we have answers, you will too. I promise that. Our thoughts and prayers are with those who were on board and their families. I cannot stress that or say that enough. Here at Phoenix Airlines, we are dedicated to our customers. We hope to find signals emitting from the black boxes, if the plane crashed into the Pacific Ocean. We have several ships setting off from Hawaii, which was the closest land where the plane was last seen on the radar systems. Now, I will take a few questions from the media and answer them the best that I can."

"Do you think this was an act of terrorism?" one reporter blurted out before several other questions were spit at Royce. It sounded like a buzz of angry bees. I felt sorry for Royce at that moment. I could see his face turn a shade of pink, and his forehead was beginning to sweat. I could almost imagine the heat in that room, from not only the general mood of the audience, but from the camera lights and flash photography.

"One question at a time please," Royce yelled at the press line. "You!" He pointed at a woman reporting for NBC.

"Will Phoenix Airlines be releasing the final recordings from the last conversation with the pilots and the Hawaiian air traffic control tower?"

"Um," Royce thought for a moment. "Not at the moment. We don't see the need to yet. We released a transcript of the last words. It was pretty much just one of the pilots telling the tower 'good morning' and nothing more. There really isn't any indication of anything suspicious. It was business as usual before they went silent. Next question…you!"

A reporter from CNN spoke up. "Can you tell us about the business you were sending your employees on in Beijing?"

"As I said earlier, that is a private and confidential business matter for the time being," Royce said with frustration in his tone. "There is no relationship between that and why PA 619 disappeared."

There was a sudden disturbance in the press conference. I could hear a door burst open. The camera that was on Royce then panned to the back of the room, and I saw several individuals. They were a few of the families of the missing passengers. There were howls and cries of anguish. There were mothers yelling for their sons and daughters and placing blame on Phoenix for the disaster. They kept shouting and demanding answers. I felt pity for them. They were not in their right states of mind. They had all lost people they loved. Security had to forcefully escort the angry families out of the room. The camera then panned back to Royce. He looked even more uncomfortable. He was whispering into Natasha's ear. Natasha nodded and stepped off the stage.

"I'm going to take one more question," Royce said. "I have to run."

There were boos and yells from the crowd, because they had obviously expected more time to question the CEO of Phoenix Airlines. Now many of them were going to be left scratching their heads and reviewing voice memos they had recorded on their smartphones for their reports.

"CBS," Royce pointed at the reporter, "I'll take yours."

The CBS reporter spoke into her microphone. "How come no aircraft or ships deployed as soon as you all realized that the plane disappeared from radar? According to reports, they were not dispatched until noon, when it was confirmed that PA 619 had not landed at its scheduled arrival time in Beijing."

"We were making sure it was really lost," Royce said. "If the transponder was off, then it would have been invisible, and we needed to verify it wasn't landing in Beijing."

The reporter spoke again, "Fair enough; however, radar systems could have identified an object flying in the air, unless it was flying at a low altitude so as not to be detected by the radar. There were no reports of an airplane flying low over China that morning."

"I said only one question," Royce said. "And air route surveillance radar systems can usually detect up to two hundred nautical miles from land. That means parts of the ocean are blind to radar detection. I'm sorry, but I must go."

Royce stepped off the stage to more heckling and annoyed buzzing voices from the reporters. I turned off the entertainment system and decided to listen to music for the rest of my flight to Montana. Music was my escape. The crisp, clear sound vibrating inside my ears was bliss for me. For someone with a mind that never really liked to shut off or knew how to be at peace, I found music to be the ultimate distraction. It calmed me. It took me out of my element and gave me the ability to not think. All I could think of since I had narrowly missed Flight 619 was finding answers. I, like most of the country and the world, was very curious and fascinated with this tragedy. The classical music blasting into my ears took those questions out of my mind, and I imagined sitting in an amphitheater, listening to a live classical orchestra playing the tunes that were digital notes emitting from my digital music player.

Music had another interesting power over me. It helped me relive old memories. Whenever I would hear a song that I associated with an event in my life, I could picture that memory in my head, clear as day. There was one particular song about a break-up from my favorite country band that always reminded me of my split from my last girlfriend. The song I was playing at that moment was from a country band that I had seen perform at the Hollywood Bowl with a string quartet. I attended the performance because Jim had an extra ticket, and he'd taken me as his plus one earlier that summer. Remembering that moment in my life had reawakened my mind.

We had been seated in box seats that were maybe three or four rows away from the stage. I was drinking a glass of my favorite red wine; we had been allowed to bring our own alcoholic beverages to this particular performance. Jim was hastily typing away on his smartphone. He said he had to write a work email. When he finished, he put his phone in his pocket and continued to watch the show. I glanced at him from the corner of my eye. He was looking at the show, but he was not *watching* it. He seemed to be elsewhere in his mind. It was obvious that he was bothered by something, but I did not want to ask him what it was.

"I'm going to run to the restroom," he said midway through the show, and he left me alone in the box. I poured myself another glass of wine, and before I knew it, I had finished it. I decided to go check up on Jim, who had not returned after fifteen minutes. I walked up the row in the direction of the nearest bathroom. When I went in to investigate, he was nowhere to be found. I walked out and saw him on his cell phone, having what looked like a heated conversation, judging by his constant hand movements and gestures. I walked in his direction and felt the inclination to eavesdrop. He was in a back corner, where much of the sound from the amphitheater was blocked off. Once I was in earshot, I heard a few bits of his conversation.

"Are you sure they know?" he asked the person on the other end of the line. "Could our phone lines be tapped right now? Do you think they are listening in?"

My attention was piqued at that moment. I wasn't sure who "they" were, but they were apparently making Jim paranoid. I could see his hands shaking. I ducked behind a trashcan in case Jim turned around. I did not want him to know I was listening in.

"We need to discuss this project in person instead of on our phones. You don't want to tell me where you're hiding, do you? Right—not over this line. Let's discuss it on Monday. Bye." Jim ended his call and rushed back to our seats.

When I arrived back at our box, I told him I had to use the restroom myself. The rest of the night was a blur because I apparently had too much wine, which was probably why I only now recalled that memory of Jim's phone conversation.

I opened my eyes and pulled off my headphones. I stared blankly at the entertainment screen in front of me that was shut off. Jim must have been talking about the project they'd wanted to let me in on. Perhaps that was why they had not wanted to tell me while we were on U.S. soil. He was extremely paranoid. Had he thought someone was watching him and his every move closely? Somebody might have been onto them. But who? Who was he talking to, and why were they hiding?

I arrived on campus with my briefcase in one hand and a bottle of water in the other. Several students kept looking at me and whispering. It was evident that they had heard I'd missed Flight 619. I received several "hellos" and "good to see you, sirs." It was an awkward feeling, knowing that I had become famous—and I say *famous* lightly—overnight from being a drunken fool who was late to the airport.

And then the worst thing that could happen, which I had completely not expected, happened. There was a rush of reporters from several major news outlets sprinting out from a corner near the student union. Apparently they had been interviewing students about me. A student of mine was having information pried from him by a reporter. When that student saw me, he pointed at me. It was as if a herd of cattle had been let loose from the confines of their barn. There were shouts and questions being yelled over each other, and I could not tell what they were asking. My eyes widened in shock, and I turned on my heel in the opposite direction of my class.

"Security!" I heard our dean, Dexter Brandon, shouting. "Please escort the media off the grounds! They are disturbing education in progress!"

I was thankful for Dexter. A team of maybe five campus security officers intervened with the persistent news reporters. They were able to hold them back long enough for me to backtrack in the direction of the building where my class was. I mouthed "Thank you" to Dexter, and he nodded with a thumbs-up. He then put his hand up to his ear to represent a phone and mouthed back "Call or visit me after your class."

The disadvantage of teaching a summer class was that the odds of the students showing up were much slimmer than in the fall or spring semesters. Many of them felt the need to skip to bask in the sun or party a little harder than usual, since it was summer. I was counting on this. When I opened the door to my classroom, I was surprised to see every seat taken. There was even an overflow of people sitting on the stairs who did not even belong in my class. Their whispers stopped as soon as I walked in, and they looked at me with wide-eyed interest. It was as if they were looking at a ghost.

"Okay," I cleared my throat. "I know that there are some people here who are not registered for my class. I need to ask you to leave right away, or I will be speaking to the dean."

At least twenty random students picked up their bags and shuffled out of the room. Once they had cleared out, I pulled out my aeronautics textbook and turned it to the chapter we had left off on during my last session with them. I began to write some notes on my blackboard. I turned around and saw that all my students were staring at me with piqued interest. For once, there was not one single person on a phone or laptop. Nobody was tweeting or Facebooking. They were focused. I felt like laughing at that point, and then I did. My students were not sure how to react to my random, awkward laughter.

"I think you all are more interested in a different kind of lesson," I said, once I regained my composure. "You want to talk about the missing Phoenix Airlines flight, don't you?" Everyone nodded and said "yeah" in unison.

"Fine then." I decided to appease them. "It has been over a day since the plane disappeared off radar and failed to land in Beijing. Yes, I was supposed to be on the plane for business and had originally canceled this class, but decided I would come back after that fiasco. I needed an escape from Los Angeles. Now, the search is pretty fresh, but so far nothing has been found. We have no clues as to what happened. Not even my employer, Phoenix, knows anything. Let's discuss theories. I think today's lesson should be based on this real world scenario that I, as a professional engineer, will be dealing with until the plane is found. Does anyone want to tell me what you think happened? I'm all about hearing your theories. And think like engineers, please."

"An alien abduction?" one of my students by the name of Jack shouted, which was followed by an annoying amount of laughter from the rest of the class.

"Sure, that could be a possibility," I replied seriously. "Who knows what is out there in the universe. Maybe it was abducted and sucked into space." A few people chuckled at my sarcastic response. "Anyone else?"

"Perhaps the pilots intentionally diverted the plane and crashed it—maybe it was a suicide mission, or they were hijacking it for reasons unknown," a girl whose name I did not know said from the back of the class.

"Okay, that is possible," I replied. "You there!"

A male student near the front row who had his hand up responded, "Perhaps the plane had technical difficulties or a malfunction that caused a fire to spread quickly, knocking out the plane's communication systems, like the transponder."

"That's a theory news networks have been debating, for sure," I said. "And you?"

Rachel was sitting in the first row, flushed with excitement at her opportunity to speak. "My theory is a government airplane shot down Flight 619 by accident, or perhaps they realized it was hijacked and did not want to risk another September 11 incident from happening. Maybe they want to hide the fact that they had to take the plane down?"

"Interesting," I said while scratching my chin in thought.

"What's your theory?" Rachel asked.

"That's a great question," I said. "I don't know what to make of it just yet." I did not want to publicly say any of my theories, for the fear of them being misconstrued or talked about in the press. I wanted to research and study this mystery, since I had almost been on that plane. I could have been part of the mystery that was captivating the world. I wanted answers too.

"Surely you must have some kind of idea," Rachel spoke up again.

"It's been a whirlwind over the last twenty-four hours. My mind has yet to process this. I lost three colleagues who were on that flight. It's a very difficult time," I said honestly. Rachel looked uncomfortable, as if she had said something horrible. I clarified my response to her. "Don't worry, it's okay. We are all intrigued by this strange disappearance, and it is fine to ask these questions. I simply have not asked them yet."

"Professor Baldwin," my student Mark now spoke up with his hand raised.

"Yes?" I replied.

Mark cleared his throat and eloquently asked a very burning question. "I think it was an inside job. How does an airliner go missing in this day and age without some kind of satellite or GPS tracking? It's funny that the communications went offline and that the wireless Internet system was down too. I understand you work for the airline, but do you think there could have been some kind of cover-up?"

I looked at Mark for a while, as if only just seeing him for the first time. I knew his name, so he was a student who had caught my attention in the past. He was smart and very logical. He was also not socially awkward like most of my colleagues or other engineer friends and students. Mark was refreshing to have in my class. I smiled, and then answered him.

"Another very good theory," I said. "I can honestly say that Phoenix Airlines is as baffled about this mystery as you and I are. My boss, the CEO of the company, has been frazzled and stressed out about this since the news broke."

"What if the plane comes out of a wormhole and lands in Beijing days later," one of my students joked.

"Well, this isn't a science fiction movie," I answered, "but maybe wormholes exist and the plane was sucked into a vortex and into an alternate universe."

I received a couple of chuckles from the class; I grinned at them in appreciation for receiving my sarcasm well. Sometimes intelligent people are so deeply immersed in their studies that something as simple as a sarcastic joke can go over their heads.

"Any other theories?" I asked. "You…in the green shirt."

"Hi, I'm Luke," my student said. "I think a terrorist group might have hijacked the airplane and landed it in their country. I believe they might paint the plane so that it is unmarked and unrecognizable. Then they might fill it with explosives for some kind of terrorist attack somewhere else in the world."

"Fascinating," I said. "That's an interesting theory, no doubt." Another student by the name of Virginia raised her hand. She was seated near the back of the classroom auditorium. "How about you?" I pointed to her.

"The news is calling this the next biggest mystery in the history of aviation since the disappearance of Amelia Earhart's round-the-world flight in 1937. Back then, technology was not as advanced, and after an extensive search party, she or any traces of her airplane were never found. Do you think that they'll find this airplane, seeing as analysts are trying to figure out where to even look since the plane diverted off course?"

"Well," I answered, "I would hope so. It's too early to tell right now where they need to look, but you can trust that Phoenix Airlines is doing everything they can to scour the seas. Personally, I hope the airplane is found. It would be a travesty if this mystery remains unanswered like Earhart's tragedy."

We spent the next half hour debunking some of the more radical theories that, in my opinion, seemed too crazy to be real life. One theory that we debunked right away was the idea that some sort of Bermuda Triangle-like event occurred. Some students continued to toss around the words "wormholes" and "abduction," but I wanted to stay focused on what could have really happened. There was something in the back of my mind that I kept private from my students. A part of me felt that maybe the top-secret project that my colleagues were working on might have had something to do with PA 619's disappearance. I kept that to myself for fear of my students talking to the media about anything personal I shared.

The bell rang and my students scrambled out of the classroom. Many of them left with friendlier-than-usual goodbyes, which might have been out of sympathy from everything I had just been through in regards to the missing flight. My student Mark Crane lingered around until all the students had left.

"Professor Baldwin," he addressed me, "Could I have a quick word?"

"Sure," I said.

"Do you know what happened? I mean, do you really *know*?"

"I do not," I responded honestly. "I was being truthful. I wanted to utilize all your brilliant minds for ideas as I try to figure this out along with the rest of the world. Some of the ideas were very farfetched. I'm sure excessive binge drinking has cost a few of your classmates some brain cells, but there's still plenty of time left in the semester for them to redeem themselves."

We shared a nice laugh at my quick-witted sarcasm. I liked Mark. He was my top student. I saw a younger version of myself in him.

"Ah, to be in my twenties again," I said. "More freedom and the ability to make mistakes to learn from."

Perhaps it was because I was teasing myself for being middle-aged, but I had a perfectly timed coughing fit. Mark was nice enough to pull out an unopened bottle of water from his satchel for me. It was lukewarm, but I gladly accepted it and took three huge swigs. Mark closed his bag. I noticed a rainbow-colored pin on it.

"Excuse me," I apologized. "Not sure where that cough came from. Now that I have you here, I actually want a quick word with you as well."

"Oh?" Mark sounded surprised.

"I want you to come intern for me at Phoenix," I told him. "You exhibit the qualifications of a true *rocket scientist*. If I talk to Dean Brandon, maybe we can work something out for your fall semester, which is just around the corner. September will be here before we know it."

"Really?" Mark had a huge smile on his face.

"I want to mentor you," I said. "My professor in college mentored me, and it's a big part of why I have been so successful in my career. His name is Professor Bernstein. In fact, because of him, I chose to teach part-time, because I felt that one day I could inspire a bright, young mind much like you. He took a unique interest in me for some reason. He never had kids nor married. I believe he always viewed me as the son he never had. Bernstein is one of the most brilliant men I have had the privilege to meet over the years of my studies. "

"You should bring him in to be a guest speaker some time," Mark suggested.

"Ah," I said nervously, because I had reached a point where I felt the need to take a break from teaching. I was coming to a decision in my mind to quit, but I needed to speak to Dean Brandon before I could come to terms with it. I pressed on, "So, does the internship with me sound like a good idea?"

"Yes! I'm in," Mark replied excitedly. "One hundred percent."

My office was located on the floor above my classroom auditorium. I locked myself in there after sprinting down an empty hall. I sighed with relief that I had not run into any of my students or colleagues. The last thing I wanted was to be hounded with more questions. My class had taken a lot of energy out of me. I turned on the TV in my office out of habit. It was on a primetime network channel. The show that was airing was called *Live with Chris Harrington*. He was a well-known on-air news reporter who had started his career working on the battlefronts of America's war on terror. He found much success in his career and was offered his own talk show. On this specific episode, he was interviewing a wife of one of the PA 619 passengers. Her husband was on the airplane.

"Has Phoenix Airlines been updating you and your family since you first got word about the airliner's disappearance yesterday?" Chris asked the woman. There was a caption on the lower third of the screen that read the woman's name, Mary Lou Tomlin.

"We only know as much as the rest of the world does, unfortunately," she said as she wiped a tear from her eye with a tissue.

"Do you think they are telling you everything?" Chris pressed on. "The *whole* truth regarding this matter?"

"I think they are telling us all they can right now," Mary Lou replied. "I wish they would offer the families of those on board that flight some more information."

A few images of the woman's husband and personal family photos were put on the screen for the audience to view. It made it feel so personal. There were so many lives impacted by this missing flight. I felt a tinge of frustration knowing that Jim, Dylan, and Charles had been on it and perhaps lost. And then there was the small bit of information I had hid from everyone I knew and the media. They had been planning a secret mission that even I was still unclear about. Was it crucial I tell authorities this information? Was there a connection? Could it help them find the plane? I had no idea. My mind was exhausted thinking about that pressure and burden I was secretly carrying with me.

I met with Dexter regarding Mark's internship. Dexter agreed to allow Mark special privileges to have an internship out of state and still get school credit. Once business was out of the way, the next question Dexter asked was the one I had been waiting for.

"So, do you have any idea what happened to that Phoenix airliner? For Christ's sake, you were almost on it!" he said in the most melodramatic way possible. It was almost as if he had rehearsed that sentence over and over in his head before seeing me.

"I do not," I answered, the same answer for the hundredth time that day. "It's been a rough day."

"Sorry I asked," Dexter said, looking slightly embarrassed. He got up and pulled a bottle of wine out of his desk drawer. "Care for a glass of this pinot noir?"

"No, thank you," I replied politely while thinking about how alcohol had recently saved my life.

"Your loss," Dexter replied.

All I could think about was how much I had lost recently. Jim was on my mind for a while as Dexter sipped his way through his glass of red wine, jabbering about who-knows-what. I had tuned out at that point.

Then, I came to the abrupt decision to tell Dexter my plan to retire from teaching. I had decided during my class, and I mulled it over in my head before speaking out loud. I loved my job, but with the new promotion and the extra work that would come with losing three important engineers, I knew that my plate would be very full. The fact that I was given a second chance at life meant that I would have another shot to fulfill my own personal desires and goals. Traveling every weekend to Montana did not allow me much of a social life or the opportunity to date. I was not getting any younger, and I had dreams of getting married one day. I clenched my fists under Dexter's desk. My palms began to sweat. I felt nervous. I even felt guilty, thinking about how I would let my mentor, Professor Bernstein, down by walking away from this position he'd prepared me for.

"Ahem," I cleared my throat, but it was mainly to interrupt Dexter's incessant rambling about Phoenix Airlines. "I've reached a very important decision. I want to give you my verbal resignation now, but with acknowledgement that I will be giving you an actual letter of resignation in a couple of days."

Dexter was speechless. He almost dropped his wine glass. He looked at me as if I was joking. Perhaps he thought I was at first. His face looked like he was trying to decide between laughter and disappointment.

"You're joking!" he said, a little more loudly than was necessary. "You can't just quit!"

"The last day has been intense," I told him matter-of-factly. "I lost three colleagues. I nearly lost my own life. I need to take some things off my plate; I bit off more than I could chew. I will need to step up at Phoenix because we lost some key engineers, and I just got a promotion."

"Patrick," he tried to compose himself, "you're one of the best professors on campus. Your students need you. It will be difficult to find a replacement."

"You can give my class to Professor David Chen," I told him. "He will be more than happy to pick up my summer class. After all, we only meet once a week."

"I understand that you have been through an ordeal," Dexter said, sounding defeated, but I knew he would come around. "This is your life, and you have another go at it. You get to see another day. If this is what you truly want, then I can't beg you to stay. But rest assured—I would be on my knees in a heartbeat to keep you around, if I thought it would help."

"Thank you," I said. I really was thankful. I was afraid quitting would be much more difficult because I knew I was one of Dexter's favorite instructors.

"Do you want to give a formal goodbye to your students and colleagues?" Dexter asked.

"There's no time," I said. "I'll have to draft up a farewell email. I still want Mark to intern for me this fall."

"Very well," he responded.

"I have to go," I said abruptly. "Do you think I can sneak out, or is the media still staked outside somewhere?"

"Security removed them," Dexter replied. "I'd be happy to call an officer or two to escort you back to your car."

"That will draw attention," I said. "I'll be fine. It's been a pleasure, Dean Brandon."

Dexter looked slightly annoyed with my quick escape from his office. He did give me a firm handshake and a pat on the back with a forced smile. He must have hoped for a much longer conversation with me, what with the bomb I had just dropped, but I was exhausted from my long day of flying and my two-hour class. There were no sightings of reporters on the walk to my rental car. I got into the car and locked the doors. The feeling of freedom and the weight off my shoulders was very calming. I felt a sense of relaxation washing over me.

The drive through Montana was spectacular, as always. The summer days were long, so the sun was still high in the sky even though 7:00 PM was rolling around. The mountains and green trees took my breath away every time I looked at the picturesque scenery. I asked myself why I lived in the sprawling city of Los Angeles. I had always said I would move back to Montana, but with every three-day weekend I spent there, the monotony of the town made me realize why I lived in Los Angeles. Usually by Saturday night I was bored as hell and felt the urge to be around *normal* people and not those country folks. When I say *normal*, I meant people who were cultured and had seen the world outside of my small town.

My cabin was in Missoula, Montana, a few hundred miles away from our capital, Helena. The cabin was in the woods just outside the city limits, and there was a lovely lake not far from my doorstep. My favorite thing about my cabin was that I could truly *disconnect* from the world. I had no cable or Internet service in the house. My cell phone reception was very spotty and practically useless. The nearest gas station or house was three miles away. I felt secluded and alone. However, when I pulled up to my house, I let out a groan of annoyance. There was a pickup truck parked right in my carport. It was Georgia and Albert.

"Hello, Mom…Dad," I said when I got out of my car to greet my parents, who were sitting on the rocking chairs on my cabin's front porch.

"Were you going to make time to see us?" my mother asked, sounding slightly offended. She was pushing well into her eighties, but she was sharp as a tack. My father, who was almost ninety, had slight memory issues and was usually in his own world. Today, he seemed slightly coherent.

"I'm so glad you missed that flight, Patrick," my father said, and he gave me a tight embrace. "It's nice to have you back home."

"I'm happy to be standing here," I said honestly, and I really meant it. I hugged my parents. I loved them dearly, even if sometimes their unannounced visits annoyed me. "Would you like to stay for dinner? I have some pasta in the house I can whip up."

"That would be lovely." My mother smiled and pushed her thick glasses up her nose as if to get a better look at me.

Dinner that evening in my Montana cabin turned out to be a lovely affair. You really do not appreciate the love of family until you have had a brush with death…I mean, if you wanted to call me missing the plane a brush with death. I also did not have a wife or girlfriend, which my mother kept bringing up over and over at the dinner table. I wished she would not remind me every five minutes. Other than that slight annoyance, it was truly good to be in my home state in the middle of nowhere, where I could not access the local or national news.

"Speaking of news," I interrupted my father, who was talking about some man who won the lottery in town and was all over the local news, "I have something to share with you. I resigned from my position at the university."

"What?" both my parents replied in unison.

"You're not going to that space camp?" my dad asked.

"Honey," my mother replied to my father, "that was his childhood, Albert. He's a grown man now. Remember?" My mother then turned to me and whispered, "His memory comes and goes. I thought he was having a good day today."

My mother spent the rest of our meal talking my ear off and making sure I would make time to visit Montana even though I would not be coming every weekend now.

"I'll wash the dishes, dear," my mother said once we were done. "Go watch some TV with your father in the living room."

"I don't have cable," I reminded her.

"We had our neighbor, who works for the cable company, install an antenna receiver the other day," she said.

I groaned.

My father's memory was fading. He had Alzheimer's disease. I had accepted that he was gone a few years ago when he was first diagnosed. Today he seemed to be alert and was talking to me just fine. We flipped through the channels to find something we could watch. I avoided all the news channels because I was not in the mood to talk about PA 619. Apparently, my father had not grasped the concept that the plane I was supposed to be on had vanished. My mother had told him about it, but it appeared as though he had forgotten, even though he had spoken of it before dinner.

I found a home improvement reality show. My father used to be an architect. I figured this program would help him recall some memories from his past. I was right.

"Remember when you were about ten years old, Pat?" he asked me. "I renovated the farm house on the ranch and designed it to look like the one from your favorite TV show?"

"I do," I said. "You did an amazing job. And it's still standing on your property."

"That it is," my father smiled. "Time flies, doesn't it? You and Charlie really loved that barn."

Charlie was my older brother. He was fifteen years old when I was born. My father used to joke with me that I was an accident because my parents had me at such a late age, but he assured me that they had always wanted two kids. It took a while for my mother to conceive their second child, me. I don't remember my brother Charlie very much. He was killed when he was nineteen years old. I was only four. Charlie was visiting home one holiday. He had been enrolled in college in upstate New York when he passed away. A presumably drunk driver hit him one weekend evening while he was driving back to our house from catching up with some high school friends. I always felt this small bit of sadness in my heart. It felt misplaced. Charlie was my blood and family, but he was a stranger to me. I never knew him. I could not even remember what his voice sounded like. They never found the driver who hit him. He or she had sped off into the Montana night.

"You should stop by the cemetery before you fly back to Los Angeles," my father suggested. I thought about his words for a moment. It was nice to have a seemingly normal conversation.

"Of course I will," I replied. "I'll go first thing in the morning."

My mother came and joined us on the couch. She rested her head on my father's shoulder. Her yawns gave away her fatigue. I always considered myself an only child, and while technically I was now, the truth was that we could have been a family of four. There was something very comforting about being with my elderly parents. They seemed happy. Their lives in Montana were so quaint, while my life in Los Angeles was fast-paced. I imagined what it would be like to be retired. My mother's biggest worry was my father's mental health, but on a day-to-day basis, her normal problems were really just mundane concerns, such as what she would cook for dinner or how crowded the service at their church would be.

"I think it is time for us to head home," my mother announced once the home improvement television show had ended. "Care to walk us out, dear?"

"Gladly," I said, and I walked them to their car. My mother and I helped my father get into their old Chevy pickup truck. "Drive carefully," I told them once they were both inside the vehicle.

They drove off into the Montana evening and back toward the city where their home was located. I looked at my cabin and smiled. It was a pity that I would be visiting it less frequently, now that I had resigned from the university, but I always embraced change. The extra free time would serve me well.

July 16, 2016

The following morning, I paid a visit to the local cemetery. I had to walk several yards up a hill to get to the location of my late brother's tombstone. My parents had a plot reserved a few feet away from where my brother was buried. I had even reserved one for myself. Montana was home. There was nowhere else I would rather be buried than with my family. The backdrop of beautiful mountains and forests added serenity to the cemetery. Whenever my time would come, the patch of grass that I was standing over would be my final resting place.

Charlie's tombstone read "Charles Anthony Baldwin: 1957-1976." I placed my hands on the tombstone and brushed off some dust. It still felt as though I was grieving for a stranger every time I came to visit Charlie's grave. It pained me that I never had the opportunity to know him. I had asked my parents when I was a teenager about him, so that I could have some sense of who he was. I was told he was smart, witty, and loyal. Since he died when I was young, I did not recall the grieving process my parents went through. I could only imagine how difficult it was for them. Had I not been born, they would not have had any children to see them grow old. This thought gave me guilt about spending less time in Montana, now that I was working only for Phoenix Airlines.

I plopped myself on the grassy knoll and took in the fresh, crisp air. The smell of pine trees wafted through the air and into my lungs. It gave me life. These were the simple pleasures that I was deprived of, living in a metropolitan city. Montana would always be my home, and it was important that I embraced my roots. In the last two days, that was the most at peace I had felt since learning of PA 619's disappearance. There were no cameras or reporters hounding me. I was alone. Well, at least as alone as I could be, since six feet under me were thousands of dead bodies. That was a morbid thought, but death was natural, even if sometimes our lives were cut short, like my brother's.

We all die, I said to myself. *I'll be with you one day, Charlie. Maybe, on that day, I will be able to fill you in on everything that has happened to Mom, Dad, and me. Maybe you already know. I can only assume that you are with our grandparents, watching over us. Can you say hi to Jim for me—if he's dead? I want to know what happened to him, Dylan, and Charles. I never thought about it before, Charlie, but you share a name with one of my colleagues who disappeared two days ago. It's funny how I never associated his name with your memory. I guess that is because I call you Charlie and him Charles. Charlie has character. Mom and Dad said you had character. Your name is so fitting and uniquely you. I love you, dear brother.*

I was never religious. My parents were devout Christians, but I was never a big fan of church. I walked by the church on the cemetery lot before leaving. It looked so eerie, sitting on the edge of the forest, void of people.

Strange, I thought. *There's nobody around today. No staff, no nuns, no priests, and no visitors to the cemetery. I like this emptiness. This quiet.*

It was not really quiet, though. There were crickets and birds chirping in the distance. It was not *quiet* like when I was parachuting down to Earth from my first skydive, where I could hear nothing for miles up in the air.

July 17, 2016

I begged my mother not to drag me to church the next morning. I was not ready to be the center of attention. I enjoyed my alone time in the cabin, and it would be a rude awakening to be gawked at by the families I grew up with during the service.

"It's a special Sunday service," my mother pleaded as we walked up the steps and into the church. "I told Father Emerson to say a special prayer for you in today's service. You are the talk of the town. Being here today in the flesh is a miracle from God, dear."

"What's a miracle?" my father chimed in. "What did God do?"

"Your son survived a plane crash," my mother told him.

"You survived a plane crash?!" my father shouted, and several people turned in our direction with their hands over their mouths. A few people pointed and clapped.

"Technically," I corrected her, "they have yet to find any trace of the plane, so to say that it crashed is misleading. Also, as I was not on the actual plane, you can't go around saying I survived it."

"Why didn't you tell me about this plane crash?" my father asked. He sounded hurt.

"Dad," I said, "Mom is exaggerating. It's nothing." I did not feel like explaining the scenario to him again, since he had forgotten.

As expected, the service was focused on my "survival" of Flight 619. Strangers and familiar churchgoers hugged me and wished me many prayers throughout the service. Father Emerson spent a good ten minutes dedicating a prayer to me and the families of those lost on the plane. I was pretty sure my face was red the entire hour I was seated in the pew beside my mother and father.

When the service was over, I avoided the gazes of several members of the church. My mother stayed behind to talk to her friends. I rushed to my rental car and waited with my father.

"That was a lovely service," my father said.

"I guess," I replied. "I don't like this attention."

"What attention?" he asked.

"Oh, um…" I struggled for a few words. It was nice to have someone around not gawking over me for being a "survivor." I kind of liked the fact that my father was oblivious due to his condition. "Oh, there's Mom!"

I bid farewell to my parents and took off to the airport an hour later. It was strange not knowing when I would be returning. It would probably be during the Christmas holidays, which were a few months away. I checked in for my flight upon arrival at the Phoenix Airlines counter. The woman at the counter did a double take and looked at me over her half moon glasses. I handed her my ID so that she could look up my flight record. She was overly polite as she took my checked bags and put them on the conveyor belt behind the ticketing counter. She gave me back my boarding pass and ID with a toothy smile.

I said "Thank you," and walked off.

"Oh, Mr. Baldwin!" she yelled from behind me. "I wanted to say how lucky you are to have not been on that flight the other day."

"Thank you," I replied awkwardly. I felt my face turn red as a few customers in line stared at me and whispered among each other.

6

July 18, 2016

Royce Killington's office had sent me an email calendar invite to report to his office as soon as I arrived at work that Monday morning. His assistant Natasha greeted me. She phoned Royce to announce my presence.

"He's ready to see you, Mr. Baldwin," Natasha said.

I took in more details of Royce's office than when I had been there last, a few days before. His office was the size of a conference room. It was spacious, and all of his furniture was made of fine oak. He had bookshelves along his walls, making his office look like a library. His desk was the size of a piano. He had a few folders on top of it that were labeled "Confidential."

"You needed to see me?" I said while I took a seat in the chair in front of his desk.

"The search is in full force. They've come up empty-handed over the weekend, but search teams are continually searching the Pacific. Australia has sent their teams to aid us in the search for Flight 619. Some images from a Chinese satellite picked up what appears to be debris in a certain area of the ocean. We have some ships on their way now to search. It's the only lead we have at the moment."

"I hope we get answers," I said, "but sadly, that means everyone on the flight is most likely dead, if the plane crashed. I want to remain hopeful that there's a chance it did not crash and we find an explanation for its disappearance."

"Many of the families are hoping too," Royce said. "To them, no news is good news. However, no news also means that their tempers and frustrations are running high. I brought you in here today to give you some restructuring updates for your department. You'll be leading a team of engineers now, since we are down three men, for obvious reasons. I know this might seem too soon, but we need to continue our safety initiative. We need to get on board even more so now, after this international disaster. I'm going to be interviewing candidates to fill the empty high-level spots."

"I understand," I said, but deep down inside, I was horrified with how quickly Royce was planning to move on. I was still grieving. "Do you need me to help with the interview process?"

"I've got that covered," Royce said. "I like to take control of who gets to work on these big projects. It's my company and brand."

"I see. I guess I should let you know that I resigned from my professor position and will now be coming to work on Fridays."

"Good," Royce replied. "You'll have a lot on your hands soon. As do I. I cannot let this incident tarnish the Phoenix brand or my name. My father would be so upset if that happened. He worked all his life to make Killington a brand in itself."

Royce appeared to have been speaking his mind out loud when he spoke of his father. He quickly looked at me and turned red.

"Sorry," he said. "I..."

"No worries," I said quickly as the atmosphere began to feel awkward. Royce walked over to his oversized desk, pulled out his chair and sat down.

"Everything all right?" I asked.

Royce ran his hands through his hair. He had flecks of gray in his blonde hair that the sunlight from his office windows illuminated white. He stared at me for a second, then reached for a frame on his desk and turned the front of it so I could see the photo. It was of his father, Jackson Killington.

"He never liked to be called Jack," Royce said in a low voice. "It was always Jackson or Mr. Killington. He was a proper Englishman who came to America when he was in his twenties. He became a gentleman here in the States. His footsteps are very hard to follow."

"You're doing a great job," I added automatically.

"Thanks, Patrick," Royce replied. He got up from his desk and walked over to his bookshelves. He read the spines of the books on one of the shelves until he found the one he was looking for. "This is his biography. It was written by his best friend."

Royce handed the dusty book to me. The jacket cover had a professional headshot of Jackson Killington on the cover, and the title read *Jackson Killington: The Man Who Made a Killing and a Ton of It.*

"Brilliant title," I commented.

Royce smirked. "Yes, a very good play on our surname. You can have that copy. It pains me to talk about my father...especially his death. I think you will find this read interesting, because at the end of the day, his fortune is what started Phoenix. He inspired me. Perhaps his story can inspire you as we work together to make history."

"Are you sure you want to give this to me?" I asked.

"Please," Royce said, "I have hundreds of copies at my house. I can replenish my bookshelf tomorrow. This book has many answers, yet also opens up many questions. My father was a mystery. He shares something in common with PA 619." Royce had a strange look in his eye for a second, as if his thoughts were somewhere else at that moment. He frowned, and then turned to me with a stoic and quiet expression, as if he were studying every pore on my face.

"Thank you," I said to Royce awkwardly before bidding him farewell. I put Jackson Killington's book in my messenger bag for safekeeping. I walked out of Royce's office and into his lobby. There was a man in a gray suit seated in the waiting area. He looked foreign.

As soon as I was outside, Royce called out to Natasha, "Send in Zyphone Communications, please."

Natasha prompted the man to go into Royce's office. "Mr. Wong, Mr. Killington is ready for you now."

The TV in the lobby was turned on to the news, which was reporting updates about Flight 619.

"Any new developments?" I asked.

"No sign or trace of the plane," Natasha replied. "There are some satellite images that show what appears to be debris in the ocean, and the search in those coordinates is taking place now. No word yet."

The report was showing the path that the airplane took from Los Angeles to where it disappeared after passing over Hawaii. Flight 619 was only near Hawaii because it was taking a unique flight path due to storms in the north portion of the Pacific Ocean. A graphic showed two possible routes the flight could have taken as it diverted from its original flight path. One direction showed the plane heading north towards the Bering Sea, near Russia and Alaska. The other direction showed the plane could have possibly flown to the Southern Sea, near Antarctica. As the transponder was off, satellites could not pick up any of its pings, but some data suggested these two possible routes.

I stepped outside for some fresh air during my lunch break. There was a grassy courtyard in the back of our offices with several benches. I picked my favorite under the shade of a tree and sat down. Even though we were close to the beach, it felt hotter than usual that day. Maybe it was because the offices were in close proximity to the airport and the long runways were reflecting heat. Maybe it was the jet fuel released into the atmosphere from the constant takeoffs and landings from the commercial airliners that was causing the air to feel warmer than usual. I loosened up my tie and unbuttoned the collar of my shirt. I could feel my feet sweat inside my dress shoes. I wished I had been wearing something more casual. I looked ahead of me and saw a fascinating creature.

I laid eyes on this woman for the first time while seated on that bench. She had light brown hair that was wrapped into a simple ponytail. She was wearing an emerald suit blazer and a matching skirt. She wore black high heels, and her nails were well manicured and painted red. She had a purse slung on one shoulder. In the other hand, she was carrying a notebook. She caught my eye and smiled. I felt my face turn red. It was as if the temperature in my cheeks became significantly hotter than the temperature of the weather. I began to feel self-conscious. I knew my forehead was sweating, and the coolness around my armpits meant that I was sure to have pit stains on my shirt. If I were to raise my arms up and wave at this woman, she would see the embarrassing wet stain on my armpits.

She's walking toward me, I thought. There was no one else in the courtyard but us. There had to have been at least ten other vacant benches. Why was she walking straight for the one I was sitting on? I had never met or seen her in my life, yet she had that look in her eye as if she knew who I was. Part of me was hoping she was coming to say something to me. She was a beautiful woman, and she had these piercing green eyes. They were locked dead on mine, as if she was on a mission and could not lose eye contact with me.

"Hi," I stumbled for words awkwardly, once she had stopped in front of me with only two feet of distance between us.

"Are you Patrick Baldwin?" she asked courteously.

"I am," I said. My heart was beating heavily. She knew my name. If she knew who I was, then it could only mean one thing. And my worst fears were realized. My heart sank at her next words.

"My name is Francesca Fields," she said while extending her hand to shake mine, "I am a journalist for the *Los Angeles Times*."

It was as if her beauty slapped me on the face and taunted me. *She's part of the media*, I thought.

"Um, hello," I said softly. "I'm not talking to the press."

"How daring of you to assume I came to see you for anything press related," she said sharply. That caught me off guard.

"Well, I…" I trailed off.

"Do you assume you are someone noteworthy that I should interview for the newspaper?" she added.

"Excuse me?" I was annoyed now. "What can I help you with…" I looked at her hand and noticed she was not wearing a wedding ring, "… Miss Fields?"

"I am curious about one thing and one thing only," she answered. "My team has tried to speak with Mr. Royce Killington on the matter of Flight 619, but all press inquiries have been deferred. I know that you are not allowed to speak to the media, but I was hoping we could talk…*off the record*."

"No!" I said flatly. "Can't you people leave me alone?"

Francesca looked at me closely as if she were trying to read my mind.

She looked well for her age. She must have been in her mid-thirties. She took a seat right next to me and turned her head in my direction, with her hands elegantly placed on her lap, and said, "You don't know any more than I do, do you?"

"You're right," I said.

"Why were you going to Beijing?" she asked.

"I thought you were just saying I'm not someone noteworthy enough to be interviewed," I said sarcastically.

"This is not an interview," she replied. "I told you, it would be off the record. A friend of mine had a daughter who was on that airplane. If I may be honest here, the truth is…I was waving around my press badge because I thought I could use that power to get answers for my own personal use, to help my friend who lost his daughter on PA 619. He was a childhood best friend, and his daughter was like family to me. I want to help him find closure. Do you know what it's like to lose someone and not have closure?"

I racked my mind for a few seconds. She looked very serious and stern. There might have been a trace of tears glistening in her eye, but she played it off as something getting caught in it. Her beauty was mesmerizing, and it was perhaps due to that fact that I spoke more freely than I intended to.

"Why yes, I do, Miss Fields," I answered. "I lost my brother to a presumed drunk driving accident decades ago. I was only four years old. I never had the opportunity to know him. I'll never really know who he was, except for the anecdotes from my parents. It's hard to have closure from something you don't remember, but was a part of your family's life for several years. He died at nineteen. That means there was almost two decades of his life that I will never know much about. So, yes, I know what not having closure is like. The alleged drunk driver never stopped. It was a hit and run. My parents never met the person responsible for his death. I might die one day never knowing who killed my brother. Sadly, your friend may not ever know what happened to that plane. I don't even know. Royce does not know. Answers are being searched for, and all we can do now is wait, like the rest of the world, with bated breath. I'm only lucky that I'm alive today, with the ability to wait with the world for those answers. And I lost *three* colleagues on that plane too."

I felt myself heat up even more from the rant I had gone on against this woman who was a stranger to me. A part of me felt satisfaction because she looked at a loss for words. She stood up abruptly and began to walk away.

"No goodbyes then?" I called out sarcastically.

She turned around and stared at me. Her cheeks looked flushed, as if she was blushing from embarrassment. "I'm very, very sorry. I do not know how to respond to your statement."

"It wasn't a statement," I retorted. "Nor was it something for you to write about. I see you are holding a notebook with a pen. How could you have the audacity to come up to me and pretend that you are trying to help your friend when you have *journalist* written all over you—and your notebook?"

"I was not lying," she said, and the next thing that happened was unexpected. She began to cry.

She walked slowly back toward me and put her notebook on my lap. I reached for it and opened it up to the first page. There was the name Mallory Cooper written in ink. It was my guess that the notebook belonged to this Mallory person. It was a college student's science notebook, with very neat handwritten notes on every page. It was not what I had expected. There were no notes about Flight 619 or anything news related. This notebook did not belong to Francesca. I felt my face turn red.

"Why does the name sound familiar?" I said aloud without meaning to. Then I had a flashback of the CNN report I had recently seen. Mallory Cooper was on the flight. Then there was a photo of her parents. I had recognized the father as the man I had spoken to at the airport. He was the father of the girl who was going to study abroad in China. That girl was the owner of the very notebook I was holding. Chills went up and down my spine. I turned my head up and looked into Francesca's piercing eyes, which had silent tears streaming from them. "I...I briefly spoke to her father at the airport. I saw her parents on the news. She was on my flight—the one I should have been on."

"Craig is a dear old friend of mine," Francesca said with a hoarse voice. She cleared her throat and continued. "I grew up with Craig...Mallory's father. His family and mine are very close. I don't care about writing a story.

I don't care about what happened. All I care about are answers and hoping that she might still be alive out there somewhere."

"I'm sorry I was harsh." I stood up so that I was not awkwardly looking up at her.

"Don't be," she replied. "It was rude of me to intrude upon your privacy like this, especially because I write for the paper. You were just defending yourself. I can only imagine how you must feel. You've been through enough, I'm sure."

Something daring was building up inside me. I felt it swell like a volcano that was prepared to erupt. Words were bubbling at the surface of my lips, and I was unsure how to spit them out. I took a deep breath and said, "Would you like to talk more over drinks? I mean—I don't feel comfortable here at work. Someone might see us and get the wrong idea that I'm speaking to the press."

"Oh right, yes," she said with a look of surprise. She squinted her eyes, as if trying to frame me into focus. "When and where?"

"Why not tonight?" I asked. The truth was, I was attracted to her. Perhaps this was not going to end up as a date, but part of me felt like it could not hurt to get to know this woman more. "There's a pretty quiet dive bar we can go to in West Hollywood. It's called The Goat's Head."

"Sure," she said with half a smile. "I can meet you there. Does 8:00 sound good?"

"That will work," I replied.

"Then I will see you tonight," she said, and she bid me farewell before walking out of the courtyard.

When you have something that you are really anxious for, time tends to laugh at you and move excruciatingly slow. The rest of my day at the office felt like years. I kept glancing at the clock on my computer screen and to the clock on my wall, to see if they were actually in sync or if time was playing a trick on me. I tried to pass the time between 5:00 and 6:00, before I could leave for the day, by looking up images online and in one of my men's style magazines. I was searching for style tips on a perfect way to dress for what I pretended in my mind was a first date with Francesca. I was an engineer. Fashion was not my forte. Once 6:00 PM arrived, I darted out the door and was on my way home to prepare for my meeting. My only hope was that traffic would not be a nightmare, but as is typical at that hour in Los Angeles, it was.

Eight arrived much faster than anticipated. *The irony*, I thought. I found myself only ten minutes late for my meeting with Francesca. She was sitting at a corner of the bar and sipping on a glass of white wine. She stood up at the sight of me and extended her soft hands for me to shake, which I willingly did. The bar was lacking patrons that evening. There were maybe only five other people besides the waitstaff.

"Sorry I'm a few minutes late," I said, pushing my hair back and wiping nervous sweat off my forehead with the cuff of my long-sleeved red plaid shirt.

"Don't worry," Francesca said. "It's quite all right. It's only ten minutes past eight."

The bartender stopped by our table and asked for my drink order. I chose rum and Coke. My hour and a half with Francesca was electrifying, to say the least. I learned so much about her. She was born in San Francisco, but attended the University of Southern California for journalism fifteen years ago. She had lived in L.A. ever since. She was very attentive and she locked eyes with me so intently. The more rum and Coke I drank, the easier it was to have a conversation. She seemed to be enjoying herself. At one point, my hand brushed up against hers. I felt my face burn with embarrassment. It must have showed, because it appeared as though she smirked, and then she ended it with a smile and a flash of her pearly white teeth. It was also comforting that she did not bring up PA 619 once during our meeting. I was tempted to ask her about Mallory's father Craig, but I decided that since our conversation had been going so smoothly, I would avoid the subject entirely.

"You keep glancing at your phone," she said while catching my eyes locking onto my phone's screen. "In a hurry?"

"No," I said to her. "It's a habit. I always have to know what time it is. I rarely ever go out for drinks on a workday. I tend to go to bed pretty early. If I stay up later than eleven, it feels way too late. Ha! I sound like an old man now, don't I?"

"Not at all," she giggled. "It's always nice to go to sleep at a decent hour when you have a full-time job Monday through Friday. I usually continue to work from home after leaving the office. It's nice to shut down my work life tonight. I'm glad you invited me to hang out. You've been a good conversationalist."

"I'm glad to hear that," I smiled. "Should we close our tabs soon?"

"Yeah," she agreed. "I'm ready for bed. I have an early call tomorrow."

Once our bill had been paid for, split equally on our credit cards, I walked her to her car. She drove a red BMW. It was sporty and clean, as if it had been washed that day.

"Thanks for taking the time to hang out," she said.

"We didn't talk about your friend," I finally brought up the subject.

"That's fine," she said. "I was more interested in getting to know you."

My heart skipped a beat. She really wanted to hang out with me. Was this a date? My confidence began to rise like water boiling over a pot. The result was always a splashy mess, and my next response cemented that notion.

"So, was this a date?" I asked. I wanted to hit myself on the head. Why had I asked such a juvenile question, as if I was in high school and my mother was about to pick me up from that bar? Francesca blushed, yet she was struggling for words.

"I, um…" she looked confused. "You're a really nice guy…"

There it was. The "nice guy" line. I had heard that one too many times. It felt as though my heart had been jerked out of my rib cage and squeezed like a sponge over a dirty stove. It felt as if it was being used to clean off the steaming hot burners over which that boiling pot sat. Why did I ask such a dumb question?

"What I mean to say is…I mean, why don't we set up a real date for our next meet up?" Francesca smiled at me. I stared back with a look of confusion.

"Yes! Yes, of course!" I said, a little more loudly than anticipated.

Francesca giggled, and then she kissed my cheek. "It's time for me to go. You have my number now, so why don't you let me know when it's a good time? Preferably, let's meet up again next week. I have a few work deadlines this week that are taking up my spare time."

"I'll look at my schedule and we can plan this date soon," I said. "Night, Francesca."

She drove off in her red car, and I stood there in front of The Goat's Head with a transfixed look on my face, as if I had just lived a dream. Perhaps it was the nerdy engineer side of me coming out. A beautiful girl—woman—had just asked me out. On a real date.

7

July 21, 2016

I was sitting on my living room couch with a frozen dinner on the coffee table before me. I left the contents of the processed food in its original plastic container. I felt like such a bachelor. Normally, I did not mind cooking, but with the extra workload I had been given since the disappearance of my colleagues, I literally had more on my plate than the disgusting brown frozen meatloaf I was about to consume.

It had been a week since Flight 619 disappeared from the sky and radar. The news did not change much. The questions revolving around this mystery remained the same since day one, and there were still no answers. However, more and more questions arose. A new spin on the story was focusing on the pilot. His name was Victor Cohen. He was an experienced captain who had been flying for over two decades.

The report on the news, which I was watching intently, was about a theory that Victor Cohen had malicious intent and might have maneuvered the plane off course. I did not personally know Victor, but if I was a member of his family, I would have been outraged. It felt as though this theory made Victor a scapegoat to get the attention and scrutiny of the nation off Phoenix Airlines. When I searched the Internet, I found reports that Victor's family was indeed irate about the entire situation. A search had been ordered by the FBI to raid his apartment. He was a single man living in a one-bedroom apartment in Santa Monica. Nothing suspicious was found except for a flight simulator that had been installed on his computer. To me, that was not suspicious at all. It meant he took his work home and studied his craft in the art of flying. There were anecdotes on the news reports from colleagues that said he trained on his free time so that he could be prepared for the most unusual scenarios. "He was an overachiever," one of his former co-pilots was quoted.

Speaking of co-pilots, they ruled out Victor's co-pilot, Stanley Dupree, as a suspect. His house was searched as well, with permission from his wife. There was nothing strange in his records that the FBI found out of the ordinary.

I looked up at my television screen and two photos taken from Victor and Stanley's Facebook pages were on display. Stanley had black, thick glasses. He was much younger than Victor; however, he appeared to be balding. Victor's photo depicted him in his pilot uniform. He had a black mustache and curly black hair. He looked to be in his forties. Once their photos were removed and the camera panned back to the anchorwoman, she began to talk about another passenger named Aaron Moss, who was a commercial pilot as well, but traveling to China on vacation and off-duty. He was cleared as a suspect as well when the FBI was unable to turn up anything suspicious in his background. The news report then moved to the subject of Royce Killington. I reached for my remote and raised the volume.

The anchorwoman began her report. "Royce Killington, the son and heir of the late mogul and entrepreneur Jackson Killington, was not available for comment when we reached out to him about how involved Phoenix is with the search for the missing airplane in the Pacific Ocean. Meanwhile, Australia has joined in the search for the missing airliner led by former Australian Defense Force Air Chief Marshal Ted Holt. Radar pings, or handshakes, as they are being referred to, were picked up heading south from Hawaii, where the last actual radio tower communication was made with the plane. Audio from the control tower in Honolulu has just been released to us. It was the last words spoken from the cockpit of 619."

The audio began to play during the report. "This is PA 619 checking in. We are clearing over Hawaii, en route to Beijing," came Victor Cohen's voice. "Good morning, PA 619. Copy that. Have a safe flight." Someone at air traffic control in Honolulu had responded to Victor's final contact at 5:00 AM Pacific Daylight Time, which was 2:00 AM in Honolulu. Communication was lost with the plane an hour later.

The reporter continued, "So, there was nothing suspicious about that communication. It seemed to be normal protocol. Those were the last words and the last time PA 619 was ever heard from. Air traffic officers realized the plane was missing an hour later, when it could not be located on the radar. They declared the airplane lost. It should be noted that the reason the airplane was flying near Hawaii, which is not the normal route for a flight from Los Angeles to Beijing, was due to apparent weather conditions. Aviation meteorologists who signed off on the flight route change were unavailable for comment."

I felt frustrated with the news. Almost every major news network was still talking about PA 619 as if it had happened that very day. I realized a week was not that long, and the mystery of a Boeing 787 disappearing without a trace was a huge story, but I felt they were beating this story down to the ground. I retired to my bedroom and reached for Jackson Killington's book. I had placed it on my nightstand. I'd started reading it a few days ago. It was a very interesting read. Jackson Killington was born in London to a middle class family. His father left his mother and him when he was around thirteen years old, leaving them with nothing. Jackson had to work his way up from the bottom. When he turned eighteen, he set off for America to begin a new life for himself in Texas. Every chapter was a pretty detailed account of his life. It felt as if I knew him.

I found it interesting that a British man like Jackson would end up in Texas, but there was so much affordable land and opportunity in the Lone Star State. Jackson was able to buy property, which would set in motion his path as a successful real estate developer. Jackson would eventually marry his wife Fiona, whom he had met on a return trip to visit his mother in London. He brought Fiona back to the States with him, where she eventually gave birth to their only son, Royce. Royce had grown up in Dallas, where the Killingtons resided, before he packed his bags and moved to Los Angeles. Royce had wanted to become a film producer, but did not have much success with the backing of some independent films he financed.

I was finally at the last chapter of the autobiography, *Jackson Killington: The Man Who Made a Killing and a Ton of It.* I thought the title was clever and interesting. The title of the last chapter seemed a bit too morbid, and I was unsure how any editors or publishers would have let the author publish it. The last chapter's title was "The Killing of Killington."

Jackson Killington's death was a widely known story. I never talked about it at work because of my close proximity to his son, but his death was a mystery in itself. The one good thing about this book was that the author was Jackson's best friend, Colin Shaw. Therefore, the account of Jackson's death would be the most accurate, because the media always spun things in many directions.

This final chapter was exceptionally detailed. I could picture Jackson's final day. I read the excerpt aloud.

"It was the morning of October 2, 1998. Killington checked into his penthouse office in downtown Dallas. He greeted his executive assistant, Natasha Wilkins—"

Wow, Natasha was Royce's father's assistant too? They've kept her in the family, I said to myself. I realized I had never really taken the time to become acquainted with Natasha, so I found it interesting that she was working for the Killingtons for almost two decades. I continued reading.

Natasha said she heard a click on his door, as if he had locked it. He never locked his door from the inside. Natasha knew better than to question her boss, so she continued with her administrative work. Everything that happened after the moment Jackson locked himself in his office is all speculation. What I will describe is what I believe happened to him inside.

Jackson went to retrieve a steel briefcase that he'd always kept hidden. Behind an expensive portrait of a sunrise over the horizon of an ocean that hung on his magnificent wall was a safe. Jackson entered his passcode and pulled out the briefcase. Inside the case was $500,000 in cash. This was no ordinary briefcase, though. It was the size of a large suitcase. The denominations of bills inside varied. They were mostly hundred dollar bills, but there were even one-dollar bills, fives, tens, and fifties. People found it peculiar that he did not have twenty-dollar bills in his case. Jackson, who was a billionaire, claimed he was "not that twenty-dollar bill Jackson." He had some strange superstitious belief that he could not carry or even spend a twenty-dollar bill, because the president on the note was Andrew Jackson. Jackson Killington believed he was a man who made his own fortune, and did not like the fact that money, which he was made of, had a bill with someone who shared his name. (Though it must be noted that Andrew's surname was the same as Killington's first name, and technically not the same.) Jackson once said he wanted to be remembered for this strange quirk. He never wanted to be associated with a common twenty-dollar bill.

Jackson's next move, once he pulled out the case, was extracting the wads of cash and tearing off the straps that bound them. He then tossed the bills all over his office, as if the money meant nothing to him. He let them fall on the ground. At that point, it is believed that Jackson reached for his most expensive bottle of scotch and drank it straight from the bottle. He then smashed it onto the ground. This was the next sound that Natasha heard. She walked to the door and knocked to ask if Jackson was okay. He replied, "Do nothing." Those were the last words she ever heard from him. Moments later, there was a gunshot. Natasha screamed and called 911 immediately after. She tried to kick down his door in panic, but was unable to.

Jackson allegedly put a gun to his head and pulled the trigger. Natasha ran downstairs to find help, as the entire penthouse floor was dedicated to his office. Then there was an explosion. Natasha was one floor below, and felt the ground and ceiling above her shake. The lights flickered, and everyone ducked under their desks.

Firefighters arrived on the top floor and found the door to Jackson's office blown out. A fire had started, but they were able to put it out within ten minutes. They found Jackson's wallet and the money scattered on the floor next to a gun, but there was no sign of Jackson's body. When the firefighters opened his wallet, they found his credit card, driver's license, and a twenty-dollar bill inside.

The office was treated as a crime scene. They found gunpowder residue and fragments of shrapnel. It was ruled that Jackson had blown himself up. It was thought that Jackson had shot the gun for fun, but never intended to use it to take his own life. There were strange charges on his credit card statement that led authorities to believe he had purchased some kind of explosive which he *used to take his own life. Whatever the device, it had literally blown him into nothingness. There was no body or pieces of his body left to bury. Stranger than this very high profile and planned suicide was the fact that he had a twenty-dollar bill inside his wallet, when it was known by his close friends that he never carried or spent them. I used it as a clue to help me get closure into why he killed himself. Why would a man who has everything want to take his own life? What could he not have? My guess was normalcy. He found the twenty-dollar bill to be so common and normal. Perhaps he secretly wished his life were normal because he could not handle the pressure of his demanding, high-profile life and job. That's my guess, but this is one mystery we may never solve.*

I remembered the headlines from nearly two decades ago about the tragic death of Jackson Killington. Many people thought he was murdered, but the clues that were uncovered led authorities to believe it was, in fact, a suicide. I could only imagine the pain that Royce must have felt dealing with this. His mother passed away a few years later from cancer. He was left with a huge fortune, as he was the only son and heir.

I prepared for bed with a final thought in my mind before taking a Xanax to put me to sleep: What if Jackson had never taken his own life? Phoenix Airlines only came into fruition because Royce used his inheritance money to build the airline empire. It was strange to think how someone's life ending could mean the beginning of something else. Phoenix Airlines became a booming business that offered jobs to thousands of Americans, including myself. During a time when the economy had been rough, those jobs had been putting food on the tables of several families, and vodka in my own freezer. I laughed at my own foolish thought of how I wasted my money on alcohol. I closed my eyes, and before I knew it, it was another day.

July 22, 2016

Friday had come at last. I had set dinner plans with Francesca for that evening at a restaurant in the Hollywood Hills, nestled in the canyons, called Peace. I had taken a cab from my condo in Westwood because I was sure that I would be having several glasses of wine with my dinner. Peace had the best pinot noir in town. I usually ordered a bottle with dinner. When I was ten minutes away from the restaurant, Francesca called my cell.

"Hi, Patrick," she said. "I hope you don't mind. I know this was going to be a dinner date, but, well, I felt bad…and…well, he was feeling really down, so I invited him. He wants to meet you."

"What are you mumbling about?" I asked.

"Craig. Craig Cooper—Mallory's dad—my friend," she answered.

"He's joining us at dinner? But I only made a reservation for two." I began to feel annoyed. I had not seen her since we had drinks at The Goat's Head, and this time around it was supposed to be a proper date. Now I had a third wheel to deal with, and I knew that the table conversation would be nothing but questions about Flight 619.

"I'll make it up to you, I promise," she pleaded. She sounded sincere and honest. "He was feeling very lonely tonight. He separated from his wife a few months ago, and this tragedy has only made them grow further apart. His ex-wife, Charlotte, is in shock and does not want to be around him right now."

"Oh…okay," I answered. "I'll see you shortly."

Francesca was standing outside the entrance to the restaurant in a black dress with floral print. Her hair was in a ponytail, and she had a black clutch at her side. Next to her was a man with blond hair and stubble on his face. His eyes looked bloodshot, as if he had not slept in days. He was wearing a blue button-down shirt with a teal green tie and brown chino pants. His shirt was not completely tucked in properly. I recognized him immediately.

"Mr. Baldwin," Craig said, extending his hand for me to shake. "I did not think we would ever cross paths again."

"I'm sorry for your loss," I said truthfully.

"I'm sorry for yours too," Craig replied. "You had three colleagues on the flight, didn't you?"

"I did," I replied. I looked over at Francesca, who gave me an apologetic look.

"Craig and I are old family friends," she spoke up.

"I'm sorry to crash your dinner," Craig added. "I know you two were planning on a one-on-one meeting. I pretty much begged Francesca to drag me along. I felt that, by meeting you, I could begin to get closure with this tragedy. I haven't slept much in days." He really looked like he had not.

"I'm not sure I can truly help you with closure," I said honestly. "I, myself, have yet to find my own."

The hostess sat us in a back corner of the restaurant. We all ordered glasses of wine and a few appetizers. Craig wasted no time in jumping to the subject of Flight 619.

"So, you don't know anything? I mean, you work for Phoenix."

I looked at him with a smile, even though inside, I wanted to grab him by the tie and choke him out of annoyance. "As I've told everyone else in my life, I am as clueless as the public."

"She really wanted to study abroad in China," Craig went on. "I was so supportive—on the outside. On the inside, I was afraid of sending her to a foreign country. I keep asking myself, 'What if we had booked an earlier or later flight?'"

"You cannot blame yourself," Francesca added. "There's no way you could have known 619 would disappear. Let's be hopeful that the plane will be found, and we receive good news with a reasonable explanation."

"It's been over a week," Craig said sadly while fidgeting with a roll of bread. "I keep trying her cell phone in hopes that she will answer. It goes straight to voicemail. I have left several messages for her. I want her back. She is my only child."

The meal consisted of Craig telling us anecdotes of his daughter's upbringing. When our food arrived half an hour later, he barely touched anything on his plate. Francesca was eating her salad and nodding with interest at everything Craig was telling us, but I could tell that she started to feel fatigued with this third party conversation. I gave her a couple of looks that I made sure silently spoke my frustration with her change in our dinner plans. Her eyebrows furrowed in what I perceived as embarrassment. Craig seemed to be in his own world as he kept going on and on about Mallory's sweet sixteen birthday. The waitress came back and asked us if we were interested in dessert.

"Mallory's cake was beautiful. We put sixteen sparklers on the top to signify her age," Craig said after the waitress handed us the dessert menus.

She gave Craig an inquisitive look that went unnoticed by him. She shrugged her shoulders and said, "I'll be back for your order. I recommend the chocolate soufflé."

"I'm sorry," Craig said a few minutes later. "I've been going on and on and haven't let either of you speak. It's been so difficult. I'm going to start a fundraising group to raise money to help with the cost of the search party. A group of the other family members of 619's passengers have a fear that the search will become too expensive, and if they don't find the plane soon, the search may be disbanded due to incurring costs."

"That sounds like a positive thing for you to do to keep busy and hopeful," I said absentmindedly. "You know what? I'm going to skip dessert. Here's some cash. This should cover my portion of the meal. I need to run. It was a pleasure meeting you, Mr. Cooper."

"Call me Craig," he responded, and he seemed slightly put off by my obvious disinterest in being at the table. Francesca looked taken aback, but I could tell she knew it was her fault that I was not pleased with the added dinner guest.

"I will be praying for your daughter as well," I added, even though I was not going to actually pray. I had not even prayed for my own friends who were also lost on board. I only said it as a figure of speech. I waved farewell to Craig and Francesca and left the restaurant without a glance back.

I was lying in my bed, watching some random reality show about a redneck family that owned a gun store in Arkansas, when I received a phone call from Francesca. I answered it after five rings.

"Hello," I answered.

"Patrick," she said, "I'm very sorry. I thought that he could work on finding closure by talking to you."

"He expected me to have answers because of my affiliation with Phoenix," I replied sternly. "You put me on the spot. I thought we would have a first official date tonight. I was hoping to get to know *you* more. Not your childhood friend, who just so happened to have a family member on board PA 619."

"Can I please make this up to you? I promise, no more talks about the plane or even my work at the newspaper, if that will put you at ease," she pleaded.

I was silent for a few minutes, mulling over her genuine and apologetic request. "Fine. However, I'll let you plan out the date."

"Fair enough," she said. "I'll be in touch soon, then."

"Okay then," I said. "Talk soon."

Part of me felt as though I was playing some kind of game. I liked to be forward and upfront when it came to dating, but she had crossed the line and put me in an uncomfortable situation. If she wanted to make it up to me, then she would have to woo me over again. I was still uncomfortable about her work and investigation on Flight 619, but I wanted to give her the benefit of the doubt that she legitimately had a romantic interest in me.

Jackson Killington's book was still on my nightstand. I opened it up again and perused the pages. I opened the book to the final chapter, where I had used a twenty-dollar bill as a bookmark for the sheer irony of it, and reread the chapter. Nothing new stood out to me. I wasn't sure what I was looking for. His death was so bizarre and tragic, much like the disappearance of Flight 619. To this day, there were no real answers as to why he killed himself in such a fashion. I flipped to the beginning of the book and found the dedication page. It read:

To TOM,

My inspiration, intellect, and reason for being. My adulation for you all,
and the conception of The Presence.

Curious, I thought. What a strange dedication. Who was Tom? Why would the author, Colin Shaw, not dedicate the biography of Jackson Killington to Jackson Killington himself? He was, after all, one of his best friends. I did a Google search for a "Tom Killington," thinking it might have been a family member of Jackson's. I found nothing. I then searched "Jackson Killington's biography dedication page." A few blog articles turned up in the query, but nothing interesting. With everything I read online, I could not find any conclusion about the dedication page.

Colin Shaw never commented or answered any questions about it either.

I found one blog that was purely a conspiracy theorist site. It alleged that Tom was Jackson's killer, and that Colin Shaw knew the real truth, but was forced to write the biography to emphasize that Jackson had committed suicide. There were many theories about Tom's identity, but none of it seemed to make any real sense. It was a bunch of farfetched fictitious ideas. The theorists had researched anyone who knew Jackson, and they could not come up with anyone named Tom.

I was preparing to go to bed when a sudden idea popped into my mind. I opened up the book to the dedication page and reread it. A few things stood out. Tom was spelled in all caps: "TOM." Another interesting part of the dedication page was that the first letters of the words "The Presence" at the end of the sentence were also capitalized.

I Googled "Jackson Killington The Presence" and found only one related article. My jaw dropped when I saw the author of the article on this random journal that came up in my query. His name was just below the description of the search results—"By Professor Claude Bernstein."

It was my former professor…the man who taught me all I knew about aviation and inspired me to teach. He had taken a personal interest in me for some reason. He once asserted, "Patrick, you have the ambitious fire inside you to burn forever. Never give up." I looked out my window at the Los Angeles night sky with a feeling of guilt in the pit of my stomach, as I had recently resigned from my professor position.

I moved my mouse over the link to the journal and clicked on it. My heart sank. It went to a webpage with an error message: "Not Found. The requested URL was not found on this server."

August 3, 2016

The last few days were extremely busy for me. Royce hired two new engineers instead of three, whom I was to manage. His assistant Natasha had informed me that they wanted to make cuts to the headcount overhead, because airfare sales declined for Phoenix in the month of July more than they ever had since the company's inception. Royce was being cautious. He was hopeful that the small plummet in sales was only because of the bad publicity Phoenix Airlines was receiving from the media while the search for the flight continued. Weeks had passed, and not one single piece of debris had been discovered.

I attended a meeting with our two new engineers and two of our publicity team members. It was so strange to meet with publicity because of the vast difference in our fields. It was because the two new engineers had not been media trained. The company wanted to make sure they knew the importance of not speaking on behalf of Phoenix during this difficult period. There was internal concern that the media would begin to hound them, in hopes that since they were new, they would be naïve enough to give away private information.

The first engineer was an Indian man named Pravish Patel, who graduated from Harvard and had been working with an airline company in Singapore before moving to America for this job. He was around my age and wore clear-framed glasses. He had black medium-length hair that was long enough to cover his ears. The other engineer was an Italian woman named Paola Andreoni. She was from Rome, but had been working at a competitor airline in the United States for over ten years. She still had an Italian accent. She was thirty-four years old, with straight black hair that she wore in a ponytail. She had a light complexion with freckles and green eyes. She had good looks and an impressive résumé.

Brad Warren was our head of public relations. His assistant, Sara Brady, was taking notes as he spoke to us in the small conference room where our meeting was being held. It was the same conference room where Royce had informed me of my promotion, where I'd had my last meeting with Jim, Dylan, and Charles.

"This is the most updated information we have," Brad said, after he concluded his long drawn-out media training for Pravish and Paola. I looked at them both, and I could tell they had come back to reality from a daze. I held the urge to laugh. Brad continued, "The search is still going strong. There have been a few false alarms where some satellites picked up what appeared to be debris; however, when the ships arrived at the coordinates given, there was nothing to be found. Extensive research on the flight data of 619 was done, and it suggests that the plane made a deliberate turn south after it flew over Hawaii, in the direction of the South Pacific Ocean. Data infers that it was flying in the direction of New Zealand and Australia, but we aren't too sure, since communication with the plane was lost. Analysts are doing some mathematical equations to project the flight's path based on its diversion after Hawaii. They are considering the amount of fuel left on the plane and the speed at which it was clocked when last flying. We can only make assumptions based on these theories and data. There are several small islands on the projected rerouted flight path of PA 619, including Fiji, Tonga, and Samoa, to name a few. None of those islands ever reported seeing a plane, nor did they pick up anything on their radar. It's possible that the fate and resting place of this plane, if it was downed in the end, is in the South Pacific Ocean, adjacent to New Zealand and Australia. However, it could be hundreds or thousands of miles away from any land. That's all the information and facts we have for now."

Brad and Sara thanked us at the end of the meeting for our time. When they left, I addressed Pravish and Paola.

"So sorry you had to go through that," I said with a smile. "If it's any consolation, I was grilled by Royce regarding the same thing right after the plane disappeared."

"It's amazing you were not on it," Paola said. "You're a very lucky man."

"It seems so," I said. "I've been happily avoiding the media for the last few weeks. They've stopped chasing me."

"I'm glad to be on the team," Pravish said. "Many of my friends thought I was crazy for taking this job after what happened, but I know that there is an initiative to build safer planes. I want to be a part of this tremendous effort."

"That will be a very big project, and what we will be dedicating most of our time to during the fall," I told them. "Royce believes that this safety initiative will help rebuild our image. We have a meeting with him and members of the third party companies that are helping us build it later in the week. Also, our intern starts tomorrow."

I had been so distant from the University of Montana since I'd left the campus for good three weeks ago that I had nearly forgotten I'd hired my former student, Mark Crane, to be my intern. A few days ago, I'd received an email from him that made me feel guilty for forgetting my promise to him.

Dear Professor Baldwin,

I'm following up with you on the internship at Phoenix Airlines you offered to me during my last class with you. I was saddened to hear you resigned, but I have prepared to come to Los Angeles for the fall semester to work for you. I have attached my résumé, should you need my background and qualifications for the human resources department. Please let me know if you need anything further and when the start date will be, so that I can begin looking for housing in Los Angeles.

Best,
Mark C. Crane

Upon receipt of Mark's email, I gave him a phone call and confirmed that I would get his information and résumé to HR. Once his credentials were approved by HR and Dean Brandon, I was able to get him on payroll and a start date for August 4. It was earlier than the original start date in September I had proposed to him in my classroom a few weeks back.

I was also waiting for an email response from Professor Bernstein. A few weeks before, after I had done an extensive Google search regarding the strange dedication page that author Colin Shaw had written, I sent an email to my former professor and mentor. I asked him about the online journal link I found with his name attached to it, which was no longer published on the website's server. Nearly two weeks had passed and there was no response. I felt slightly annoyed, because we had been good about keeping in touch during my career as an aerospace engineer. I had not spoken to him in over a year. The fact that his name had showed up during my search to discover who Tom was felt like a sign that I should reach out.

I checked my email religiously, both on my laptop and mobile device. Nothing. It was out of the ordinary. The only explanation I could come up with was that he might have been out of the country on vacation. He was known for shutting off technology when he was on personal travels.

I spent that evening doing what had become a common practice before bed. A bottle of red wine sat on my nightstand half empty (or half full), next to a glass filled nearly to the brim. I reached for the glass and took a sip. My ritual consisted of watching a major news channel. On this evening, I had it on a conservative right-wing program called *Tact and Fact*. The anchor was going on about how the president was wasting so much money and resources on the search for Flight 619, and was insisting that billionaire Royce Killington foot the bill.

"We have so many Americans without jobs, and our Democratic president is playing Marco Polo in the Pacific Ocean with submarines and ships, looking for a plane that presumably vanished out of thin air," the anchor, Will O'Connor, was ranting. "President Howard is to blame for our recent economic downfall and national debt."

I rolled my eyes and changed the channel to a liberal program.

There was a split screen on this show. On the left side of the screen, the anchorman, dressed in a gray suit, was announcing his guest on the right split screen, broadcasting live from New Mexico. The man seemed a bit strange. He wore a fisherman's hat and vest. He had a long, curly silver beard and thick eyeglasses. Once he was introduced, he began to explain his purpose for being on the show.

"The truth is, a giant metal object cannot simply disappear into thin air," the man by the name of Percival Webb was saying melodramatically. "What goes up must come down…unless it is never found. Flight 619 never came down. Nobody has been able to report even the smallest fragment of debris in the ocean. No one saw any kind of explosion, and there was no distress signal or call for help from the cockpit. There's only one theory that can support this, and that is simply the fact that this airplane was abducted by beings from another planet."

"I'm going to stop you right there," the anchorman, Jonathan Whitmore, cut in. "So, to clarify to the audience or anyone just joining us, you are a UFOlogist and you have a theory that a species from another galaxy took the airliner from Earth?"

"That is correct," Percival continued. "I've been abducted before. I do not believe they intended to harm the passengers and crew, but I do believe they want to colonize them on the planet where they are from, which is a mystery to me. They never told me what part of the universe they came from. A few years ago, there were these strange lights in Nevada, just outside Las Vegas!"

There was a Twitter feed scrolling on the bottom of the screen with messages from viewers, saying things like "He's crazy" or "What a crackpot," in regards to Percival's outlandish theory. I changed the channel to a news station I trusted more and sighed with relief when I saw that it was reporting up-to-date facts on the missing PA 619. Well-known journalist Chris Harrington, who also had his own talk show apart from being a major contributor to the news network, was anchoring the program.

"We have some updates on the theory of Flight 619's pilot, Victor Cohen," Chris Harrington said. "The flight simulator found in his apartment seemed to show that he had mapped the airline to a remote island in the South Pacific. The FBI also stated that, while this flight path on his simulator had been originally deleted, they were able to recover it with some special technology. A spokesperson for Phoenix Airlines commented on this matter, saying quote, 'Pilots were trained to create flight paths for emergency landings based on where they were scheduled to fly, in case there were some kind of emergency.' It appears that this theory is being debunked because there is not enough evidence or anything suspicious in Victor Cohen's background. On the subject of the search, submarines are using sonar technology to create images of the seabed in various areas of the South Pacific Ocean where data suggests the airplane could have crashed after running out of fuel. This area of the ocean has never been extensively searched or mapped. These parts of the ocean remain a deep mystery, which could prolong the search. The families of the passengers on board are growing restless."

The news cut to scenes of the victims' families holding signs of support that read "Remember Flight 619" outside of LAX and the Phoenix Airlines terminal.

"There is still no sign of the missing airliner. Theories from hijackings to pilot error to technology failure have been thrown around, but until the black boxes are found, this mystery will remain unsolved. The question on everyone's mind remains…was the airplane hijacked, or did it crash into the Pacific Ocean?"

I shut my television off and set my remote on the nightstand. I grabbed my copy of *Jackson Killington: The Man Who Made a Killing and a Ton of It*, and opened it to the very last page, where Colin Shaw's "About the Author" section was. There was a professional headshot of Mr. Shaw in an expensive-looking suit. His facial expression was serious, without a hint of a smile. He had short gray hair and light-colored eyes. His photo was black and white, so I could not tell what color they were, but I presumed them to be blue or green. His jaw was square and his cheekbones were pronounced. I read his small bio.

"*Colin Shaw currently resides in Washington, D.C. He is the former head of the Central Intelligence Agency. Mr. Shaw retired from the agency in the early 2000s to spend more time with his wife and daughter. He currently* spends his retirement writing non-fiction crime novels. He has degrees from both Harvard and Yale, and also runs a non-profit organization that raises scholarships for college students with an interest in criminal justice and law, which is Mr. Shaw's educational background. He is also a weekly contributor to Will O' Connor's show Tact and Fact on the Fox Network."

I laughed out loud, because I had just been watching a segment from that very show on Fox. While it was purely a coincidence, I took it as a sign to find a way to get in touch with Colin Shaw. I wanted to know what his dedication page meant, as no one else seemed to know from my online research. Professor Bernstein seemed to have an idea, but his article no longer existed online, and he had yet to return any of my correspondence. Shaw's book had the address of his personal website. I logged on via my laptop. The website was pretty bland. It was a landing page with links to his social media pages and a few clips of him on Tact and Fact. I was hoping to find a way to contact him or his publisher, but there was no direct form of contact listed. I thought about sending a tweet to him on his Twitter page, but I decided I did not want that public.

Why were Jackson and Colin best friends? I thought. I had not said it out loud, but there was something about this strange connection and Colin's dedication page that really resonated with me, and I wanted to talk to someone about it. Then I remembered something Royce had said to me when he gave me his father's book: "This book has many answers, but opens up many questions. My father was a mystery. He shares something in common with PA 619."

What if he was being literal? I thought to myself again. What if Jackson Killington did share something in common with PA 619, and it had nothing to do with the mystery or possible death of the passengers. I said possible death because there was no evidence of a crash or debris…yet.

I felt silly. I had an aerospace engineering degree, and I was trying to make some conspiracy theory in my mind. However, I could not shake off the feeling that Royce was trying to tell me something the day he handed me his father's book. He'd had such a strange look in his eye, as if he were trying to read me. It was not until that moment, while I was lying in my bed, that I began to feel slightly paranoid that he might have known Jim,

Dylan, and Charles had invited me to a secret meeting in Beijing. Had he become aware of their work on a life-changing project that would alter mankind's quest for travel? I feared I would never know what this project was. I did not even know the name of the company in China that they were planning to meet with. To top it off, I was the only person who knew about my colleagues' intentions. At least, I hoped I was the only one. Knowing this and hiding it from the world made me feel guilty, because it could have been a clue in solving the disappearance of Flight 619.

There you go again with conspiracy theories, Patrick. I thought. *Jim, Dylan, and Charles' plans were private. It's not like they were doing anything dangerous. The only thing about it that would look bad is that they were trying to leave Phoenix Airlines and work on another project while on a Phoenix business trip.*

My thoughts, which were the reason I suffered insomnia, were interrupted by a phone call. It was Francesca. My heart skipped a beat.

"Hi there," I answered. "To what do I owe a late night call?"

"Late?" Francesca's sultry voice replied. "It's not even ten yet. I'm calling to reschedule our date. I'm very sorry about the other night with Craig. He seems to be a little more level-headed, and wanted me to tell you he was sorry for imposing."

"Well, I suppose you can make it up to me. I'm free this weekend," I responded.

"Great," she replied. "I have tickets to a jazz show at the Hollywood Bowl. A client sent them over to the *Times* for my boss, but he cannot attend. I figured a pair of box seats would entice you."

"I love a good show at the Bowl," I replied. "I'll bring a bottle of wine. What day this weekend?"

"Saturday," she replied.

"Perfect," I said with a smile that she could not see. "It's a date."

August 4, 2016

I arrived at work in good spirits, with the prospects of a good weekend ahead. I was also looking forward to being reunited with my former student,

Mark Crane. He was waiting outside my office when I arrived.

"Early!" I said excitedly.

"I did not want to be late for my first day, Prof—erm—Mr. Baldwin," Mark said. "And I did not know how Los Angeles traffic would be on my way to work."

"Call me Patrick," I told him. "What part of town did you find housing in?"

"West Hollywood," he replied. "It has a great community."

"Not a bad place to stay at all," I added. "Come in. Let me drop off my bag, and we can begin our tour of Phoenix Airlines. You will also meet my small team of engineers."

"Did you hire new people after the, um, incident?" he asked.

"Our CEO did," I said. "They are lovely people. We are three senior engineers, but we have a much larger team of junior engineers who we collaborate with on building various models of our planes. There are maybe one hundred engineers. I'm going to take you to one of our offsite hangars where we are building one of our larger models. It's a 787. Much of our work will be in the office designing blueprints, but today we will get some hands-on experience for you with the designers."

A Mercedes Sprinter picked up Mark, Paola, Pravish, and me outside the corporate headquarters. On the ten-minute drive down the street to a nearby airport hangar, I introduced Mark to Paola and Pravish and explained to them how his grades and viewpoints in class caught my attention. When we arrived at the hangar, we passed through security clearance to enter the premises. I smiled upon noticing the excited gleam in Mark's eye.

"Wow," he let out an audible whisper. "So this is where Phoenix literally gets its wings?"

"Yep," I replied.

We were standing inside a hangar the size of a football field. There were two jumbo planes being worked on. They looked completely dull and gray, because they had not yet been painted metallic silver, nor had any red markings and Phoenix logos. The nearest plane had ladders and various forklifts around it, with several workers in hard hats hammering, drilling, and welding. The noise was deafening. I pulled out four pairs of brightly colored earplugs for everyone to put on, as the drilling sounds and the screeching of saws in the distance were piercing.

This was my element—the smell of burnt metal and the clangs of hammers building the magnificent metal bird we called the Phoenix. This specific model being built before our eyes was hollow. The engines had not been installed yet. It was just a shell of the hunk of steel that would soon be flying at speeds over 600 miles per hour shortly before the beginning of 2017.

"Tomorrow, there will be a meeting held by Royce to announce the new safety systems that are going to be put in place on the airplane," I told our group in a loud voice over the commotion. "It's going to happen a lot faster than planned due to the recent tragedy with Flight 619. Many of these engineers have been working overtime. It has been kept under wraps. I find it odd that he has not shared it with any of us yet. The company meeting will be the first time he announces the new safety features, which are being built by a corporation in China. That's who I was supposed to meet with on my trip via Flight 619."

"What are these safety measures for the new planes supposed to do?" Mark asked me.

"Like I said…I've been in the dark," I replied. "It's supposed to make the percentage rate of mechanical and pilot failure virtually nonexistent. But how it's supposed to do that is what we'll find out tomorrow."

"That will be big," Paola replied with excitement. "This could be historic."

"Or a really good PR stunt, considering recent events," I said sarcastically, more to myself than to the group.

August 5, 2016

Friday arrived at lightning speed. Mark, Paola, and Pravish followed me to our largest auditorium in the corporate offices at 10:00 AM. The room had over five hundred seats that faced a stage and an enormous screen where a revolving Phoenix logo was projected. It looked much like a movie theater. There was a podium on the center of the stage adorned with a metallic red Phoenix Airlines logo. Once I found a group of four seats together, I asked my team to save me a spot while I ran outside to use the restroom.

There was a murmur of commotion outside the hall. A group of Phoenix employees were staring out a giant glass window that faced the front entrance of the building. They were pointing and speaking in rushed voices. My curiosity was piqued, so I walked over to see what was causing the ruckus. A protest appeared outside, on the opposite side of the street from the Phoenix Airlines Corporation entrance. There were over a hundred people with picket signs that read "Pray for Flight 619," "Make Killington Pay," and "We demand answers!" Some signs showed artwork of a phoenix bird on fire, signifying its death. A few police officers were working to keep the crowd controlled and peaceful. The yells were barely audible through the glass walls. Some of the individuals in the protest looked familiar. I was pretty sure that some of them were family members I had seen on TV of those lost on board 619. They were leading the protest and looking unpleased about the zero progress in finding any piece of the plane since it vanished last month.

"This is going to turn into a riot," a man next to me said. He was wearing a designer gray suit and had sleek jet-black hair that was neatly parted. He had a navy blue briefcase in one hand. "I'm Joe. I'm a consultant for Zyphone Communications. Zyphone is presenting our partnership with Phoenix at the conference today. I hope these people don't ruin it."

Joe extended his hand for me to shake. I could make out a shiny gold watch underneath his sleeve. *Zyphone must pay well*, I thought to myself.

"Well, they have the right to publicly assemble," I said. "Enjoy the presentation."

I proceeded to the auditorium after using the restroom. The presentation was delayed by fifteen minutes. Royce rushed into the auditorium and quickly straightened his tie. It was apparent that he had been caught off-guard by the protest ensuing outdoors. The audience quickly fell silent upon his entrance and stared at him with anticipation. A few late employees trickled in behind him and rushed to their seats. The lights dimmed and a never-before-seen Phoenix Airlines commercial began to play. The music moved the piece. It was edited with a powerful voiceover narrator, images of our airplanes taking off, and cut with scenes of people and cityscapes. The spot had sound effects of pilots speaking to officers in air traffic control via radio. There were even images of various forms of transportation: trains, cars, people biking, a sailboat, and a rocket ship launching. The theme was to emphasize flying as the key mode of travel. The narrator's voiceover gave me chills:

"Once you get up there, there's only one way to go. Onward. The sky's the limit. It rises from the ashes. Reborn in flames. With a flap of its wings, it tells the story. Phoenix Airlines, born to fly."

Royce walked up to the podium greeted by thunderous applause and whistling. He cleared his throat and raised his arms to silence the audience.

"Thank you for joining me today, Phoenix," he addressed the crowd. "I'm sorry I was late. I'm sure many of you noticed there is a protest going on outside. No need to worry. The police are keeping them at bay. Now, let's get on to more pressing matters and the reason why we are here today. I hope you enjoyed that new sixty-second spot that we'll be airing wide starting today. It also proudly boasts our tag line, 'Born to fly.' We are Phoenix—like the bird reborn from ashes after bursting into flames. We've had some obstacles lately, but we plan to overcome them. The sky *is* the limit. Many of you know that we have hinted at working on greater safety measures in the wake of Flight 619's disappearance. Prior to this tragic incident, we were already setting in motion plans to install a unique technological system that will make flying even safer than Phoenix's fleet already is. Sadly, three of our head engineers were headed to Beijing on official business on Flight 619 to work with a company in China that will be responsible for building these systems for us. I'll get to that momentarily. I would like to have a brief moment of silence for the three men we lost: Jim King, Dylan Sparks, and Charles Rosenberg."

I felt many eyes fall on me right before everyone bowed their heads to take their own personal silence in respect for my three colleagues. When Royce cleared his throat again to signal everyone to look up, I caught the eye of a few people looking at me. When they realized that I was making eye contact with them, they nodded, almost as if consoling me silently.

"This conference is being recorded for a webcast that will be made available to the public once we finish here," he continued. "I wanted to start by telling you all, my fellow Phoenix employees, before the rest of the world. These dark and trying times…oh…hit record!"

Two cameramen walked up to the stage and set their cameras on tripods. They signaled a countdown from three backwards, and signaled they were rolling when they had one finger up. Royce began to speak again, as if he had just started talking to us for the first time during this meeting.

"Welcome, my fellow colleagues and the members of the press and media that are watching this webcast," Royce said in a much more cheerful tone. "We are coming together today because I want to reveal a new initiative for the safety of all of our airplane fleet that we have been slowly designing with a company called Zyphone Communications in China. We are calling this initiative the Phoenix Project. After last month's tragic disappearance of Flight 619 where three of our own were lost, I felt that it should be a priority to roll out our initiatives much more quickly. We have created a computer system that will be installed in our entire fleet of planes that will be able to detect the tiniest of malfunctions to the most major. This computer system, which we are calling the Forecaster, will be able to predict when an engine or system could potentially fail even before a plane takes off for flight. Very advanced computer and technology systems will be effectively running diagnostics every single second that the airplane's engines are running. In the event of a malfunction while in the air, the computer systems will alert ground control instantaneously. If, God forbid, there is a hijacking while in flight, the systems will lock the plane into autopilot to safely maneuver it to the nearest airport, hands-free. This is a first in aviation history! However, we do not want to worry our command of pilots. We will never replace the industry with self-flying airplanes, as humans will always be needed for the use of many of the plane's controls. The self-flying protocol is for emergencies only, in the event that the pilot becomes unable to safely maneuver the plane."

There were many gasps and applause in the audience. Royce smiled and continued, "This system will also work with a special satellite system that Zyphone Communications currently has orbiting in space. The system will continuously send out precise GPS coordinates of the plane's whereabouts. This system cannot be turned off by anyone on board. With Flight 619, we lost communication because of a possible tampering with the transponder, which could only be manually turned off by someone with the knowledge and know-how. The GPS system has a chip that will be included with black boxes that will withstand crashes on land or in water to track the location of the airplane. That being said, we will be able to locate a missing airplane that might have sunk in the ocean within a day or two with exact coordinates. We will never lose an airplane again. And I won't get into it too much during this teleconference, but Phoenix will eventually get into space travel. You probably noticed the rockets in our commercial. It's foreshadowing our future. That will be something we will get more into in late 2017 or early 2018."

At these words, there was an eruption of cheers and murmurs of excitement. Even though the webcast was not streaming live yet, I could already feel Phoenix's stock going up. This was a bold and historical move indeed. My jaw was dropping, but I also felt slightly put off with the fact that he had kept this from my engineer staff and me.

"I would like to introduce you to an old friend of mine, Robert Wong, CEO of Zyphone Communications. He will talk about our safety initiatives. Oh, and to the billing department—you will be getting plenty of purchase orders from them soon, so you'll want to be best friends with his team. Ha! Robert, come on up!"

A bald Chinese man with round glasses and an expensive looking suit walked up to the podium. He shook Royce's hand and then grabbed the microphone to adjust for his height. He was shorter than Royce. I recognized him as the man in the gray suit who had been waiting to meet with Royce outside his office the day he'd given me his father's book.

"Good afternoon, Phoenix," Robert spoke in perfect English, which apparently caught many people by surprise. "We are proud to partner with Phoenix Airlines today. Zyphone has been a privately owned communications company for over fifty years. Outside of communication, our list of side projects includes satellite and geographic mapping, solar energy, research into VR—that's virtual reality, for those of you non-tech folks—and now work in the aviation industry. We will still continue to be a private company, but we are excited to enhance the safety of commercial flying for all of your customers. We hope to see increased sales and zero accidents. The missing PA 619 is a tragic story, but it is also a learning lesson. For the last month, we have brainstormed with Mr. Killington on what we need to do with the Forecaster system. Effective next week, we will begin going into production of this highly advanced computer operating system, and by the beginning of January 2017, we hope to have at least thirty percent of the Phoenix fleet equipped with the Forecaster."

There was more applause. Robert waited in silence while it died down. When it was quiet again, he continued. "To those of you who are engineers, fear not. Zyphone engineers are specialized in the creation of this computer system. Therefore, the Phoenix team will be in charge of installation of the product on all fleet. It will be a perfect relationship and great delegation of work to both companies. We are very excited to have this partnership, and we have one more surprise. Can we play the video?"

The lights dimmed and a computer-animated video began to play on the screen behind Robert. There was a 787 Phoenix airplane flying through the clouds. A few seconds into the video, one of the engines on the wing exploded, and the plane began to fall into a nosedive. People in the audience gasped at the unexpected explosion. The sound effects were of theater-quality in the giant auditorium. The next thing that happened in the video was even more shocking and unexpected. I could almost feel everyone's jaws drop. The tail of the Phoenix plane blasted off like a rocket into the sky, and out came a giant parachute held by very thick ropes...or so the animations made it appear. The airplane went from falling at rapid speeds to slowing down and safely plummeting to the ground.

The animation was very cartoonish. It seemed like science fiction or something out of a Hollywood movie. The video showed the airplane hitting nose first into an open meadow with a few trees. The parachute had softened its plummet to the ground exponentially. An inflatable cushion ejected from the top and bottom of the plane. The airplane then fell back on its side to the ground with a soft thud. Then, the exit doors opened, and a bunch of animated passengers jumped out of the plane, apparently unharmed. The final scene of the video showed that the tail of the airplane self-destructed into harmless ash in the sky.

The lights turned back on and there was a stunned silence in the audience. The only sound I could hear was a few cell phone vibrations from members of the audience who received a text or email at that moment. A few people looked over to their neighbors to exchange amused or even shocked glances. I do not believe anyone in the audience knew how to react to what we had just witnessed. Was this video meant to be serious?

So, this is why Phoenix Airlines and Royce wanted to send me and the other engineers to China, I thought to myself. And yet, I still had no idea what secretive side project my engineer colleagues wanted to work on outside of the Forecaster.

Robert Wong walked off the stage with a huge grin. Royce returned to the podium and took in the confused and shocked audience with satisfaction written on his face.

"That was the Phoenix Project," he said. "It's an initiative for the safety of commercial flights within our fleet. There will be many firsts with the project as we continue mankind's quest for travel. That video you just saw will be a last resort safety feature that will be built onto newer models of our fleet beginning in 2017. A company Zyphone has partnered with will design the parachutes. The parachute will deploy when the Forecaster system detects an inevitable crash. I would like to also note that if there is an explosion in one section of the airplane, there will be a feature where it is contained to only that section of the plane so as not to spread to the rest of the craft. We are taking flight into the future, and I am excited to have you all on our team. Thank you for your time. I will take a few questions before we end."

Almost everyone in the audience raised their hands. I was one of them. The question and answer session lasted for fifteen minutes. I could tell Royce was overwhelmed. Luckily for him, Natasha came to his aid and whispered something into his ear.

"Thank you for your time, everyone," he announced. "I have to run to an important phone call."

The crowd was buzzing with excitement during their exit out of the auditorium. I was curious to ask Robert Wong many questions, but he could not be found. He must have slipped out of the auditorium while Royce was answering questions.

"Pretty crazy stuff," Mark said to me on our walk out.

"I was not expecting anything like that," I replied honestly. "Much of that sounds like science fiction and fantasy."

"It really does," Pravish added.

We were almost to the elevators when I heard a crash and the sound of glass shattering. Screams and the stomping of heels and shoes running in our direction followed. I turned around and saw through the now broken glass wall of our building that the protesters had started a riot. One of the rioters had thrown a brick through the glass. The officers outside were in shock at the sudden outrage from the previously peaceful protesters. One of the officers had been knocked over by the crowd as they rushed toward the offices.

"RUN!" I yelled in unison with some of my other colleagues.

We made our way to the nearest stairwell and ran upstairs. Mark, Paola, and Pravish followed me all the way to the top floor. There was a door to the rooftop labeled "Do not enter." We had no other choice, so I kicked it open. A few other people had followed us onto the rooftop. I looked over the edge of the building and saw a huge cloud of smoke erupt. To tame the angry rioters, the cops had unleashed gas canisters. Several more officers and police cars joined in, helping keep the rioters at bay. The sirens were blaring louder than the panicking crowd.

"Oh my God!" Paola cried. "Have they infiltrated the building?"

"I can't tell," I said, looking over the edge. My stomach squirmed; I was not a fan of heights. Then I saw two men in jumpsuits run into the building through the broken glass. I heard gunshots, but was not sure where they were coming from. There were screams coming in all directions. It was as if a war had broken out. I could hear fire engines and ambulances joining in the cacophony of sound, as well as the beating of propellers from helicopters hovering above us. I gestured for Mark, Paola, and Pravish to hide behind a ledge in the distance. They obliged and ran as fast as they could, followed by a few others who had joined us on the roof.

I ran to the stairwell door and closed it. I saw a large metal canister randomly propped near the door, and pushed it in front of it to keep the door blocked, in case any of the rioters came up to the roof. I sat down in front of the canister and began to breathe hard. I felt a coughing fit coming on. I had not experienced one in a while. It felt as if I was going to throw up my lungs out of my mouth. I clenched my chest. It felt really hard to inhale. Dizziness swept over me as Mark came to my aid.

"Still have that cough?" he asked, pulling out a bottle of water from his satchel like he had done for me when I had a similar coughing fit in front of him in my classroom back in Montana.

"It feels as though I'm out of shape," I said through heavy breaths, "but I work out often."

There was a sudden banging on the door. Someone yelled inside the stairwell, "The door is locked! Wait—I think something is propped against it! There must be people up here. We need to find him. One of ours said he came up here."

I looked at Mark and whispered, "Help me get up. We need to get far away from here. Those rioters could be armed. I heard gunfire earlier." Mark gave me his hand and pulled me up. I had a sudden head rush and coughed again.

"Are you a smoker?" Mark asked me. "Your cough sounds dry and hoarse."

"I was when I was in college," I answered. "I quit ages ago. I guess this is the aftermath of all those packs I inhaled while doing my studies." I clutched my chest again, because I felt pain and tightness after my last cough. A few seconds later it subsided, and I felt normal again.

"C'mon!" Mark urged, and we ran to the ledge where the rest of our group was hiding. "Let's join the others. There's safety in numbers."

There was a huge crash behind us. The door had been smashed open and knocked clean off its hinges. Two men in blue jumpsuits pushed the canister out of the way. They were wearing sunglasses and red bandanas over the bottom halves of their faces, covering their noses and mouths. They did not look like any of the protesters I had seen earlier.

"YOU!" One of the men yelled and pointed at me.

"STOP!" The other man pulled out a small handgun, and said to Mark, "Get on your knees and put your hands over your head."

I quickly looked over at the ledge where Paola, Pravish, and the others were hiding. They were not visible, having hidden when they saw the men crash through. Mark obeyed the orders of the armed man. I took a closer look at his jumpsuit. There were no patches or markings on them. It reminded me of an Air Force uniform, but theirs were plain and free of any labels.

"What do you want?" I asked them calmly.

"Are you Patrick Baldwin?" one of them questioned.

"Yes," I answered. "Who are you people?"

"Our presence is not important," one said. "What do you know about S.R.K.?"

"What?" I genuinely sounded confused. I had never even heard of S.R.K. before. "I don't know what that is."

"Tell us!" he snapped, angrily brandishing his gun. "Do not lie. *They* told you. You were planning a side trip in Beijing!"

"What?" I replied, and then it dawned on me that *they* meant Jim, Dylan, and Charles, and the side trip was that secret mission, which I honestly knew nothing about. "I promise you, I do not know what you are talking about."

The next thing that happened felt like a blur. There was a loud gunshot. I fell to the floor. I smacked my face on the ground, and my nose began to bleed. The man holding the gun fell to the ground and dropped his weapon. He fell face first. Our eyes met when his sunglasses fell off. We were both lying face down on our stomachs with our cheeks pressed to the rooftop. Blood was gushing from under his stomach. His dark brown eyes eerily stared at me. They were lifeless. There was another gunshot. This time, the victim was the police officer who was holding the gun that killed the assailant threatening to kill me. The other man in the blue jumpsuit had shot the police officer who did his job and saved me. Two other officers ran onto the roof from the stairwell and quickly sent two fatal gunshots into the chest of the last standing gunman. He fell onto his back with a loud crunch as his skull hit the surface.

"Is everyone all right?" the officer asked while running to his partner who had been shot.

"Yes," I called out, wincing in pain.

"Officer Barnes is down," the officer yelled into his radio. "He's dead! I'm on the rooftop of the building. I need backup. We took down two armed men in jumpsuits. One of them shot Barnes. It does not look like these men were part of the protest."

Mark, Paola, and Pravish came to my side. I got up on my feet and shook dust off my jacket. I was still dizzy. Everything felt as though it had happened too fast for my brain to process. The world began to spin. The colors began to swirl and blend into one. Then there was blackness.

I woke up in a hospital, lying on a bed with a bandage over my head. There was an ice pack by my side. As soon as I was conscious, a nurse came to my aid.

"What happened?" I asked.

"You fainted," she told me. "No worries. You went through an ordeal. Do you remember anything at all? Do you know your name?"

"I'm Patrick Baldwin," I answered. "And I do remember what happened. I saw three men killed on the rooftop of my office building. There was a protest that turned into a riot."

"I'm very sorry you had to experience that," the nurse said to me. "We want to examine your head in case you have a concussion. It was probably the stress that caused you to lose consciousness. You poor thing."

"Okay," I sighed.

"Your coworkers were here earlier, but they have gone home. I can update them on your status. There is a woman outside who says she is a friend of yours. Should I call her in?" The nurse walked to the door when I nodded yes and waved in the visitor seated outside in the hall. It was Francesca.

"Oh my goodness!" she said, running to me and giving me a tight embrace. "I was so worried. I was at the scene while you were being taken into an ambulance. I was sent to report on the protest. Then I saw you. I'm so sorry. I heard what happened on the roof. Your intern, Mark, told me. Killington asked the *Times* not to mention your name in any of the reports I write, because you've already been in the press so much. I agree. But you need to see the news."

I tried to open my mouth to reply, but I felt so weak. Francesca turned on the television to CNN. There was a story being reported about Phoenix's new safety project. Within the few hours I was unconscious, news had apparently traveled fast since the conference webcast had been uploaded online. The reporter was covering the attack on the Phoenix Airlines offices that followed after.

"I'm not sure what set off those people," Francesca said. "They were protesting peacefully. I was looking at some video footage caught on cell phones, and it looks like it was only a handful of people in the crowd who got out of hand. None of the protestors that were related to 619 victims were part of the riot. In one video, I saw two men in blue jumpsuits run straight into the building while all the officers and employees seemed distracted by chaos. It looked almost like a diversion. Mark told me that they asked for you by name on the roof."

"Can you give us some privacy?" I asked the nurse, who nodded and walked out of the room, closing the door behind her. "That's true, but you cannot write about this."

"Of course I'm not," she said, sounding offended. "I'm trying to protect you. Mark said they asked about something with initials."

"Right," I replied. "They did, but I don't know what they were talking about. They assumed I knew something about…"

I trailed off. I had not told a single soul about my private meeting with Jim, Dylan, and Charles prior to our scheduled flight. I did not feel comfortable confiding in Francesca because she worked for the L.A. Times, and I was still getting to know her. I had not formed a strong trust yet.

"I don't know what they assumed I knew," I continued. "But something strange happened on that roof. I was targeted and I need to know why."

"Yeah," Francesca agreed. "I think those two men in blue jumpsuits had nothing to do with the protest at all. They used the protest as a cover. Police are doing some investigations. I know Killington is trying to work with them to get to the bottom of it, but all this is being kept from the media. Out of respect, I won't write about it publicly, but my journalistic instinct wants to investigate and figure out what the attack was about and why they tried to kill you."

I sat up on my bed and looked at her beautiful eyes. "I'll work with you. How can I help?"

Francesca smiled. "How about you tell me more about the Phoenix Project Forecaster system? I could write about that, and I need a big story for the Sunday edition."

"I know as much as you do," I said honestly. "Royce kept us in the dark. Are you now asking me to trade information for your time?"

"What?" Francesca blushed. "Instinct. That's who I am. I have to pay my bills. Besides, I have those box seats for us tomorrow at the Hollywood Bowl. I mean, if you are still up for it and feel well. I really do want to spend time with you."

I reached for my forehead. It felt as if a bomb had exploded inside my head. I could still hear the gunshots ringing in my ears, as if they were distant echoes that would not stop reverberating in my mind. I tried to force the memory of the officer being shot out of my head, but it was pointless. It kept replaying in my mind like a looping video. I had never witnessed something so tragic. I could feel tears stream out of the corners of my eyes. Francesca sat on the bed next to me and caressed my arm. I could see sympathy in her eyes. She put her hand over my shoulder.

"It's been a rough day," I said.

"If you want to cancel tomorrow's plans, that is totally fine," she said.

"I still want to go with you." I smiled at her. She returned the smile, and her face moved closer to mine. I could feel my heart beating faster, and since her hand was still on my shoulder, she was able to pull me in. I must have flushed red in the face. She smirked as her lips touched mine. We kissed feverishly for a minute before we broke apart.

"Our first dates seem to be cursed. Hopefully tomorrow will go without a hitch," she told me.

August 6, 2016

Francesca and I were seated at a box at the Hollywood Bowl. She had brought us sandwiches, and I came with a bottle of wine. The summer evening was perfect. The weather was in the seventies and the sky was clear. The sun had not set over the horizon yet. Francesca and I were deep in conversation prior to the start of the jazz band that was set to perform.

"I'm glad my name was kept out of the news from yesterday's fiasco," I told her. "Thank you for sparing me."

"Of course," she said. "I'm sorry I get a bit journalistic at times. It's in my blood."

"That's fine," I said to her. "Sometimes I'll start talking about random aeronautical engineering stuff. It won't make sense and it will sound nerdy. So, thanks in advance for not getting bored with me."

Francesca laughed. "Oh, tell me something *nerdy*."

"Okay," I replied. "An object falling from the sky will fall at 9.8 meters per second with the gravitational pull of Earth. If Flight 619 hit the ocean, it definitely would have broken into hundreds of pieces. It's so bizarre that not *one* piece of the flight has yet to be found almost a month later."

"Do you think something more is going on?" Francesca asked.

"I think I'm ready to admit it out loud—and just to you—*off* the record," I said. "Yesterday was eye-opening. The men in jumpsuits asked me about something only three other people would have known about."

And then I told her everything about Jim, Dylan, and Charles' secret meeting with me, and how they were planning some secret mission in China to work on a project that would change the aviation industry forever. I told her that the men in jumpsuits asked me if I knew about S.R.K. That must have been the name of their secret project, or so I deduced.

"S.R.K.," I said. "Sparks, Rosenberg, and King. Each letter matches their last names. But I have no idea what it means. The last time I was here at the Bowl was with Jim King. He went to the restroom during the show. I followed him and overheard a paranoid conversation he was having about feeling that they were being overheard or watched. He mentioned that their phone lines might have been tapped. Those men in jumpsuits knew about this project. I don't even know what it is! Did they ever identify those men?"

"Not yet," Francesca said. "It's actually really strange. They had no wallets or any form of identification on them. Their pockets were empty except for a few unused bullets. They had no keys either. Their fingerprints and DNA samples are not matching to anyone in the police database. It's as if they do not exist."

"How do you know this?" I asked, sounding impressed.

"I have my ways," she smiled. "I have a source with LAPD. This isn't being reported in the news either because it's alarming. People are going to want to know who these men were, and I think they are going to play off their identities as random homeless people or just give them fake identifications."

"How can someone simply not exist?" I asked.

"When you find that answer, let me know. It will make a thrilling story," she said.

"Yes, it will," I agreed. "I think I'm going to take a few days off this week. I was hoping Phoenix would shut down for a bit after that attack, but Royce still wants everyone to continue about our business as usual, since there is much work to be done for our future."

"Well, then you should take some personal days," she suggested. "After all, you were attacked and ended up in the hospital."

"Perhaps so," I said, and then I changed the subject. "Tell me more about you. How long has it been since you last dated someone?"

"A year," she said, blushing. "He broke my heart and got back together with his ex-wife. I cut off communication with him after that. He wanted to remain friends, but I had invested too much of myself to forgive him for that. Sorry for the overshare. I don't date much, since I'm married to my job."

August 7, 2016

On Sunday night, I wrote an email to Royce saying I needed some time to recover. Before I went to bed, I turned on the news and saw a report about the two men in blue jumpsuits. The reporter said that the two men were not American citizens. It was ruled that they were acting as radicals in retaliation for the minimal progress Phoenix had made with the recovery of finding PA 619. I rolled my eyes in disbelief. The men did not have foreign accents. Francesca was the only person besides Mark who knew those men were intentionally after me, and I could not say anything because I felt my life was at stake. There had to be a connection between Jim, Dylan, and Charles and their secret S.R.K project with these two mysterious men. I had a lead on the mystery of PA 619, and I was probably the only person in the world who did—and I felt I was in danger.

10

September 20, 2016

August came and went, and September was nearly over when I finally decided to take two weeks off from work for an actual vacation. For the past month, I had been knee-deep in work on the Phoenix Project. With the need to begin rolling out the safety features on some of the planes by early January, I knew that I was probably not going to have much of a Christmas break, so I booked a trip to Hawaii.

Nothing else major had happened since the riot on Phoenix Airlines grounds. I had been keeping to myself, and the press seemed to have lost interest in me. Thankfully, the only person in the press that I did not want losing interest in me was Francesca. She and I had become much more serious in our relationship. It was very exciting for me, especially because I had asked her to join me on my trip to Hawaii. The prospect of this trip made my last day in my office before vacation much more bearable. I also had an unexpected visitor that day.

I was finishing up reviewing some drawings of the mechanics of the Forecaster when Mark walked in.

"Patrick, there's a woman here to see you," he announced.

"Who?" I asked.

"Her name is Melissa King," Mark replied.

My heart sank. Melissa was Jim's wife. I had not reached out to her since PA 619's disappearance.

"Tell her to come in," I said, as I absentmindedly brushed my hair back with my hands and straightened my tie.

She was a sight for sore eyes. Melissa had red hair, a light complexion, and freckles. She was in her sixties. She had a pearl necklace around her neck and was wearing a black dress. She was wearing a rather large black hat, fit more for a horse race derby than my office.

"Hello, Pat," she said softly.

"Melissa…" I tried to find something comforting to say. "I'm so sorry I have not reached out."

"That's quite all right," she responded.

"How are you holding up?" I asked.

"Well, with no sign of the plane or any debris, still," she said, and she took off her hat and set it on my desk, "I feel hopeful. No news is good news, right?"

"It's been over two months though," I said. "We have to face reality. I have. How are your sons holding up?"

"They are fine," she replied. "They've been spending a lot of time with me. Their wives and my grandchildren have been coming over in their spare time to keep me company. It has been nice. I love my family dearly. I miss Jim."

"I miss him too," I said, and I walked over to my door and closed it. I pulled out my desk chair and offered it to her to sit. "Can I ask you something?"

"Yes, dear," she said.

"Did Jim ever mention a confidential project he was working on?" I asked.

Melissa looked at me for a moment with blank eyes. She nodded her head from left to right to signify no.

"I am asking because he was working on something top secret, and I have no idea what it was," I continued.

"He was?" she asked with piqued interest. "Well…he always kept himself locked in our house basement. He created an office and workshop down there. He was always working on something late into the night. It peeved me, to be quite honest."

"I had no idea he had a workshop at home," I said with intrigue. I took a deep breath and asked, "Would you mind if I do some digging around? I think there is some unfinished work he would have, um, wanted me to complete."

"I don't see why not," she said. "When would you like to stop by?"

"Well, I leave early tomorrow for Hawaii for two weeks. Could I swing by this evening?" I asked.

"Yes, that should not be an issue," she said. "It's really nice to see you. Phoenix gave all the families of those on board 619 five thousand dollars. It feels disgusting. Money can't bring back our loved ones."

"I know," I said quietly.

"I wish Jim had missed that flight like you did," she said. "I'm sorry; that was a bit awkward."

"Er, it's okay," I replied, but I did feel awkward. "Is there any reason in particular that you came to see me?"

Melissa fidgeted with her purse for a few seconds before looking at me. She stared at me for almost a minute before she spoke.

"Yes, there is something," she said, and she had tears forming at the corners of her eyes. "Jim was acting paranoid the month leading up to his disappearance. He kept thinking our home was bugged with surveillance, or that he was being followed. I did not know what he was paranoid about until maybe a week before he boarded that flight to China. I have never told anyone this. Not my sons, not the police, not the FBI, and not even the media. I came here with that intention, thinking I would sound crazy to you, but then you asked me about some project he was working on. Could there be some connection?"

"Maybe there is a connection," I said. "I also advise you to keep this quiet. I'm glad you came to me. I overheard him having a phone call when we were at a show at the Hollywood Bowl earlier this summer. He definitely sounded paranoid. I'm not sure what this project he was working on was, but he wanted to tell me; however, I had to wait until we arrived in China to learn about it. It was something that would revolutionize modern-day travel. I believe the project was called S.R.K.—'K' for King, and the 'S' and 'R' were for the letters of the other engineers' surnames who worked with us."

Melissa stood up and said, "I need you to help me look through our basement as soon as possible then. Can you come now? I had a feeling you might be able to help me."

The Kings' home was located in Hancock Park in Los Angeles. It was a beautiful two-story Victorian home. We walked into the living room and through a hallway until we reached the door to the basement. Melissa pulled a key out from her pocket and unlocked the door.

"I haven't had the courage to go down there since he went missing. This will be the first time anyone has been down here in over two months. Please don't mind any dust that has collected," she said.

She flipped a light switch on, which revealed a staircase that led us down. The workshop was filled with several computers, a giant tube, and random machines. It did not look like a workspace any kind of engineer I knew would have. It looked more like the workspace of an inventor.

"This place is impressive," I said aloud.

Melissa pulled out a washcloth and wiped dust from a photo frame on Jim's oak desk. It was a photo of a young Jim and a tall, muscular man in an army uniform.

"Jim and his father," Melissa said softly. "They've been estranged for years. I wonder if he knows that his son was on Flight 619."

Melissa looked so sad in the dim lighting of the basement. I felt so much sympathy for her. There was some awkward silence, so I reached for the desk drawers and began to pull out files. There were several folders filled with sketches of airplanes. I found a logo of Phoenix Airlines on one document. There was even the offer letter that Jim had received for his employment at Phoenix Airlines. It listed his salary offer, which was much higher than mine.

"Nothing out of the ordinary here," I said. "I'm not sure what to look for."

"I rarely ever came down here," she said. "He never said I couldn't come down here, but I got the impression he preferred peace and quiet. He hinted that he wanted his alone time whenever he came to work down here."

"Is this his cell phone?" I asked, pulling out an old flip phone that was probably from the early 2000s.

"It was his old mobile phone from years ago," she replied. "I doubt it works."

I pressed the power button, and it turned on. The battery bar signified that it had about ten percent of charge left. I was pretty sure this was the same phone I had seen him use when our meeting ended on the day we were scheduled to fly to China.

"I don't think he's used that in over a decade," Melissa said.

"Well, why does it have some battery power?" I asked. "Cell phones lose charge if they've been sitting around unused for a while. And there's barely any dust on this. Why would he keep it in his top drawer?"

"I have no idea," she said somberly.

"Maybe he wanted to use a phone with old technology so as not to be tracked?" I asked curiously. "There's only one contact in this phone: 'J.K.'"

"That's probably his own contact info. Those are his initials," Melissa added.

"There's a text message exchange. Only one and it's to 'J.K.' Ugh—it's in old school format. The entire conversation is in various windows and not in one conversation window, like you would find on a smartphone. Technology problems of the first world."

I read through the message exchange, which began in the year 2002 and ran up until July 13, 2016—the day Jim boarded Flight 619. It appeared as though only about two text messages were sent per year, making the twelve-year conversation seem short.

"So he's been using this phone for nearly twelve years to either communicate with himself or with someone of the same initials. Wait a minute…"

I turned the phone around to examine it. I took off the battery cover to reveal the SIM card. It was a prepaid card.

"This must be a burner phone!" I said excitedly, as that was my initial theory. "He used this to communicate with someone he did not want people to know about or be able to track."

I scrolled through the exchanges. They were all very short and concise.

They also seemed to be speaking in code, as the conversation did not make any sense. I handed the phone to Melissa to read, but she could not decipher anything. I read twenty-five text messages out loud:

Received: "Thx for finding me well."
Sent: "Beginning funding. Sun is set to rise."
Received: "Election is near. Rules will change."
Sent: "Election won."
Received: "Everywhere. Watching. We See."
Sent: "Caesar was killed by his own."
Received: "Brutus will not know."
Sent: "Update?"
Received: "Tan. Sand. Beaches."
Sent: "Update 2?"
Received: "More have joined. The seeds will grow."
Sent: "Secrets must stay buried – sea, sand, or snow."
Received: "It is the only way, be well."
Sent: "Update 3?"
Received: "Alive."
Sent: "I need answers."
Received: "How is my sun shining?"
Sent: "Your sun is shining well. Plz I need answers."
Received: "Answers are forthcoming."
Sent: "When/where/what?"
Received: "My sun rises this year."
Sent: "He has risen, as you predicted. I'll join."
Received: "They know the plan."
Sent: "What?! Tell me more!"
Sent: "Hello?"

"This conversation took place over twelve years?" Melissa asked. "And it makes zero sense."

"It's code. This means something though. Dammit!" The phone's battery was dying. I searched the desk for a charger, but could not find one. "Do you know where he kept the charger for this?" I asked.

"I don't," she said. "I think we should destroy this phone. It confirms that someone was aware of whatever Jim was doing. We need to protect him. What if he is still alive somewhere?"

"I need to transcribe those texts," I said. "They might mean something to me later. I'll write them into a journal I have to keep a record of things."

"Keep the phone then," Melissa said. "I'm sure you can find a charger for this model somewhere online or at an old used phone store."

"Thank you," I said. "Should we continue digging around for anything else?"

It was nearly 10:00 PM when I called it quits in my search around Jim's basement. The only useful clues I found were the cell phone and a drawing of "S.R.K" in one of Jim's notebooks, but there was nothing else, except his attempt at what looked like a logo for the letters. This confirmed S.R.K. was tied to Jim, Dylan, and Charles, but any evidence of what S.R.K. meant was lacking. I could not even figure out what the machines in the workshop did exactly. They had random switches and light bulbs.

I dusted myself off and was heading up the stairs when one machine caught my eye. The lights on it were flickering orange. I went to the machine to examine it. Melissa followed behind me. Then I pulled the machine away from the wall, which subsequently shut it off, as it became unplugged. The orange lights instantly went out. There was a label on back of the machine that read "Moving Picture Props, Inc." with an address and phone number. I reached for my smartphone to do a quick search. I had no service.

"Use my Wi-Fi," Melissa said. "It's called 'The Kings,' and the password is 'RoyBob123.' We named it that after our sons' names."

"Thanks," I said, and then I was online and found the business, Moving Picture Props, Inc. It was located in Los Angeles. "It's a Hollywood prop shop. These machines…"

I walked around the room and realized that every random machine in his workshop was just for show.

"They're props! They're not real machines!" I exclaimed.

"I don't understand," Melissa said with confusion.

"I don't either," I added. "Why would he create a fake workshop and lab environment with all these high-tech looking machines if they are not real?"

"To hide in plain sight?" Melissa suggested.

"You may be right!" I said, sounding very excited. Melissa looked surprised at her own suggestion.

"It's getting late." Melissa sounded tired. "Perhaps we can reconvene when you return from your trip?"

"Yeah," I replied. "I'm not sure what to make of this yet, but Jim was very smart. If he wanted to hide something, he could. He could probably even hide a dead body. Sorry—that was morbid."

I took one last glance at the room filled with fake machines, Jim's desk, and a random clear cylinder-shaped tube that was standing vertical against a wall, and then I headed upstairs.

September 27, 2016

It was a beautiful day in Hawaii. I had become accustomed to waking up ocean side every day to the smell of salt in the air and sunscreen lotion on my skin. Francesca was working remote via her laptop and submitting stories to the *Times* every evening. On this particular evening, we took a sunset stroll down the Honolulu beach just outside of our hotel. I looked into Francesca's eyes and kissed her. Then I got on one knee and handed her a flower I had picked from a garden outside our hotel.

"Will you be my girlfriend?" I joked.

She smiled at me and said, "Yes. Duh. I figured that part was assumed, since I came on this trip."

We had not put a serious label on ourselves until that moment, but it felt really nice to know that I would now have a partner.

After dinner, we returned to our hotel room. Francesca was checking her email on her phone. She had received an interesting message that made her excited. She jumped and said, "Oh my God! I have some news!"

She handed me the phone, and I read the email. It was from a control tower supervisor from the Honolulu International Airport.

"Why were you emailing this guy?" I asked.

"I figured if we were going to be in Hawaii, I might as well look into the tower that had the last communication with 619," she said excitedly. "I reached out to one of the supervisors, and he has agreed to meet us today!"

"I thought we were separating ourselves from all this while on vacation?" I asked her.

"I know. I'm sorry, baby," she said flirtatiously. "But maybe we can get some inside information? He's especially intrigued to meet with you."

Against my better judgment, we met this man at a coffee shop a mile away from the airport. He was dressed in slacks and a white button-down shirt with a navy tie. He wore aviator sunglasses and did not take them off, even though we were inside the coffee shop and it was evening.

"Patrick Baldwin," he said, reaching for my hand to shake. I politely gave it to him. "And you must be Miss Fields?"

"Hello, Mr. Theiriot," Francesca said.

"Call me Baxter," he said.

"Thanks for agreeing to meet us," she said.

A waitress brought us iced coffee, and before I could take a sip, Baxter spoke, "I have nothing new to tell you that I haven't told any other members of the press in the last two months. My last words to 619 were 'Goodnight, PA 619.' And that is all. There was nothing suspicious, and Pilot Victor Cohen sounded alert and coherent. I'm not sure what went wrong when we lost communication about thirty minutes later."

"Thirty minutes?" Francesca piped in. "I thought it was an hour later that everyone realized the plane went off radar and had turned course?"

"Things get misconstrued in the media—you should know that, Miss Fields," Baxter stated.

"If you knew that it was off radar and had potentially diverted to a route completely off its flight path that early," I said, "why was there not a drastic search or action taken until nearly around the time when the plane was scheduled to land in Beijing?"

"We've been grilled on that many times, Patrick," Baxter replied, "but the truth is, we were all confused and did not want to cause alarm. Most people in America were asleep at the time this was happening. We didn't want to cause panic that something like another September 11 hijacking was occurring."

"Well, if the plane turned deliberately," I added, "do you think there was a possibility that it had been overtaken?"

"I mean, we don't know, do we?" Baxter said with frustration. "Look, I know as much as anyone else does. We are not hiding anything. Maybe the plane's compass system malfunctioned and they were not sure which direction they were going. Maybe they tried to come back to Honolulu to land because something happened. I don't know. The plane just vanished off radar."

"How many years have you been working in the control tower?" Francesca asked.

"Over twenty. Why?" Baxter replied.

"Just curious," she said. "Have you ever experienced anything similar to this?"

"Not as strange as this occurrence," Baxter admitted. "Usually we'll find debris in less than a week after a plane disappears off radar. You would have thought that something would have washed up by now. I know the Hawaiian beaches have been searched in case it crashed close to the islands, but nothing has turned up. No pieces of the fuselage. No luggage. No seats. No bodies."

"That's the weirdest part about this," I said. "I almost wish I could have been on that flight, just to know what happened."

"But then you wouldn't be here, Patrick," Francesca said with horror. "Don't say that!"

"Sorry," I said. "Baxter, what about your dealings with the government?"

"The U.S. government came and did their investigation. They questioned all of us," he said.

"What kind of questions?" Francesca asked.

"They wanted to know who was at the tower at the time of the communication. Why we did not act fast enough. They probably did a background check on all of us. I don't think they had any real reason to be suspicious of my team, but they were following protocol, I presume. I want this to be over. It has been a lot of stress. I'm actually retiring in a few months."

"What are your plans after retirement?" I asked politely.

"I have a place in Alaska," he said. "I plan to live in the mountains. I have a boat as well, and plan to spend lots of time sailing with my wife."

"That sounds lovely," I said. "So, the Coast Guard did a sweep around the islands here, but Australia is involved with this search too, since analysts believe it might have flown way down south. Is that right, Francesca?"

"It is," she responded. "They believe that the plane's resting place could be somewhere in the South Pacific Ocean near New Zealand and Australia. It's all speculation from equations that some scientists came up with or something regarding the flight path the plane might have taken when it went off course."

"Do you have any information from the Australian search teams?" I asked.

"We're not involved in their matters. I'm sorry, but I don't. Look, I want answers too," Baxter said. "My voice has been on the news, and is all over the Internet with the Flight 619 cockpit final recordings. I'm just as curious as everyone else. If I knew something, I would not be this stressed out. But I have no answers. That is the honest truth."

We bid farewell to Baxter. I asked for his business card in case I ever needed to reach out to him. He knew what it was like to be linked to this flight without having actually been on it. Francesca seemed flustered. She had hoped he would have known something we had not already heard on the news.

"Do you believe him?" Francesca asked me as we walked back to our hotel.

"Yes," I said. "I really do think we're all on the same boat. And in the dark. I mean…look at me. I work for Phoenix Airlines. If they know something happened, they are definitely not keeping me informed."

"I suppose you're right," she said, defeated. "I just can't shake off the feeling that somewhere out there, somebody knows the truth. The question is, who? A government official, perhaps? Or maybe Royce Killington?"

11

For weeks, I had been trying to get hold of my former engineering school professor, Dr. Bernstein, to no avail. We were good at staying in touch, but he was not responding to any of my emails or phone calls. Two weeks prior, I had sent him a letter via regular mail after returning to Los Angeles from my trip to Hawaii. I wanted to know what that article he had published online about Jackson Killington was about. More importantly, I wanted to pick his brain about what his thoughts were on the missing Flight 619. I was offended that he had not once reached out to me regarding my survival by missing the plane's final boarding by minutes. He would have seen my face and heard my name on the news. October came and went, and I began to worry. I started to research his family online, to see if I could find anyone to reach out to. I knew he'd never married, and therefore had no children. If memory served me correctly, he had a younger brother. I could not find anything about his brother online or through any kind of social media, such as a LinkedIn or Facebook profile.

November 1, 2016

The day after Halloween, an answer showed up at my doorstep. It was Tuesday morning, and I was recovering from a Halloween party that Francesca had taken me to in the Hollywood Hills. I had been dressed as a vampire, and I was pretty sure I still had makeup on my face. I answered the door to a woman who was probably in her twenties.

"Mr. Baldwin?" she asked.

"Yes, how can I help you?" I asked. I really wanted to ask her how she got up to my floor, as my lobby had a concierge who was very strict. I held back that thought when she told me her name.

"I'm Bernadette Bernstein," she said, crossing her arms over her green cardigan. "Claude's niece."

My jaw dropped, and I opened my door wide.

"Please come in!" I said excitedly. When she walked in, I gestured for her to have a seat on my sofa. "How did you find me? I've been looking for Claude's family for ages. I did not know he had a niece."

"Yes," she said. "I'm Ben's daughter. Ben is Claude's brother."

"So, how…why…you're here!?" I said, not being able to string a normal sentence together.

"You were easy to find," she said. "I was picking up mail at Claude's house in Montana and found the letter you wrote him." She pulled my letter out of her bag to show me. She continued, "I read it and saw that you had been trying to get in touch with him. I also realized you were the survivor of Flight 619."

"Well I wouldn't say *survivor,* as I merely just missed my flight," I said. "Why didn't you call or email me? My contact information is in that letter."

"Claude would have wanted me to speak to you in person," she replied. "And, well, the news is easier to break in person. Claude's been missing since last April. He failed to show up at our family Easter brunch, and after twenty-four hours of no responses from his phone, we filed a missing person's report."

"Dear God, I had no idea!" I said. "It was unlike him to be radio silent."

"Claude was obsessed with the Killington family," she continued. "You mentioned his article about Jackson Killington in the letter. I did not know about it, so I Googled it and found the same error page you did. I did some digging around his house and sifted through some of his old hand-written journals. They did not have anything about the Killingtons. I did, however, find a mound of ashes in his fireplace. He had apparently burned some files. Or, at least, somebody did. There was a piece of paper that flew out of the pit and did not burn completely. It was the corner of a document. 'Jackson' and 'Tom' were two of the few names I could read off it."

"Do you still have that piece of paper?" I asked.

"I do." She pulled it out of her pocket. I glanced over it. I could not make out the sentences, but the name 'Jackson' was on it and so was 'TOM,' again in all caps, like the dedication in Jackson's biography.

"I think this was a hardcopy of his article," Bernadette said after a few silent seconds.

"What could have happened to him?" I asked. "He's been missing for nearly, what, seven months now?"

"Correct," she said sadly. "But I don't think he was kidnapped or anything of that nature. I think he's alive and in hiding."

"And why do you say that?" I asked.

She pulled out a photocopy of a passport from her purse and gave it to me. It was Claude Bernstein's face, but it was not his name.

"Wilbur Wright!" I exclaimed, and I nearly laughed in shock. "Couldn't he have been more original?"

"The name of one of the Wright brothers! The first successful inventors of the airplane." Bernadette said excitedly. "It took me a moment to put two and two together."

"So, what is your theory?" I asked.

"He fled from something," she replied. "That's my guess. Although, I'm not sure what he would have gone into hiding for. Do you think he knew something...something *dangerous*?"

"He lit his work on fire. He must have known something interesting he didn't want anyone else to see," I said. "But as strange as it was for a large 787 to disappear without a trace, the same can be said of a person vanishing under similar circumstances. But...what happened?"

"Disguised himself? Witness protection? Address relocation, perhaps?" Bernadette threw out her ideas. "I don't know."

I scratched my head in serious thought. Bernadette looked around my condo, pulled out a half empty Diet Coca-Cola bottle from her bag, and took two sips. Then, she put it back in her bag and said, "I want to find my uncle. I feel that *you* can help me. You knew him well."

"I'm curious about something," I said suddenly. "When I was searching Dr. Bernstein online, I did not find any news articles about him missing. Why is that?"

"It was in our local news. It's a small town. Not sure it would have received larger coverage than that. I don't think our local newspaper has an online version. Perhaps that's why a search would have turned up nothing," she said matter-of-factly.

"Ah, okay," I said, still feeling shocked from learning that my mentor was missing. My theory, after considering the photocopy of his passport, was that he was, in fact, still alive and hiding on purpose. "How long are you in town for?"

"I'll be leaving tomorrow," she said. "Back to Montana. I should get going soon, though. I need to pack for my return flight. Thank you so much for your time."

"If you think of or hear anything new, please call me. My cell phone number is in that letter, after all," I insisted.

"Absolutely," she said. "Thank you for taking the time to see me. I hope to find my uncle. I miss him dearly. You can keep that copy of his passport. I have another."

"Okay," I said, and I set it on top of my coffee table. "Thank you, Bernadette."

We shook hands and I walked her to the door. I closed the door behind her and walked over to my couch. My head was spinning from this startling news. For over two months, I had been trying to contact my mentor, and finally I had an answer as to why he was silent. Now I was left with even more questions.

November 7, 2016

Mark walked into my office with a draft of installation instructions for the Phoenix Project. We were getting ready to install the safety features on some of the newer planes that had been built over the summer and were not in service yet. We took a quick ride down the road to one of the hangars and met with the mechanics who were installing the systems on board. I ran into Royce and Robert Wong when we walked into the hangar. They were talking to some of the builders. Royce caught my eye and gestured for me to walk over.

"Hi, Royce," I said. "This is my intern, Mark Crane. He was a former student of mine."

"Welcome to the team," Royce said quickly, then turned to me. "Patrick, we are getting some parachutes delivered later this week that will be implemented into the tails of the new models. If all goes according to plan, we can probably have a demo mid-December, before the holidays. We will be able to garner a lot of press, because it's also one of the busiest times for travel. I want to have this demo a few miles outside of Palm Springs, in an open area of the desert, and hold a demonstration of a crash-landing scenario. I want to show the world the marvel of our ultimate safety feature. We have had many people criticize us because of how ridiculous it sounds for a parachute to deploy out of the tail of an airplane. People don't think they'll be strong enough to hold a heavy airplane from crashing to the ground. I want to prove them wrong."

"I see," I said. "Well, I want to see that for myself as well. Who will you get to pilot this airplane? Since this will be the first demonstration ever, it could be dangerous. Don't you think your first tests should be private versus public for the world to see, in case something goes wrong?"

"We're confident it will work," Robert Wong chimed in. "I stand by my company's product."

"I'll be right back," Royce said. "My assistant keeps calling me. It must be urgent." Royce walked outside of the hangar and left Robert alone with Mark and me.

"Want to take a look at the Forecaster module?" Robert asked.

"Sure!" Mark jumped in.

Robert walked us to one of the 787s. We climbed a ladder and into the plane where he guided us into the cockpit. There was a black box with an LED touch screen that had a 3D model of the 787 rotating 360 degrees.

"You can touch sections of the plane to zoom in and see if there are any issues," Robert said. "Parts of the plane will illuminate red if there is some kind of mechanical failure. It also has a voice command for hands-free operation. It's very nifty."

"ROBERT! ROBERT?" yelled Royce from the hangar. "Where are you?"

"In the plane!" Robert called out.

We climbed down the ladder and out of the plane and saw Royce running towards us. He looked extremely pale. There was a look of horror in his eyes. He was panting and trying to catch his breath.

"What's the matter?" I asked.

"Th-there's been another...*another* accident," he panted. "A 787 was shot down over Turkey. It was one of ours."

12

After the tragedy of Flight 619, I had not thought things could get any worse for Phoenix Airlines. It was as if the phoenix bird had erupted in flames that Monday afternoon, and any chance of it being reborn from the ashes seemed like a distant, intangible option at that moment. It felt as though my ears were ringing when Royce was telling us the news. We rushed to the coffee break room in the hangar and turned on a television. Every news station was reporting the news that Royce had just broken to us.

Phoenix Airlines Flight 425 was flying from Istanbul to London. They were ten hours ahead of our time zone, so it was evening there. About forty-five minutes after takeoff, the Boeing 787 exploded in the sky like a firework and plummeted to the ground in a ball of fire. There was cell phone video footage from civilians who witnessed the incident. The remains of the airplane fell over a rural town in Bulgaria. There were firsthand accounts of people saying that bodies had fallen through the roofs of their homes. Luggage, pieces of the fuselage, chairs, and more bodies were spread within a five-mile radius from where the explosion happened in the sky. The images were graphic.

Flight 619 had vanished four months prior, and now Phoenix Airlines was in the news again because of another downed plane. This one was not lost, however. It had been shattered into thousands of pieces, and the theory was that it was an act of terrorism. Theories were being thrown around as to what happened. The biggest theory was that a terrorist group from the Middle East shot it down. It had just happened, so no one was sure, but the plane was deliberately taken down.

"How could this be happening?" I asked tensely to Mark as we drove back to the headquarters. "This is not good at all."

"This was probably an act of terrorism," Mark said. "It's not like the plane had a malfunction."

"This could affect our launch of the Phoenix Project," I added. "The company has already lost so much money since 619 went missing; I can only image the costs that are going to come out of this. Two major tragedies for Phoenix in 2016. This is not good at all."

Much like the day PA 619 went missing, nobody at headquarters was getting much work done. People's phones were ringing off the hook, but the employees were too glued to the TVs to bother with them.

"President Howard is about to hold a press conference regarding the downed airplane," Paola said, rushing into my office.

I followed her out, and we walked into a conference room. Pravish and Mark were watching as well. President Howard's live press conference was being broadcast from the White House. The president was dressed in a navy suit with a matching navy tie. He had perfectly parted jet-black hair and thin black square-framed glasses. He had a clean-shaven face and bright blue eyes. He gestured for the crowd to fall silent.

"My fellow Americans," he began, "it is with great sadness that I must address the tragedy of Phoenix Airlines 425. My heart, sympathy, and prayers go out to those families affected by this tragedy. We have confirmed that out of the 234 passengers on board, fifteen were Americans. The airliner is American. While this incident did not occur on American soil, you can rest assured that we will do our best to investigate this matter. Any party responsible for these horrific actions will be met with justice. As of now, we do not have any information regarding who is to blame. We do believe this was *not* an accident."

November 11, 2016

Over the course of that week, there were still questions to answer regarding who was to blame in the shooting down of Flight 425. Half of the bodies had been recovered and were put in a train and sent to London, where families were waiting to bury their loved ones. Forensic scientists had done tests on some of the bodies and found metal particles in them that were not from the plane. It was then deduced beyond reasonable doubt that a surface-to-air missile had taken down PA 425. The burning question was who launched the missile?

Francesca had spent many long nights that week working on articles regarding the incident. She had interviewed a few ex-Phoenix Airlines employees, as current employees, like myself, were not allowed to speak on behalf of the company. During Francesca's incessant research on this tragedy, she found conspiracy theories regarding the incident. One of them was that this had been an inside job by the U.S., so that President Howard could go to war with certain countries in the Middle East. One theory that piqued my interest, even though I knew it was farfetched, was that Flight 425 was actually the missing Flight 619, disguised under a new number. The theory alleged that this flight was preparing for a terrorist attack on London, and U.S. intelligence had received a tip quickly enough to prevent such an attack. The U.S. intervened and shot down the airplane, and made it look like a radical terrorist group had done the deed.

"Phoenix has had a pretty rough year," I said to Francesca. We were sitting on my balcony and having dinner al fresco.

"Two tragedies in the same year, and only months apart. One missing. One shot down. And we can't forget about that riot attack on the headquarters," Francesca added.

"Maybe I should think about switching to another company," I said sarcastically.

"How is the progress of the Phoenix Project coming along?" Francesca asked.

"Stalled," I said. "Royce has put everything on hold as he deals with all the Flight 425 drama. He's getting pressure from investors and the company that built the systems to keep moving forward, and use this accident as a motivation to bring the Forecaster to the public."

"Okay," Francesca said suddenly. "Those safety features will not safeguard a plane from a missile attack. It would explode in seconds, even with the Forecaster system."

"The features are meant more for mechanical failures and human error," I added.

"I know," Francesca replied.

November 15, 2016

Natasha called me to come up to Royce's office. I arrived on his floor, and she told me to walk right in. Royce was seated at his desk staring off at the ceiling as if deep in thought.

"You wanted to see me?" I asked.

"Take a seat," he gestured over to the chair in front of his desk. "I'm getting a lot of pressure regarding the fate of the Phoenix Project," he said. He looked extremely sad. "I've had investors pull out. The media is back to reporting on PA 619 again. It died down slightly in the past weeks, but with the shooting down of 425, all anyone is talking about is how we've had two airplane tragedies this year alone, after having a record of zero incidents."

"What's going to happen?" I asked.

"I want to have a live testing of our parachute deployment of one of our latest 787 models," he said, "but it would be an ambitious business move. If it's successful, then we could garner positive press."

"I think you should test this in private before showing the world. I know Wong is confident that it'll work and wants to test it for the first time for a live audience, but it's risky. After all that has happened to the company recently, I would suggest we have all the kinks worked out in private."

"Patrick," he began, "I know that would be the smart thing to do. However, I'm a man of big risks. I want to do this demonstration in Palm Springs I was telling you about last week. I want you to help convince our staff. I had an executive meeting yesterday, and the common consensus in the company is that our project is a lost cause. I want the Forecaster to become reality. I strongly believe in it. Wong and his company are the best in the business."

I sat in Royce's chair, transfixed on a cloud in the sky outside of his window. I had a random thought. I wanted to skydive again. It had been over twenty years since the last time I had done it. I was going through a mid-life crisis at that moment. The stress of the Phoenix Project was a huge burden. I had been hoping that Royce would pull the plug on it, because it did seem like a lost cause after the tragedies the company had experienced. I ran my hand through my graying hair and took a deep breath that ended in a small coughing fit.

"Need some water?" Royce asked.

"I'm fine," I said stubbornly. "Ahem. So—the thing is…well, Royce…I…"

"Please tell me you're excited to see this project through," Royce insisted. "You're my top engineer. Do it for me. Do it for Jim, Dylan, and Charles. Do it for the future of aviation and this company. I need you to believe in it. If your colleagues see you pushing forward on this, it might change their minds."

I struggled with finding the right words to say. I had been on the brink of telling him he should scrap the whole plan, but I saw a look of desperation in his eyes. I truly felt sorry for him. He was the face of the company, so any feelings people had about the brand were directed at him. It was easy to understand why he wanted to see this project through. Failure was not a word in his vocabulary. I took another deep breath that was absent of a coughing fit and lied through my teeth.

"Yes, I support it. I will stand by you to see this through."

"Good," Royce said with a smile and a look of relief. "I'll need to have the teams working through Thanksgiving so that we can be ready for a December 15 demonstration event. In return, I'm giving everyone two weeks paid time off around Christmas and New Year."

"Okay," I replied, dreading the next couple of long weeks.

I spent the rest of the afternoon briefing Paola, Pravish, and Mark before I sent an email to the rest of the engineering teams. Mark was very eager to work on the project, even through the holidays. Paola and Pravish did not take the news well, as they had planned to take some time off to spend with family.

"Everyone will be getting a large bonus right before Christmas for working through the holiday," I pleaded to Paola and Pravish. "I need you two on my side. I know this isn't what you had in mind for Thanksgiving, but after the Flight 425 tragedy, all Killington wants is for us to continue perfecting the Phoenix Project."

"I guess we have no choice," Pravish said with frustration.

"I will cancel my flight back home to Italy," Paola chimed in unhappily.

Mark and I walked out of the building in the direction of our parking garage that evening around 9:00 PM. It had been a very long day. I did a double take when I saw a familiar man standing by the entrance of the garage, smoking a cigarette. It was Craig Cooper.

"What are you doing here?" I asked him.

"Another plane down. Another *Phoenix* plane down, may I add," he said.

"This one was an act of terrorism," I said. "But seriously, what are you doing here?"

"That doesn't make it much better," Craig ignored my question. "For all we know, PA 619 was, in fact, hijacked by terrorists too. What if the 425 plane was Flight 619, and the passengers from it, including my daughter, were on board and obliterated as a cover up?"

"I think you need to stop reading conspiracy theories," I said. "The bodies that were recovered were not from PA 619. You should know that. We have a manifest of the victims that boarded that airplane in Istanbul. Craig, what are you doing here? Seriously."

"I was waiting for you," he said.

"You could have called or emailed me," I replied, feeling a tinge of annoyance. It was late and I was ready to get some sleep.

"You've been getting serious with Francesca," he continued. "She talks about you all the time. And you haven't told her anything confidential that could help me get answers as to where or why my daughter disappeared."

"What are you talking about?" I was livid now. "I don't even know anything. I'm as in the dark as you are. Nobody in this God damn airline company knows, for Christ's sake."

Mark shifted uncomfortably next to me. I had a quick coughing fit, and then I cleared my throat to continue my outrage.

"Are you interrogating my girlfriend?" I spat.

"I'm surprised she's not interrogating you," Craig said.

I took a whiff of his breath. He smelled like whiskey. He had been drinking.

"She knows I know nothing more than the rest of America," I spat again. "We were all baffled by that tragedy. Remember, I lost colleagues too. Three of them."

"Francesca got close to you so she could not only find answers for me, but also to get some juicy details for a big story," Craig said. "She needs something big if she wants to advance at the *Times*."

I was silent for a few seconds. I clenched my fists. Craig was apparently very drunk. In my mind, there was no way that his statement could have been true. Francesca had never pressed me for any personal information.

"You're lying," I said through gritted teeth. "I'm embarrassed for you. I will call you a taxi. You need to go home."

"Am I?" he taunted. "Did you notice that I stopped speaking to major news outlets a few weeks after the plane went missing? Did you notice that I haven't been around Francesca much?"

"I've been avoiding the news," I said semi-truthfully.

"Well, I was prepared to start a big ruckus to bring scrutiny on Phoenix," he said. "Then some Phoenix Airlines lawyers kept calling me and saying that we should meet. I finally obliged. They forced me to sign a non-disclosure agreement and paid me a lump sum to keep my mouth shut."

"What do you mean?" I asked, not convinced I believed anything he was saying.

"Take a look for yourself," he said, and he handed me a rolled up sheet of paper.

I perused it quickly. My mouth dropped in awe. There were three paragraphs. From memory, it essentially said that Craig was to no longer publicly or privately speak ill of Phoenix Airlines. He was to be paid fifty thousand dollars and he could not tell anyone else about his payoff, especially other families of 619's victims. It was a small settlement.

"See," Craig said. "They went all out to do damage control for their image. That's all they care about. Your boy Royce Killington's signature is on that NDA."

And so it was. That was Royce's signature. I had seen it many times as an attachment to one of his emails or in the contracts he had to sign off for me during my work with the Phoenix Project. I looked Craig in the eyes.

"Why did you sign it?" I asked. "What did you mean by saying you were forced to sign this?"

"They told me that there would be 'repercussions' if I were to continue my public rant," Craig said, as he put the word "repercussions" in air quotes with his fingers.

"Did they elaborate?" I asked.

"It was very threatening," Craig continued. "I ignored them, naturally, and went on CNN the next day. That evening, I was driving to my house and saw a black car parked in my driveway. My first thought was it could have been someone from the media, waiting to get some sound bites from me. I parked my car on the side of the street and walked up to the black car. Two men came out of it. They were wearing these aviator sunglasses with blue lenses."

"The lawyers?" Mark jumped in.

Craig and I both looked at Mark as if we had forgotten he was there. Craig turned back to look at me only, then answered Mark's question.

"It was not the lawyers. I don't know who they were. But they told me that there would be much more harm to other members of my family if I didn't mind my own business. They had no weapons, but they were tall and muscular. They were clenching their fists threateningly."

"What did they tell you, exactly?" I asked.

"It was just vague threats about the safety of my family," he said. "They were not specific, but I could tell they were very serious."

Craig stopped talking and ran toward a nearby trashcan and proceeded to throw up. Mark and I cringed as he poured his guts into the trashcan. It was as if pouring out these secrets he was telling us had made him sick; however, it was actually due to his excessive drinking.

"I can't handle whiskey like I used to," he panted. "I'm sorry. Liquid courage is what fueled me to talk to you. I have not told anyone about this. Not my ex-wife, not my parents, and not even Francesca."

Craig put his back to the wall of the garage and slumped down to the ground to sit. He began to cry into his jacket.

"I miss her so much," he sniffled. "Mallory was my pride and joy. My only child. She was so bright. I knew she had a great future ahead of her. I just want to know what happened to her so that I can finally sleep."

I felt pity for Craig. I knew his rudeness from earlier was alcohol induced, and that he was a broken man who had lost a loved one. He had been silenced and blocked from his hope to find out what had happened to his daughter. I understood his genuine heartbreak. I wished I knew what happened to Jim, Charles, and Dylan. I was in the same boat as Craig.

"There, there…" I consoled him. "Get up. I can help you get home. Let me give you a ride."

Craig tried to regain balance and stand up. I had to lift him up by holding him under his armpits. He stumbled slightly and burped.

"Oh, I should also mention what they were wearing," he said. "They had on these blue uniform jumpsuits. There were no labels on them, but they looked almost military-like."

13

My heart began to beat fast at those words. An image of the riots at Phoenix Airlines Corporation popped into my mind.

"What do you know about S.R.K.?" one of the men in blue jumpsuits demanded of me on the rooftop of the office.

Then I saw both of those men in jumpsuits fall to the ground. Blood was spilling from under them as their lifeless eyes stared back at me. There were yells and the smell of gunpowder wafting in the air. I could hear sirens in the distance and the rush of police officers running onto the roof.

I came back to reality and looked at Craig. He was not looking at me. He was staring over my shoulder with a look of horror. He then turned on his heel to run, but in his drunken state, he lost balance and fell.

"Seize him!" I heard Royce Killington yell from behind me. "That man is a nutcase. Call Kingsley!"

Two Phoenix security officers tackled a flailing and screaming Craig to the ground.

"What are you doing?" I asked Royce.

"This man has been sending me threatening messages and leaving me deranged voicemails," Royce said with a look of pure loathing for Craig. "I had to put a restraining order on him."

Royce handed me his cell phone and showed me a long list of emails from Craig's address. They were, in fact, threatening. Most of his messages said the same thing. He wanted to expose Royce for his lies.

"He claims I had two lawyers make him sign a NDA," Royce said angrily. "I never did such a thing."

It all made sense to me suddenly. It was there in black and white on the screen of Royce's phone. Craig was a broken man. There was no NDA signed. He was not threatened. And he must have seen the report of the riots and saw the men in blue jumpsuits. He tried to make me think they were silencing him. I looked at Royce with guilt. I had almost believed Craig. I smacked my head absentmindedly and thought about the most obvious part of Craig's delusion. Why would Royce cause a public riot on purpose to attack his own company? Phoenix was struggling with a major national tragedy and the declining price of the company's stocks. It was absurd.

"He was drunk," were the only words I could say. Mark was silent, and I was thankful for that. I was not sure what he had made of Craig's encounter with me.

"He's not allowed on these premises," Royce said. "He has accused me of being the reason 619 went missing. He has called me every horrible name imaginable. He has even been caught sitting in a car outside my home in Brentwood. He will be taken to jail, and I will be pressing charges."

Craig cried and screamed as three officers arrived on the scene and attempted to shove him into the back of one of their patrol vehicles. After a few tense minutes, Craig was handcuffed and locked away in the back of a car. The last words he said before the door closed on him to muffle his cries, was, "I never wrote those emails. He framed me, Patrick! You have to believe me. He's evil. All he cares about is the public image of his company and himself."

It was almost midnight when Francesca arrived at my apartment. I had a glass of wine in hand. Her eyeliner was smeared all around her eyes. She had been crying. She gave me a hug as soon as I opened the door and began to sob into my shoulder.

"He's not c-c-crazy," she cried.

It took about ten minutes for her to calm down. I handed her a box of tissues.

"I saw the emails he was sending Royce," I told her. "He suffered from depression. He was recently divorced. He probably became unhinged."

"Unhinged?" she said, not sounding happy about my use of the word.

"I'm sorry," I apologized. "Poor word choice."

She began to sob into one of my sofa pillows for a few minutes. When she came back up for air, she asked, "What did he tell you, exactly?"

I explained to her that Craig was drunk and that he alleged he was forced to sign a NDA so he would not publicly or privately speak about Flight 619 or Phoenix Airlines negatively. I told her he insisted that there were two men in jumpsuits who threatened his family if he did not keep quiet. Then, without thinking, I asked her something I should have waited to ask at another time, when she was not as upset or vulnerable.

"He also said that you started dating me so that you could earn my trust and see if I really had inside info about the missing airplane. Is that true?"

Francesca looked as though I had just slapped her really hard. She began to cry, and through tears and barely audible words, I stringed together her response.

"My ch-ch-childhood best friend was drunk and depressed. He was arrested on a lie. He d-d-did not have a restraining order. I know Craig well. He would never threaten the CEO of a company like that. I also know he would ne-never make that accusation about me. And even if he did, how dare you believe him? Why the hell would I do that to you? I-I-I really care about you!"

"I'm sorry." I tried to comfort her by putting my arms around her, but she pushed them off. "He really did say that. I was confused at first, and that's why I thought I would ask. He seemed so believable."

Francesca continued to cry into my pillow. There was a good five minutes of awkward silence until she finally stopped. It was as if she had run out of tears to spare. She looked up at me, absent of the tears she'd had before disappearing behind the pillow.

"I'm sorry," she said. "Craig was drunk. That's true. I did once tell him I was going to date you to help him. To see if I could find out anything on the inside."

Now I was angry. I stood up and walked outside onto the balcony. I felt like screaming, but my voice would wake my neighbors and carry over to Beverly Hills. I turned back inside and closed my balcony door much harder than I had intended to.

"Are you serious?" I asked. "How the hell—why the hell would you—"

"I didn't!" she cut me off. "I didn't do anything. I told him that at first, but as I got to know you, I knew you had no information, and you were just as lost as anyone else following the story. I honestly began to fall for you. I promise."

"I think you should go," I said angrily.

It was not something I had meant to say, but at that moment, I felt slightly played and betrayed. The look in her eyes was real. She was genuinely hurt by my request for her to leave. Her green eyes filled with more tears. Her lips trembled. She opened her mouth as if to say something, but then stood up and reached for her purse. She walked out of my condo without a glance back. I had no energy to run after her or say anything. I felt I was too harsh, but if she had really only agreed to initially see me for a story, then that was plenty hurtful to me.

November 24, 2016

I woke up on the morning of Thanksgiving feeling very alone. Francesca and I had not spoken since our fight at my condo. I had refused to back down and send her any kind of text message or call. It was apparent that she had felt the same. It was 6:00 AM, and I had to be at work in an hour. I was not worried about rushing to get ready, because everyone else in L.A. was on holiday. I had to report to work to continue the Phoenix Project initiatives for the December 15 safety test launch in Palm Springs.

The news was on in the background as I poured myself some cereal. It was rare these days that there were reports about PA 619, as it had been nearly five months since it had disappeared, but the network I had my TV tuned to was reporting something that caught my attention.

"The Australian government, which has teamed up with the U.S. and Chinese governments in the search for the airliner that disappeared from the skies last summer, has issued a statement that they will begin scanning the South Pacific Ocean a few hundred miles off the coast of New Zealand in between Antarctica, where it is believed that PA 619 could have ended up. Several analysts have used advanced calculations, based on the fuel and speed of the plane, to determine its final resting place. This area of the ocean is a mystery itself. It is very deep, and not much is known about what lies beneath. Sonar technology will be used to map the ocean floor, but it is believed to have very deep canyons and mountains. Finding the airplane is like finding a needle in a haystack, but the search teams are hopeful and almost certain that this is the right place to be looking."

I was expecting to see news reports about Craig being arrested, but it seemed as though Royce made sure our public relations team kept things quiet. Since he was a public figure, the incident would have made the news, but his influence most likely prevented anything from getting out. He'd probably grown tired of the public relations nightmares he had to endure over the past few months.

The drive to Phoenix Airlines Corporation was quick. I was able to speed down the 405 with no traffic en route to El Segundo. Many of the Phoenix Airlines employees who had to work that day did not seem thrilled to be there. I was surprised to find Paola and Pravish in good spirits, however.

"You both seem like the only ones happy to be here," I told them. "I guess this is an American holiday—you don't even celebrate it in your own countries."

"Well, I am sad I could not use the time to travel to see my family," Paola said, "but we will have some time during Christmas. I am happy to say that Pravish and I were granted green cards by Mr. Killington for our dedication and hard work on the project. Can you believe that? We'll be full citizens soon! No more visas for us!"

"Wow, congratulations!" I said. "That's very kind of Royce."

"I'll have to write him a nice thank-you email," Pravish gushed. "What a nice man and company!"

It felt like our Thanksgiving was Christmas, because later that day, more surprises from Royce arrived. An email was sent around noon informing us that he was hosting a Thanksgiving lunch for us in our company's commissary. It was no ordinary feast. It was catered by one of the top chefs in town, who owned several prestigious five-star restaurants. The food was beyond delicious. People's spirits seemed to lift as they dove into their holiday meal full of turkey, veggies, and pies. Each person was even gifted a bottle of wine.

"Ahem," Royce spoke into a microphone system as dessert was being served. "I know that many of you had to take time away from your families, whether you are local or live out of town. The Phoenix Project will change our business forever. December 15 will be a massive day for us. Now, with the holidays approaching, I wanted to let you all know that your holiday bonuses will be arriving electronically into your bank accounts at midnight. The amount of your bonus was determined by your time of service here, but I think you will be very happy with the compensation for all your hard work and trouble. Happy Thanksgiving, team Phoenix!"

Everyone applauded and cheered. The mood from the morning seemed like a distant memory from the cheers and excitement running through the commissary. I had to hand it to Royce; he was his own public relations team when it came to how he was perceived by his employees. Only a few weeks ago, I had heard murmurs from some of my junior engineers, bad-mouthing Royce for his "dictator-like" leadership when we were all told we would have to work through Thanksgiving and perhaps some weekends. Now, it was as if that had never happened. I saw some of those same engineers shaking Royce's hand vigorously as he made his way around the tables. Royce arrived at our table and took an empty seat next to Mark and me.

"Good morale is the key to success," he whispered to me. "I think you'll be happy with your bonus."

I smiled back and replied, "That is very generous of you. I do thank you for keeping up the morale. It hasn't been an easy few weeks."

"I know," Royce said. He then turned to Mark. "Mr. Crane…"

Mark turned red. I do not believe he thought Royce knew his name.

"Yes?" he asked timidly.

"When do you graduate?" Royce asked.

"This spring," Mark answered. "My internship here ends right after the test launch. December 20, to be exact. I have loved working here every day."

"Well, good," Royce smiled. "Because I am going to approve headcount for a new position on this team. I think you should be the one to fill it. I would like you to begin in January. We can figure out a way to finish your last semester while working full-time in L.A."

Mark dropped his fork onto the floor in shock, and then vigorously shook Royce's hand with a large smile and several "thank yous."

Royce could have been a politician that day. He had won the votes of everyone in that room. I was skeptical. There was something strange about all the strings he had just pulled. It was as if he'd bought everyone's approval with the wave of a magic wand. He appeared genuine, but it seemed too excessive.

It was at that moment that I made the decision. I was going to put in my letter of resignation after the December 15 event. There were too many bad memories from the past five months alone. I had lost faith in Phoenix. Jim, Dylan, and Charles had apparently lost it as well, since they were planning this S.R.K. Project, whatever it might have been. I wanted closure, and walking through those halls every week made it very difficult. I decided not to tell anyone about my plans to resign until I had written my letter and personally handed it to Royce.

I quit teaching, and now I'm going to quit Phoenix, I thought. *This isn't like you, Patrick...*

We were out of the office by 4:00 PM that day. I did not have family in town, so I was not rushing to get back home. Instead, I had a strange idea to pay a visit to Craig and ask him a few questions. I hesitated doing so, but I wanted to talk to him in a coherent state. We met up at a coffee shop near my condo.

"I must say, I'm surprised to see you," Craig said. He had bags under his eyes and a beard. He had abandoned his clean-shaven look while he had been in jail for a short period. "No Thanksgiving with family or Francesca today?"

"No family in L.A. Francesca and I have not talked since you were taken by the cops a few days ago," I said.

"She did not mean to hurt you," Craig said. "She wasn't going to really use you. I just hoped that she would. I think she told me she would get to know you better to make me feel like there was hope to get answers. I think she realized soon enough that it was not worth hurting you. She really cares about you."

"I believe that," I said, finally admitting out loud that I might have been too harsh on her.

"Did you believe him?" Craig asked.

"Believe who?" I questioned.

"Killington," Craig answered. "That I am crazy?"

"Are you?" I asked. "That's why I wanted to meet up. To determine that, and see if anything you said drunkenly was a misrepresentation."

"I'm not," Craig said. "Maybe I'm crazy because I'm missing my daughter, and a father would go to any lengths for his child, but I was not harassing Killington in that manner. Those emails were not real. He set me up."

"I'm going to ask him to drop the charges he filed against you," I said. "I think I can convince him if I talk to him."

"Why would you help me?" Craig asked. "I've done nothing but burden you. I was a drunken fool the other night. I did not send those emails to Royce. Someone sent them on my behalf—that, or Royce framed me."

"Something is off, for sure. I could use your help," I said. "We both want the same thing: answers. I want to find my colleagues—or at least learn what happened the night 619 went missing. And you want closure for your daughter, Mallory. Maybe we can team up?"

I watched tears pour down Craig's unshaven face. He smiled as though he had not done so in years. He had a hopeful gleam in his eye.

I continued, "I found myself on the rooftop of Phoenix Airlines on the day of the riot. Two men in plain blue jumpsuits forcefully questioned me about something only my colleagues who were on the plane and I would have known. It was then that I knew there was some kind of connection—or at least there might be some relation—as to why the plane disappeared. You mentioned that two men in jumpsuits threatened you to stop speaking publicly about Flight 619. Coincidence? I think not. I believe there was foul play, and it has to do with them and quite possibly me."

It was then that I admitted for the first time out loud that I might be the key to learning about what might have happened on that fateful morning of July 14.

December 14, 2016

On the day before the Phoenix Airlines test launch in Palm Springs, Craig Cooper was dismissed from court, as all charges against him had been dropped. It took a few weeks for me to convince Royce to do so, but in the end he had agreed because I told him Craig was my girlfriend's best friend. I failed to mention she was currently my *ex-girlfriend,* but we'd never had a break-up conversation, so it was murky. The one stipulation for dropping the charges was that Craig had to agree to a three-year restraining order, and was not allowed anywhere near the corporate offices or within one hundred feet of Royce.

Craig had called me filled with gratitude on the morning he learned the news. I told him that I would reach back out to him once I was out of my contract with Phoenix.

"Then, and only then," I told him, "can we begin working together to find some answers. I have a few days left in the office, and I'm going to hang back late tonight to do some research. I have an early morning drive to Palm Springs."

"I understand," Craig replied. "I saw Francesca an hour ago. She said you both are still not talking, and that you've essentially broken up."

"Well," I added, "we never officially broke up; I guess that is, in fact, where we are at."

I stared at my computer screen quietly for five minutes after I ended my call with Craig. I contemplated calling Francesca for closure; it seemed ridiculous that we had not spoken in over two weeks. Five minutes became fifteen. I decided to take a walk in the courtyard when I made up my mind to not call her. I had a big event the following day to prepare for, and all the eyes of the world would be on the project I had poured my heart and soul into over the last few weeks.

As I approached my favorite bench in the courtyard—the one where I first met Francesca, ironically enough—I saw Robert Wong's familiar face walking in my direction, with a designer workbag over his shoulder.

"Ah, Mr. Baldwin," he said when his eyes made contact with mine. He had a cigarette in his free hand, which he put out on the edge of a trashcan, then threw the butt inside it. "Are you ready for tomorrow? It's a big day!"

"As ready as we can be," I said truthfully. "The 3D model computer system simulators show it working perfectly. Now it's just up to the demonstration to go without a hitch so that we shine in the eyes of the press and the world."

"I know you might have thought we should do a private testing first," Robert replied. "But the satellites have been up and running for the last week. All systems will be a-go tomorrow afternoon, and I feel confident everything will run smoothly. The stage is Phoenix's for the taking if it is successful."

"We hope to make history tomorrow," I said, trying to sound confident, even though my gut told me this was a recipe for disaster. *How could we test something for the first time in front of millions of people, watching all over the world?* I thought.

"Here's my card," Robert said, handing me his business card. "I'll be in town until mid-next week, finishing up a few things before I return to Beijing. We should grab drinks. I'd like to hear more about Royce's number one engineer."

I felt myself go red while my ego was being stroked.

"I'd love to," I said. I took his business card and put it in my wallet. "I'll email you soon to set a time and place."

"I am looking forward to it," Robert said. "See you tomorrow in Palm Springs!"

Later that evening, I swiped my badge into one of our labs once the last remaining junior engineer had left for the day. It was around 7:00 PM. The only people left were the janitorial staff. All the employees had planned to leave the office early, as every department had been asked to attend the launch event tomorrow.

I approached a filing cabinet that belonged to our record maintenance group. They were labeled by date. I sifted through July 2016. There was a folder labeled July 13, 2016. In that folder, there were tabs that sub-divided different cities where Phoenix Airlines flew out of. I arrived at Los Angeles, and saw that the maintenance records for all of our flights on that day were missing. I was not surprised, however; they had probably been taken during the investigation of PA 619, since that was the date the plane took off on what would be its final flight.

I scratched my head and began to think hard. There had to be digital records. I turned on one of the computers in the lab, but it was password protected to the manager who worked in that department.

"Crap," I cursed under my breath. "Of course it would be secured."

Then I heard the sound of a door being opened. My heart sank. I ducked under the desk as the blinds on the window of the door swung and made a jingling noise.

Heavy footsteps followed the opening of the door. My heart began to race. I could hear it pounding against my rib cage. I clutched at my shirt with my right hand, in hopes that it would muffle the sound. Apparently, I was under the impression that this stranger who had entered the room could hear my heart.

"Mr. Baldwin, are you here?" an unfamiliar voice called out for me.

I nearly peed my pants. Who knew I was in that room?

"Mr. Baldwin," the voice continued in a whisper, "I got an alert that you swiped into this laboratory. It's after hours and this is not your department, so I wanted to check in. My name is Kingsley. I'm head of security."

I took a deep breath and got up from hiding. I'm not sure what gave me the courage to do that, except for the fact that either way, I was caught. I should have known that my badge would be traced in some way when I swiped to enter the lab.

"Hello," I said timidly. "I, um..."

"May I ask what you are doing here?" Kingsley questioned me. His voice sounded friendly and gave me comfort. I also recognized him from seeing him around the building and outside of Royce's office waiting area once.

"Nothing." That was all I could muster as a response.

Kingsley looked over at the maintenance cabinet I had been digging through. I bit my lip in frustration, as I had left the cabinet ajar.

"They took the files," he told me. "The FBI, that is. After the plane went missing, they came by to investigate. They found nothing suspicious with the mechanics of 619. There was routine maintenance the day that plane took off. You won't find the hard copies on the premises."

"I..." I struggled with an answer again.

"Don't worry," Kingsley said nicely. "I understand your curiosity. You were meant to be on that plane."

I took a deep breath and felt at ease, knowing that I was probably not going to be in trouble. I decided to be honest with Kingsley. For some reason, I trusted him.

"I want answers," I said truthfully. "So, there was nothing in those records?"

"No," Kingsley said, "nor in the digital files. The airplane was up to date on maintenance. Unless something was missed when they looked at the plane's diagnostics the evening it departed, there was no evidence of mechanical failure. It kind of makes the mystery of the airplane more intriguing, doesn't it?"

"Did they tell you this?" I asked. "Did they tell you the records were normal? So, the plane was free of any maintenance issues?"

"I'm head of security," Kingsley said. "Part of my job is to make sure these records get input into the system. I saw the original report. And no, they were not tampered with either."

It was strange that he ended his sentence that way. I had been mulling over the idea that perhaps the records had been tampered with.

"Phoenix is not hiding anything, Mr. Baldwin," Kingsley said. "Nothing goes through this facility without me knowing."

I looked intently at Kingsley. He was a tall, very fit man with a tan complexion. He appeared to be in his late seventies or early eighties and was bald. His face gave away his elderly age, but his athletic body was much more youthful looking. He was wearing a short-sleeved security uniform and had a tattoo sleeve down one of his arms. It was a snake that intertwined from what I guessed was the top of his shoulder all the way down to his hand. The snake's menacing head and red, glaring eyes stared at me with a wide-opened mouth and sharp teeth. A flame erupted from its mouth, and it ended on his hand in between his pointer finger and thumb. The snake was dragon-like in appearance, and judging by the fact that it was breathing fire, it was most probably a dragon and not a snake, as I had originally believed. It was sinister in every aspect, but it was artistic. It coiled around his muscular arm and looked almost life-like. He must have had that tattoo for decades. It seemed odd for a man his age to have one, but I figured he received it during his youth. And he was really buff for an older gentleman. As tough as Kingsley appeared physically, his voice and demeanor were kind.

"I apologize for my unauthorized late-night entrance into this lab," I said abashedly.

"Your card grants you access to this lab," Kingsley said. "You've done nothing wrong. At least, nothing worth noting to my superiors." Kingsley winked at me and smiled. By superiors, I assumed he meant Royce.

"Thank you," I said. "It's been a rough few months."

"I can imagine," he responded. "I suggest you get some rest. Tomorrow is a big day. I wish I could attend, but I'm holding down the fort here while most of the company is in Palm Springs. Besides, we are using the time while everyone is out of the office to fix a water issue in one of the hangars. Traces of radon were found in the bathroom faucets. It's probably from the soil and foundation the hangars are built over."

"Right," I replied. "Have a good night."

I walked out of the lab with a heavy sigh and feeling extremely thankful that Kingsley was very understanding. I had been sure I had put myself in a predicament, but I was glad that I was walking out with an understanding of discretion between Kingsley and me.

December 15, 2016

The big day had finally arrived. I left my condo at 5:00 AM to beat Los Angeles traffic, and arrived in Palm Springs shortly after 7:00 AM. All Phoenix employees were to meet at one of the local hotels. We parked our cars in a garage and boarded several charter buses that took us a few miles out into the desert, where the demonstration was being held.

When we arrived at the location, which was about two miles away from the nearest major interstate, we found hundreds of folding chairs placed before a podium and stage that had been erected for the event. There was a giant white banner with the red Phoenix logo on it right behind the podium. In front of the podium was a press line, with several major news outlets and camera crews buzzing with excitement.

"This is really exciting," Mark said as we disembarked from the bus. Pravish and Paola followed behind us.

"I think we've put a lot of effort into the Forecaster and this project in general," I said. "We have some of the most brilliant minds on this project. I hope the test is seamless." Overnight, I had been able to calm my anxiety because of that mere fact. Phoenix had employed some of the best engineers in the world. Knowing that, I had a good feeling that this demonstration would, in fact, proceed without any issues. I was comforted by the confidence that some of the junior engineers on my team had exhibited while taking their seats in front of me.

"Save my spot," I told Mark. "I'm going to run to the restroom."

I walked over to the restroom line. There were thirteen people in front of me waiting for only two portable stalls. I groaned to myself. *Couldn't they have provided more toilets? I'm sure they had the budget.*

A man in front of me turned to face me and asked, "Do you have a lighter?" He was holding a pack of cigarettes. I recognized the short gray hair and light colored eyes. I had only seen a photo of this man in black and white. In real life, his eyes were light blue. It was Colin Shaw, the author of *Jackson Killington: The Man Who Made a Killing and a Ton of It.*

"I don't—sorry," I said in surprise. "Are you Colin Shaw?"

Of course, I already knew the answer. His face was unmistakable, as I had seen his author head shot in my copy of Jackson Kilington's biography.

"I am," he replied. "And you are?"

"Patrick. Patrick Baldwin." I extended my hand for him to shake, and he reached for it. "I work for Royce. I'm his head engineer."

"Well," Colin replied with interest, "that's very impressive. I'm a family friend of the Killingtons, so they were kind enough to invite me in person to this launch. I flew in from D.C."

"I enjoyed your book on Royce's father," I said, making casual conversation. "Royce gave me a copy."

I teetered in my mind on whether I should blatantly ask him about his dedication page to TOM. Then I realized how weird that would be. *Should I ask, 'Who is Tom?'* I pondered. *No, you don't want to sound like you're suspicious.*

"I'm glad you enjoyed it!" Colin replied gleefully. "A few minutes until show time. Now, if only this line would move quickly."

My conversation with Colin pretty much ended there. It was his turn to use the restroom, and after he finished, he waved goodbye to me and proceeded to find his seat. He was seated near Natasha. After giving each other a welcoming embrace, they spoke as if they were old friends. Since Natasha had once worked for Royce's father, it made sense that Colin would know her.

At 9:00 AM, the show began. Royce took the stage to tumultuous applause and the flashing of several cameras. Everyone seemed too excited to care that the temperature was quite cool that morning. It was in the low forties. I buttoned up my wool blazer because I was shivering; however, it might have actually been my nerves getting the best of me.

"Ladies and gentlemen…welcome to the live demonstration of the Phoenix Project!"

More applause erupted. I noticed Robert Wong in the front row, clapping his hands overenthusiastically.

"Today will be historic," Royce continued. "For the first time in the history of aviation, we will witness a distressed commercial airliner land safely, thanks to the workings of our very intelligent computer system that we've dubbed the Forecaster. We have cameras around the desert to capture the event. We even have cameras inside the cockpit of the airplane, which is being piloted by Brick Walters, a well-known Hollywood stuntman who has done work in several hit action blockbuster films. The newly redesigned model of our Boeing 787 is currently taking off from the Palm Springs airport just a few miles away. Ah—there we go!"

There were two large LED screens to the left and right of the Phoenix banner. On the screen, the audience could see the airplane take off from the airport. There were more cheers. At that moment, I was tapping my feet with anxiety.

"You're shaking," Paola whispered to me. "Are you okay?"

"Anxious," I said. I did not feel like speaking, in fear that vomit would pour out from my queasy stomach.

Royce continued, "Many of you have seen our safety 3D model video we released a few months ago when we had our unveiling. Today, you are about to witness this prototype in real life. Are you excited?"

More cheering commenced. I could feel bile rising up to my esophagus. I was clenching my mouth. It felt warm with a burning sensation as it brushed against my vocal chords. I could no longer hold it in, so I ran out of my seat and straight to the portable toilets.

"Is he okay?" I heard Pravish ask.

Several people whispered as I ran to the bathroom. Thankfully, there was no line to wait in this time. The toilets were vacant, as anxious on-lookers had taken their seats.

I opened the door and immediately began to puke into the toilet. I clenched my nose with one hand, because it smelled terrible. I tried to keep my face as far away from the toilet seat as possible. Some of my vomit had landed on the seat. There was blood.

Strange, I thought. *Does one normally throw up blood when they are nervous as hell?*

The putrid smell of the toilet made me gag again and more fresh vomit projected out of my mouth. I coughed again, and wished that a bottle of mouthwash would magically appear, so that I could wash the taste of bile out of my mouth. My stomach felt empty. I had lost my entire breakfast from that morning, which had consisted of a croissant and coffee from a bakery.

I wiped my mouth and walked outside. I could see Mark, Pravish, and Paola craning their necks to see where I had gone. I gestured two thumbs-up at them, to communicate that I was fine. Everyone else was busy looking up at the sky. In the distance, I could see the silver 787 with the red Phoenix Airlines logo on its nose flying in our direction.

My nerves were still worked up. I felt a small pain in my chest. I needed to throw up again, but I had no contents left in my stomach to expel.

I heard a buzzing of murmurs from a nearby tent. Out of curiosity, I walked over to it. It was the control room for all the audio and visual equipment that was broadcasting the event. A digital sign blinking over the tent read "LIVE." The event was airing live on the web and on several major television news networks.

I saw two men rush out of the tent in a hurry. They were wearing…

"*Jumpsuits!*" I gasped, and my heart pounded in fear. Then, my adrenaline got the best of me, and I decided to run after them.

"We need to hurry!" yelled one of the men. "It needs to be timed right."

The two men arrived at a four-door pickup truck. They opened the driver-side door and pulled out what looked like a remote. My eyes widened in shock. The remote was a red flag for me. Out of shock, I began to look around the vicinity for some kind of weapon. I found a few large rocks on the ground and picked two up. I clutched them tightly in my hands, then took two hoarse coughs and clutched my chest. The rocks fell back onto the desert sand. I collapsed for a few seconds before regaining my strength to pick up the rocks. One of the men saw me and looked at me with concern.

"STOP!" I yelled hoarsely. "STOP!"

I had the feeling that these men were about to set off a bomb in the crowd of on-lookers. That's what my anxious mind believed the remote was for.

"It's okay!" one of the men told me. "It's part—"

"SHOOT THE DAMN THING NOW!" the other man yelled, and he shoved his colleague, who pressed the button on the remote just as I hurled a rock at him.

It felt like everything was moving in slow motion. I could also hear the engines of the airplane flying overhead. Its sound had reached my ears. There was a loud explosion from the distance that echoed across the desert canyon. The rock I threw had hit the truck's tire after the man with the remote ducked and avoided being struck by it.

"What the hell, man!?" he screamed in anger.

His yell was then drowned by screams from the audience watching the event in person. There were cries, and a few on-lookers had left their seats in haste in the opposite direction of the airplane.

The explosion had taken place miles away from the audience and up in the sky. The members of the audience who had not leapt out of their seats in shock were looking and pointing up at the disaster. Many of them had their hands clasped over their mouths in awe. I followed their gazes and looked up at the sky to witness something far worse than I had anticipated. The explosion was from a missile that had been launched from the ground and aimed directly at the 787.

15

The missile made contact with the left wing of the 787. The explosion was deafening. An orange cloud of fire erupted like a firework followed by black smoke. The audience's bloodcurdling screams rang in my ears. I fell to the ground in shock. Royce was standing on the podium with a huge grin on his face, looking at the terrified crowd. I looked at him with disgust. Was he behind the attack? He looked ecstatic about the scenario unfolding.

I turned over and saw the two men in blue jumpsuits. They had taken their eyes off the airplane, and were apparently pleased with the fact that the missile they'd launched had struck it. The man I'd nearly hit with the rock then walked over to me. He seemed upset, but not as angry as he was when I had nearly smacked him on the head. As he got closer, I was able to read a label on the front of his jumpsuit. It read "Weapons & Materials Research Group."

The man knelt down by me and said, "I'm sorry if we scared you. This was all part of the demonstration."

Royce spoke to the frightened crowd as the 787 began to plummet toward the desert, confirming what the man said to me. "Silence!" he yelled. "This is all part of the show. Put your attention on the screens."

The screens on the stage cut to the interior of the cockpit. Brick Walters seemed unfazed by the attack. He was pressing several buttons on the Forecaster computer module. He then pulled on his seatbelt to make sure it was fastened, and the cameras changed to an exterior shot of the airplane. The cabin of the plane deployed from the shell of the 787. People's screams were exchanged with cheers and applause at the realization that a parachute had deployed, and the missile attack was all for show.

The cockpit of the plane hurled toward Earth with smoke billowing out behind it, making it look like a comet. It crashed in a desolate part of the desert and exploded upon impact. The sound was heard throughout the canyon.

The shell of the airplane was making its descent slowly to the ground, with a giant white parachute holding it up vertically. There were murmurs of excitement in the crowd. I could see Royce beaming with satisfaction. I was in awe. The entire cabin of the 787 was about to be saved. I wished Royce had told us he was going to shoot down the plane, but I was guessing the dramatic effect was worth it for the spectators. I had to admit, this was a historic day. If a missile had made contact with the main body of the airplane, much like what happened to Flight 425, it would not have stood a chance. However, I understood Royce's controversial choice to use a missile for the demonstration. The missile only hit the wing, keeping the main cabin intact, and therefore giving the plane a fighting chance for the Forecaster to do its job.

There were several all-terrain vehicles with police lights rushing to where the plane's cabin was about to crash land. The screens zoomed in as the cabin hit the desert sand. It then fell onto its side, right side up. The emergency exit door of the cabin opened, and an inflatable slide was released. Brick Walters surfaced at the frame of the door to a tumultuous round of applause and a standing ovation. I felt goosebumps running up and down my arms. Music began to blast from the stage's speakers. The press line's cameras were flashing and buzzing with fervent excitement.

I dusted my pants off and walked back to my seat in the audience.

"That was insane!" Mark said, patting me on the back. "Did you know they were going to shoot it down?"

"No—did you two know?" I asked Paola and Pravish.

"No," they both said in unison.

Royce cleared his throat into the microphone, and the audience quickly settled down.

"Today, Phoenix Airlines has made history. We've had a really rough year. Our prayers go out to the families and victims of PA 619 and 425. We hope that this demonstration will show you the drastic efforts we have been working on long before these tragedies occurred, highlighting our priorities in making air travel safer than ever. Starting next month, we will begin to slowly release our fleet of planes with these safety features to an airport near you. We will begin to phase out our older models."

"Old? Those planes aren't even three years old yet!" I heard some lady sitting in front of me whisper to her neighbor.

"I'd like to invite our special guests, the press, and my Phoenix Airlines family to the Palm Springs Oasis Hotel for a reception and luncheon. There will be plenty of food and drinks. Please join us for this celebration. The charter buses will be loading shortly. Thank you!"

The crowd began to shuffle onto the buses. I was preparing to board mine when Royce called for me. Natasha was by his side, wearing a very fashionable red blazer and matching skirt with designer heels. How she was able to walk in heels in the desert terrain was anyone's guess. She also had on a white neckerchief. It looked like the uniform female Phoenix flight attendants wore.

"I need a word," he said. "Mind riding in my car?"

"Um, sure," I responded, and then I turned to Mark, Paola, and Pravish. "I guess I'll see you all at the hotel."

"Sorry to take you away from your colleagues," he told me once I approached him and Natasha, "but I want to go over a few things. We'll be taking this black car. Natasha—you, Robert, and Colin will take the other."

"Okay," she said, and she walked off to grab Colin Shaw and Robert Wong.

Royce's driver opened the door for me and gestured for me to get in. He was an elderly man with a white Santa Claus-like beard. He was wearing leather gloves and a wool black suit with a matching black wool golf cap. He had on a pair of silver-lensed aviator sunglasses that I could see my reflection in. I got in and found a bottle of water on the seat waiting for me, which I thankfully took. My stomach was still queasy from throwing up earlier. Royce jumped in and smiled at me as he buckled up.

"Today was an amazing day. Your team did well. Zyphone turned out to be a great partnership in helping us with the Forecaster invention. I'm overjoyed."

Royce's phone kept vibrating. I found the buzzing sound to be very distracting.

"Twitter mentions," he said. "We are trending worldwide!"

"It's the talk of the industry and the world right now," I added. "Congratulations, sir."

"We invested millions on this project," Royce continued. "I think we will see a nice return. People will be choosing our fleet of planes over the competition easily. I think we have truly outdone ourselves to get out of the PR nightmare of the missing Flight 619 and the terrorist downing of 425."

"Did they confirm that the downing of Flight 425 was a terrorist attack?" I asked.

"Not officially," Royce replied, "but we are pretty sure that it was terrorist related, and the government is looking into it. Usually terrorist groups will claim responsibility and boast about it, but the Middle East has been quiet."

"And do we have any updates on 619?" I asked curiously.

"We have ships using advance sonar technology hundreds of miles off the coasts of Australia and New Zealand, working day and night to map out the bottom of the ocean. We've found a few sunken ships from the 1900s, but no sign of plane wreckage. I'm hopeful that we'll find something. We are looking in the right place, based off the equations a team of researchers presented of the possible turn 619 took on the path it diverted from."

"Well, I hope we get answers soon," I said. "So, what did you want to talk about?"

"I want to talk about Jim, Dylan, and Charles," Royce said matter-of-factly. It appeared as though he meant business. He straightened his tie and then fidgeted with a handkerchief in the breast pocket of his designer suit.

"What about them?" I asked.

"I've been doing my own research into the 619 disaster," Royce said. "Off the record, that is. I had our company cell phone carrier provide call records from the business phones of our three missing engineers. They even provided voicemail records. I had the cell phone company wipe the record of one particular voicemail that was left for Jim, because I found it to be of interest, and I wanted to ask you personally about it before going to the authorities, in case it leads to any kind of clue."

I took a deep breath. I could feel my palms sweating. My heart was beating so hard I felt it would burst, and I would vomit all over again inside the luxury sedan.

"Ahem," I cleared my throat. "What do you mean?"

I tried to play dumb, but I knew he was going to ask me about the voicemail I left for Jim after I received knowledge that the plane went missing.

"The voicemail in question…" Royce said to me with an inquisitive look, "well, let me play it for you to refresh your memory."

He played the voicemail from a sound memo on his smartphone: "One new voicemail, received Thursday, July 14, 2016 at 7:28 PM… Jim, it's Patrick. I hope nothing horrible happened. I pray you get this voicemail. I wish I would have known more about this side secret project."

I closed my eyes and kept wishing I would wake up from this nightmare. I could feel Royce's gaze on me.

"What was this 'side secret project' you spoke of?" he asked me after a few seconds of silence.

"The one we were heading to Beijing for," I said, trying to sound as if that was the most obvious answer. "The Forecaster—even though we didn't know the name of it at the time."

Royce did not seem convinced. He put his hands together and then brushed his chin with them. He reached for a bottle of champagne that was being chilled in a small bucket of ice, and poured himself a glass without offering me any.

"Were you going there on business other than for Phoenix Airlines?" he asked flat out.

"I…" I did not want to lie. "They mentioned something to me, but they didn't tell me what it was."

I felt as though I could no longer keep that secret. I had only told Francesca, Craig, and Jim's wife, Melissa, about the secret project. Perhaps it was information I should have mentioned a long time ago. It might have been the key to finding the airplane, which at this point, seemed like it would be lost forever.

"Elaborate," Royce asked.

"It was a secret project they were putting together that would conflict with the interests of Phoenix. It was outside of the work you were sending us there for, with some company I do not know the name of. They told me nothing more. All I know was that I would find out in person in Beijing, and it would change the way people traveled commercially. It would compete against commercial airlines, apparently."

"Why did you keep this silent?" Royce asked angrily. "Do you know how awkward it would be for us if this voicemail was released to authorities and the press five months too late? It looks suspicious."

"I'm sorry," I said honestly. "I was scared. I didn't know what to do. I was in shock from this fiasco because I was supposed to be on that flight."

"Do you think that what they might have been planning could have had some connection to this disappearance?" Royce questioned me.

"It was not until the riots at the corporate headquarters that I felt that there might be something more. There was something about those two men in jumpsuits. The ones who were shot on the rooftop of our building... well...they asked me about some project called S.R.K. I don't know what this project is, but I deduced that it was initialed after the surnames of Jim, Dylan, and Charles. Sparks. Rosenberg. King."

"I've been trying to find the smoking gun in the case of Flight 619," Royce said with hushed urgency, "and all of this time, you had this information and never came forward. This will make it look as if we, as a whole company, were hiding something. Since you are under my employment, it will make the entire corporation look bad. This is not good, Patrick."

Royce had been aging very well until the disasters of 619 and 425 occurred. His hair had a few more grays, and I could see more wrinkles building up around his eyes. He looked as if he had been given a death sentence. I could see he was trying to figure out his next move by the look of terror in his eyes. It was then that I knew Royce Killington was just as clueless as I was as to what happened that fateful morning of July 14.

"So, there must be a connection between our three engineers and the airplane going missing," Royce said. "And those two mysterious men in jumpsuits who were never identified wanted to question you about it? Is it possible that someone wanted to silence our engineers?"

"Yes," I said. "Maybe someone powerful out there wanted to silence them—and me?"

Royce looked at me. For a fleeting second, it seemed like he was giving me a look of pity, but then his eyebrows furrowed and he became business-like again.

"What project could they have been working on that was so secretive it would become their death sentence? You honestly do not know what they were working on?"

"I've told you all I know," I responded. "The truth."

"We are almost at the hotel for the banquet," Royce said. "We will need to talk about this tomorrow, first thing in the office. I'll have Natasha schedule us an appointment. Do not speak of this to anyone else. I need to think about how we will move forward with this. I may have my friend Colin Shaw advise me. He used to be the head of the CIA."

The driver opened up the door for Royce. He buttoned his suit jacket upon getting out of the car, and briskly walked into the hotel. I pulled out a few dollars from my wallet to hand to the driver. He said, "No need," and went back to the driver's seat.

Upon entering the Palm Springs Oasis Hotel, I saw Natasha and Colin Shaw in what appeared to be a heated conversation or argument of some sort. I walked by them, but they took no notice of me. Royce was speaking to several of his security personnel. Paola and Pravish were at the hotel bar getting drinks. Mark was chatting excitedly with a dapper blond-haired man who was about his age. Both of them were grinning ear-to-ear in what appeared to be an engaging conversation.

"I thought you would beat us," Paola said. "You had a much nicer ride than us."

"How was it?" Pravish asked.

"Interesting. We spoke about business things and whatnot. It was nothing very pressing," I lied.

Mark joined us a few minutes later looking cheerful, and we all walked into the hotel ballroom where the event was taking place. There were several dining tables set for the luncheon. We had been handed tickets that designated where we would be seated. My team and I were assigned to the same table, which was set for eight people. Four other junior engineers had joined us; all of them were men in their twenties. *The future of this company*, I thought to myself.

A waiter came by and offered our table a bottle of red wine. I raised my glass to signal him to fill it up. As I was about to take my first sip, I saw a woman in a pink blazer from across the room. It matched perfectly with her pink heels. There was a photographer following her around. I nearly dropped my glass. It was Francesca. We had not seen each other since before Thanksgiving. It was as though she could feel my gaze. She turned around and looked right at me. I quickly turned around, as if I had not noticed her.

The waiter brought our appetizer salads. I was thankful for the timely distraction of eating lunch. I was starving, since everything I had eaten for breakfast had been expelled from my stomach at the demonstration. I felt fine, and my stomach was no longer queasy. I figured it would be safe to eat without getting sick again. It only took me one minute to finish my salad.

"Hello, Patrick," came Francesca's voice from behind me. "May I have a quick word?" She had walked over to the table while I'd had my back to her. I let out an inaudible groan.

"Hi," I said, turning red and feeling sweat escape from my armpits. "Sure."

Francesca led me to a courtyard outside of the ballroom. There was a fountain in the middle and several palm trees strategically planted around it.

"We haven't spoken…" she began, but I cut her off.

"I know," I said. "I imagine you are here with the *L.A. Times*?"

"Obviously." She pointed to a badge she had clipped to her blazer that read "Press."

"What do you want to talk about?" I asked.

"Us," she said. "Look, at first I might have been considering getting to know you to get a story. Journalist instincts got the best of me. But I got to know the real Patrick, and I started to fall for you. Craig was drunk that night. He apologized to me profusely about saying what he did about me to you. You know I would not do anything to hurt you. I really do care about you. Craig is my best friend, and he's been through a lot since his divorce. The fact that Flight 619 is still missing, and we have no idea what happened to his daughter Mallory, makes matters even more challenging."

"I've accepted the fact that my friends are dead. Craig should accept the fact that Mallory's fate is the same," I told her rather harshly.

"He wants evidence—even a piece of the airplane would suffice for closure. Any proof it crashed into the Pacific," she said. "But enough about 619. I'm here to talk about our relationship. Where do we stand? We have not communicated in over three weeks."

"It's hard to have trust once it's been broken," I told her. "I've been hurt before. That's why I've been single for so long. I've been lied to and cheated on by girlfriends. I don't want to feel like you are using me for a story and to further your career."

"Don't say that!" she snapped. "You know I know things you've confided in me that I have not told anyone about—not even my editor." My mind raced to my conversation with Royce earlier about my voicemail on Jim's phone. I felt panic again.

"Now is not a good time, Francesca," I told her. "I'm here for work. I have a lot on my plate right now, and I don't think I can move forward with us."

"That's fine," she said, and she pursed her lips. "Good luck with the Forecaster. I hope it's a successful launch for Phoenix. See you around."

She stormed off without a glance back at me. I felt really sad at that moment. I cared for her, and I truly did believe she no longer had any interest in prying for private information for a story. It was my own insecurities that were getting in the way. Besides, my mind was more focused on my own safety, because I did not know whom I could trust right now. Royce learning about the side business Jim, Dylan, and Charles had planned in China was enough to make me sick with worry again.

The rest of the event went by quickly. Royce made a big speech about the successful test launch. The press was buzzing with excitement and punching their laptop keyboards at every word he said. From those keyboards, the news of that day's event continued to spread like wildfire throughout the world. It followed me back to Los Angeles and tried to go to bed with me, as I watched some primetime television shows before calling it a day. Every news outlet kept replaying the video of the 787 parachuting down to safety, and Brick Walters sliding out of the cabin to deafening cheers.

December 16, 2016

I walked into the lobby of Royce's office. The scent of pine trees hit me as I walked in. There was a large Christmas tree with expensive glass ornaments hung so elegantly on it.

The holidays, I thought to myself. *Whatever Royce has to say to me… it won't change my desire to resign.*

I was carrying a binder in one arm. In the pocket of that binder, I had a copy of my letter of resignation. Now that the launch was over and I was to receive a bonus, I was ready to part ways with Phoenix. There were too many unhappy memories post-Flight 619. The energy felt bad, and every day, all I could think of doing was walking out the door to go home at the end of the day without looking back. Now, it was my time to look forward and away from Phoenix. It also did not help that Royce was aware of the existence of Jim, Dylan, and Charles' secret project. It was possible that Royce might have asked me into his office to fire me.

Natasha was nowhere to be found at the receptionist's desk. Royce's office door was ajar, and I could hear sobbing. Curiosity got the best of me, and I walked over to peek into Royce's office. I saw Natasha with her arms over her head and face down on Royce's desk. She was seated in his chair. I knocked.

"Are you all right?" I asked her.

She looked up at me. Her mascara had run down her face. She was a beautiful woman, but at that moment, she was very disheveled.

"I'm here for my meeting with Royce that you set up for us," I said, acting as if her crying was completely normal. I felt so awkward, and that was the first sentence that came to mind.

"Royce…" she sobbed, with tears streaming down her face and onto Royce's oak desk, "…is dead."

16

December 25, 2016

When I was a child, Christmas morning meant waking up before my parents and running to the Christmas tree in our living room. It entailed opening up presents from "Santa," spending the morning having a family breakfast, and sledding outside in the snow. I missed having white Christmases. Thinking about our yard covered in bright white snow and sipping hot chocolate by the fireplace brought back so many memories of warmth and happiness.

Normally, I would fly home to Montana to visit my parents. I had not been back home since I resigned from the university. My parents had become accustomed to seeing me every weekend. I canceled any plans of traveling home due to the major shake-up at Phoenix Airlines. I was seated at my dining table with a cup of piping hot coffee. I had a copy of the *L.A. Times* in front of me that was a few days old. Francesca had written the cover story. And it was a major story indeed.

ROYCE KILLINGTON FOUND DEAD AT 43 IN
BRENTWOOD HOME
By Francesca Fields

In the early morning of December 16, 2016, a housekeeper for the
Killington estate found the lifeless body of Royce Andrew Killington on the

floor of his bedroom. There was no sign of foul play. Autopsy reports are expected back in one week.

Mr. Killington was found the day after the test launch of his Phoenix Airlines safety system, the Forecaster, which representatives of the L.A. Times attended. His death came as a shock to the aviation industry. Killington was single and had no children. He will be cremated in a ceremony next week. Two decades ago, his father, Jackson Killington, committed suicide…

The article went on to talk about Royce's achievements and questions about the fate of Phoenix Airlines and what would happen next. That answer came to us the following week at work. Natasha Wilkins had been a staple of the Killington family for almost thirty years. She was the assistant to Jackson and then Royce. Everyone who worked there knew she was very well informed on all things Killington. She knew the company back to front, and Royce had felt he could trust her. It was in his will that she would become the rightful heir to the Killington estate and would take on the role as CEO of Phoenix Airlines. It was like she won the lottery. She did not even have to marry into the family. I found it strange that Royce had no family. It would have made more sense for his family legacy to continue, but he'd never had children. Natasha seemed very overwhelmed over the course of that week. She kept herself out of the public eye. It was my understanding that she felt uncomfortable with the jealous stares of several Phoenix employees. Some employees went as far as to spread rumors that she'd had intimate relationships with both Jackson and Royce.

Since Royce's death was untimely, I held onto my letter of resignation, because Natasha had not yet fully transitioned into her role. It would happen the first week of January. I pitied her. She was about to run one of the most valuable companies in the world. Overnight, she became one of the most powerful and richest women in the world.

I took a swig of my coffee. It was lukewarm after ignoring it while reading Francesca's article for the thirtieth time. I took a deep breath, and my thoughts fell on Royce's death: *How did he die? Was it natural or unnatural causes?*

January 19, 2017

About a month after Royce's death, the world received closure to its mystery. The autopsy results were finally released to the public. It was strange that they took so long, but I believed they might have wanted to be sure there was no foul play. It appeared as though his death was from a drug overdose. His test results came back and showed there was a mixture of anti-depression medications, alcohol, and cocaine in his system.

We were at the office on that Thursday when Natasha called a staff meeting in the main Phoenix conference room. She stood before the entire corporation to tell us about their findings before it was released to the press. There was silence in the room. Money was not everything. The multi-billionaire must not have had a happy life behind closed doors, and if we thought back about the fate of his father, we knew it was the same for him too. Money does not buy happiness. It only brings problems on top of problems and endless piles of stress. *Poor Royce*, I thought.

There was one thing that was nagging at me about his death. First and foremost, I felt sad about his passing. He was a colleague, and he had given me a career-changing opportunity at Phoenix Airlines. But deep down inside, I felt relief. We were supposed to talk about the fact that he had become aware of my voicemail exchange with Jim. He was aware that there was a secret project being plotted behind his back, and I was the only person connected to it and living. I was relieved that I never had to deal with that difficult circumstance. With his death, his and my secrets were buried. The voicemail he had pulled from my wireless carrier would be forgotten and lost forever. It almost felt too convenient this had happened.

January 31, 2017

The end of the first month of 2017 had arrived. I decided that I would put in my resignation at long-last. I invited Paola, Pravish, and Mark (who was now working full-time at Phoenix while finishing his university courses online through a special agreement with Dean Brandon) to my office. I briefed them on what I was planning to do. They were very saddened to hear that I had chosen to resign from my position, but they understood why. The stress and memories from PA 619 haunted me every day I walked through the halls of those offices. There was not a corner I turned that did not remind me of times when Jim and I would be racing down them to our next meeting.

After speaking to my team, I walked by the conference room where I'd had my last meeting with Jim, Dylan, and Charles, the afternoon before our flight to Beijing. I reached the elevator bank and headed up to the top floor to Royce's office. Only now it belonged to Natasha, and she had a new assistant sitting at the desk where she had once sat. It was a young man. He must have been freshly out of college. He had a suit on and plastic clear-rimmed glasses. The head of security was waiting in the lobby. Once he saw me, he smiled and made his way toward me.

"Hello, Kingsley," I said. I had not seen him since he'd caught me looking for Flight 619 maintenance records.

"Mr. Baldwin," he said happily to me, and he put one of his large hands on my shoulder. "She knows what you are about to do. I guess rumors fly around quickly. She wanted to make sure that I escort you out after you resign, and that I get your badge and any other company-owned items that are on loan to you. Oh, and I had a car service called for you. I know you must have driven to work today, but you'll want to take that ride."

"What do you mean?" I asked in shock. I felt suspicious.

"It'll help you learn about that night—the night in question that prompted you to sneak into those maintenance files the other day, out of curiosity for the truth. I'm on *your* side."

"Mr. Baldwin," Natasha's new assistant called for me. "Miss Wilkins is ready for you."

Kingsley winked at me and whispered carefully into my ear, "You will be reunited with someone from your past."

Kingsley walked into the elevator, and said he would return in five minutes. I was left dumbfounded. Natasha's assistant urged me to hurry into her office, and I obliged in haste.

My conversation with Natasha lasted only ten minutes. She offered me a glass of cucumber spa water as I took a seat. She had heard I was leaving from some of my junior engineers, who had apparently taken note of the recent changes I'd made in my office. I had spent the last week slowly moving items out of my office. She was understanding and very warm. She offered me a very nice benefits package as a favor, which would carry me over for at least eight months of unemployment.

"Royce spoke very highly of you," she said. "We are going to miss you. I wish we could do something to make you stay."

"I appreciate that," I told her as I took a heavy sip of my water. "It's just my time to move on and close this chapter here. I'm sure the Forecaster system will turn out great."

"I hope so," she said. "We had to push back the launch to March due to Royce's death. I've been talking to Robert Wong, and he reported that there have also been some manufacturing issues. We may not be able to launch until summer if these issues are not rectified soon." We spoke for a bit on that subject before I stood up to exit.

"I wish you luck," I told her before I left her office. "Thank you for your time."

Kingsley was waiting for me by the elevator. He took my badge, office keys, work phone, and laptop. He escorted me out of the building after a quick final goodbye to my team. The walk to the main entrance of the building felt like it took a decade. For a fleeting second, I had a bit of remorse for resigning. The thought of having to look for another job seemed intimidating, but with Phoenix Airlines under my belt and the successful demonstration of the Forecaster, I would more than likely have no issues finding a new gig.

"So, why do you want me to take this ride?" I asked Kingsley once we were outside of the building.

"You'll find some answers, but you'll also get more questions," he said matter-of-factly. "We will be crossing paths again, but not for a while. Your driver will take you to a safe location for a quick conversation."

A black sedan was waiting for me outside of the offices. It was the same one that I'd rode in with Royce after the Palm Springs demonstration. It even had the same driver with the Santa Claus-like beard.

"Hello, Patrick," he smiled and winked. "Get in."

The driver was silent for the first few minutes as we drove toward the ocean. He kept eyeing me through the rearview mirror. I started to feel a sense of panic and suspicion.

"Kingsley said we are to have a conversation..." I said, trying to sound calm.

"That is correct," the driver replied. "I just want to make sure we are in a safe location. I would not want us to be, um, overheard."

"Overheard?" I asked suspiciously. "By whom?"

"Never you mind," he continued. "We'll arrive shortly."

Ten minutes later, we found ourselves parked in a secluded area of the beach. It was close to LAX. Airplanes were taking off every two to three minutes right above us.

"Patrick," the driver said. "Now that you are no longer working for Phoenix, it will be harder to seek the answers you want. Kingsley told me you tried to look at some PA 619 maintenance records. You need to be careful. There are powerful people out there who want the truth hidden and buried forever. I, myself, don't even know what happened that night, but I have some information and a few leads to help you. I think we can help each other. I was also friends with Jim, Dylan, and Charles. I want to know what happened to them."

"You knew them? How?" I asked, wondering how a personal driver for Phoenix Airlines and Royce Killington could have any connection to my engineer friends.

"There's not enough time right now for that," he said, rushed. "I have to head back to the offices to pick up Natasha for a meeting in twenty minutes."

"Are you saying you know something about the missing plane?" I asked.

"Yes...and no," he replied. "Something devastating happened. I don't want to sound like I'm making up a conspiracy theory, but I have knowledge that proves something more sinister than engine trouble could have set this plane off course and into the dark abyss of the night. I promise to share more of this later, but time is of the essence. I need you to become friendly with Robert Wong. Reach out to him. Pretend you are interested in working for him, to get closer."

He handed me a blank card with only a phone number handwritten on it.

"My cell phone. I'm Will," he said. "I'm on your side. Kingsley is on your side. Robert is the key to learning more about Phoenix. His communications company might have more information about those final pings from PA 619. I have a feeling he is hiding a lot information from the public."

"How do you know that?" I asked.

"I've crossed paths with him before," Will answered. "You'll find what you are looking for as long as you look for *TOM*…"

"TOM?" I said, more to myself than him. "Is '*TOM*' spelled in all capital letters?"

Will smiled at me with a triumphant twinkle in his eye. He looked at me with great pride before resuming his serious demeanor. He continued, "TOM is the link. TOM is the cause. Colin Shaw and Robert Wong are linked. They shared a car ride while you and Royce rode with me. I know Colin and things about his past. He was buddy-buddy with Robert, and therefore Robert must have information that you—*we* seek. TOM is the key. You're also the key, Patrick."

Will drove me back to the corporate headquarters without another word. I kept asking him questions, but he completely ignored me and then proceeded to take a phone call. He dropped me off without another word, leaving me dumbfounded.

I proceeded to walk to my car, which was parked in the parking garage adjacent to the building. When I got into my car, I remembered that I had told Robert I would email him to plan drinks while he was in town after the Forecaster demonstration launch. I had completely forgotten about that conversation in the wake of Royce's death, but I realized that would be my way in to meeting up with him. The only issue was that he lived in China. I dug for my wallet in my back pocket and pulled out the business card that he'd given me the day before the demonstration event in Palm Springs. I read his business card. It had his name, work number, cell phone, email, and his title. It also had the name of the company: "Zyphone Communications, Inc."

"Oh my God!" I yelled out loud inside my car.

Underneath "Zyphone Communications, Inc." was a sub line of text that read, "A TOM Telecommunications Company."

The link! I thought to myself. *Robert is connected to whomever or whatever this TOM is.*

I felt adrenaline rushing through my veins. If Robert's company owned the satellites that monitored all of Phoenix Airline's flight paths and tele-communications methods, then there was a high probability that he knew something more, and that Will's hunch might have been right. I felt wary about these mysterious Will and Kingsley characters, but perhaps their need for discretion and secrecy was not so strange. If powerful people could be behind the plane's disappearance, then I had to tread carefully. I had to be on my guard; I felt like I was a pawn in a dangerous game.

I pulled out my smartphone and sent an email to Robert, in hopes that the next time he was in Los Angeles, we could have a conversation.

17

March 8, 2017

My body was shaking from head to toe. I looked down and could see several farms and a few trucks trudging along dirt roads. In the distance, I could see snow-capped mountains and tree-filled canyons. The air was cold and the wind's roar was so deafening that I did not even hear my tandem skydiving instructor say, "One…two…three."

With the roar of the wind and the whirl of a backflip, I was falling toward the ground. I looked up and saw the small airplane we had just jumped off fly away in the opposite direction. My cheeks were pressing back up against my face and into my skull. I kept yelling in excitement as the rush of the free fall took over all my senses. After about a minute, there was silence as my tandem instructor pulled our parachute cord and we began to descend to Earth ever so slowly. For the second time in my life, I *heard* that quiet again.

I looked at the clouds above me. I could see a few airplanes in the distance, and below me there were vehicles, which looked like toy cars from my perspective, driving down the roads. None of their sounds could reach my ears. My instructor remained silent. I could hear his heavy breathing, but it did not bother me. I closed my eyes and felt alive. The last time I had gone skydiving was during my undergrad years in college. It was an amazing feeling to be up in the air again, making my way gently down to the ground.

I felt a sensation in my stomach when my instructor maneuvered the parachute slightly to turn us towards the direction of the skydiving school. A few minutes later, we braced for landing. I lifted my legs so that my instructor could gain control of the landing onto the ground. Once his feet hit the ground, he held himself back so that I could put my feet on the ground as well. It was empowering to know that I had survived another jump. My instructor unstrapped me, and I was freed. I knelt on the grass and took a deep breath.

"So, are you considering taking skydiving courses?" my instructor asked. He was a tall burly man with reddish hair and a matching beard.

"I think I might," I said matter-of-factly. "I'm in between jobs, and I have a lot of free time."

The skydiving school had a locker room where I had stored my belongings. I pulled out my backpack and changed out of my skydiving jumpsuit. I grabbed my cell phone out of my backpack pocket and saw that I had an email from Robert Wong. A few weeks back, he'd confirmed that he would be in L.A. around the second week of March. At long last, I would finally be able to meet up with him that evening.

I arrived at the Beverly Hills Hotel, where Robert was staying. I valeted my car and proceeded to the hotel's restaurant lounge.

"I'm meeting a guest of the hotel," I told the hostess. "Robert Wong."

"He is waiting for you," she replied. "Follow me."

Robert Wong was wearing a trendy beige suit and a red tie. He greeted me with a firm handshake and wide toothy smile.

"Mr. Baldwin!" he exclaimed. "It's so great to see you. Phoenix is not the same without that brain of yours."

"Thanks," I said, trying to come off as modest. "How are things at Zyphone?"

"Well," Robert said, "since the tragic and untimely death of Royce Killington, getting the Forecaster planes up in the air has been a challenge. Natasha, Royce's successor, knows a lot about the company, but she does not have leadership experience. It has been, uh, very trying times. However, we plan to finally get our fleet up in the air by May or June. A little later than planned, but it will happen."

"Good," I said.

"Have you lined up a new gig since your resignation from Phoenix?" he asked me.

I took a deep breath and said, "Truth be told, I wanted to take a little bit of a working hiatus to clear my mind. I've also been a bit sick lately. It's nothing serious. I have a cough that does not seem to want to go away. However, I'm enjoying the time to rest and sleep in. It's been nice. The reason I wanted to meet with you—and I apologize for not reaching out right after the Forecaster demonstration in Palm Springs—is to see if you could use an experienced engineer in your ranks. Namely…me. Not right away, but in the near future."

Robert smiled. "I was hoping you would say that. Much of our work is done in Beijing. To take on a full-time and distinguished position at Zyphone, you would have to relocate to China. It would make sense to get you on the team that's building and perfecting the Forecaster systems."

"Well, I am very familiar with the product," I joked. "I was hoping to stay in Los Angeles, though."

"Our warehouses and factories are in Beijing," Robert said seriously. "It's our home base. I would need my team to be based there."

"Well, that's unfortunate," I told him.

"I know your expertise is in aeronautics, but have you thought about working with satellites?" Robert asked.

My interest piqued instantly.

"I would not be opposed to it," I said. "I do not have much experience in working with satellites. Come to think of it, I have a question about your company. Your company began building satellites first, right?"

"Yes, that is correct," Robert answered. "We made satellites that I've donated to the Chinese and American governments. Our satellites are also the ones used to track all of the Phoenix Airlines flights."

I thought about what Robert had just said, and as if he was a mind reader, he told me, "PA 619 was the only time our satellites lost contact. Someone must have turned off the airplane's transponder, which in turn cut out the tracking of its GPS coordinates to our satellite. We've used our satellites to send high quality images of the oceans to authorities and the search parties involved, in hopes that we would find debris. Anything we found, however, did not turn out to be floating debris."

"So, even Zyphone was in the dark the night the plane went missing?" I asked.

"Indeed. They're calling it the biggest mystery in aviation history," he said in a dramatic tone.

"Can you tell me more about your company?" I pressed on, and I pulled out his business card. "I noticed that underneath your company's name, there is a sub line of text that reads, 'A TOM Telecommunications Company.'"

"TOM Telecommunications," Robert said, "is our parent company. I'm actually working to phase out that name."

"TOM is in all caps," I said, trying not to sound too suspicious. "Does it stand for anything in particular?"

"Um…" Robert seemed caught off guard by the question. "Tom was a name we used as a code word back in the 1960s when we were working with the government on satellite communications projects. We referred to our satellites like they were people. We capitalized the name just for personal preference. It does not stand for anything."

Robert smiled after he finished his answer. His eyes danced around the room as if he had to distract himself by people watching. I felt that his answer was a completely fabricated story.

"Are you gentlemen ready to order?" Our waiter had arrived at our table and proceeded to take our drink and food orders.

Robert fidgeted with his necktie and then asked me, "Would you like to come to our on-site North American satellite facilities and get a sense of the work we do? We have a local office in Pasadena. If you find it worth your while, we can talk about potential employment with one of our engineering groups. Personally, I'd rather have you in China working on the Forecaster, but if you want to remain in Los Angeles, I completely understand."

"That sounds amazing," I said. "When can you have me over?"

"How about this Friday? You can shadow one of our engineering leaders," Robert suggested.

"That would be wonderful," I said.

"Your presence will be most welcomed," he said ecstatically.

I might not have figured out who or what TOM was, but I did learn it was associated with Zyphone's satellite development arm. My hope was that I would be able to learn something by getting a tour of their facilities on Friday. The rest of my dinner with Robert was casual, and we spoke more about our personal lives than work.

I walked into the lobby of my condo after dinner and waved at our doorman. I did a double take. To my surprise, I found Francesca sitting in the waiting area of the lobby.

"She's here to see you, Mr. Baldwin," my doorman said.

Francesca locked eyes with me, smiled, and then waved. She got up and walked towards me.

"What brings you here?" I asked curiously.

"Can we talk upstairs?" she asked me.

"Sure," I agreed.

We walked into my condo and I poured her a glass of her favorite red wine. She sat on my couch, took a huge sip, and spoke.

"I've been thinking about a few things regarding PA 619."

I groaned. "Are you fishing for a story?"

"No!" she snapped. "This is personal. Who knows about what the men in blue jumpsuits asked you besides Craig and me?"

"Um," I thought for a moment. "My former intern slash colleague Mark knew a bit about what they asked me on the roof. Why?"

"My LAPD contacts are stumped," she continued. "It's been seven months since that riot. The identities of those two men still remain a mystery. No fingerprints exist for them in the police database. No DNA samples match anything on police record. No IDs, no wallets, and not one single shred of evidence to help link them to identities. They might as well have not existed."

"That's bizarre," I said. "The police are keeping that quiet from the media, but not from you?"

"They know I'm not going to write about it," she said. "Especially because it may help protect you. These men knew something about those three engineers and the secret project they were working on. It's really crazy that just a handful of us know there is something much more shady regarding the disappearance of Flight 619. Craig was even threatened by men in blue jumpsuits to stop prying into Flight 619. Remember?"

"I do," I said.

"Craig wants to work collectively as a team," Francesca said. "He mentioned you all spoke about that."

I nodded, then decided to fill Francesca in on my recent dinner with Robert Wong and how the mysterious Kingsley from security and Will from transportation at Phoenix Airlines had become allies of mine, helping me seek answers. Francesca was overjoyed with these recent developments and insisted they could be the keys to finally figuring out what happened to the airplane.

"When you shadow at Zyphone's satellite facilities, you need to see if you can somehow find out if there are images of the GPS coordinates they traced on the night of July 14. They could be hiding something even though they've said the transponder was off. Whoever this Will guy is, he seems to know things. Maybe he and Kingsley infiltrated Phoenix Airlines to get inside information to help whatever their cause is. We have to be wary of Robert Wong and even that Colin Shaw character. Robert and Colin, from what you told me, seem to be old friends and have long ties with the Killington family. If Will is on to something, then Robert and Colin know something the public does not."

"I have this feeling that whatever we may uncover will be like opening Pandora's box. Once we open it, it can never be closed again. Who knows what we'll find," I said.

Francesca had a strange look in her eye. It was a look of passionate hunger. She did not blink for thirty seconds as she looked into my eyes. I felt my palms sweat. Without a warning, Francesca kissed me. We kissed for several minutes. It was intense. It was as if we were picking up where we had left off. We were bound together by this knowledge that the rest of the world was oblivious to regarding PA 619. She was an amazing woman, and I trusted her. She had no interest in splashing a fancy story in the headlines of the *L.A. Times*. She wanted to help her friend Craig learn the fate of what happened to his daughter, and she wanted to help me find closure as well.

Francesca stayed the night. It was not a dream. I woke up during the middle of the night next to her. I rolled over and stared at her as she breathed peacefully in her slumber. I felt a glimmer of happiness. The four months we'd spent broken up felt like a waste of time. I was relieved to have her in my arms again, and I was even more excited about the prospect of working with her and Craig to uncover the truth about PA 619.

March 10, 2017

I arrived in Pasadena, California at 9:00 AM sharp. The receptionist, a woman by the name of Jenna Lin, greeted me upon checking into the facility.

"Welcome to Zyphone Communications," Jenna said cheerfully. "Would you like some coffee before I take you to Stephanie Anderson, head of the satellite engineering group?"

"I'm good," I told her. "But thank you."

I had a nervous stomach. My anxiety was getting the best of me, and I knew caffeine would make me feel sick. We walked through a few badge-accessible doors, until we arrived at a suite that read "Worldwide Satellite Operations."

Upon entering, I saw a beautiful woman with strawberry blonde hair. Her nametag read "Stephanie Anderson." She was wearing a white laboratory coat and green-rimmed glasses. Her hair was in a ponytail, and underneath her lab coat was a gray blazer and skirt.

"I've heard so much about you," Stephanie said while extending her hand for me to shake. It felt smooth to the touch. "Not only did you manage to miss getting on Flight 619, but you have set the bar high when it comes to aviation safety with our implementation of the Forecaster at Phoenix Airlines. Very impressive credentials, Mr. Baldwin."

"Thank you," I said humbly, feeling my face turn red with embarrassment. "It's a pleasure to meet you. I'm sure Robert has told you about my interest in joining your team?"

"He has," she smiled. "I would like you to shadow me today so you can see if this department would be of interest to you. Robert will join us at the end of the day."

Shadowing Stephanie was very useful for two reasons. The first was that it helped me realize I had zero interest at all in working with satellites. It was mundane and lacked the creativity of designing airplanes. The uses of satellites were very interesting, but it was not something I felt would be my next career path. Pretending to be interested was the most difficult part. I had to suppress a few yawns from my boredom. The other reason was that I felt closer to classified information that could help me find Flight 619.

"Our work with the government is crucial," Stephanie said, while showing me prototypes of satellites the U.S. government used to observe the Middle East during times of warfare after the September 11 attacks. "These satellites control our drones and give us up-to-the-minute images of the territories we are observing."

"By observing, do you mean spying?" I asked, a little more sarcastically than I'd intended to.

She laughed and replied, "Naturally, yes. How do you think we found bin Laden? Satellites played a major role. It was also confirmed that a radical terrorist group from the Middle East was responsible for the surface-to-air missile that shot down PA 425 back in November. I'm sure you know that by now. They wanted to start a war with Turkey. The United Nations is dealing with how to take action with that group. It's quite sad that those innocent lives were lost. One of our satellites helped us find answers by tracking the images of Flight 425's route that fateful day."

"So," I began, "that's very interesting. If the satellites helped solve that attack, then why did they lose track of PA 619? Why aren't there any answers for us from that data?"

"Ah," she said while fidgeting with a computer in the laboratory, "the transponder was turned off. I'm sure you've heard that on the news. It was also night, so satellite images are not going to easily photograph an airplane from above. It was as if the plane was invisible to all eyes and technology that night. It's quite tragic that happened. I'm sorry for your loss, by the way."

"Thank you," I said. "Do you think that the transponder malfunctioned, or was it purposefully shut off?"

Stephanie looked around the room. The other engineers appeared too busy with their work to take notice of us.

"There's an 'off' switch on transponders," Stephanie said. "Someone would have to know how to manually turn it off; subsequently, it would conceal the plane's location. Of course, there is the chance that maybe there was an electrical fire, or it malfunctioned and was giving incorrect readings. That would force the pilots to shut it off. There could have been a few scenarios, but I'm not sure it was a malfunction. We have maintenance records from the day before takeoff, showing that all systems were working properly."

Stephanie typed a few things into the computer and then printed out a document. She pulled it from the printer and handed it to me. It was the maintenance record from the morning before the plane went missing. It was dated July 13, 2016. This is what I had been looking for at the office of Phoenix Airlines when Kingsley confronted me and told me the FBI had taken the hardcopy version of it.

"Nothing unusual, right?" Stephanie asked. "I have clearance to access these records, as I'm part of the satellite team and it was part of the evidence we looked at when monitoring satellite activity from that night. Phoenix Airlines shared it with us here at Zyphone."

"Everything checked off as cleared," I said. "So, what do you think happened—in your professional opinion?"

"You're not really here because you are interested in satellites, are you, Mr. Baldwin?" she asked me bluntly.

"Um," I stuttered for a second and felt myself sweat. I let out two nervous and hoarse coughs that hurt my throat.

"It's okay," she whispered. "Follow me to my office."

We walked down a hallway until we arrived at her office. She let me in and then followed behind me after closing the door.

"Take a seat," she said.

"Look...I..." I began.

"I understand your curiosity," Stephanie said. "I would be doing the same thing if I were meant to be on that flight and lost friends with its disappearance. You want answers. I get it. To be quite honest, I thought you would have more answers, since you worked at Phoenix."

"Nobody does," I said. "We're all in the dark. Royce was too, apparently."

"That's because we actually don't know what happened," Stephanie said. "We've shared most of Zyphone Communications data with the FBI, government officials, the press, and Phoenix Airlines. The search area in the South Pacific is happening because of this data. Much of it is guesswork from calculations based on projections of the airplane's alleged change in trajectory, but it is the best data we have from the most brilliant minds in the world."

"You said you've 'shared most' of the Zyphone data," I pried carefully. "What do you mean by 'most?'"

"Simple," she answered. "All of our satellite data is authorized to be shared when needed for emergencies like this tragedy. We do have one satellite that is controlled by an agency of the government that none of us have clearance for. It's controlled by..."

She trailed off and looked out of her window. She had a look of concern on her face.

"Controlled by whom?" I pressed on.

"I'm not allowed to talk about that," she said. "If you worked here, you could gain access to that information, but since you are not an employee of Zyphone or under TOM Telecommunications umbrella, it would be a violation of my contract to speak about it. I've already said enough."

"If there is a satellite that might have information about that night," I continued, "wouldn't it be in the best interest of this government agency to look into it?"

"They must have," Stephanie said, "and probably found nothing useful, as we are still searching for the plane."

I took a minute of silence to think about something in my head. Robert Wong had been working with the government for years. He was apparently friendly with Colin Shaw as I saw them together at the Palm Springs demonstration. As per the "About the Author" section of Colin's book on Jackson Killington, he was the former head of the Central Intelligence Agency.

"Is that satellite controlled by the CIA?" I asked suddenly, once the remarkable thought had processed in my head.

Stephanie opened her mouth, but did not say a word. The look of surprise on her face told me all I needed to know. I was correct in my assumption. Then my next thoughts brought me fear: *was the government behind the disappearance of PA 619?*

"We should probably continue our tour of the facilities," Stephanie said, in a feeble attempt to change the subject.

"I'm right, aren't I?" I ignored her change in subject.

"Mr. Baldwin—" she added.

"Call me Patrick," I said.

"Fine," she took a breath, "*Patrick*. I have no authority to talk about these private matters. Zyphone is privately owned by Mr. Wong, and these matters are of utmost sensitivity. Can we agree to drop this subject, please?"

"Nod yes or no," I told her. "I'm trying to find out what happened. I will not give you away. This could be an amazing lead."

I was not sure why I told her that much information. I felt that I could trust her, but I panicked. The truth was, I was not exactly sure who I could trust.

I continued, "Something happened on the morning of July 14 at 35,000 miles up in the air just off the coast of Hawaii. I lost three colleagues. There were 241 souls on board who are still unaccounted for after all these months. Not one shred of evidence has surfaced, but I know that there are some individuals out there who must know something. I don't want to get deep into it, but I have reason to believe that the plane's disappearance was not an accident or an act of God. I believe it was intentional."

"I understand," Stephanie whispered. "I can assure you that this government agency cannot and must not be hiding anything."

"The CIA is shrouded in secrecy," I stated. "If they did find out something, like perhaps that it was a terrorist attack, they would have their own reasons to keep it quiet if it meant helping their cause in tracking down those responsible. What is the CIA hiding?"

"I don't know," Stephanie said, and then she clasped her hands to her mouth. She turned red and her shock became anger. "You should go. *Now*! I'll tell Robert you were not feeling well. This conversation never happened. I wish you luck on your, um, endeavors."

Stephanie rushed me out of her office. When I got to my car, I reached for a white card in my wallet that had the handwritten phone number of the driver, Will.

It rang three times before he answered, "Hello?"

"Will, it's Patrick Baldwin."

"I was wondering when I would be hearing from you," Will responded.

"Sorry it took so long," I said. "Two days ago, I met with Robert Wong. TOM Telecommunications is the umbrella company name of Zyphone. Robert wants to phase out that name soon, but for now it remains intact. TOM is spelled in all caps as if it stands for something, but Robert said it does not. I don't believe him, though. There's a satellite system that the company built that is being controlled by the CIA. Robert is friends with Colin Shaw, who was the former head of the CIA. You said they are both linked and that TOM is the key. I think the key is to find out how to get access to that satellite. That is how we'll find our answers."

"You need to be careful about openly speaking of sensitive matters over the phone," Will said in a serious tone. "It's not safe. I'm proud of you, though."

"Are you going to tell me more information about the theory you mentioned back in January when you gave me a ride in your car?" I asked.

"Not over the phone," Will sounded irritated, "but when we meet again."

"When will that be?" I asked.

"I'll come to you when I can," Will said. "We need to be very careful. Anyone could be listening in. Look, I have to go, but I'll be in touch."

"But—" Will ended the call before I could say another word. I began to question if I could even trust him. Why was he shrouded in so much mystery?

18

Will's phone number had been disconnected. I had tried to reach out to him again over the weeks that followed our last conversation. I felt uncomfortable with the fact that he mentioned the next time I would see him, he would just show up. I kept having paranoid thoughts that I was being watched. I could not shake off the foreboding feeling.

PA 425 had found itself in the headlines again. News had splashed the major networks for a few days, revealing the attack from the terrorist militant group that Stephanie Anderson had mentioned to me. Some arrests and seizes had been made of those responsible. A few individuals connected to the attack were still hiding in Istanbul. The story opened the old wounds regarding PA 619 and brought the mystery back into the spotlight, but then there was a mass school shooting that took everyone's attention from the missing airliner to issues regarding gun control in America.

Robert Wong was persistent. He'd kept calling and emailing me since our last meeting, to see where I stood on the possibility of working for Zyphone, since I had rushed out after shadowing Stephanie and was unable to speak to him in person that day. A part of me wanted to take him up on his offer, to gather more information about this mysterious satellite that was controlled by the CIA, but as I had already made things uncomfortable with Stephanie, I felt that it would be too risky. There was always the chance she could tell Robert that I was putting my nose in their business. In the end, I politely declined Robert's offer to place me in one of his satellite operations teams. He seemed disappointed on my last call with him, and mentioned that he would probably see me next at the Forecaster launch party that was to take place Memorial Day weekend. Phoenix Airlines was finally ready to go public with their new fleet, and since I had been an integral part of its development, I would be receiving an invitation to the launch party.

April 2, 2017

I'll never forget this day. It was one of the worst days of my life. I felt like a half-written book after receiving some devastating news. I was at dinner with Francesca that evening at this hole-in-the-wall pizza joint. As I took the first bite of my pizza, I began to have a coughing fit. I was used to them by now. I had this annoying chronic cough that did not want to go away. I excused myself and went to the restroom. I walked into a stall and pulled a few sheets of toilet paper to blow my nose. Then I began to cough again, and I covered my mouth with the paper. I could taste iron in my mouth. It was a familiar taste. When I took the paper off my mouth and examined it, I saw specks of red. It was blood. I stood there, transfixed for a few minutes, staring at the toilet paper. This was not the first time I had coughed up blood; the last time was on the day of the Forecaster test launch in Palm Springs, when I was throwing up inside a portable toilet stall. I started to shake as worry set in. I made the conscious decision then that I would make an appointment to see my physician as soon as possible. This incident was not normal, and I had ignored it for far too long.

"Are you okay?" Francesca asked me when I returned to our table. She gave me a look of concern, probably due to the one on my own face.

"Um," I thought for a moment. "I'm not sure. My chest is hurting a bit."

"We can take our pizza to go if you're not feeling well," she suggested.

I nodded in agreement, "Let's do that."

We arrived at my condo. I could still taste blood in my mouth. My appetite for dinner had disappeared. I felt a small tinge of panic. I did not want Francesca to worry, so I told her that I needed to get some rest. She seemed put off by our date night ending abruptly, but she did not argue. Once she was gone, I waited ten minutes before going down to the garage to get my car. I decided to drive myself to a twenty-four hour emergency room.

The energy in the Beverly Hills clinic felt cold and stale. The fluorescent lights did not help me feel calm either. There were about fifteen people coughing, wheezing, crying, and complaining in the waiting room. I rolled my eyes and took a deep breath.

This is not how I wanted to spend my Sunday night, I thought to myself. I signed in at the reception window and filled out my personal information on a set of forms I was given. Once I filled them out, I took a seat next to a gentleman who had his arm in a sling.

"I recognize you," he said once his eyes met mine.

"You do?" I asked curiously. "Do we know each other?"

"No," he said. "I saw you on TV last summer. You're the guy that was supposed to be on PA 619, right?"

"Oh," I felt myself go red. "Good memory. Yeah, that was me."

"You're a very lucky man," he said softly. "My father was killed in a plane crash. September 11, to be exact."

"Was he on one of the flights that was hijacked?" I asked with piqued interest.

"It was American Airlines Flight 11. It crashed into the North Tower of the World Trade Center that morning," the man said. "It prompted me to go into war. I was in Afghanistan for five years. Lost my leg…" The man pointed to his leg and lifted his jeans slightly. He had a prosthetic leg.

"Thank you for your service to our country," I told him automatically. "May I have the honor of knowing your name?"

"Jack Reed…and remind me yours? I seem to have forgotten it from the news reports."

"Patrick Baldwin. Pleasure to meet you."

"Thank you," Jack replied. "You are lucky indeed. It's strange that in this day and age, what with GPS and all kinds of tracking devices, they have yet to find a single piece of that aircraft. I sympathize for the families. I know what it's like to not have a body to bury. I signed up for the army the following year instead of going straight to college. I'm glad to have lived after my service, but as you can see, I'm a little banged up. Well, this broken arm was from a football accident a few weeks ago with my buddies. I need to have the cast looked at. I might have cracked it."

"I see," I said, taking a look at his cast. "May I ask you how you felt that morning, when you saw the news about Flight 11? Flight 619's disappearance was such a unique and surreal moment for me, and it's not something I've ever really talked about with anyone who could relate."

"I will never forget that day," Jack said. "I lived in Boston. I remember saying goodbye to my father around five in the morning before he left for the airport. I was half awake. He was heading to Los Angeles for a work trip. It was a quick 'see you later' type of goodbye. My mother kissed him farewell, and he drove to the airport. I was eighteen years old. That morning was like any other morning. I had my bowl of Cheerios, and then I took the bus to school. I was in my senior year.

"It happened during first period. I had a welding class, which was located at the vocational building adjacent to the main campus. I was sitting in my class, waiting for my teacher to walk in. When he finally stepped into the classroom, he had a somber look on his face. He told us an airplane had crashed into the World Trade Center. He pulled out a rolling cart that had a TV set on top of it, and turned it on to a news channel that was airing a live feed of the North Tower ablaze, with dark black smoke billowing from where the plane had made impact. Then he told us that the airplane had left from Boston that morning. Almost instantly, the anchorwoman mentioned it was American Airlines Flight 11 and it had been headed for Los Angeles, but it had been hijacked about fifteen minutes into its route and then diverted to New York City.

"My heart just dropped. Suddenly, I felt dizzy. I thought I was going to throw up. I began to shake. My classmates took notice, and I began to cry. I wasn't sure what the flight number of the plane my father was on was, but I knew it was his plane. I began to sob out loud, and the entire class consoled me once they realized why. Some of the girls burst into tears. The principal showed up at my classroom ten minutes later to tell me in person that my mother was in his office. He looked at the state I was in, and then to the TV playing in the classroom. He knew that I had already figured out the horrible truth as to why my mother was at my school."

I looked at Jack for a minute without saying much. I could feel tears forming at the corners of my eyes. Jack's eyes looked bloodshot.

"I'm very sorry for your loss," I told him. "This wasn't public knowledge, but I missed my flight because I overslept and was slightly drunk off a few cocktails. It was a stupid mistake, but it saved my life. I only wish I knew what happened, but I am trying to do something about it. I had three coworkers on that flight. Even my luggage made it on board."

"Thanks for sharing," Jack said. "I'm so glad we dealt with most of the terrorists responsible for this. If it wasn't for a satellite, drones, and the Central Intelligence Agency, I'm not sure how American life would be right now. Would we be sitting ducks, waiting to be attacked again?"

"What kind of satellite?" I asked out of curiosity.

"The CIA called it the 'Peeping Tom,'" Jack said. "The military did not have access to it, but the CIA controlled it and was able to give us coordinates of where we needed to go to find the most wanted targets."

Peeping Tom, I thought to myself. *Tom? Coincidence? Probably not.*

Jack was called into his appointment, and I shook his good hand farewell. I sat in that waiting room with my thoughts. *Did this random stranger just happen to give me a lead? Did I just get intel on the code-name of the potential satellite Stephanie had been telling me about at Zyphone?*

And then it was my turn to see the doctor. I explained to Dr. Mary Goodman, who had come to the room I was placed in, what had happened to me at dinner. I proceeded to explain my chronic cough. She took some blood work, looked at my throat, and asked me a slew of serious questions. She had a concerned look on her face.

"We should take some X-rays," she suggested.

Twenty minutes after my X-rays had been completed, she returned to the room I was waiting in. She brought the photographs of my scans and put them on a screen to enlarge them for viewing.

"Mr. Baldwin," she began, in a very serious and sympathetic tone, "we found an abnormal mass in your lungs. It's a tumor."

I felt like it was a death sentence. Anxiety got the best of me, and my body began to shake as if I was cold. My teeth started to chatter.

"What does that mean?" I asked.

"A pulmonologist will need to confirm the tests, but it looks like your cancer is in its third stage," she said. "I wish you would have seen a doctor sooner. Right now, our best bet is to start off with surgery and then chemotherapy. I would like to get you into surgery within the next couple of weeks. I'll be honest with you, Mr. Baldwin; the chances of survival are very slim at this stage. We can buy you time, but ultimately you could have maybe a year at best if the procedure goes well."

"But I haven't smoked since college," I said in shock.

"You can also develop it through exposure to other elements or family history," she informed me.

It was as if time had stopped and everything stood still for the next few days. I told Francesca I had fallen ill to give myself space to process the news. I could not even muster the energy to tell my parents. I spent nights crying into my pillow. I had not thought I was even capable of producing so many tears. I'd always had thick skin. I found it ironic that I had cheated death by missing PA 619, yet months later, I was lying on my bed, thinking about how it would be a very painful last few months on Earth. Death had found me again.

April 17, 2017

I decided to keep the news that I had lung cancer a secret from everyone I knew and loved. The only exception was Mark Crane. I needed someone to take me to the cancer center for my surgery, as I was going to be put under anesthesia. I had filled Mark in on everything the week before, and he agreed to drive me to the clinic.

"What happens if the surgery is not a success?" Mark asked me on the drive to the clinic.

"I don't know," I answered. "Maybe radiation or chemo. I'm supposed to go through chemo after the procedure anyways. You must promise me that you will never tell a soul about my cancer unless I give you permission."

"I won't. Thanks for trusting me," Mark said with gratitude.

"I see myself in you," I told him. I'd never had a son, but he felt like one to me. "You reminded me of a younger me. You'll do big things for Phoenix. Once this procedure is over, I want us to work on uncovering what really happened to PA 619. I don't want to get you in trouble at work, so I won't ask you to do anything sneaky. I need help getting a hold of this guy named Will, however. He works as a private driver for Phoenix. He used to drive Royce around, and now he's Natasha's personal driver. I had his number, but it's now disconnected. He has been helping me figure out who or what TOM is."

Mark had been briefed on some of my post-employment adventures, which mainly consisted of trying to get answers as to the whereabouts of the missing airplane.

"Will?" he asked. "Do you mean Wilbur? That driver's name is Wilbur Wright."

"No way!" I yelled, so suddenly that Mark hit the brakes of his car on instinct. "Sorry, I didn't mean to startle you. Are you serious? That's his name?"

"Yes, like the actual Wilbur Wright who helped invent the airplane! Kind of ironic that he drives for an airline company," Mark finished.

I was in awe. It was starting to make sense. Wilbur Wright was the alias that my mentor Claude Bernstein was going by. His niece Bernadette had come by my apartment months earlier, and told me he'd gone missing. However, she'd found a copy of his fake passport, and it was under the name Wilbur Wright. What was he on the run from? Why was he in hiding? I had decided to keep Wilbur's true identity to myself until I was able to confirm it was him. I was so excited to learn that Claude was in good form and was helping me find answers.

The bright fluorescent lights on the ceiling were blinding. I had an oxygen mask put over my mouth. I could feel the anesthesia begin to kick in. The surgeons were fidgeting and buzzing about the room, which began to swirl in a pool of color. The lights started to dim, but in actuality, I was dozing off into a deep sleep. The sounds of drills and the heart monitor faded out like the end of a song. I could feel a cold chill settling into my bones. I wanted to move my hands and touch my chest, but I could not move. I was unable to feel my fingers or move my toes. I felt like a statue.

Is this true quiet? I thought. It felt like the same quiet I'd experienced the two times I'd gone skydiving. I could not hear or feel anything. I was blind. There was nothing but darkness. I tried to open my eyes, but they were forced shut. I could no longer hear the beeps from the heart monitor or the doctors fussing over me.

There was a man standing on the side of the road by a vehicle that had been flipped over. He was crying over the body of another man who was lying face down in the snow. I could see blood splattered onto the fresh white snow. Moments later, two police cars and an ambulance arrived. The officers spoke to the man. I was unable to hear what he was saying through his yelps and cries. He was eventually handcuffed and put into the back seat of one of the police cars. Paramedics examined the lifeless man and turned him over. They pronounced him dead.

I saw a pickup truck pull up a few minutes later. A man and a woman walked out of the car. The woman was yelling and demanding to see the body.

"My son!" she screamed bloody murder. "That's Charlie! My Charlie! Oh, Albert..."

The woman hugged the man she was with and cried onto his shoulders. I felt chills run up and down my spine. I was maybe twenty feet away from the couple, whom I recognized as my parents. They were significantly younger. And then it dawned on me. The dead man on the ground was my brother Charlie. The brother I'd never met, who was killed by a drunk driver when I was four years old.

How? I thought. *Have I gone back in time? I thought Charlie's death was a hit and run? Who was the man who was arrested?*

I heard a baby crying from the backseat of my parents' car. It was me. I walked over to the car and saw my four year-old self. It was such a strange feeling. I tapped on the foggy window and waved at my toddler self. He—or rather I—stared right back at me. I smiled.

"Patrick..." I heard a distant voice say. Then, all of a sudden, there were bright lights. I regained consciousness. The doctor was shining a light over my eyelids to help wake me up. A swirl of color appeared, and then the hospital room came into focus. It was apparent that I had not gone back in time. Instead, I'd had a lucid dream about my brother's death. It was surreal, but not accurate as to what had really happened. My family never knew who was responsible for Charlie's death. A witness said they'd seen a car hit him and swerve as if the driver was intoxicated, but they never found out who it was, and it was too dark to make out the make and model of the vehicle.

The procedure had gone as well as could be expected. The surgeons explained that while they had removed most of the tumor, they could not get some of it out. The next step would be to start chemotherapy, but I decided to wait on a decision on when to begin it. I was in no hurry to poison my body with chemicals and lose my hair. The removal of most of the tumor would stall the process of the cancer spreading, but I would still meet the same fate. Cancer would win. It was possible that I would be given a year, but that was not guaranteed. I was stubborn, and decided a few days later that I would start chemo if the tumor began to grow again. That meant that I would have to get a check-up at least once a month. My doctor respected my decision, even though he did not recommend it. We ended up doing radiation therapy a few days after my surgery to ensure that the remaining cancer cells were destroyed. The results were satisfactory, according to my doctor.

I knew that I had bought myself more time. My focus was on utilizing the time I had left to find the answers I was looking for regarding the missing flight. I could care about nothing more. It had become an obsession, and I was not going to let my health get in the way.

The next couple of weeks started off fine. I was not coughing or wheezing as much as I had been before. I was still keeping my health issues to myself. I had not told anyone else about it. Francesca had been a much-needed distraction. We had been going on at least three dates a week. She spent many nights over at my condo. I could feel us becoming more and more serious.

April came and went, and before I knew it, it was almost time for the Forecaster launch party that was to take place on Memorial Day. I officially received my invitation in the mail, on behalf of Phoenix Airlines and Zyphone Communications, for my work on the Phoenix Project.

May 29, 2017

I had a glass of wine while I dressed into my suit for the launch party. I was multitasking by ironing my shirt, eating a frozen mac and cheese dinner, and folding some laundry. Francesca had to work on a deadline that evening, even though it was a holiday. She was my plus one to the launch party.

"The news never takes a vacation," she told me on the phone as I was fixing my tie.

"That's okay, baby," I said to her. "I'll meet you at the party. Do you have the address? It's at Zyphone's corporate offices in Pasadena. Your name should be on the guest list."

"Great," she said. "I'm sorry I'm not there at your place helping you get ready, handsome. I can't wait to see you later tonight!"

"Likewise," I smiled. "I'll see you soon."

I received a text message from a car service that arrived to pick me up. The car service was a courtesy of Phoenix Airlines. I grabbed my keys, wallet, and cell phone and ran down to the lobby. A black sedan was waiting for me outside.

"Hello," I greeted the driver as I got into the car.

He lifted his right hand and waved at me, but never turned to look at me. I looked at my phone and began reading a few emails to pass the time, while the driver maneuvered through the traffic on the drive to Pasadena.

The driver drove me about a mile from my condo and turned into a quiet neighborhood in Beverly Hills. I found this route to be strange. My initial thought was that he knew a faster route to avoid traffic. Then, he parked the car on the side of the street. My heart started to race in panic. What was he doing? He turned to face me, and I saw a familiar white beard. He reached for his beard and pulled it off. Then he took off his sunglasses. The face staring back at me was one that I knew very well. The name was not his original name, but I had come to learn not too long ago that he'd taken the alias of Wilbur Wright and had gone into hiding.

"I've been searching all over for you, Claude! Your phone was disconnected!" I said, staring at the face of my mentor and friend, Claude

Bernstein, who had been reported missing by his family. Claude appeared to have aged a bit since I last saw him, but he was still proudly wearing his Star of David necklace.

"It's time we talk," he said. "I told you I would just show up. Tonight is critical. I have an important task for you to carry out while at the party. I know you were probably excited to enjoy a night of fun, but this is our only chance to find some crucial information regarding PA 619. Now, let me tell you how I play into this mess."

19

"You've been missing since last April," I said in awe, staring into my mentor's eyes as if he was just a dream. "Your niece came to L.A. to tell me in person."

"I went into hiding," he said.

"That was my guess," I said matter-of-factly. "But why?"

Claude took a deep breath and began his story.

"I have had an obsession with the Killington family for as long as I can remember. It was my own personal fascination. I never really told anyone about it. A billionaire tycoon was something to marvel about. My obsession might have been somewhat unhealthy. I'll admit that. I wanted to meet Jackson Killington several years ago, when I was finishing up my PhD. I had this grand idea that if I could befriend him, he would fund an aviation project I was developing. I wrote him a letter giving him my background and credentials, and told him it could be a worthwhile investment, should he be interested in becoming an investor. I don't think he ever saw my letter. I finally met him at a fundraising event that I paid an arm and a leg for just to attend. I watched him have a few glasses of wine before I felt he might be tipsy enough for me to talk business. I struck up a conversation with him and his assistant Natasha. I pitched my idea of a program that would make air travel safer, but I told him I needed funding to help me patent my idea. He agreed to a meeting, which I took a month later. It was the earliest he could squeeze me in. By then, he had forgotten we had met, but it all came back to him when I began talking about my invention. I called it Project Firebird. Fast forward almost two decades later, and his son unveiled a framework called the Phoenix Project. It was the *exact* same invention I had proposed to Jackson nearly twenty years earlier."

"You're kidding me?" I interrupted him.

"I wish I was," he went on. "The Forecaster was my idea. I had sketched drawings of the parachute launching out of the tail end of a 787. Back then it seemed like science fiction, but Jackson was very much into it. For the next two years, he funded me while I began blueprinting my ideas. He was interested in getting into the aviation industry, even though his background was in real estate. I had to sign a NDA with him. I was to keep all of this a secret until we did a joint press release to the public. Obviously that never happened, so by law, I was bound to keep it a secret from many of my colleagues. Even you. He stole my idea and kept it under wraps for a very long time."

"That's unbelievable," I replied in shock. "And I got to see that project through this past fall."

"Fate," Claude said. "At least it was in the hands of someone I trust...*you*."

"So, why didn't you ever have a press release?" I asked.

Claude continued, "Because I was bound to Jackson in a manner more powerful than the legal document I had signed. I was recruited into a top secret society, of which he was a member. It was made up of the most brilliant minds in the world. He saw me as a leader of the future of technological advancements, and knew I would be a perfect fit for his organization. He told me it took him over a year before his fellow members agreed to recruit and initiate me."

At that point, I was dumbstruck. A secret organization? This story was taking a turn down a crazy path.

"It sounds absurd, I know," Claude said in a barely audible whisper, as if he could read my mind, "but I know things that will change the way you see our world. It isn't political leaders that run this country or the world in general. It's the smartest and richest businessmen and women who walk this Earth. The Killingtons are just a part of this secret society's dynasty. In an email you wrote to me, you asked about this article I published. It was an article outing the secret organization. It only lasted ten minutes online before my blog was pulled down. I don't think anyone ever saw it.

I had a hardcopy of it at home, but I returned one day to my house and found it in shambles. They'd burned that copy and left my home office in a state of destruction. It was a warning to me. I had turned down the invitation to join their organization back in the day. Apparently, it's not an option. You can't turn them down. I was the first person in history to do so, because I did not trust their scheming ways of controlling the human population. It's this type of fear that made me go into hiding and to ignore your attempts at communicating with me. I wanted to make sure you were safe first."

"You're freaking me out," I said honestly. "What is this organization, and how did they try to recruit you?"

"I'm sorry I didn't tell you more about TOM in our last in-person conversation, even though I already knew who they were, but I will now. They are called TOM for short. It stands for 'The Omniscient Minds.' They are a group of intelligent men and women from all walks of life. Their members are inventors, entrepreneurs, celebrities, and high-ranking officers in political organizations. Many of their endeavors have shaped the world in the last couple of centuries. Albert Einstein was a member…Steve Jobs, Bill Gates, Amelia Earhart, and the Wright Brothers, to name a few. Omniscient is the all-wise, all-knowing, all-seeing. That's their way of life. They are one giant brainpower, and they led advancements in technology, computing, warfare, and even travel. They remain secret and anonymous to the world, yet many of their names are high profile and famous. Not all, but many of the leaders were and are public figures. They refer to themselves as '*The Presence.*' They are everywhere and nowhere at the same time. They could be your brother, your sister, your teacher, your father, your mother, your neighbor, your lover, or your best friend."

I recalled the dedication page in Colin Shaw's biography of Jackson Killington:

To TOM,
My inspiration, intellect, and reason for being. My adulation for you all,
and the conception of The Presence.

"Was Colin Shaw a member? I read his book about Jackson Killington. His dedication page is what prompted me to do a Google search, which led me to your deleted page," I said quickly. I could feel excitement building inside me.

"Yes," Claude said. "And as former head of the CIA, he had so much power to keep TOM invisible."

"You never told me how you were recruited."

"One night," he said, "they came to my house. All of them wore these blue jumpsuits."

My jaw dropped. *Blue jumpsuits...*

"There were no labels or patches on them," he went on. "There were ten men in my living room, led by Jackson. He told me about their organization and how he had an idea to create a new airline company that would one day implement my invention. He said it would be the only guaranteed way to gain control of the aviation industry, but he wanted to manipulate his son into one day starting the company on his behalf, as a test to recruit him into TOM. I was surprised that Royce was not a part of TOM already. Apparently, he had not proved his worth to them, and simply being an heir to one of the richest men in the world did not count as being qualified.

"As they informed me about TOM and the ways of The Presence, I became terrified. I turned them down, and it was not pretty. They threatened me in many ways. They promised to ruin my credit, mess with my bank account, and more. I feared their threats to destroy the life I had built for myself.

"A week passed and nothing had happened. I stayed quiet and went about business as usual. I knew I could no longer work on Project Firebird, so I decided to go back to teaching. I think the reason that nothing ever happened to me, apart from staying quiet and never talking about TOM to a single soul, was that Jackson killed himself a week after my attempted initiation. I think The Presence had their hands full with that PR nightmare, and needed to deal with the loss of one of their most influential leaders. I think at that point, they got to Royce, without revealing their identity to him, yet. It would not be until several years later that Phoenix Airlines would metaphorically rise from the ashes of Project Firebird. Royce's plan for the Phoenix Project had been in the works from before launching his airline business. After two years of Phoenix's establishment as a public and commercial airline, the Forecaster was introduced. The Killingtons wanted control over the entire aviation industry. The hope was for other airline companies to buy and license the Forecaster system and begin implementing them into their own fleets of planes. It was TOM's goal to control people's way of travel and be the leader of the aviation industry—from behind-the-scenes, of course."

"This is all so much to take in," I said, sounding exhausted. "I'm in utter shock. So Jackson and Royce were members of TOM?"

"Jackson was indeed. He lived the life of The Presence," Claude said. "I'm pretty sure he was the leader of TOM. I don't think Royce was a member yet, nor did he know about it. I think someone had been pulling his strings—using him as a puppet until he played out his father's plan correctly. Then, and only then, did I theorize he would get initiated. I heard him question you on that drive to the hotel banquet on the day of the Forecaster's demonstration back in December. I was your driver then, as you may recall."

"You were indeed," I said in awe. "How very sneaky of you."

"Royce was close to being recruited. Colin Shaw was going to see to that," Claude continued. "I sensed it. I also knew that once he was recruited, he would tell TOM about his suspicions of you working on that secret project with Jim, Charles, and Dylan."

"How do you…" I asked in surprise.

"I'll get to that," Claude cut in. "Everything is connected to Flight 619. But there are many missing pieces, and together we can figure them out. All I know is this—someone in TOM got wind of the S.R.K. Project that your friends were recruiting you to join. I don't know if TOM knew what the project was, but they knew it was something aimed at thwarting them from worldwide domination and power. You must be wondering how I know about this secret project, and the fact that it's called S.R.K. after your colleagues' initials? Well, S.R.K. was my next invention, and I linked up with your colleagues in secret a year ago to begin the process of taking TOM down by beating them at their own game. The plan was to take down the industry they had gained control over."

"The aviation industry?" I asked.

"Yes," Claude replied.

"So, what is this invention?" I asked excitedly. "Obviously, I was never able to learn what it was, as the secret disappeared with them on that flight."

"I will tell you, eventually," Claude said. "As I mentioned to you before, your three colleagues were friends of mine. But you are safer right now being ignorant about it. That's the only reason you are still alive. They knew you did not know what the project was, so when you missed the flight by accident, you were never targeted or silenced."

"Silenced?" I gulped.

"The Omniscient Minds have their shady ways," Claude said. "They will do anything to make sure their secrets stay, well, buried."

"How do I come into play with helping to find more information?" I asked him.

"You've already done a great deal," Claude said. "The information on the CIA satellite was a great lead. I had my friend Kingsley—whom you've met, and is head of security at Phoenix—look into some files. Phoenix does not have access to this satellite per se, but Kingsley found a record of someone accessing it at the corporate offices. That means someone there has clearance to unlock whatever the satellite is observing from space. My theory was that it could have been Royce, but he's dead now, and I'm positive he had not been fully recruited into TOM prior to his death. Kingsley does not know who at Phoenix could be part of the secret society, but whoever that person is, they got wind of what Charles, Dylan, and Jim were up to. Their project was a conflict of interest to Phoenix and The Presence."

I looked at my watch, then back to Claude.

"We should get going, or I'll be late to the launch party," I said. "What is the task you have for me?"

"You need to gain access to the satellite," Claude said. "I know it sounds crazy and impossible, but you need to find a way. Perhaps you can schmooze with Robert Wong? I think he's connected as well."

I kept going over possible scenarios in my head on the drive to Pasadena. Admittedly, it gave me great anxiety. The last thing I wanted to do was something that could get me in trouble. It did not help my fears, knowing that anyone at this party could be part of TOM or undercover security. I could feel my body shivering with anxiety from the complicated task ahead. Claude seemed composed playing the part of a Phoenix Airlines driver, but I was curious to learn more about how he came to meet Jim, Charles, and Dylan. He knew what they had been working on because it was *his* invention, but he was adamant about keeping me in the dark.

I finally arrived at Zyphone's corporate office. There were spotlights, and a red carpet rolled out for the event. I bid farewell to Claude, who then told me he would pick me up by midnight. He gave me a new burner phone number, as he had shut off his previous one. I walked up the steps to the entrance of the building and gave my name to a woman at the check-in table, who then gestured for me to go through security.

Once inside, I found that the atrium of the building had been transformed into a reception. There was a bar, catering, and small high tables for people to stand around and set their drinks or food on. I found Pravish, Paola, and Mark right away. Mark had brought a guest with him, whom I recognized as the dapper blond-haired man he'd been talking to at the banquet reception for the Forecaster test launch in December.

"Hello, old friends," I waved at them.

"Patrick!" Pravish said while giving me a hug.

"Good to see you again," Paola smiled.

"They pulled out all the stops for this party," I said nervously. "It was like going through TSA to get through security here."

"They don't want to risk anything," Mark said. "Even though there haven't been any more PA 619 riots lately, they didn't want what happened at the Phoenix office, back in August, to happen here. Oh, by the way, this is Travis." I shook hands with Mark's party guest.

I spotted Colin Shaw with a beautiful woman who looked ten years younger than him, with wavy strawberry blonde hair and an elegant dress. I presumed she was his wife, since they were holding hands.

"I'm going to get a drink," I said. "Francesca should be here within the hour."

I checked my phone in case I had any missed messages from her, but my notifications were blank. I walked over to the bar and grabbed a glass of red wine. I glanced over to the opposite side of the atrium and saw Natasha and Robert deep in conversation. Mark had come to join me at the bar.

"June 1 marks the beginning of it all. Our 787s will launch with the Forecaster system," Mark said. "Two days to go. The first plane flies out of LAX at 9:00 AM that morning. It's a big deal. At long last, this wave of the future will become reality. The aviation industry will change forever."

"It's remarkable," I said. "Who is that friend you brought as your guest?"

"Travis?" Mark asked.

I nodded. "Yes, I saw you talking to him at the Forecaster demonstration banquet in Palm Springs last fall. He's quite a sharp dresser."

"Yes, I met Travis that day. He works for the agency Phoenix's marketing team uses for advertising." Mark blushed. "He's my—"

We were interrupted by Natasha's voice. She had taken a stand at a podium in the center of the room and began to speak.

"Thank you all for coming," she said. "We are excited to have our colleagues, friends, and families with us as we embark on what will be a historic journey for us all. We are Phoenix Airlines. Born to fly. Now, we've had a difficult year thus far, with the loss of our fearless leader, Royce Killington. I would like to ask everyone to observe a moment of silence."

Everyone bowed their heads for about thirty seconds before Natasha began to speak again.

"We had a little bit of a delay, but our Forecaster system is ready and it will be a game-changer. Here is CEO of Zyphone Communications, Robert Wong, to tell us about the systems his company built for our fleet of aircraft."

There was a round of applause and whistling. I felt a tug at my side and smiled. Francesca had arrived. She looked stunning in a red cocktail dress. I gave her a kiss followed by a tight hug.

"Glad you could make it out of the office," I whispered into her ear.

"Me too, baby," she replied and then kissed me on the cheek.

"Welcome, everyone," Robert Wong began his speech. "We launch in two days! I can't be more thrilled and proud of the years of work and research I have done with the Killington family. This is not common knowledge, but the idea of the Forecaster was the brainchild of the late Jackson Killington. Back then, it seemed impossible that such technology could be created. But here we are—two days away from what once seemed like science fiction, now becoming science non-fiction."

I rolled my eyes and clenched my fists. *It was Claude's invention, not Jackson's*, I thought to myself.

He continued, "From Amelia Earhart to the Wright Brothers, to the planes we used in World War II, to the first man on the moon—man's quest for flight has been a wonder of the twentieth century. Now, the twenty-first century is about taking the trials by error of our past and perfecting them. We want flying to be even safer. We don't want to lose any more human lives in the skies. We don't want another tragedy like 9/11 or PA 619. We want people to travel across the world and explore their interests and broaden their horizons without the worry of expenses or safety. Teaming up with Phoenix Airlines was a no-brainer. It was devastating to lose my friend and colleague Royce Killington, but his successor Natasha has taken the reins of this company, and we will finally get to live out a dream that was once an idea written on paper. We are the first to implement a safety system of this nature. Some people made fun of us. We were spoofed on late night comedy shows. The blogs and press said our idea was straight out of a sci-fi movie. Well…it looks like the joke is on them. We are about to make history, and each and every one of you in this room played a role in making our dreams come to fruition. For that, I'm eternally grateful."

There was thunderous applause and cheers following Robert's speech. During that exchange, I dragged Francesca outside of the atrium and into a hallway to give her an update on how I had come face-to-face with Claude Bernstein. After explaining to her that I would have to find a way to gain access to a top secret CIA satellite, she nodded in agreement, as if my mission was completely normal.

"It has to be done," she said. "Especially if Claude thinks that this satellite might have had access to where PA 619 was the night it went off radar."

"Yeah," I agreed. "I'll need to get some time with Robert, but he's going to be swamped with attendees trying to speak to him right now. I'll let him schmooze and have more booze. Then, I'll find a way to pry into his mind."

"I can't believe this whole thing is about a secret society," Francesca said. "At least now you know what TOM is. If only Claude could have told you more about this *thing* your colleagues were planning to work on in Beijing."

"He said it's best I don't have that information yet," I said. "I guess it's dangerous to know the truth."

"I always thought someone out there, somewhere," Francesca began, "knew something about the airplane. We could be close to finding out its final resting place. The ships that are mapping the bottom of the ocean floor with sonar technology aren't finding much. The biggest discoveries they've made so far have been the sunken remains of nineteenth century ships. No sign of a Boeing 787."

"Right," I said. "Okay, I'm going to poke around. Keep your eye on Robert, and text me if you see him alone for a moment."

"Deal," she said, and then she walked back into the atrium.

I was not sure what I was going to poke around for, but I felt compelled to explore the currently abandoned halls of Zyphone. I could not get far, because most of the hallways were restricted access for employees only; as fate would have it, I ran into Stephanie Anderson, whom I had met when I came to shadow at the Zyphone offices.

"Mr. Baldwin," she said with surprise. "What are you doing outside of the party?"

"Oh," I replied nervously. "I needed some quiet space to make a phone call."

"Why don't you use my office?" she suggested.

"Um, sure," I said.

She swiped her badge on one of the doors leading to a restricted access hallway, and I followed her until we arrived at her office.

"Take a seat," she said.

I obliged and sat in the seat directly in front her desk. She then sat on her chair facing me. She put her hands together and intertwined her fingers while giving me a pensive look.

"But seriously, Mr. Baldwin," she said sternly, "what are you doing away from the party?"

"The call…" I lied again. She did not buy it.

Stephanie got up from her desk and pulled the blinds on her office door down to shield us from view.

"Do you have a girlfriend?" she asked me by surprise.

"I do," I replied. "Why?"

"You're a handsome man," Stephanie said. "You seem like a good man too…a good man who does not want to go looking for trouble."

"What do you mean?" I was nervous at this point and began to cough. I was glad that no blood projected out of my mouth.

"You're prying," Stephanie said. "I told you about that satellite the day you came over to our offices back in March. I did not mean to give you that information, and since I still have my job, it appears that you have not spoken a word about it."

Except to Claude, Francesca, and Mark, I thought to myself.

"I need to warn you," Stephanie said seriously. "If you want to stay out of danger, for yourself or the sake of anyone you care about—even your girlfriend—you should stop prying before someone finds out what you are up to. Trust me, you don't want to go down this path. There's no turning back."

"Is that a threat?" I snapped.

"Not from me," she replied. "I don't know everything that goes on behind closed doors here. That's the truth. Mr. Wong is back and forth from China to our offices here, but he's had many closed-door meetings and gatherings before. I'm not dumb. I know there must be something going on, and I do believe he has been working with the government—or at least the CIA. That satellite helps keep our country safe. Or, at least, that's what I've been told."

"Does *Peeping Tom* mean anything to you?" I blurted out.

Stephanie looked at me with surprise. She stared me down for a few seconds before opening her mouth. "You've looked too far into this. I advise you to stop while it's *safe*. How did you learn about the code-name?"

"An army guy I randomly met at a hospital told me about his days of service," I answered honestly. "Dumb luck. Does someone related to Zyphone know what happened to PA 619?"

"I don't know," Stephanie said. "That's an honest answer. Don't give me that judging look."

"Okay," I said. She sounded truthful. "Do *you* think someone knows?"

"I think," she began, "if someone knew something, they would have reported it to the authorities. I don't see the CIA keeping this under wraps unless it was for the safety of our country or for diplomatic relations."

She made a good point. It was one I had never theorized before. Could the government know something about PA 619 that it had to keep a secret from the world, because it meant keeping the country safe from terrorists or some sort of international threat?

"Robert Wong and Jackson Killington did not come up with the Forecaster," I told her. "They stole the idea from a mentor of mine. Did you know that?"

"I did not," she said. "That's a serious accusation to make."

"You keep silent and faithful to Zyphone because you have to," I said, looking at photos on her desk of presumably her children and husband. "You want to provide for your family, so you keep yourself out of the shady business that is happening under your nose. You get paid very well here and have full benefits. It's a perfect life."

Stephanie looked like she was on the verge of tears. I seemed to have hit a chord.

"Two hundred forty-one people vanished that early morning on July 14," I told her slowly. "Innocent lives. They might be dead. Or maybe they are being held hostage somewhere. I don't know. I do know that I want to know the truth. And I don't care about opening up Pandora's box, because this is bigger than you or I could possibly fathom. I met a man named Craig Cooper. His daughter Mallory was on that flight. She was in college and was going to study abroad in China. He will never see her again. By the looks of that photo on your desk, you have two daughters. As a mother, how would you feel if your daughters had disappeared along with that plane?"

Stephanie began to cry. She pulled a tissue out of a box on her desk and wiped her eyes. After composing herself, she spoke up.

"Robert used to have an assistant. I heard him yelling at him one night when I was working late. His assistant had apparently gained access to some sensitive material, from the bits and pieces of shouting I heard. 'You will regret this' was one of the things I heard from Robert's office. His assistant came out crying after the screaming match and almost ran into me in the hall outside of Robert's office. He looked horrified when we locked eyes. He said that he'd learned something about Robert, and he was terrified about it. He whispered to me something along the lines of, 'He's in a secret organization.'"

"That's true," I told her. This confirmed that Robert Wong really was connected. He was part of TOM. The confirmation was useful knowledge. "I learned about this organization earlier today. Never mind how I know, but know that it is a scary thing to have been made aware of."

"Oh dear," Stephanie said nervously. "This is why I don't want you to pry. The next day, Robert's assistant jumped to his death from his apartment balcony. His name was Edgar. He was a brilliant young man. Robert did not seem fazed by his death, nor did he acknowledge it, publicly or to our staff. I always felt there might have been foul play, because the poor boy looked scared for his life when I last saw him. You should have seen the look in his eyes. I don't think he would have killed himself. I don't want you to get mixed up in whatever he's hiding. If he's working on something top secret with the CIA or some government agency, then just let them be."

"I need to find information about this satellite," I demanded. "I won't get you involved. Just tell me how I can access it."

Stephanie closed her eyes and appeared to be deep in thought. She opened her desk drawer and pulled out a badge.

"I'm going to give you this temporary badge," she said. "It's not programmed to any person in particular. Anyone who uses it can remain anonymous when going through restricted areas. My badge is assigned to my name, so that anywhere I go in the building, I am tracked. This can't be traced to anyone. I took this badge from Robert's office one day when he was not looking. He had several stashed away in a drawer. I once heard him mention it to a colleague in passing. Apparently, he always misplaced his own badge. I have been saving it for a rainy day. If you want to bring on the storm, then you can have it. Just leave me out of this."

I felt my phone vibrate in my pocket. I pulled it out and saw a text from Francesca, "He's alone. He looks tipsy."

I wrote back, "Distract him. I think I can get access to what I'm looking for."

She responded, "Be careful. I'll flirt with him. I'm not sure he knows I'm your girlfriend. Besides, I've done this before."

I smiled and texted back, "You have some real journalistic integrity."

I took the badge from Stephanie and examined it cautiously.

"Don't worry," she assured me, "this is not a trick."

"What about security cameras?" I asked. "This place is probably full of them."

"There are many," she replied, "but I have access to shut them down from my desktop computer. I'll handle that. You need to take a left outside my office and walk down the hall. Make a right, and at the end of the hall, you will see a blue door. That's it. Use the badge I gave you. When you get inside, you'll find a round room with a computer in the middle. The password is Tom's Presence."

"Of course it is," I mumbled to myself.

"What?" Stephanie asked.

"Nothing," I shrugged. "Anything else I need to worry about? Will there be people in there?"

"No," she said. "Security is preoccupied with the party, and all the employees of Zyphone are mingling with the employees of Phoenix out there. It's now or never."

"What made you decide to change your mind?" I asked her seriously.

"It's the right thing to do. I'm going to resign tomorrow," Stephanie answered. "I can't work for a corporation I do not trust."

"Here's my business card." I handed her a card with my number. "Let's get in touch later. I can fill you in on what I learn."

I left Stephanie at her office and followed her directions down the hall. I arrived at the final stretch to the room I needed to gain access to. The blue door was standing between potential answers and me. I reached for the badge and swiped it on the keypad to the right of the door. A red light on the keypad turned green, followed by a chime that signified I had unlocked the door. As I walked in, a hand reached for my shoulder and startled me so suddenly that I dropped the badge.

"Francesca!" I sighed with relief. I reached for her face and kissed it. "You scared the hell out of me. Aren't you supposed to be distracting Robert Wong?"

"He became preoccupied with Natasha and Colin Shaw," she said. "They were having some kind of serious discussion. I assigned Mark to tail him, though, so he'll be keeping an eye on him and will send me text updates. I thought it would be more fun to help you. I love this kind of stuff—sneaking around for answers."

"I would have preferred you stay out of this," I told her seriously. "It's dangerous. And how did you get past the first secured doors into this hall?"

"I followed someone through," she said nonchalantly. "I like to live on the edge. They didn't see me sneak behind them."

"Fine," I said, and then I walked into the room with her behind me.

The circular room behind the blue door was brightly lit with fluorescent lights. Francesca and I had to squint to adjust to the harsh lighting, which was a dramatic difference from the hall we had just been in. The walls were concrete and bare. I looked at my phone and realized I had no service. The walls were blocking my access to cell reception. I moved on to more pressing matters. As described by Stephanie, we found a computer module in the center of the room. It was the only thing inside the small room, which was about fifteen feet in circumference.

"Now what?" Francesca asked.

"I have a password," I told her. "The woman I shadowed a few months ago gave it to me."

"Just like that?" Francesca asked with curiosity. "The journalist in me finds that suspicious."

"She knows Zyphone is shady," I explained to her. "She had a change of heart and decided she wanted to help me. I trust her."

Francesca shrugged as I pressed enter, and the computer monitor woke up from sleep mode. There was a bar on the screen, and the text "Enter Password" above it. I typed in "Tom's Presence," and instantly we had access to the database. There was an image of a satellite as the wallpaper of the desktop. I presumed it was an actual NASA image of the satellite code-named Peeping Tom.

My palms were sweating on the mouse as I scrolled through files, trying to find anything that might provide any insight to PA 619. I kept checking my phone for the time.

"Hey," I said suddenly, making Francesca jump. "I found a database of maintenance records. This has nothing to do with the satellite, but this computer is linked to Phoenix's network, so it can probably access all kinds of material! Let me type in PA 619's flight number in the query search. You can look up flight records by flight numbers."

I input "PA 619," and the final record on file was dated July 13, 2016. There was nothing unusual about the record. It was the same as the one Stephanie had once showed me. The airplane was in working order. There was a signature of the person who authorized the maintenance service. The name read "Joseph Conroy." Below his name, it stated that his title was "in-charge flight attendant."

"This Joseph guy was on PA 619 that night," Francesca said. "I remember the name from the flight manifest. So sad."

Francesca pulled up her phone to show me a document she had on file. It was a story she had written about Joseph. There was a photo attached to her story. Francesca held up her phone to my face. The man was blond with green eyes. He looked familiar.

"I feel like I've seen this man before," I said.

"Maybe at the airport on that fateful day?" Francesca suggested.

"I was late to my flight, remember?" I said matter-of-factly. "He would have already been on board."

"Right…of course," Francesca replied.

I continued looking through the files and typing in queries in the desktop search finder. No words like "TOM" or "Peeping Tom" or "The Presence" were turning up any results. I found people by the name of Tom who were employees of Zyphone, and a few references to TOM Communications, Inc. There was nothing that stood out. I began to desperately search file folders for anything labeled with the word "satellite," but nothing interesting showed up. I felt frustrated.

"Nothing," I said. "I can't find anything. Stephanie did not give me clear directions on what to search for. She gave me the password, but no further instructions."

"Well," Francesca said, "maybe we should just throw in the towel. I'm getting nervous. What if we get caught?"

"Shh!" I whispered urgently.

I could hear the sound of heels clicking down the hall on the other side of the door. I pressed my ear on the door and heard the sound of footsteps approaching the room we were in.

"Hide!" I whispered urgently to Francesca.

"Where?" Francesca said, looking around. "There's nowhere to hide in here."

She was right. There was a beeping sound on the other side of the door. Moments later, it swung open. Stephanie was standing there.

"Did you find what you were looking for?" she asked. Considering I was supposed to be alone, Stephanie did not seem surprised by Francesca's presence.

"No," I said with relief when I realized it was her. "Can you help us? You did not give me further instructions on how to find the satellite information."

"Let me access—we need to hurry," she said in a rush.

Stephanie approached the computer and put a storage drive in the USB port of the computer. She clicked a few files and typed a few things on the keyboard.

"Okay, I'm pulling up Z-1550. That's the code-name of the satellite. I forgot to mention that," she said apologetically. "All right…yes…come on…come on. Great! I downloaded all the files on the satellite. It was launched about five years ago, so you should have its lifetime."

"Thanks for this," I told her. "What kind of files are they?"

"Spreadsheets, presentations, and word documents," Stephanie answered. "Only Robert and the CIA have access to this information. Admittedly, I've never looked into them, even though I was able to procure the password from Robert's desk once. Hide that USB drive and be very careful. I don't know what you'll find, but I imagine there are some dark secrets in that drive. It's all in the palm of your hand."

I looked at the drive and examined it before putting it in my pant pocket for safekeeping. Francesca kept eyeing her watch nervously. She tapped me on the shoulder.

"We should get back to the party," she suggested. "I don't want anyone to realize we've been missing for about half an hour."

Stephanie closed the door to the room, and we began to walk back down the hall. When we were by her office, she stopped dead in her tracks. She had a look of horror on her face.

"I forgot to sign out of the computer!" she whispered. "Let me go shut it down or someone will know there was a breach!"

Stephanie ran down the hall as quickly and quietly as she could in her heels. I felt my phone vibrate in my pocket. Mark had sent a chain message text to both Francesca and me. "I lost Robert. Not sure where he went."

"Let's wait inside Stephanie's office," I suggested to Francesca. "Mark lost visual of Robert."

I heard two male voices coming down the hall. I opened Stephanie's office door and grabbed Francesca's hand. She followed me into the office, and then I shut the door softly.

"It's Robert," Francesca whispered, and we both ducked behind Stephanie's desk.

For a split second, Robert walked by the office door, and I was able to make out his frame through the window on it. Colin Shaw was walking alongside him. My heart dropped. *What were they up to?* I thought.

"Do you think they are headed to that satellite room?" Francesca asked nervously. "Stephanie…"

Robert and Colin's voices drifted off. I heard another set of footsteps.

I saw another person pass by Stephanie's office door. It was Mark. I quickly got out from behind Stephanie's desk and ran out into the hall. I whispered urgently for Mark to turn around. When he did, I signaled for him to come back. He walked briskly over to me, and joined us inside the office.

"I was tailing Robert and Colin," Mark said. "I found them a few minutes after I texted you."

"We should get back to the party," Francesca said. "It's opposite the direction of that room. They won't see us if we leave now."

"But what about Stephanie?" I said. "She could be caught."

"Right," Francesca said. "There was nowhere to hide over there. She's been found. There's no doubt about that. We need to get out of here. Let's hope she doesn't give us away."

I opened the door slowly, with just enough space to fit my head through. I looked left and right. The hall was abandoned. I waved for Mark and Francesca to follow me, and we walked briskly back in the direction of the atrium where the party was taking place. The closer we got to the party, the louder it became, as hundreds of buzzing voices greeted us.

"I don't feel right about leaving Stephanie behind," I told Francesca as we walked into the atrium. "Should I go check on her?"

"You don't want to call attention to yourself," she said sternly. "Besides, she works here, so it's less suspicious for her. Let's just play it cool and pretend to be enjoying ourselves."

Fifteen minutes later, Robert Wong reappeared at the party. Colin Shaw had not returned with him. Robert grabbed a glass of champagne and walked over to Natasha and some other board members of Phoenix Airlines. He whispered something into Natasha's ear. She had a worried look in her eyes, but then nodded to him as if she understood whatever he had just communicated to her. She continued her conversation with the board members as normal.

Pravish, Paola, and Travis had joined Francesca, Mark, and me at a small table. They brought over a few slices of cake from the dessert bar.

"I'm going to run to the restroom," I said suddenly.

Francesca gave me a concerned look. I put my hand on her shoulder and massaged it gently.

"I just need to use the restroom," I lied.

I could feel Francesca's gaze on the back of my neck as I walked back out to the hall which we had come from earlier. The restrooms were located in that area. Once I was out of Francesca's field of vision, I began walking briskly back to Stephanie's office. The badge-access door to the hallway of her office was propped open by a roll of toilet paper. I assumed it was Colin's doing, since he was not a Zyphone employee. As I neared her office, I heard muffled and angry voices. My heart began to race.

"The security camera system was down." I heard the familiar voice of Colin Shaw. "Did you do that?"

"No," I heard Stephanie cry from inside her office. "I don't...I don't know what happened."

"Why were you in that room?" Colin demanded angrily. "You know that Zyphone has a partnership with the CIA. That computer contains highly sensitive material."

"I was looking for a notebook I might have left behind earlier," Stephanie said quickly. "And with all due respect, Mr. Shaw, aren't you retired from the CIA?"

I peeked through a crack in the blinds of Stephanie's office window. I could see Colin's face. He looked red with anger, and there was some sweat on his forehead. He must have been nervous as well. Stephanie was deathly pale, with fear in her eyes. I could see her trembling slightly.

"That is true. I am retired," Colin said with disgust. "My successor, Randolph Smith, and I are still very close. He will not be happy to learn that an employee was poking around in that room. How and why were you looking for a notebook in there? You don't have clearance. How did you get badge access?"

It was the nail in the coffin. Stephanie was struggling for an excuse, but I could tell she had hit a brick wall. Sweat began to pour out of her temples. She looked like she was about to cry. I began to tremble with anxiety myself. *This is it*, I thought. *She's going to give me away.*

In the distance, I heard a pair of heels clinking on the concrete floor down the hallway. I made a dash for the nearest door. It turned out to be a janitorial closet. Thankfully, it was unlocked. It smelled like wet garbage, but I held my breath and squeezed inside between a few mops and a shelf of cleaning supplies. I left the door slightly ajar so that I could peer through. The heels I'd heard down the hallway belonged to Natasha Wilkins. She appeared at Stephanie's office door. She knocked twice, then let herself in and closed it shut behind her. I wanted to walk out of the closet and peer through the window again, but my nerves got the best of me. I did not want to risk getting caught. What was Natasha up to? She and Colin were having a heated argument at the Palm Springs launch event back in December. And then earlier, Robert had whispered something into her ear. She was Jackson Killington's right-hand woman, and now a successor to Royce Killington's coveted CEO position. She had been with the family for years. There was no doubt in my mind that Natasha was a member of TOM. She had to be.

I heard a yelp from Stephanie's office that sounded like her. It sounded as if she was hurt suddenly and was taken by surprise. I heard a thud of something hitting a piece of furniture. It might have been a desk. My heart began to race again. I started to cough nervously. It was my cancer taunting me. I began to open the door slowly, then stopped dead in my tracks. Robert Wong was returning to Stephanie's office. He was walking so fast that he had not noticed the closet door was ajar.

Robert entered Stephanie's office. I heard some hushed muffled voices, but I could not make out what they were saying. I felt my phone vibrate suddenly. It was a text from Francesca, asking why I was taking so long in the restroom. She then sent another follow-up text, urging me not to pry into the situation at hand, because she had seen Robert head back down the hallway I was in.

I wrote back to her, "I'm fine. I'm caught in a dilemma, but I'm hidden." She was not happy with that response, and sent three more messages pleading for me to return to the party.

Natasha walked out of Stephanie's office and looked in both directions down the hallway. Then she darted straight for the closet I was in. She was reaching for the handle. I felt dizzy with fear and anxiety. She was about to find me hiding inside.

"Not in there," Robert yelled to her, peering out of Stephanie's office. "The garbage bin is near the freight elevators two corridors down."

"Got it," Natasha said.

I sighed with relief as she headed down the hall putting space between her and me. *That was too close,* I thought. I had never peed my own pants in my adult life, but there was no doubt I had been very close to doing so at that moment. My body was trembling.

Natasha returned with a giant trash bin reserved for janitorial use. She pushed it into the office. I heard a bit of shuffling and heavy heaving from both Colin and Robert. The worst thoughts crossed my mind. Did they hurt her? I remembered something Claude had told me on the ride earlier:

"They knew you did not know about what the project was, so when you missed the flight by accident, you were never targeted or silenced."

"The Omniscient Minds have their shady ways. They would do anything to make sure their secrets stay, well, buried."

Buried. I feared that Stephanie might have been *silenced.* That was just a euphemism for killed. I did not want to believe it. The truth was not technically confirmed, but I stared in stunned silence as Colin and Robert wheeled out the garbage bin and headed down the hall opposite of where the party was taking place. Natasha nodded to them and headed back to the party.

Is she in there? I thought. *She must be.*

Once all three of them were out of sight, I ran out of the closet and headed to her office. It looked like there was a sign of a struggle. There were papers from her desk all over the floor. There was no sign of blood or anything that would suggest she had been killed. I tricked myself into believing she might have been knocked out. Even if that was true, something sinister and dark had just happened because Stephanie was caught in a room she had no business being in. The dark truth sank even further into the pit of my stomach…it was my fault.

Francesca ran up to me and hugged me tightly when I returned to the party.

"What happened?" she asked when she saw my startled face. "You look pale."

"I think…" I could not admit it out loud.

"What?" Francesca urged.

"Silenced." I could only utter one word. I wanted to pass out. I could feel vomit from my stomach rising up my esophagus. I could taste some of the cancer medication I had taken earlier that morning. I forced myself to take a deep breath. The last thing I wanted was for a room full of people to see me throw up all over the atrium floor.

"Did they kill her?" Francesca whispered.

"I don't...not sure...they rolled her out of the office in a trash bin. But...I...don't know," I struggled to say a complete sentence.

Francesca had a look of surprise in her eyes, and then it turned into a forced wide-eyed excitement, complimented by a fake smile. I turned around and saw Natasha approaching me. Francesca put on an act in her presence.

"Patrick!" Natasha said excitedly, as if nothing had happened in the last half hour in Stephanie's office. "It's so good to see you. Thank you for coming. You've been an integral part in the development of the Forecaster. We are so appreciative, and you are missed."

"Hello, Natasha," I said. She looked composed, and her clothing was pristine and ironed. The polish of her well-manicured nails seemed intact. It was apparent she had not done any of the *heavy lifting* in Stephanie's office. "It's been a few months, hasn't it?"

I tried to speak nonchalantly, but in my mind, the image of her pushing the garbage bin while wearing her designer heels made me want to throw up again.

"I haven't seen you since you gave me your letter of resignation—Hi, I'm Natasha," she said, reaching for Francesca's hand. "Have we met?"

"Not officially." Francesca shook her hand. "I work for the *L.A. Times*. I did a write up of the launch event in Palm Springs. I'm Patrick's girlfriend."

"Oh, how wonderful," she said happily. "That was amazing press. We are so thankful."

"How has your role as the new head of Phoenix been?" I asked, trying to make casual conversation.

"How did you land that role?" Francesca cut in. I gave her a side eye with a what-are-you-thinking-asking-that kind of look.

"I have some big shoes to fill," Natasha said with a small frown, but she was not taken aback. "I've worked for the Killingtons for years. I graduated with a degree in political science from Yale, and ended up in Dallas, Texas after chasing my fiancé down there for a job. We called off the wedding because we were not ready for marriage, but it turned out we just weren't in love. I needed to find a job, so I applied to be Jackson Killington's executive assistant, and I never left that position. He treated me well. Royce brought me on as his assistant when he started Phoenix and, well, I ran the show from behind-the-scenes. Long hours paid off, I guess. I was part of the family. Jackson saw me as a daughter and Royce considered me a sister."

"I see," Francesca said, trying to hold back another rude question.

"Well, I have to say my goodbyes before heading out. So wonderful to see you, Patrick—and to meet you, Francesca. If you want to come back to Phoenix, the door is always open."

"Thank you," I said automatically, and she left us. I turned to Francesca. "What were you thinking?"

I heard a familiar voice call my name before Francesca could answer. It was Jim King's wife, Melissa.

"I was hoping I would see you here," Melissa said. "Hello…"

"Hi," Francesca said to Melissa when she acknowledged her. "I'm Patrick's girlfriend."

"Oh!" she said happily. "I had no idea you were seeing someone, Pat."

I blushed slightly and put my arm around Francesca. "Yes, I am indeed. I had no idea you were going to be here."

"Me either," Melissa said. "They invited me a few weeks ago. I think it was out of respect, since Jim was an employee of Phoenix and he was a part of the early development stages of the Forecaster."

Melissa's eyes became watery. I could see the pain and hurt on her face.

"I think about him every day," she continued. "I miss him. I want answers. I can't consider him dead because they never even found a single piece of the airplane. I sometimes hope they are alive somewhere. Maybe if the plane was hijacked, they are being held hostage somewhere."

"I know how you feel," I told her truthfully.

"I met Natasha Wilkins," Melissa said. "I told her how much Jim loved working for Phoenix. I even let her know about his laboratory in our basement. I said, 'He loved to bring his work home,' and she seemed very impressed by that."

I glanced quickly at Francesca. She had the same look of concern I did. If she'd told Natasha about Jim's laboratory, then there was no doubt she might inform Colin or Robert. The basement was where Jim was working on the S.R.K. Project. This project was a threat to TOM. I thought back to the rooftop, where those men in jumpsuits had threatened me and asked if I knew about the project. I'd still had no idea what it was, except for the fact that it was a conflict of interest to these people. If Natasha was part of that secret society, then her getting wind of this laboratory was not a good thing.

"We need to catch up," I told Melissa while checking my cell phone for the time. "It's getting late. We'll need to go. My driver should be arriving soon. Will you call me if you ever need anything?"

"Of course, dear," Melissa said.

Francesca and I walked outside of the building and found a line of black cars waiting to pick up their clients.

"I'm worried," I told Francesca. "They now know about Jim's lab. Maybe we missed something."

"Do you think Jim's wife is in danger?" Francesca asked nervously.

"I'm not sure," I said. "But something just happened to Stephanie. I wouldn't put it past them. There's Claude."

I spotted the black car Claude was driving. We approached the car, but stopped dead in our tracks when we saw Natasha tap on the window. Instinctively, I reached for my pant pocket to check that the USB drive was still in there. It was.

"Hi, Mr. Wright," she said. "I didn't know you were picking me up."

Natasha got into the car and they drove off. Claude gave me a shrug and an "I'm sorry" look. He was caught off guard by her assumption that he was her driver for the night.

"I guess we'll have to call a taxi," I said to Francesca.

May 30, 2017

The next morning was a busy day for the local news. Francesca was summoned to the bureau early that morning for a breaking story. She left my condo around 6:00 AM. She called me on her drive to work to explain what the news was. Melissa King's home had burned down around 4:00 AM. She had been inside asleep at the time. Her body had been found in the ruins. Firefighters said that the fire had started in the basement, and the cause was most likely electrical.

"That's not true," I cried with anger in my tone as she told me about Melissa's death. "They did it. The Omniscient Minds. Or whoever the hell they are. This is horrific."

"Natasha knew about the basement. She found out last night," Francesca said. "And they took out Melissa and burned that laboratory down to bury Jim's work forever."

"We were just talking to her last night," I sobbed. "We need to stop these people. The sad thing is, the basement was full of props from a Hollywood shop."

"Even if we believed the props were just for show," Francesca said, "there might have been something hiding there."

"Right," I said. "Hiding in plain sight...maybe."

"That's not all," Francesca blurted. "They found Stephanie dead. It was from a car accident not too far from the Zyphone offices. The police say she ran into a pole. They will be checking her blood in the autopsy, as they assume it was a drunk driving accident. I think both you and I know the truth. They killed her last night. Robert, Colin, and Natasha were accomplices in her murder. That accident was staged—somehow."

I was so upset. Poor Melissa had lost her life. She would never know what had happened to her husband. Stephanie Anderson had been found dead. How many more people would be silenced for the sole purpose of hiding a secret? And were we being targeted? So far, we had been able to learn about TOM under the radar, but the more we kept uncovering secrets, the more I couldn't shake off the feeling that we could be caught.

When I hung up the phone with Francesca, I dialed the new number that Claude had given me. It rang three times before he picked up.

"I was going to call you soon," Claude answered. "She—Natasha, that is—asked me to drop her off at Jim's house last night. I drove away, but parked near enough to keep an eye. I saw her approach two men in jumpsuits. There's no doubt she is a part of TOM. They burned down Jim and Melissa's home."

I told Claude everything that had happened at the party, and how we believed Stephanie had been killed there. I told him how Robert, Colin, and Natasha had been a part of it, thus confirming further that Natasha was part of the society. It was obvious at this point. He was happy to know that I had been able to procure a USB drive with all the files from the satellite's computer system at Zyphone. He urged me not to open any files on my computer until I met with him in person, in case there was spyware attached to them.

"The worst part is," Claude went on sadly, "the basement is gone. That's where we built it."

"Built what?" I asked.

"The invention," he said slowly. "Let's meet in person. It's time to tell you about the S.R.K. Project. It's, without a doubt, the real reason why PA 619 never landed in Beijing."

21

June 19, 2017

It was a few weeks before I was finally able to meet with Claude face-to-face. He had to reschedule our meeting many times out of paranoia he was being watched or followed. It was beyond frustrating, because I was left in suspense, waiting for answers regarding the S.R.K. Project; time was of the essence, because every day, I was battling cancer. At long last, I met with Claude at a motel in Van Nuys, a suburb of Los Angeles. When I got to his motel room, Claude looked around outside after letting me in, as if he'd expected me to be followed. He closed the door and locked it.

"I'm sorry for the delay," Claude apologized. "I wanted to make sure I could throw off anyone in case we were being tailed, watched, or our phones were being tapped."

"Don't you think that sounds a little paranoid?" I asked.

"Melissa and that Stephanie woman died on the same night," Claude said. "It's our fault Stephanie was killed—killed and made to look like it was an accident—so that we could get our hands on sensitive files on a USB drive. You did bring it, right?"

"Here it is." I handed him the drive. "As promised, I have not opened it."

"Good," Claude said. "There's a chance that the files could have tracking malware. I have a laptop with a special program that blocks any kind of malware, spyware, or viruses. We can access the files on it."

"Stephanie downloaded the entire hard drive on that USB," I said. "It holds about four gigabytes of data. When I was combing through them briefly on the Zyphone computer, I could not find anything."

"You need to know what you are looking for," Claude said. "I might be able to find something, but depending on how many files there are to sift through, it could take some time. I may even need to hack some of the files; I presume some will be encrypted."

"Claude," I took a deep breath and felt excitement coursing through my veins. "Can you tell me about the S.R.K. Project now? I know you said it's dangerous for me to know about it, but I truly think we are off TOM's radar. Besides, you've gone missing, so they don't even know you're in town."

"Yes, it's time you learn," Claude agreed. "After all, you would have been part of the team. Maybe they would have changed the name to S.R.K.B.—B for Baldwin."

"What about B for Bernstein?" I added. "Wasn't this your invention? You admitted to working with Jim, Dylan, and Charles."

"Yes," Claude said. "This is what you need to know..."

I sat on an armchair in the room while Claude took a seat on the corner of his bed. He rubbed his cheeks and eyes as if trying to wake up, and sighed while looking up at the ceiling, deep in thought.

"Let me begin," he said, "with how I connected with your colleagues. I told you a few weeks ago that I had been recruited to join The Omniscient Minds. I denied them, but was able to remain alive and well because I kept my mouth shut. Jackson Killington stole my idea for the Forecaster. It was launched a few weeks ago, after several months of successful testing, but they took the idea I'd proposed decades ago. It has now come to fruition. One day, one of the Phoenix planes may malfunction and crash. The Forecaster will save their lives, and I will never get credit. I should have been the next big inventor. I would have been worth millions...maybe even billions, one day. But that will never happen. I was destroyed. I went back to teaching. I met you and mentored you. I saw a bit of myself in you. Your hire at Phoenix was no accident. I had a headhunter seek you out and recruit you. Jim, Dylan, and Charles were going to groom you to become part of my new invention, which would overtake the aviation industry I had once hoped to make better. I guess, technically, I did make it better, but I will never receive credit for the Forecaster.

"My next idea was something out of science fiction. It sounded crazy, but I began to work with Jim, Dylan, and Charles after meeting them at an industry conference. After learning of their credentials and lead roles at Phoenix, I decided I had to meet them. The opportunity came when I went to the convention they were all attending. We struck up conversation at a mixer and became acquainted. Over the next few months, I gave them information about TOM and how they were going to propose a new safety invention that they had stolen from me. They were skeptical and reluctant at first, but during a private meeting we had one day, Jim stood up and urged Dylan and Charles to join me. For some reason, Jim took a leap of faith in me and believed my tale about this ominous secret society. Dylan and Charles trusted Jim, and eventually they began to buy into the idea of my new invention that would change the way humans traveled forever. And for the year leading up to the disappearance of Flight 619, they began to work out of Jim's basement. I urged them to use discretion when working on our project—especially since they worked for a company connected to some of the members of TOM. I had to work with them from afar, because anyone connected to me would be in danger if members of TOM got wind of what I was up to. Then, they were ready to begin work with a facility in China that would host our new workshop."

"And what was the invention?" I asked with anticipation, as if I had been waiting a millennium to find out. The truth was that I had been waiting for almost a year, but I felt it was worth the wait to finally learn about this revolutionary invention for commercial travel.

Claude got up from his bed and pulled an art easel from the closet. There was a blank poster board on it. He reached for a black marker that was on the desk and began drawing an abstract map of the United States.

"I'm not the best artist," he said, "but this is our country. Here is L.A."

He drew a dot over where L.A. was located on his abstract map, and then drew another on the opposite side on the East Coast.

"And this is New York City," he added. "Now, let's connect these two dots with a line. Typically, via airplane, this trip takes about five to five and a half hours one-way. What if we could change that to two to three hours?"

"That would be amazing," I said. "Is there a way to make an airplane fly faster? Physically, it would not be safe."

"Oh," Claude said with a sly smile. "We are moving out of the aviation industry for this. Remember, they were shaking in their boots when someone, somehow, got wind of the S.R.K. Project."

"So, how do you get from point A to point B in the time you mentioned earlier?" I asked.

"The S.R.K. Project," he began, "is a code-name for a mode of transportation we have dubbed the HyperTube. Let me draw this out."

Claude began to sketch a cylinder-shaped tube. He made a note over it that read "Hard glass transparent body." Then he drew these shapes inside that looked like the letter L.

"These are seats," Claude explained. "These glass canisters or tubes are what people can sit in. We were designing them to fit about one hundred people per tube. Each tube is inside a larger tube that is also transparent. These tubes or pipes are the tracks of the HyperTube. Think of the canisters tellers use at a drive-thru bank. You put your money in the canister and then send it through the teller machine, and it moves up a pipe through air pressure. It then ends up inside the bank for the tellers to complete your transactions. The tube is pushed and pulled by a vacuum and air pressure. This is the same concept we are using for the HyperTube. It will allow the tubes to launch across the country at high speeds, but all passengers inside will have a very safe and comfortable ride. It will also be much cheaper than airfares. We planned to sell tickets at least fifty percent cheaper than Phoenix's domestic flights. Each tube will have compartments below the cabin seating where passengers can store their luggage. The HyperTube is a reality. We have the technology to bring it to life, but it will take decades to create and to build out the tracks. We are also posed with the challenge of making tracks over the oceans, as we would want to expand to international travel."

I sat in stunned silence. It was such a simple concept, and the idea made so much sense. This was the project I was supposed to be recruited to secretly work on. Nearly a year had passed since I had that meeting with Jim, Dylan, and Charles after Royce assigned us to travel to China. Now I knew what they had been planning. It was a huge question that had finally been answered.

"Wow," was the first word I could say after Claude's explanation. "It really is something out of science fiction, isn't it?"

"But it can be reality," Claude said excitedly. "The tubes have no mechanical engines, and the only need for power is for air conditioning, lighting, and communication on board. But they are pushed through a vacuum at speeds unimaginable right now. No fuel needed!"

"When I poked around Jim's basement lab last fall," I said, "I found a bunch of fake mechanical pieces and machines that were props from a local Hollywood shop. I was—"

"Wondering what the point of the props were?" Claude cut in. "To throw off anyone who went down there without our authorization. The pieces were random. That way we could hide our project in plain sight."

"That's what I thought," I said. "I remember seeing a clear tube in the basement when I was last there. Was that a piece of the track?"

"It was," Claude said. "We created a prototype track and built it out of the strongest plastic and glass materials available. The passenger tube had not been built yet. We were going to build it in China, and the company we planned to work with also gave us acres of land to build test tracks on. That's where we left off. Once PA 619 went missing, so did some important notes and files that Jim, Dylan, and Charles flew with. They were also my entire team. I could no longer work on the HyperTube. I knew that the plane must have been intentionally diverted from its original course so that it could be buried at sea along with the minds behind one of the most important inventions of the twenty-first century—that may now never see the light of day."

Claude sat back down on the bed and buried his face into his hands. I thought he was going to cry, but instead he rubbed his face in frustration again and stared back up at the ceiling for a few seconds. He came back to reality and turned to face me.

"I would not talk about the HyperTube in writing, over the phone, email, or in any other way that can be traced," Claude said. "It's dangerous that you know about this project."

"Can I tell Francesca and perhaps Mark?" I asked. "Or Francesca's friend Craig—his daughter was on PA 619."

"That's up to you," Claude said. "I think it will give some closure, but if you do tell them, they must follow the rules to keep it tight-lipped. Look what happened to Jim, Dylan, and Charles—and the rest of the souls on board that flight. They're gone. Perhaps…forever. I must also note that I've been in hiding for over a year to ensure they wouldn't silence me. I had to uproot my life and take an alias. It was pretty risky to pose as a Phoenix personal driver to Royce and Natasha for the last several months, but it gave me the opportunity to keep a close eye."

"Thanks for telling me all this, Claude," I offered him. "I'm glad you're alive and well. I'm sorry you have to be in hiding, but we need to expose TOM, so *they* can't hide anymore. It's the only way to take control of what they took from you and me. They took our three friends and buried them at sea. That much I'm sure of. I want to find out what happened to the plane. We need to find it. If we find the black boxes, maybe they will expose TOM. Whatever happened up there in the skies that night will not be a secret forever. And if you find something in those files, please let me know as soon as possible."

"I will," Claude said. "Like I said earlier, it may take some time, but I need to be thorough."

I wanted to tell Claude that I did not have much time. Granted, I might have had a year or so left on this Earth, but my time was ticking to the slow marching beat of my heart and lung cancer.

"Oh, and happy birthday," Claude said. "I always had your birthday marked on my calendar."

"Thank you," I said with a forced smile. "I'm forty-three years young."

That evening, Francesca and I spent a quiet night alone in my apartment. I ordered dinner from a mobile app food delivery service that delivered premade meals. All we had to do was warm them up in the oven. I served us glasses of red wine, and we celebrated my birthday in the privacy of my condo. I told Francesca about the HyperTube and my meeting with Claude. I urged her to keep it to herself. I could see an internal conflict etched on her face. She admitted it was the story of a lifetime, but due to the sensitivity of the information, she agreed to keep her lips sealed. However, she did not keep them sealed when it came to locking them with mine.

After we finished eating and I put our dishes in the dishwasher, we snuggled together on the couch, where we kissed passionately. It was the most intense and intimate moment I had ever had with her. It was at that moment I knew I was in love with her. I felt my heart beating with excitement. My palms were sweating into hers as she clenched my hands tightly. Her lips pressed against my teeth, and I gently grazed her bottom lip playfully with them. She looked into my eyes, and I looked into her green eyes deeply. It was electrifying. I could hear quiet again, just like when I was skydiving. It was only her and me in this world. Time had stopped everywhere, and we were shielded from the outside world in the confines of the four walls of my home. Nothing else existed in that moment. Our hearts were beating in unison. Our bodies and minds were synchronized.

"I love you," I whispered to her for the first time.

Her cheeks flushed red, and a large grin spread across her face. Her eyes lit up with happiness. I could feel the warmth of our love embrace us both.

"I love you too, birthday boy," she whispered hotly into my ears.

I was in love. I knew it for a fact. In dating culture, it is a big step in any serious relationship to admit it to your partner. I knew I meant it, and I could tell she genuinely loved me too. It was a gift money could not buy. There was a small catch, though. I felt guilt. I'd known I had cancer for about two months. I was secretly battling it. I would hide my medications at the bottom of my underwear drawer so that she would never find them lingering in my bathroom medicine cabinet. I did not want to tell her. Giving her my death sentence would also be the ax to our newfound love. Was I a bad person for not telling her this major detail? How long could I keep up the charade of living a seemingly healthy life? Eventually the cancer would win, and my health would deteriorate. My body would weaken, and I would be unable to hide it.

June 27, 2017

I went to see my doctor about having a round of chemotherapy at the cancer center closest to my neighborhood. I was in the waiting room for thirty minutes before my doctor called me into his office. He told me that the procedure would be difficult on my body. He advised that it would make me weak, and my hair would start to fall out.

"I don't want to look like a dying patient for the last few months of my life," I pleaded with the doctor. "Can I opt out of chemo?"

"It's your choice," he told me. "But I don't recommend it. You could have other complications and your lifespan will be shortened."

"I would rather be able to taste food during my final months," I argued. "The constant taste and smell of medications lingers on my taste buds too long. I want to let nature take its course. I have decided."

"If that's your decision," he replied, "then so be it. We will have to get you to sign some forms stating it was your choice. I still want you on your medications, however."

"I can do that," I agreed.

I walked out of the cancer center with a somewhat unshackled feeling. It was as if I had taken control over my own fate and life. I loved control, so I felt that choosing to be off chemo for the last year or months of my life was liberating. Then there was my relationship. I was scrolling through my phone's camera roll, looking at photos of Francesca and me. There was no way I could break her heart with this news. I knew she would stick by me until the very end, but I wanted her to be happy. I did not want her to waste a few months or years waiting for me to take my final breath. Death was my next flight, and for that departure, I would fly alone. It was my final boarding call, and there was no way I would be missing that flight. I'd cheated death last year by minutes. It had found its way back to me, and it was singing a sad, slow song for the final moments I had to spend on Earth. The destination of this final boarding: unknown. What happens after we die? I was never religious. My family had tried to force religion on me as a kid, but it never stuck with me. My parents meant the world to me. I always imagined I would be the one to bury them, but life had a funny way of playing itself out. It seemed as though they would be burying me, much like they had my older brother Charlie. In a few months, my cancer would spread, and I would become worse. I decided that when that moment came, I would spend my final days in my cabin in Montana near my parents. They would learn the truth then, but not before. This secret was my cross to bear.

July 2, 2017

I woke up on Sunday morning to incessant knocking on my door. I ripped off the eye mask I was wearing to block out the natural light from my windows.

"What the hell," I groaned.

I grabbed a robe from my closet so as not to answer the door in boxers. I greeted my untimely guest with a look of annoyance. It was Craig Cooper.

"What are you doing here?" I asked rudely.

"The news!" he exclaimed. "Can I come in? You need to turn on the news. They found a piece of PA 619! It's not confirmed yet, but it's possible that it might belong to the missing plane."

"What?" I was wide-awake now.

"In a few days, it will be the one-year anniversary since it went missing," Craig said excitedly.

I was confused by Craig's excitement. If a piece of the airplane had been found, it meant that it had been torn off the airplane. It would most likely mean that it had crashed.

"There could be clues to help us find the airplane," he continued speaking with excitement.

"You don't still think there's a chance that your daughter is alive, do you?" I asked bluntly. "A piece of the plane could mean exactly what experts have been saying. It crashed somewhere."

"I know," Craig said, sounding defeated. "I just want hope. This could mean closure, at the very least."

"Where was the piece found?"

"Off the coast of the Philippines," he answered. "It washed up onshore."

"If it washed up onshore," I said seriously, "then that means the plane did, in fact, crash in the ocean. Maybe this mystery is about to be solved?"

But aren't Claude and I under the impression that TOM is behind the airplane's disappearance? I thought to myself as I searched for my remote, which I found under one of my couch pillows. *Is it possible that we have been wrongfully accusing them of taking down the plane? No, what am I thinking? They could have crashed it into the ocean themselves.*

There was no doubt in my mind that TOM was up to shady business, but my belief in this matter was about to hit a brick wall from the news report airing on my television.

22

I could not believe my ears. I had my television tuned to CNN. The news report stated that a possible piece of Flight 619 had been found. After almost a year of searching, the answers seemed closer than ever before. The very first debris of Flight 619 was in the hands of Philippine law enforcement.

"We are a few days shy from the one-year anniversary of when Phoenix Airlines Flight 619 disappeared off radar on its journey from Los Angeles to Beijing. The last contact with the plane was over Hawaii. It was then that the plane diverted off its path to China, and was believed to have veered south in the direction of New Zealand, off the South Pacific Ocean. After a year of searching the seas, a remarkable discovery was made off the coast of the Philippines near a small city called Mati. Locals reported that a piece of metal washed up on the shore of the beach. While the suggested scientific research showed the flight diversion of 619 crashing far southeast of New Zealand, it is possible that currents pushed the debris all the way to the shore of the Philippines. The piece of metal in question is, in fact, from a Boeing 787 aircraft. Authorities from Australia and the U.S. will be doing tests on the piece of debris. We can confirm that it is a flaperon, which is part of an airplane wing that combines the functions of the flaps and ailerons. The flaperon was found with barnacles underneath it, which might have formed from nearly a year of floating through the ocean. The wear of the debris is consistent with the amount of time that has passed since 619 went missing and allegedly crashed. If confirmed by authorities that this is an actual piece of PA 619, we could be closer to finally solving one of the biggest mysteries in the history of aviation. This comes two weeks before the one-year anniversary of the disappearance, and a few months before the underwater mapping of the search area in the South Pacific Ocean comes to an end. By October, ships using advanced sonar technology will have mapped the entire area where scientists mathematically calculated the airplane might have crashed. If nothing is found by then, the search will end, and the plane may be lost forever. Over eighty million dollars have been spent on the search for PA 619. If the rest of the airplane isn't found soon, the countries involved with the search party will have exhausted all their resources. The only other hope would be for a private investor to fund a continuing search. We reached out to Natasha Wilkins at Phoenix Airlines on whether they would continue funding the search, but she was not available for comment."

"This changes everything," I said more to myself than to Craig.

I felt my phone vibrate. It was Francesca. I answered her call, "Hey, babe."

"Did you hear the news? They found a piece of 619!" she said excitedly. "I'm on my way to the office now to work on a story for tomorrow's paper and for today's digital edition. Do you think it belongs to the plane?"

I looked at the TV report. The report was showing a group of Philippine authorities carrying the piece of the airplane out of the water. I had worked on several Boeing 787s during my time at Phoenix. The piece of the plane that was found was white, much like the wing color of the Phoenix models—the main body of the Phoenix planes were silver, but the wings were white with red tips. It definitely belonged to a 787, but it would need to be analyzed to prove it belonged to 619. I communicated this to both Francesca and Craig.

"Let's chat later this evening," Francesca told me before we ended the call. "My editor is on the other line. Love you."

Craig took a seat on my couch. He was glued to the TV. I could see silent tears streaming from his eyes. I sympathized with him. He'd had a rough year, from losing his daughter, to a divorce with his wife, to his drunken harassment of Royce Killington last winter, which had landed him in jail for a short while. I was looking at a man who was holding on to any hope for answers. Our first encounter had been at LAX, after I'd missed the final boarding call for my flight, which his daughter had been on. Back then, I'd had no idea that fate would bring us together again.

"I want to help you," I said to Craig. "I should fill you in on a few things, as Francesca might not have told you some developments we have had in the last few weeks regarding PA 619."

We talked for nearly two hours. I told Craig all about my mentor and former professor, Claude Bernstein, and how he'd played a role in helping me uncover a few answers. Craig's eyes opened wide and his jaw dropped during my story. He was up to speed on everything regarding TOM, the deaths of Stephanie Anderson and Melissa King, and the invention of the HyperTube that my colleagues had been trying to recruit me to become a part of.

"After hearing everything you had to say," Craig said, "you believe that the plane was taken from the skies?"

"Well, it takes a person to turn off the transponder," I said. "It did not malfunction. It was intentionally shut off. I feel like everything we've uncovered so far is pointing in that direction. We are just waiting for Claude to find a file in a USB drive I gave him that has all of the CIA's satellite information on it. It's taking longer than expected because some files may be encrypted. He has to hack into them, I believe."

"But what about this piece of the flaperon?" Craig pressed on. "How would it have drifted off to the Philippines? I'm starting to believe it probably did crash, that somehow the plane went rogue by mechanical error and went off course by accident. It might have flown until it ran out of fuel while on autopilot. I read a theory online."

"That's what scientists have been speculating for months," I said. "They need to prove the piece belongs to PA 619 first. Until then, let's just see what happens."

"Fair enough," Craig replied. "Are you coming to the PA 619 memorial on July 14? Families of those on board are getting together at the beach near the airport for a memorial ceremony at sunset. You should come."

"I wasn't aware, but I'll come pay my respects," I said to him.

July 14, 2017

It was hard to believe that an entire year had passed since I'd missed my flight on board Flight 619. There was an empty stretch of beach adjacent to the Los Angeles International Airport. Since the runway was so close to that part of the beach, there were no businesses or houses in that area. There was a small oil plant a few yards away that left the area smelling like old garbage. Francesca and I found parking a ten-minute walk from the location of the memorial in a neighborhood. When we arrived, we found several news vans parked in the vicinity. Francesca wanted to pay her respects without having to work, so she had another reporter from the *Times* cover the event. There were several family members of the passengers and crew at the memorial. Each person was holding a candle. A giant Phoenix Airlines logo was built out of sand on the beach and painted red to match the company's logo color. There was a pair of praying hands over the logo and the words "Remember PA 619" written in the sand over the logo and hands.

The sun was beginning to set over the ocean's horizon. The candles, all of which were lit by a single flame, gave off a warm orange glow that clashed brilliantly with the fiery orange sky from sunset. Craig and his ex-wife joined us. They brought us each a candle. Craig used his to light each of our candles.

"Patrick," Craig said after he lit my candlewick, "this is my ex-wife, Chelsea."

"Hello," I shook her hand. She had reddish brown hair and green eyes. I had seen photos of their daughter Mallory. She had resembled her mother more than Craig.

"I'm sorry for your loss," Chelsea said, fighting back tears.

"I'm sorry for yours as well," I said somberly.

"You are a very lucky man," she said. "You cheated death."

I felt anything but lucky. I was the only one there who knew death was still coming for me. I nodded and smiled awkwardly. I was not sure how to respond to such a statement.

"There's still no word on that flaperon, is there?" Craig asked Francesca.

"Not yet," she reported. "The results should be in any day now. A research team in Australia is doing the testing on behalf of Phoenix Airlines."

"Speaking of Phoenix…" I said with slight disgust when I noticed both Natasha Wilkins and Robert Wong getting out of a black sedan. They were both dressed in black.

"They are making appearances," Francesca spat. "All for publicity and their public personas. Like they give a damn about the victims."

Chelsea looked confused by Francesca's statement. I decided to draw everyone's attention away by pointing out that the mayor of Los Angeles had arrived with his wife. The press was snapping photos of them upon their arrival.

"This is quite a spectacle," I whispered sarcastically to Francesca.

The memorial was a very quiet affair. Most of the time there was silence, interrupted only by the occasional cry or blowing of someone's nose. The mayor walked up to a podium that was propped in front of the sand-made Phoenix logo and addressed the crowd right around sundown.

"Hello, my name is Mayor Grayson Hutchison," he spoke into a microphone. "Thank you all for coming. Today, we offer our prayers and remember the 241 passengers and crew on board PA 619. One year ago on this day, the airplane went missing. Not a day goes by that we don't think about that tragic morning. There are hundreds of men and women in the South Pacific Ocean, as we speak, combing the ocean for the airplane's final resting place. Two weeks ago, a piece of the wing washed up onto the shore of a city in the Philippines. The piece is being analyzed to confirm it belonged to PA 619. Boeing has confirmed that it was a part from one of their airplanes. Since there is only one Boeing 787 that is unaccounted for, we are almost certain that this piece is, in fact, from the missing airliner. Phoenix will be holding a press conference to present the results of the findings, as analysts are currently looking over the piece carefully. We hope to give closure to all of you who had loved ones on board. I know it has not been an easy year. Phoenix launched the Forecaster on their fleet earlier last month. This is a huge step in the right direction; this will prevent us from ever losing an airplane again. I want to announce here today that we will be erecting a statue on this spot. It will be a memorial for PA 619. It will be a gift from the City of Los Angeles, and will pay respect to all those lost on board. The statue will be a model of PA 619, and all 241 names of those lost will be engraved onto its side."

There was soft clapping after this statement. I caught a few of the family members whispering, looking, and pointing at me. They had recognized me as the man who missed the flight. I shifted uncomfortably and held onto Francesca's hand. I saw Natasha and Robert sneaking out of the crowd quietly, followed by a man in a gray suit. He must have joined them at the memorial, because I had not seen him arrive with them. He had a fedora on and was still wearing his sunglasses, even though the sun was setting. They quickly disappeared into their black sedan and drove off. I rolled my eyes in disgust.

By 8:30 PM, the event ended. Many of the candles that were lit for the vigil had gone out. The only sources of light were the moon, stars, and a few streetlights that were spaced out on the road that ran parallel to the beach. Francesca, Craig, Chelsea, and I were walking in the direction of our cars when I heard my name being called out.

"Mr. Baldwin!"

A man's voice rang out from behind me. He had an Australian accent. A short and portly bald man with a black beard came up to me. His face looked weathered and sunburned.

"Yes?" I replied.

"Hi—how ya goin'?" He took a deep breath and continued in a thick twangy drawl. "My name is Ted Holt. I'm a retired Air Chief Marshal of the Australian Defense Force. I'm running the search for PA 619. I came to L.A. to pay my respects and meet with the head of Phoenix about the possibility of getting funding to extend our search if we come up dry by October. That's when our search is scheduled to conclude. I recognized you from last year's news reports. You're one lucky man, mate."

"Hello," I said, and shook his hand. "Nice to meet you."

"It's been a crazy journey," Ted continued. "We had some rough weather lately and had to slow down the search. We should be picking back up in a few days. If you ever find yourself in Sydney, look me up. I would be happy to show you around the city. Or if you want to come on board one of our searches, you might find it cathartic."

All of a sudden, my interest was piqued. Ideas began to flutter through my mind.

"Do you have a business card?" I asked him.

"Absolutely, mate," he replied, and he pulled one of his cards out of his wallet.

"I might take you up on your offer for an expedition," I said. "I really want to get closure and would be interested in getting a behind-the-scenes look at how the search is going."

"Brilliant," he said with a smile. "You're welcome any time. Shoot me an email some time when you figure out when you want to come down under."

"Most definitely," I said.

Francesca and I drove back to my condo. I held her hand and kissed it during our commute. She looked so beautiful that evening in her simple black dress.

"What was that all about with that Australian guy?" she asked. "You want to go on an expedition?"

"Here's my thought," I said. "I want to run this by Claude, but I have an idea. Once we get a location of where the plane might have flown off to—that is, if that USB drive contains any vital information about what happened that night one year ago—we may need to go to Australia and take a ship out from there. Maybe we'll find out where the plane sank in the ocean."

"Claude has had that USB for almost a month now," Francesca said. "Don't you think he would have found something by now? Are you hoping that the CIA tracked Flight 619 with the Peeping Tom satellite?"

"Maybe," I said. "They had eyes in the sky. That's the only satellite that no one else has access to. We know that Robert can access it, and he's a member of TOM. We know that Colin Shaw is a member of TOM, and he still has ties with the agency. There must be some kind of clue that will help pinpoint a location for us. Maybe some lines of latitude and longitude?"

"Wishful thinking," Francesca said. "He's been combing through those files long enough to have found something. He has yet to report any conclusive findings."

"Regardless," I added, "at least we have an option."

"You don't really think we could just go out to sea on an adventure, do you?" Francesca looked at me with concern. "It doesn't seem realistic."

As I raced against time with cancer, anything was possible. I wanted to make it my final life's work to find this airplane. I had been documenting everything I uncovered and learned in a journal, in case I could not complete my journey. I felt it was my destiny to find Flight 619 once and for all.

23

July 17, 2017

It was Monday evening. I had invited Francesca, Craig, Mark, and Claude to my condo to view the live press conference being held by Phoenix Airlines at 8:00 PM. The results of the analysis of the flaperon were going to be announced. The conference was taking place at the Phoenix corporate offices. Mark opted to not attend it in person so that he could come to my viewing party.

Claude was the last one to arrive. I opened the door and found him wearing the Wilbur beard as a disguise. He was still in hiding, so I was unfazed by it. He pulled off the fake beard and took a seat in my living room around the TV. I had pizza delivered for us. Everyone was happily eating their first slices as we waited with bated breath until the clock struck 8:00 PM at long last. The live news feed switched over to a shot of Natasha walking up to a Phoenix Airlines podium, which was handsomely adorned with a metallic red Phoenix logo in front of it.

"Good evening," Natasha began. "We welcome the Phoenix family, members of city council, Mayor Hutchison, and the press to our offices today. A few days ago, we had a memorial for the one-year anniversary of PA 619's disappearance. A few weeks ago, a flaperon—which is part of an airplane's wing—washed up onshore in the Philippines. The discovery was exciting, because it aligned with the theory that the airplane made a sharp turn and diverted south of the Pacific Ocean from its path to Beijing.

Analysts, using data from satellite pings that morning, found that the plane might have flown for about seven more hours from when we lost contact with it. We have not been able to determine what might have happened up in the skies, whether it was intentionally diverted, malfunctioned, or the consequence of human error. No piece of the airplane had been found. We've had the seas searched for debris, but all seemed lost. Australian scientists have analyzed the piece. Boeing confirmed it was one of their parts and it did, in fact, belong to a 787, which was the same model of airplane as PA 619. Since PA 619 was the only plane unaccounted for, it was highly probable that the flaperon belonged to the missing airplane. Results have come in, and the code numbers that were engraved onto the part confirm, without a doubt, that this is a piece of PA 619. The numbers had some wear, but after careful scrutiny, they were able to decipher them. This confirms that the airplane did, without a doubt, end up in the South Pacific Ocean, as previously theorized by top data analysts and scientists using data from a company called Zyphone, which we at Phoenix Airlines partner with for satellite communications."

There was a loud murmur and buzz from the audience. A few photographers were aggressively taking pictures of Natasha. Several audience members raised their hands for questions. I turned over and looked at Claude.

"So maybe it did crash into the ocean," I said.

"Maybe," Claude replied. "But it could have still been intentionally overtaken. Someone wanted S.R.K hidden and buried forever. We've hypothesized that much. There are easier ways than taking over an airplane to silence someone, but TOM took the hard way. Our three colleagues had data and plans on their computers and in their luggage. TOM would have wanted that destroyed and unrecoverable. I don't doubt it."

Francesca spoke up. "Call this my instinctive journalistic approach, but the facts are before us. They found a piece of the airplane. The first and only piece ever found after an entire year. It washed up in an area that aligns with the data the satellites show the airplane could have ended up in."

"That satellite data is from Zyphone," Claude interrupted her. "We both know who runs that ship. Robert Wong. This could all be for show. I always theorized that perhaps the data was falsified to lead the search party in the wrong direction, so that the culprits could properly hide and dispose of 619. It's all corrupted."

"Are you insinuating that this piece of the plane is a ploy or something that was planted?" Francesca asked.

"Anything is possible," Claude said. "TOM is everywhere."

"I think the plane simply crashed into the ocean," Craig said sadly. "They may never find the entire plane or the black boxes to help solve this mystery, but if a piece of the airplane washed up onshore, it's evident that it broke apart onto the ocean. My dear Mallory…"

Craig trailed off and began to sob into one of my pillows. Francesca put her arm around him and gave him a tight embrace.

"There, there," she whispered to him.

Mark chimed in, "Mr. Bernstein, have you had any luck with those USB files from that Zyphone satellite?"

"No," Claude sighed. "There's nothing that links us to PA 619. I can't seem to find the files that track the movements of the satellite in space either. That's what I've been looking for. If I could see where it was on July 14 of last year, maybe I can find closure with this."

"I think we are wasting our energy," Francesca said matter-of-factly. "As a journalist, I have to think about the evidence presented."

"But The Omniscient Minds are real," Claude insisted. "They are a secret organization, and they tried to recruit me. They must be behind its disappearance. My own personal experience is enough evidence for me."

Francesca whispered in my ear and asked me to join her in the kitchen. I followed her and we spoke in private.

"Do you believe him?" Francesca asked. "He is kind of old. What if he's adding to a conspiracy theory? I mean, he did attempt to write a blog about this secret society."

"It was taken down immediately," I added. "Someone didn't want that information public."

"We don't know that for sure," Francesca added. "Besides, he's also been in hiding. His own family did not know what happened to him. I'm tired of giving false hope to Craig. I think he's accepted his daughter is long gone, along with the plane. Funds are running out, and the search will cease in October. I highly doubt Phoenix is going to fork over cash to continue the search. It would be good publicity for them if they did, but it's a waste of money at this point. Looking for that airplane is like trying to find a needle in a haystack. A very large haystack of hundreds and thousands of miles of ocean."

"So you're giving up on this?" I asked. "This could be the biggest story of your life. I need you. If we find out the truth, you can expose these traitors to the world. You'll get your splashy headline at long last. Maybe dating me will come with a huge payoff."

Francesca gave me a dark look. She shook her head angrily and said, "I'm not dating you for a story. I thought we were past that."

"I know," I said. "But if we find out something, I want you to write a hell of a story for the world to read. I want TOM exposed."

July 31, 2017

I woke up in the middle of the night to a coughing fit. I ran to the toilet and threw up. There was blood in my vomit. I looked at myself in the mirror. I was pale and my cheekbones were showing. I was losing weight and the color drained from my skin. I opened my underwear drawer, where my medication was hidden, and I took my dosage. I polished them off with a swig from my water bottle and then took a prescription-strength ibuprofen for the pain. My stomach was hurting from the medications. I could feel the acid in my stomach disintegrating the pills. It felt like poison, except this poison was slowing my demise from the cancer.

I tried to fall asleep, but the anxiety of my illness kept me awake. The sun was beginning to rise at fifteen minutes past six. I put on a light jacket and sandals and then walked outside towards the nearest coffee shop. I noticed a black SUV parked in my building's driveway. As I walked down the sidewalk of my street, I had the feeling that the vehicle was following me. I casually turned, and my heart began to pound. It appeared to be tracking me. I picked up my pace and did not turn back until I got to the coffee shop. I walked inside, then looked out the window. It stalled outside for a few seconds before driving away. The windows were deeply tinted, so I could not make out the driver. Panic began to set in.

"What would you like to order?" the female barista asked me at the counter.

I could not concentrate on coffee. I ignored the woman, then walked back out of the coffee shop and ran back to my condo. Once I was in the safety of my living room, I called Claude.

"I'm sorry for the early call," I told him once he answered. "I think I was being followed by a black SUV when I went out for a walk this morning."

"By whom?" he asked curiously.

"I don't know. I could not make out who was driving."

"You mentioned it was a black SUV?" Claude asked.

"Yes," I replied.

"They've started to keep an eye on you," Claude said with urgency. "They might be aware you know something. But how?"

"What do I do?" I asked nervously.

"First, I told you we can't keep talking on the phone like this. Just in case," Claude said, sounding irritated. "Second, we cannot be seen in public together—you and I. Continue your normal routine. If you see another vehicle or get the feeling that you are being watched, do not let them know you noticed. Act cool. This was beginning to happen to Jim right before he boarded PA 619. He had the feeling he was being watched."

"I was at the Hollywood Bowl with him a few months before that flight," I said. "I overheard him on the phone. He sounded paranoid."

"He was on a call with me. Someone got wind of our secret project," Claude said. "Thus the urgency to work on their project and talk about it with you in China, where they felt they were safe from prying ears."

"Am I in danger?" I asked.

"They are only keeping tabs on you at this point," Claude replied. "They won't take more action unless they have a reason to believe you might know more than you should. I wish I had not told you about the Hyp—*project*. This puts you more at risk. Ugh! I don't like that we're having this discussion on the line."

"Do you think Mark, Francesca, or Craig might be tailed too?" I pressed on.

"I'm not certain, but I would advise them to be vigilant," Claude demanded. "I'll check in with Ki—*King Kong* and see if he's heard anything behind the walls of *Firebird*."

I took "King Kong" to be code for Kingsley, and "Firebird" to mean Phoenix. I ended the call with Claude feeling foolish for speaking so openly over an unsecured cell phone connection.

August 3, 2017

Dexter Brandon, my former boss at the University of Montana, came into Los Angeles for a work trip. He had emailed me the previous day and asked if I could meet him for drinks. I recommended a bar at the Marina Del Rey Yacht Club. I was a few minutes late to our meeting, since L.A. traffic was horrendous, as usual. I found Dexter seated at the bar with a beer in front of him. His face lit up when he saw me.

"Patrick!" he exclaimed with raised arms. "It has been over a year since I've seen you!"

"Hello, Dexter," I said, taking a seat next to him. I flagged down a waiter and ordered a pint of my favorite ale. "Welcome to Southern California."

"Why, thank you," he said with enthusiasm. "I can see why you moved down here. The weather is nice right now. Listen—let me cut to the chase. I want you back at the university. You were one of my top aerospace professors. I heard you resigned from Phoenix earlier this year. What are you doing with all your free time? Or do you have a new job?"

"I've been…preoccupied," I said. "I've taken a meeting or two with a few companies, but nothing has tickled my fancy."

"Well," Dexter went on, "why don't you come back and teach full-time? You'll be close to your family again."

I took a few minutes to mull over his offer. I was not planning to leave L.A. until I had answers regarding PA 619. I considered living out my last months in Montana before the cancer won. I thought about Francesca and felt pangs of guilt in the pit of my stomach. I knew I would have to leave her behind without telling her what was truly going on with me. There would be no happy ending in whatever decision I made.

"Is everything all right?" Dexter asked with concern. "You seem distant."

"I have some unfinished business here," I answered. "If and when I can accomplish it, I will happily move back to Montana. I could see myself retiring up there."

"Splendid," Dexter said with excitement. "When do you think your unfinished business will be complete?"

"That is undetermined," I said.

"Well, let me get the next round," Dexter said, and he patted me on the back, which caused me to spill some of my ale onto the bar counter and my shirt. I reached for a napkin to wipe myself off as he apologized.

"Let me go dry off in the bathroom," I told him. I walked to the back of the club to find the men's restroom.

As I was about to reach for the door handle, I noticed a man in a navy blue suit and matching navy blue fedora smoking a pipe in the far corner of the club. He had a copy of the *L.A. Times* in front of him. One of his eyes was hidden behind it, but the other was staring directly at me. We made eye contact. I could feel the hairs on my arms rise with chills. He did not blink. It was as if he wanted me to know he was staring at me. He never bothered to advert his eyes to avoid the awkwardness. I had seen this man before. He was the man who'd stepped into the car with Natasha and Robert after the PA 619 one-year anniversary memorial. I took my eyes off him and walked into the bathroom. It was a single stall, so I locked the door behind me and quickly texted both Claude and Francesca about that strange encounter. Then I proceeded to push the hand dryer on in an attempt to dry off the spilled beer. A call from Claude came through. Once the dryer stopped, I answered it.

"You sure he looks familiar?" Claude asked immediately.

"His face was half hidden, and he was a few feet away," I said. "But I know it's the same guy who was with Natasha and Robert. I could tell by his frame, and the suit and hat were similar to what he wore that evening."

"Get a good look at his face," Claude urged. "And if you can take a photo of him discreetly, do so! He's probably one of The Omn—dammit, I can't be speaking openly on the phone like this. Be vigilant."

"Okay," I told him, and then I ended the call.

I walked back outside and looked at the corner where the man had been seated. He was gone. I looked around the bar and could not find him. I clenched my fists in frustration and sat back down with Dexter. We continued to catch up and fill each other in on everything we had done over the last year since I'd resigned from the university. Once the sun began to set, I bid Dexter farewell and walked back to my car. I received a group text message from Claude that read, "Meet at my Van Nuys motel room. Midnight. Tonight." Francesca, Mark, Craig, and another unknown number were attached to it.

August 4, 2017

Francesca and I arrived at Claude's motel. Mark arrived around the same time and parked next to my car. I knocked on the door, and Craig opened it slightly and peered through. When he saw us, he smiled and let us in. We entered and found Claude and Kingsley sitting on the bed. I deduced that the unknown number in the group message from Claude had belonged to Kingsley.

"Thank you for coming," Claude said. "All of us in this room have one thing in common. We know about The Omniscient Minds, but are not a part of the society. You also know about the HyperTube invention that I was working on with Jim King, Dylan Sparks, and Charles Rosenberg. A few weeks ago, the news reported that a missing piece of the airplane was found, confirming that it most likely crashed in the Pacific. Kingsley here is the head of security at Phoenix Airlines Corporation, for those of you who don't know him. He's been keeping an eye on Phoenix for us, working as a double agent. Earlier today, Patrick said he saw a man in a fedora watching over him at a yacht club. He said he looked like the man he saw get into a car with Natasha and Robert at the PA 619 memorial."

"He's been to the offices many times over the past year," Kingsley said. "Sometimes he wears that hat, and other times he doesn't. We've deduced he's a member of TOM, since he appears to be in close ranks with Natasha and Robert, who we can also undeniably agree are a part of the society.

Claude asked me to bring surveillance footage of this man so that you know his face, in case he begins to tail any one of you. We have sensitive information that TOM does not want us to have, and if they are aware we do, then we are in serious danger."

"Let's see it then," Francesca said with piqued interest.

Kingsley pulled out his tablet computer and played a high definition video with a watermark on it of the date of the memorial: July 14, 2017, at 10:05 PM. The camera captured Natasha, Robert, and the man in the fedora walking into the lobby of Phoenix Airlines. The man in the fedora took off his hat and walked right by the camera. Kingsley paused the video file to give us a clear view of his face.

"I recognize that man!" I said in disbelief.

"Oh my God!" Francesca said while clapping her hands to her mouth. "So do I!"

I turned and looked at her. I could see the color draining from her face. She had a look of shock, but her face read terror.

"Where do you recognize him from?" I asked Francesca. "I once saw him at the Phoenix offices. He had the same slick, jet-black hair. He was wearing a nice suit on the day I saw him, during the conference of the Forecaster unveiling. It was the same day of the riots and my encounter with the men in blue jumpsuits. I remember speaking to this man.

"This is going to turn into a riot," the man had told me on that day, about an hour before a riot broke out. *"I'm Joe. I'm a consultant for Zyphone Communications. Zyphone is presenting our partnership with Phoenix at the conference today. I hope these people don't ruin it."*

I'd shaken hands with this Joe character. I remembered he was wearing a fancy designer suit and a very expensive gold watch.

"I recognize his face from news reports last year. He was blond then. I know his name. It was on the manifest of PA 619. His name was, um, well, *is* Joseph Conroy. And he's supposed to be dead—or at least missing—as he was on Flight 619."

There was a stunned silence in the room. I could feel chills running up and down my arms. My jaw literally dropped.

"You don't mean to say," I said slowly, "that this is the man you mentioned was the in-charge flight attendant on 619? I recall you mentioning his name when we were digging for those files on that computer at Zyphone. Is this same guy whose name was on the maintenance records from Flight 619 and gave it an all-clear?"

"What!?" Mark and Craig said in unison.

"Yes," Francesca replied. "I did a report on him once. I know that face very well, but now he has a different hair color."

"So, you're saying," Claude said, looking at Kingsley then back to Francesca, "that's the man you saw *alive* a few days ago, being flanked by Natasha and Robert, both at the memorial and in this surveillance video? The video before us is from that same day…this…man…is someone who was on Flight 619?"

"Yes! I know he does not have a twin brother, because when I did research on him, I learned that he only had a sister," Francesca added.

"So, now it begs the question," Mark said. "How can a man who was supposed to have perished with the airplane still be alive? It has been a year since the plane vanished, and the only known person to have escaped the fate of that flight is standing in this room!"

All eyes fell on me. I felt my face turn red. I shrugged awkwardly.

"This is the key we needed," Claude said excitedly. "Joseph Conroy was on that airplane. If he's still alive—"

"Mallory might be alive too!" Craig cried with joy and began to sob.

"That's plausible," Claude admitted. "But as I was saying…if this man who was actually on the plane is alive, then it did not crash. And he most certainly must be behind what happened to it."

"This confirms he must be a part of TOM," I said. "They live in anonymity. It must be convenient for him to have the world think he's dead; now he can walk about freely, doing the deeds of the society."

"So, if there's a chance the plane never crashed…" Mark asked, "what about the piece they found?"

"That's something I wanted to share with all of you," Kingsley said. "I learned this recently, and did not want to put it in writing or speak about it over the phone. Claude, you'll want to brace yourself for this new tidbit. I looked into some files from a year ago, and found a work order for a third party company to build a flaperon. It was a one-off work order that was processed after PA 619 took off on July 14, 2016. It was an exact replica of the one installed on 619. The company created the flaperon with the exact Boeing coding to match the flaperon on 619. This third party company went bankrupt a few months after PA 619 disappeared, so any records of it are gone, but this work order exists in the Phoenix database."

"Holy crap!" Francesca said in awe. "Now we're getting somewhere."

"Jesus!" Claude clasped his chest. "Things are only getting crazier. How did you come across this file?"

"By luck. The flaperon that was found washed up on the shore of the Philippines was a ploy," Kingsley said. "They built it and let it weather in the ocean somewhere. Then it was strategically placed onshore to be found. That's my theory. And guess whose name was on that work order?"

"Who?" I asked.

"Natasha Wilkins," Kingsley said with a grin. "She had clearance to process the work order right under Royce Killington's nose."

"So Royce didn't have anything to do with it?" I asked.

"It's evident that he had not been recruited into TOM prior to the airplane's disappearance," Claude stated. "If you recall, I mentioned he was probably going to be recruited right around the time of the Forecaster demonstration in December, but then he had an untimely death. He obtained that voicemail you left for Jim, Patrick, and he spoke to you about it on our car ride to the Palm Springs hotel."

"Right." I recalled what Claude was talking about. He had posed as a bearded driver named Wilbur Wright. He was driving us to the launch after-party that afternoon. "Royce's accidental death was very convenient for me..."

"It was," Claude said. "They would have silenced you by now if Royce had told members of TOM that you were recruited into the S.R.K. Project."

Claude reached for a bottle of water from his nightstand and began to drink it so fast that it spilled out from the corners of his mouth. He started to shake, and then the color escaped from his face.

"Are you okay?" Craig asked him.

A sudden thought popped into my head. I slapped my face suddenly in anger for thinking of such a formidable scenario in my mind, but I had to ask Claude a very serious question. I took a deep breath.

"Did you drive Royce home that night?" I asked him gently. "That evening, on December 15, from Palm Springs back to his home in Brentwood?"

Claude began to tear up. I could tell he knew what I wanted to ask him without directly saying it. He reached for a tissue on his nightstand and wiped his eyes. Everyone in the room was quiet.

"You were in danger," Claude said in a hoarse voice. "The Killingtons were trouble. Royce was destined to join the ranks his late father once held with TOM. I was sure of that. I could tell he was nervous on the drive back to L.A. He took a few phone calls. He was speaking in code. Members of TOM discussed their plans openly when in the presence of non-members by speaking words that would make sense only to other members. I'm not sure who he was talking to, but he was obviously briefed in how to communicate with TOM members. I recognized a statement he made. He said to the person on the phone, 'The sun once set forever, but a new sun has risen. It is the year of this sun to shine. Its bright light will make the seeds grow.'"

That statement sounded familiar to me, but at that moment, I could not figure out where I had heard such a strange and similar sentence.

"When he said 'sun,'" Claude continued, "he was not talking about the star at the center of our solar system that gives us daylight. It was a play on words. He meant *son*. He was talking about himself rising to power as the son of Jackson Killington. I knew then he had just joined The Omniscient Minds."

"Do you know who killed Royce then?" Francesca asked.

Claude looked at her but did not answer. I could feel it in my bones, but I wanted Claude to verify the truth that my intuition was taunting me with.

"Royce was drinking straight out of a vodka bottle he stashed in the car," Claude spoke up after a few seconds of silence. "He appeared to be stressed over his recruitment. He looked absolutely terrified. I saw him snort a line of cocaine from the rearview mirror. He was already drunk, so he did not care about discretion. It was around midnight when we arrived at his estate. He was passed out in the back seat. I prodded him vigorously to wake him up. He did not budge. It was about twenty minutes later that he finally came around and allowed me to guide him up the steps to his front door. I pulled the keys out of his jacket pocket and opened the door. His two dogs greeted us. They began to lick us both, but I kicked them away. Royce was not coherent. It took me another fifteen minutes to get him up to his bedroom. I told him that I was going to get him some ibuprofen to help prevent a hangover. I walked into his bathroom and found his anti-depressant medication. I emptied the pills onto his bathroom counter and smashed them into dust. Then I grabbed a water bottle from his bedroom and poured the grounded pills into it. There were at least twenty pills that dissolved into that water bottle."

I felt my heart beating fast. I knew this was coming. I looked around the room. Mark's eyes were blank. Francesca had her hands over her mouth. Craig was sobbing into his shirt. Kingsley seemed unfazed by this information.

"And then what?" I spoke up.

"Well," Claude said. "I forced the water down his throat and encouraged him to drink the last drop. He drank the entire contents and within a few minutes his body was convulsing and he passed out. His breathing began to slow. His chest rose up and down until at last his body was still."

I put my hands over my face and rubbed my eyes. Claude had killed Royce. Everyone sat in stunned silence, too shocked to string two words together.

"I did it to protect you, Patrick," Claude said. "I had to make it look like an accident."

I put my hands on Claude's shoulders and squeezed them, to signify I understood. He began to cry. I gave him a hug and whispered into his ear.

"I understand why you did it."

"It was murder," Francesca said. "How is this okay?"

"Royce would have told TOM that Patrick was aware of the S.R.K. Project," Claude said. "The only reason Patrick was never silenced after missing the flight was because TOM was confident he knew nothing about the project. That was true; however, you knew there was something secretive that Jim, Dylan, and Charles were working on, but you didn't know exactly what it was, so you weren't a threat to them. I'm not proud of what I did, but think about the 241 lives that were lost. Phoenix is fueled with corruption."

"But they may be alive," Craig added. "We know the airplane did not crash into the ocean. Plus, there is one person we've realized is still alive. We know that the flaperon found was not the original part that belonged to Flight 619."

"The truth is, we still don't know exactly what happened last year to PA 619," Francesca said. "But how are you any better than TOM if you're willing to kill someone? Especially a high-profile figure like Royce Killington?"

"Francesca," I tried to calm her down. She had become worked up from hearing the news about Royce's death. "We are much closer to finding this airplane. Let's just stay calm and put our minds together so that we can expose these sons of bitches."

Francesca hugged me and nodded in agreement. She took a seat on the edge of the bed and mouthed "Sorry" to Claude.

"It's okay," he said to her. "Anyway, I have my laptop and the USB drive with Zyphone files at hand. Remind me what the name of that flight attendant who was on board Flight 619 and is allegedly still alive is?"

"Joe Conroy," I said. "Well, Joseph Conroy. He introduced himself as Joe when I spoke to him on the day of the Forecaster reveal."

"Thank you," Claude said, and he began to type a search query through the file drive containing Zyphone's satellite information. He typed in "Joseph Conroy."

"Interesting," Claude said. "A few files pulled up. The first one is the maintenance record from the night before the plane went missing."

"We saw that one back at Zyphone," I said, recalling the day we were in the Peeping Tom computer room.

"Hold on a minute!" Claude shouted excitedly, making everyone sitting on the bed next to him jump. "No wonder we could not find the GPS coordinates of the Peeping Tom satellite. Someone changed the satellite's file names to 'Joseph Conroy.' Look!"

Claude pulled up his laptop for us to see. He found a file that showed where Peeping Tom was located over Earth on the day we pulled the files from Zyphone. It showed a dot over a satellite image of Earth. At that time, the satellite was hovering over the South Pacific Ocean, hundreds of miles off the coasts of Australia and New Zealand. The Peeping Tom file name was labeled "Joseph Conroy."

"There's a drop-down menu," Claude said. "I can look through data for a specific date. I'm going to find July 14, 2016."

Claude scrolled through the drop down menu until he found the exact date. He sifted through the data until he arrived at the time frame of when the plane disappeared off radar that morning.

"This is it!" Claude shouted.

The file was in video format. Claude was able to fast-forward the position of the satellite. It was hovering over Hawaii, and then it headed south for the next several hours.

"It was tracking PA 619!" Claude said excitedly. "This matches the pings from the other satellites that helped analysts hypothesize that 619 might have diverted south. They weren't that far off."

The Peeping Tom satellite remained stationary over the ocean after a certain time frame, in the early hours of that morning until around dusk.

The location was also the same as the final location logged prior to copying over the files onto the USB drive.

"That's where the final resting place of the airplane is!" Claude said with excitement. I need to get the GPS coordinates. Hang on..."

Claude extracted the coordinates and gave them to me, and asked me to enter them into my phone's web browser so that we could search for a map. A link to a Google map populated. When I opened up the map, the coordinates showed a body of water.

"That's where the satellite stopped following the airplane," I said. "It did crash into the water after all."

"Why would this satellite still be hovering over this location as of a few weeks ago?" Francesca asked.

"Maybe to keep track of any search ships that sail by?" Mark added. "Perhaps they want to make sure it stays buried at sea."

"But Joseph Conroy is alive," Craig piped in. "If he's alive, it means the plane did not crash. We've discussed this several times."

"Let me see the map," Francesca said. I handed her my phone.

She scrutinized the map on my phone closely. After about a minute of intense staring, she smiled.

"This map has been tampered with," she said matter-of-factly. "See here—the ocean was cropped over something. It looks to me like something has been hidden from this satellite imagery. My guess is it's a body of land."

"Wow," I said, finally seeing what she meant. It looked as if someone had copied a section of the ocean and pasted a duplicate of it over a certain area. You could tell by the fine lines that there was a square-looking patch of ocean that did not look smooth against the ripples on the water. It looked like a bad attempt at Photoshop. "There must be land there, but it's intentionally hidden from the public."

"And that is where PA 619 is!" Craig said excitedly. "What do we do now?"

"The ships scouring the South Pacific Ocean are not looking in the right place," Francesca said. "The route where analysts predicted the plane would have crashed, based on its fuel and the pings they discovered, is not that far from this location. They aren't searching this area, though. The search party is still probably hundreds of miles off."

"Fascinating," Claude said. "This is the biggest lead we could have hoped for. Craig, if you want to find your daughter, then we will have to travel to the Southern Hemisphere."

"I know just the person who can help us!" I said. "Ted Holt—he's running the search teams. He lives in Sydney. He approached me last month at the memorial. Why don't I contact him and see if he can charter us out to this location, based off the GPS coordinates from the USB drive?"

"Wonderful!" Claude said excitedly. "We should keep this under wraps. Since he's running the search party, he'll want to inform his teams and the media. Let's keep the fact that we might know where the airplane is a secret from him...for now. How we convince him to take us there will be a challenge."

August 7, 2017

Setting up a private ship tour with Ted Holt was surprisingly easy. He was more than ecstatic to allow Francesca, Claude, Mark, Craig, Kingsley, and me to get a behind-the-scenes look at the work going into the search for PA 619. Everyone booked their tickets to Sydney, and we chose a departure for the following week on August 15. Thanks to Mark, we were all able to get Phoenix Airlines employee discount tickets, even though the flight to Australia via Phoenix was pretty affordable already, due to their push for cheaper airfares for everyone.

Mark and Kingsley requested two weeks of vacation from Phoenix, and Francesca told her boss she was working on a story about PA 619's search party. She was given the clearance to go, although her boss was reluctant because he felt the story was old news. She reassured him there would still be interest, since a piece of the airplane had been found the previous month. Craig worked for a marketing firm, and they were not going to allow him the time off to travel, so he quit his job.

"Nothing is more important than finding my daughter," he told me on the phone after confirming he had purchased his ticket. "I'm not going to tell my ex-wife. I don't want her to get her hopes up. She'll probably just think I'm crazy."

There was a strange clicking on our phone connection, and then a strange static sound crackled in my ear. For about two seconds, it sounded like there was a gush of wind, and I could no longer hear Craig. Then, his voice came back.

"What was that noise?" I asked him. "Was that on your end?"

"I didn't hear anything," Craig replied.

I ended the call and put my cell phone down on my kitchen table. I could not shake off the feeling that someone had tried to interfere with my call. Was somebody trying to listen in? Jim King had once feared his phone was being tapped. I felt nervous. If my phone line had just been tapped, then some unknown party knew we were about to fly to Sydney.

"You're being paranoid," I said out loud to myself.

August 14, 2017

I walked outside to my balcony to watch the sun set over Los Angeles. I began to reminisce of that day on July 13 when I sat on my balcony having a cocktail, hours before I was to board Flight 619. In the present moment, I opted for a glass of red wine. It helped take the edge off the stress of the task that lay ahead. I used my wine to swallow one of my medications. My journal was on top of my bistro table. I had a pen placed on top of it, ready for me to scribe a very important letter I had been conjuring up the courage to write. I decided that after we returned to L.A. from our adventure to Australia, I would tell Francesca I was not ready to commit to her. The truth was, I was more than ready, since I had been single for quite some time. I did not want her to see me suffer any more as my cancer progressed. I was already losing color in my face and losing weight. My belts were running out of notches. I knew that it was unfair to not let her decide to stay with me or not. That part of my plan was selfish. I was not sure how much time I had left on Earth. It could be one year, or it could be three months. I wanted her to find happiness. This news would devastate her. I figured if she did not know about it, then she could move on much faster. I knew that leaving her would make her very upset, and maybe even angry. I was banking on the fact that she would be angry and want nothing to do with me. It would help her to move on and find someone who had a body that was not decaying internally before her eyes. I knew this was a very cruel plot, but it was the only clean escape I could think of. I decided I would move to Montana and spend my final months with my family while living comfortably in my cabin. If I had enough strength, I could probably go back to teaching to pass the time at the University of Montana. Dexter had put the offer on the table; however, he did not know I was dying.

I began to write my letter to Francesca. It was the most difficult thing I ever had to do. I thought my grad school dissertation was difficult, but this was taking all the strength from my body. If I stuck around with her while my health failed, it would break my heart to see her hurt. It would probably make me sick, and I would die sooner than later. I knew myself well. The depression would make me weak. I was better off away from the pain of losing the opportunity to be with the woman I loved. Paragraph after paragraph were grueling to my soul. I kept crying silently.

How could you tell someone you love them, I thought to myself, *and just walk away from them? I told her I loved her on the night of my birthday, two months ago. How could I tell her something so raw and so powerful, and then just turn my back on her and tell her I can't commit to her or be her boyfriend anymore?*

I struggled with my thoughts. I was about to turn my back on someone I had spent almost a year with. Sure, we had broken up for a short time, but we had invested a large amount of time together. She would never get that time back. The memories we'd created together were something I would cherish and hold close to my heart. She was one of the strongest women I had ever met. I knew she would be fine eventually. She would have to be strong and move on. I recalled a story she had told me regarding her last boyfriend. He had broken her heart by leaving her for his ex-wife. She had cut him out of her life completely. I knew she would probably do the same to me. It brought me a great sense of sadness.

The sun had set and the stars began to sparkle in the sky. I finished writing my letter and folded it up. I tucked it into the middle of my journal.

Before I closed my journal, I saw an entry from last September. I had written about a visit to Jim King's home basement. There was a strange text message exchange I had found in what appeared to be an old burner phone in his desk. I had jotted the messages in my journal. I reread the seemingly cryptic texts that were addressed to someone named "J.K.:"

Received: "Thx for finding me well."
Sent: "Beginning funding. Sun is set to rise."
Received: "Election is near. Rules will change."
Sent: "Election won."
Received: "Everywhere. Watching. We See."
Sent: "Caesar was killed by his own."
Received: "Brutus will not know."
Sent: "Update?"
Received: "Tan. Sand. Beaches."
Sent: "Update 2?"
Received: "More have joined. The seeds will grow."
Sent: "Secrets must stay buried – sea, sand, or snow."
Received: "It is the only way, be well."
Sent: "Update 3?"
Received: "Alive."
Sent: "I need answers."
Received: "How is my sun shining?"
Sent: "Your sun is shining well. Plz I need answers."
Received: "Answers are forthcoming."
Sent: "When/where/what?"
Received: "My sun rises this year."
Sent: "He has risen, as you predicted. I'll join."
Received: "They know the plan."
Sent: "What?! Tell me more!"
Sent: "Hello?"

I read and reread the messages at least twenty times before slapping my forehead with a thought.

"They used the word sun in this exchange," I said out loud. "Sun…*Son.*"

It was as if the actual sun had shone a bright light in my mind, even though it was nighttime. A few days ago, Claude had explained to me that he had recognized Royce using code during a phone call. Royce had used the word sun the night Claude drove him back to his estate. Claude confirmed that it was code for son. Royce was the sun, and literally the son. I had known that the statement had sounded familiar to me; as I had written down this text message exchange in my journal, it must have stuck in the back of my mind.

"Oh my God!" I said with shock. "Jim was texting Jackson Killington! That's who 'J.K.' is on the contacts of that burner phone. Melissa King just assumed 'J.K' could have been Jim King's own initials. He was texting Jackson…but…"

It could not be possible. The text message exchange was only a few lines, but the time stamps proved it had taken place over a twelve-year period. The only catch was Jackson Killington was dead, or at least presumed dead, from a suicide bombing in his own office building for the entire part of that conversation's time frame. His body was never found, as it was presumed he had blown himself up. Was he still alive? Why was Jim in communication with him? He wrote, "Your sun is shining well." Was he talking to Jackson about Royce? I began to cry. The deeper I was diving into this mystery, the darker and stranger the circumstances became as they unraveled. I did not want to think about it or say it out loud, but if Jim was using some kind of secret code in his text message exchange, then it could only mean one thing…

I called Claude immediately and asked if he could meet up in person, as I did not want to risk informing him about my revelation over the phone. He agreed to meet at a coffee shop.

"It's impossible," Claude said when I shared my theory. "But then again, it's not. They are *The* Omniscient Minds, after all…they are all-knowing and all-seeing. They are everywhere and nowhere at the same time. Jackson must be alive. He faked his own death. It's not really that farfetched, considering Joseph Conroy was on PA 619, and we know he's been walking around Los Angeles alive and well."

"You're missing the part that I'm more concerned about," I said. "Does this mean that Jim was a member of TOM?"

Claude was silent for a few seconds before adding, "I don't want to believe it. He was working on the HyperTube with us…"

"Do you think that's how TOM found out?" I asked. "Could he have been a double agent?"

"Jim would never. There's just no way!" Claude sounded hoarse, as though he was choked up with emotions.

"Let's keep this between us for now," I urged Claude. "Jim was a good friend to me. I'd like to give his memory the benefit of the doubt."

"Memory?" Claude added. "At this point, anything is possible, and now we have to assume that the airplane never crashed. He might be alive and well. Tomorrow, we will begin our journey to the location we found in the files of that USB drive. I agree that we should keep this text message discovery between us. I don't want to alarm the rest of our team, because we do not know for sure if Jim or Jackson Killington are still alive."

August 15, 2017

I had not been inside the international terminal of the Los Angeles International Airport since that fateful day I had missed boarding Flight 619. Francesca and I made our way down the terminal after passing through security. We found our gate and were greeted by Mark and Craig, who were seated in the waiting area with their carry-on luggage.

"The flight to Sydney is about fourteen hours," Craig said once we sat down by them. "I hope I can sleep at least half of the journey."

Our flight was a red-eye, scheduled to depart at 11:00 PM. I felt nervous sitting in that terminal, about to board one of the new Phoenix Airlines models. I knew it was safe now that the Forecaster was installed, but I kept thinking about the Titanic, and how, once upon a time a century ago, they said it could not sink; yet on its maiden voyage, it struck an iceberg and was now sitting at the bottom of the Atlantic Ocean. It had taken decades before the wreckage of the ship was found. The Forecaster system had been live for two months, and there had not been a disaster yet. I was curious to see if the Forecaster could save people during a real-world flight crisis. These were not thoughts to have when I already had flying anxiety. I could also not shake off the feeling that TOM might have been aware of us boarding that flight. My paranoid mind suggested that maybe our flight to Australia would disappear. I shook this thought from my mind, in hopes that I was only being overly cautious. I had not seen any cars or Joseph Conroy following me around in the days leading up to that flight.

Claude and Kingsley arrived together. Claude was in disguise as his alias, Wilbur Wright. He had his beard on, and he brought his fake passport to match his identity. However, if I remembered correctly, he did not have a beard in his passport photo. Thankfully, it was not an issue. I felt relief when I saw him coming through the terminal after successfully passing through security with no issues.

"I find it unnerving that we haven't had any strange interception from The Omniscient Minds today," I whispered to Claude.

"Kingsley informed me that Natasha took vacation last week to leave the country, and Robert is working out of the China office," Claude said. "I don't think they are aware that we are headed out to find the missing plane."

Half an hour before our flight was prepared to depart, a female gate attendant spoke over the intercom: "We will begin boarding Flight 714 to Sydney momentarily. We'll be starting off with our Phoenix Airlines preferred members. If you are a preferred member, please come forward to the gate entry."

"You look nervous," Francesca said as we took our seats beside each other on board Flight 714. She grabbed my hand and squeezed it gently. "We'll be fine. Should I order us some wine?"

"That would help my nerves," I said. "Maybe a glass or two of wine will work wonders."

Mark and Craig were seated behind us. Claude and Kingsley had been placed near the back of the plane. I buckled up and fidgeted with the air vents above my seat. It was cold inside the cabin, and I started to shiver. I reached for one of the blankets provided by Phoenix that was located underneath my seat and wrapped myself in it. Francesca gave me a kiss before taking one of her sleeping pills. She put on her eye mask and was asleep minutes before we took off.

A female flight attendant came over the intercom to give the flight safety instructions. I dozed in and out during her speech. "…and thank you for flying with us on Phoenix Airlines. Born to fly. Enjoy your flight."

Flight 714 sped down the runway, and the engines revved louder and louder as we began our ascent. I had the window seat, so I found myself looking below at the sparking lights of Santa Monica as we flew into the dark abyss, with only the moon and a few stars speckled across the black, clear sky, lighting the way. I took one of my medications with my first sip of wine, and then reached for one of Francesca's sleeping pills. I washed it down with my wine.

I was not sure how much time had passed when I was suddenly woken up by a violent jolt. The airplane shook vigorously, and I heard what sounded like a gunshot. I looked outside the window and felt my entire body freeze in shock. The right wing of the airplane had caught fire. The seatbelt icon sign was flashing above us. The pilot came on over the intercom.

"Please remain calm, we are experiencing trouble with one of our wings. Oxygen masks are about to descend from above you. Please put them on. All flight attendants, please take your seats for an emergency landing. We are initiating the Forecaster system now. There is no need to panic."

It was easier said than done. Everyone on the airplane was screaming and crying. Francesca was crying hysterically, and saying over and over, "I don't want to die." I could hear Mark telling Craig something along the lines of, "We will be okay. The Forecaster never failed in testing."

There was a very obnoxious alarm blaring. It was painful to my ears. I saw a few other passengers cover their ears in discomfort. I did not remember this alarm system being part of the Forecaster system. It must have been added in the months after I left the company. I was silent during this entire chaotic episode. Perhaps it was because I was in shock. I was thinking about the irony of the situation I was in. Was I finally about to die in an airplane crash? As I thought that, I felt the cabin being pulled away as it disengaged from the mainframe of the fuselage. I could see the wing begin to tear apart. The pressure of the wind ripped it as easily as paper, and it flew off into the darkness like a comet with a tail of fire. The unnerving feeling of being pulled up into the sky by the emergency parachute that had deployed nearly made me vomit into my lap. The sensation in the pit of my stomach could only be described as the feeling one gets when taking a huge drop on a rollercoaster. The screams were terrifying. Experiencing the Forecaster firsthand was scarier than I had ever imagined.

The speed with which we were falling began to minimize. I was using my arms to brace myself against the chair in front of me. Francesca was grabbing onto her armrests as if her life depended on it. The deceleration of our fall meant that the parachute was working to save us. We were going to land in the ocean, and we would be fine, as the cabin would deploy an airbag from below that would act as a floatation device. The screams and cries grew louder and louder. I could hear people praying in front of me. Some luggage had fallen out of their compartments and hit a few passengers located toward the front of the plane, which was now the bottom in our free fall.

"Are we going to live?" Francesca cried.

"The Forecaster is working as programmed," I yelled over the sound of the pressure from our fall. "It should have already sent our global positioning and a distress signal to the nearest airport tower. Have faith."

I spoke too soon. I heard a huge rip above me, and then the entire cabin shook angrily. The parachute had failed and ripped off of the tail of Flight 714. We began to tumble at an accelerated speed. Some of the airplane's windows blew out, and a gush of wind pressed up against my skin. It was like I was skydiving again, but this time there was anything but silence. The roar and sound were so intense. I thought I had gone deaf for a moment. With my eyes closed, I said a desperate prayer in my head while grabbing onto Francesca's hands and squeezing them tightly.

I opened my eyes and saw an eruption of orange flames as the nose of the airplane smashed into the ocean. There was a loud explosion that left a ringing in my ears. I could barely hear my own scream of terror.

Francesca shook me vigorously. I opened my eyes and looked around. The airplane was intact, and we were still flying smoothly. Several passengers and a flight attendant were staring at me with concern.

"You had a nightmare," Francesca said. "You yelled pretty loud. I'm sure you woke up half this cabin."

"Is everything all right?" a female flight attendant by the name of Joann asked me.

"I'm so sorry," I said with embarrassment. "I think the sleep medication I took caused me to have a nightmare. May I have a cup of water?"

"Of course," Joann replied politely. "I'll be right back."

Francesca started to massage my neck once the flight attendant left. I felt hungover, a side effect of the sleep medication. I felt groggy and dizzy. With my eyes closed, I took a deep breath. The dream was very lucid and had felt almost too real. I was unable to sleep for the remainder of the flight, so I spent the rest of the time watching films on the Phoenix Airlines entertainment hub.

August 17, 2017

It was as if August 16 had never happened by the time we landed in Sydney. Australia was nineteen hours ahead of Los Angeles, nearly a day. We had left right before midnight on August 15 and landed on the morning of August 17. It took over two hours to get out of the airport. The customs line was long and excruciatingly slow. When we finally passed through customs and were out of the airport, a SUV, arranged by Ted Holt, picked us up. It was going to take us to a hotel in an area of Sydney called Potts Point. According to Ted, it was not too far from the wharf where our ship was to deploy the following morning.

The drive through Sydney to our hotel was quiet. Mark and Kingsley appeared to have fallen asleep. Claude was looking out of the window at buildings, while Craig was checking his emails on his phone. Francesca had her head on my shoulder. We were both sitting silently until we finally arrived at our hotel. We were booked at a boutique hotel that looked like an apartment building from the outside.

"Is this a flat?" Mark asked as we got out, attempting to use Australian lingo when speaking to our driver.

"No, mate," our driver Edward answered, "it's a hotel. I promise you. This is a quaint part of town; however, if you walk down south a little, the bars are a little dodgy."

"How so?" Mark asked.

"Ladies of the night like to appear on the street corners," the driver said. "If you know what I mean. Unless you fancy company..."

"Oh," Mark said, turning slightly red. "Not my thing."

"What are the dinner plans for tonight?" Kingsley asked me as we walked into the hotel lobby.

"Ted Holt will be hosting us at his home," I said. "He sent me an email while we were in the air. I read it once we landed. He lives in an area called Dover Heights, north of the famous Bondi Beach. He'll have a car pick us up at six this evening."

"Wonderful," Kingsley said. "I think I'm going to take a nap. This jetlag is a struggle."

We all checked into our rooms for the evening. Francesca and I shared a room, while everyone else had their own rooms. I dropped my bags upon entering and sank into our king-sized bed. It felt glorious to lie on something so soft, unlike a stiff airplane seat. Francesca fell asleep almost instantly once she lay next to me. I was unable to nap for even five minutes, so I decided to go out for a walk. I found Mark and Craig sitting at the hotel bar as I was walking out. They called me over for a drink, but I told them I was going to walk to the bay and get some sunshine. Mark stayed behind to drink. He'd appeared to have been deep in conversation with the bartender who had served him a pint of local beer. Claude left Mark's side and joined me on my walk to the nearby bay.

"It's my first time to Australia," Claude said. "It's been on my bucket list. I hope we can find time to sightsee after this trip to sea."

"Let's hope it's a safe journey," I said. "Do you think we'll be fine? We are headed straight for that area of ocean that the Peeping Tom satellite has been hovering over and observing. What do you think we'll find? A body of land? A ship? Debris?"

"I'm not sure," Claude said. "I'm guessing a body of land."

"Let's say we do find a body of land," I continued. "Do we march right up to shore and knock on someone's door?"

"We'll have to cross that bridge when we get there," Claude replied.

"I keep thinking about Jim," I said sadly. "If he was in communication with Jackson Killington, and Jackson is still alive, what do we do in the circumstance that we have to confront them face-to-face?"

"Again," Claude said slightly impatiently, "you are asking questions I don't have answers to. I understand that we should probably have a plan, but we are going into the unknown. I don't know if we'll find anything, or what will happen if we do. All I know is that my life's work has been hampered by the likes of the Killingtons for far too long, and justice needs to be served."

"Is this a revenge mission for you?" I asked bluntly.

"Justice, Patrick," Claude snapped suddenly. "I'm in hiding because of The Omniscient Minds. I'm sure I would be dead by now if they knew I was still alive and plotting to expose them and the fact that they may very well be behind the taking of Flight 619."

Claude and I returned to the hotel about an hour later. Mark was still at the bar, looking smug over his pint of beer. He waved at us when we walked back in through the lobby. Claude rejoined him at the bar, and I left both of them to check out the hotel's courtyard. I saw Kingsley sitting on a bench and applying sunscreen over his arm. He was diligently rubbing in a generous amount of it over his dragon tattoo that coiled around his arm and up to his shoulder. He caught sight of me and smiled.

"Do you want some sunscreen?" he asked me. "The ozone layer is weak in this part of the world, so I advise you to wear some strong SPF. It'll help prevent cancer. I need to put some over my tattoo, because my skin is sensitive in that area."

I looked at Kingsley blankly. If only he knew that I had been diagnosed with cancer, and getting skin cancer was the least of my concerns.

"I'm fine for now," I said. "But thank you."

I'd decided to head back to my room when a thought struck me. I turned back and asked Kingsley a question.

"Do you have any more inside information from Phoenix that can help us along the way?" I asked. "The information you gave us regarding the work order Natasha placed to make an exact replica of the Flight 619 flaperon was crucial. It confirms they are hiding something. I was just wondering if maybe there was anything else? Do you think there are other members of TOM working at Phoenix Airlines?"

Kingsley looked at me with concern. He raised an eyebrow and was no longer smiling.

"I mean, Natasha can't be the only one there," I added. "And Royce was killed, so..."

"I'm not sure," Kingsley cut in. "Granted, I'm head of security there, and I should be able to see and hear more than most people there. That is, in fact, true, but these people are very stealthy, from what Claude has told me regarding the time he was almost recruited into their ranks. I would have to say I'm not sure, if truth be told. I don't know if there are any other members of that secret society working for Phoenix."

"I see," I said. "How come the FBI never obtained records from that Peeping Tom satellite?"

"Why would they?" Kingsley said. "That satellite is a part of Zyphone. They would have been unaware of its connection to Phoenix. And the CIA uses it. There would be no need to touch it."

"Well, if the likes of Colin Shaw are any indication of corruption, since he was the former head of the CIA," I added, "then the FBI wouldn't need to look into it at all. Colin Shaw would have made sure that nobody knew the real truth behind what the satellite was actually observing. He was hiding in plain sight."

"Exactly," Kingsley agreed. "That's how TOM operates. They hide in plain sight. I mean, at least that's what I gathered from Claude's description of their shady ways."

"Thanks again for being so helpful," I said to Kingsley. "I'll never forget your help the one time I snuck into that lab at Phoenix while snooping for maintenance records."

"We're on the same side," Kingsley said, with a smile back on his face again. "We're going to find that airplane soon. I can feel it. You'll finally have your truth, and I'm privileged to be part of your team."

He shook my hand, and I gladly accepted it while looking at his unique tattoo. It made him look much tougher than he really was.

A black SUV picked us up from our hotel and took us to the coast, where Ted lived in an affluent neighborhood. He greeted us at the door and ushered us in. His wife, Sharon, made an amazing spread that included meat pies, steaks, roast chicken, and an assortment of salads and vegetables. Ted went over his plans for our excursion. Claude had concocted a story about having an area of ocean he wanted to search. Ted told him it was outside the proposed current search area, and that it would be a waste of time. Claude looked nervous. Claude's attempt to persuade Ted to take us to those coordinates seemed to be failing.

"Why don't we tell him the truth then?" I spoke up.

Claude looked at me nervously, as did the rest of my team. There was some awkward silence before Ted spoke up.

"I'm sorry, Patrick, what do you mean?"

"We can't say much," I began, with the idea to tell a lie, but I decided to be honest. "Well…we might have uncovered some information about this specific area of ocean, and we have reason to believe it could be where Flight 619 has actually come to rest."

"You have my attention," he said.

"It would be a risk for Kingsley and Mark. They could lose their jobs at Phoenix," I continued, "which is why we need to keep this a secret. We came across some sensitive files from Zyphone, the company behind the Forecaster system. The files were from a government-controlled satellite managed by Zyphone that was presumably following PA 619 on the morning of July 14, 2016."

"What?" Ted dropped his fork on his plate. "Phoenix may know what actually happened?"

"The satellite is operated by the company that makes Phoenix's Forecaster systems," I added. "The information came from that company, technically, but we fell into this information while at the Forecaster launch party back in May. Gaining access to this data could mean jail or worse for all of us involved in the breach."

"I'm working on a story to expose the company," Francesca added. "If we get to this area and your ship can detect debris at the bottom of the ocean or we find something above the surface, then we can start ringing the alarms. But due to the sensitive nature of the matter, we need to be discreet and confidential."

"They're right," Claude jumped in, sounding defeated now that our agenda was out in the open. "Can we trust you?"

Ted was playing with his half-eaten chicken breast on his plate, then turned to his wife before looking back at me.

"When I met you in L.A.," Ted said, "I mentioned I had a meeting with Natasha about extending our search party. Many families have been trying to raise funds to continue our expedition. We've spent millions of dollars in this yearlong search. We are expected to complete the area of the search by October. If the airplane is not found, then it may never be found, since we'll be out of funds to continue. We were hoping to get a private funder to help us. I was sent to America to try and convince Natasha to help us continue the search. I made some real valid arguments as well. I told her it would be a good publicity move if Phoenix got involved and donated funds to continue the search for at least six more months."

"What did she say?" Claude asked.

"This is where things got strange, mate," Ted said, fidgeting with his fork. "She told me that they were not going to 'waste any more resources and money.' She insisted that the piece of the flaperon that was found in the Philippines would be enough closure for the families, because it proved that the airplane had, in fact, crashed into the ocean, and that all life was, without a doubt, lost. Then she offered me a quarter of a million dollars as a bonus for my work over the last year. I got the vibe that she was paying me off to stay quiet. She offered me money, personally, and yet she wouldn't fund the damn search?"

"She doesn't want the plane to be found," I added. "I know it's a big risk to take a leap of faith on this excursion, but it may be worth your time. For now, we need to be discreet. If we find something at the exact coordinates we have, it will have all been worth the risk."

Ted appeared to be mulling over the information in his head. He poked a piece of his chicken and took a bite. He glanced over at his wife, who had a look of concern, but she nodded her head as if to say, "You should do it."

"Well, mate," Ted answered, "tomorrow, we will head to this location." I tightened my fists in excitement and victory.

"It's several hundred miles out," Francesca added. "How long do you think this trip will take?" Francesca pulled out her cell phone to show a pin drop on a map application.

"Let's see," Ted said, pulling out a pair of reading glasses. "This journey could take about a week or so. And that's if we don't run into any weather issues."

"Well, then," Claude chimed in, "it's settled. We have a long journey ahead of us."

August 18, 2017

We woke up the following morning at around 5:00 AM and took the train to Circular Quay, the wharf where Ted's ship was set to sail from. When we arrived at the wharf, the sun had begun to rise. The Sydney Opera House was a few meters away from us. Its windows reflected the orange glow of the rising sun. Several boats were preparing to head out to sea for an early morning catch of fresh seafood. Ted's search ship was about the size of three yachts. It was called the S.S. *Forager*. The bottom of the ship was painted red and the top was white.

Francesca and I boarded the ship hand in hand. We walked up to the bow and attempted to jokingly reenact the scene from the film *Titanic* where Jack and Rose held each other.

"Do you get the feeling we are close to solving this?" Francesca asked. "This could be the biggest story of our lives—and my career. You'll be a hero. Think about it: Patrick Baldwin survives missing his flight on PA 619 narrowly, and emerges to find the airplane on a secret mission one year later. They'll write books about this, and maybe even turn it into a movie."

"I don't know about that," I said, blushing. "I definitely want the press to expose The Omniscient Minds for however they took down PA 619. So many families have wanted closure, and we are at the brink of finding it for them."

Kingsley joined us mid-conversation. He looked over the railing and stared at the Sydney Opera House.

"Is everything all right, Kingsley?" I asked him. He had a sad and longing look on his face.

"This place brings back memories," he answered. "I once brought my son here. He had always wanted to visit Australia as a kid."

"Oh, I didn't know you had a son," Francesca said in surprise.

"Yes," Kingsley said. "He passed away. He was in an accident."

Kingsley was very short with the conversation, so Francesca and I exchanged looks and decided not to press on with what was obviously a difficult memory for him. He seemed to be a very private person, so I felt as though I should respect his space.

"I'm going to settle into one of the cabins below deck," Kingsley added. "Talk to you all later."

The S.S. *Forager* took off from Circular Quay after 7:00 AM and set sail out of the harbor. We passed the magnificent Sydney Harbor Bridge and the Opera House on our way out to the Pacific Ocean. Once we were out of the port and harbor and into the vast and endless ocean, Ted joined us at the bow of the ship.

"How many crew members did you bring along?" I asked Ted as soon as he walked up to us. I had not considered the fact that manpower would be needed to maneuver the ship to the location requested. I was hoping we would have fewer people on board, since our mission was shrouded in mystery, and I did not want any more people to know. I did not know who to trust.

"Ten men," Ted responded. "I knew we wanted to be lean with a crew, since we have a sensitive mission ahead. Do you think we should fill them in on what we are doing?"

"No," I said. "Not right now. I'm not sure what we'll find when we finally arrive at the GPS coordinates your captain is guiding us to, but by then, maybe we can figure out a plan of action."

"We may not find anything at all," Francesca said. "There's no need to alarm them. We don't know who we can really trust right now."

"Fair enough, mate," Ted agreed. "I hope you'll find your cabins cozy. They are quite small."

"Is the food on board good?" I joked.

"We have prepared frozen meals," Ted said, laughing back. "It won't be like the meal my wife cooked for us last night."

I started to have a coughing fit. Francesca looked concerned and placed her hand on my shoulder. My stomach felt nauseous for a moment.

"Are you getting seasick already, mate?" Ted asked.

"I'll be fine," I said. It was not seasickness. I was having a reaction to my medication.

"You've been pale lately and looking somewhat thin," Francesca whispered into my ear with concern. "Maybe you should go lie down."

The feeling in my stomach passed. I put my hand over my forehead to wipe nervous sweat away.

"It's nothing," I said. "I feel better now."

How much longer could my body fight this cancer? I knew I was not going to beat it, but the medication was slowing down the process. I needed every bit of strength I could muster to make it through whatever obstacles in our journey we had ahead of us. I spent the rest of the day writing in my journal. I pulled out my letter to Francesca and read it over twice. Every time I read it, my heart broke into a million pieces. It was the saddest thing I had ever written. Once this trip was over, I knew I would have to break up with her. The letter revealed the truth about what I was going through, but I knew I would have to mail it to her in the future. Truthfully, I did not want her to know about my battle with cancer until after I passed. I found myself in a very dark situation. The guilt weighed my heart down so much, it was as if it would collapse into my already failing lungs.

August 20, 2017

On day two of our journey, we came across our first obstacle. A storm had been brewing over the Pacific for most of the morning. Immense, dark clouds blocked the sunlight. They were threatening to open up and pour down on us. It felt like it was dusk, when in actuality it was 11:00 AM. Since we were far out at sea, our cell phones were useless. We had no reception. The only forms of communication to land were through the ship's radio system and satellite phones. Ted urged us all to stay indoors during the storm. There was a loud clap of thunder around noon, followed by a brilliant lightning storm that danced across the sky and onto parts of the ocean in the distance. Heavy rain began to pour from the heavens. The waves of the ocean kept rocking the ship menacingly and hitting us from both the port and starboard sides.

We were seated in the dining room common area, attempting to have a very bland pasta lunch that one of the crewmembers had heated up for us. It was not the most appetizing meal. My food slid onto the floor during one especially violent shake of the ship, which I did not like. Francesca looked terrified as she stared out one of the ship's porthole windows.

"This storm can overturn us," she said worriedly.

"I've braved through worse," Ted assured her. "It'll be rocky for a few more hours. If anyone starts to feel seasick, we have ginger cookies in the kitchen. They should help with nausea."

I attempted to clean up my lunch, which was now spread all over the dining hall floor. One of the ship's crewmembers ran to my aid and began to mop up the mess. Francesca grabbed me by the arm and suggested that we head to our cabin until the storm settled. When we arrived at our cabin, we found our luggage thrown all over the room from the violent movements of the ship.

"I'm freaking out," Francesca said with worry. "This storm looks bad. Real bad. We're so far out from the mainland."

"There are a few islands in the vicinity," I assured her. "I think."

There were, in fact, a few islands in the waters we were sailing through, but they were so far out of the way that even I was terrified of what would happen, should we need to send out a distress signal. Francesca was frantically picking up some of her toiletries that had rolled onto the floor. I saw her reach for my brown leather-bound journal that had fallen out of my backpack, which I had left open on top of a nightstand. My heart sank as she reached for it. The letter I had written to her was inside the journal.

"What's this?" she asked as she picked up my book.

I swiftly walked over to her and reached for it. She gave it to me, and as I pulled it out of her hands, she gave me a suspicious look.

"It's my journal," I said truthfully. "I've been keeping a record of things regarding PA 619. It's a good way for me to go back and remember any facts we've uncovered."

"Oh," Francesca said. "Is there anything in there that I can use, in case we find the plane? I'd like to write a story for the *Times*, and I could use your account of our journey."

"Um," I tried to come up with an excuse, "not really. My handwriting is so bad that it would drive you crazy. There's nothing in here you don't already know."

"All right," she responded, not sounding very convinced.

I put my journal back in my backpack and zipped it up. I took a seat on the edge of the bed with one hand on the wall for support. The ship kept rocking back and forth. For the next few hours, the rain kept slamming up against the ship's hull. Eventually, seasickness crept up on me. I began an hour-long relationship with our cabin's restroom toilet, as the breakfast and half of the lunch I was able to devour came rushing out. I shut the door to our restroom. There was some blood that came out along with my food. This cancer was doing everything it could to make my life a living hell. After I had nothing left to throw up, I washed my face in the sink. The reflection that stared back at me had bags under his eyes. My face looked thinner, which made my cheekbones more pronounced.

Francesca knocked on the door. "Are you okay? You've been in there for a long time."

"Just seasick," I answered groggily. "I'll be a few more minutes."

The sky cleared up around dusk. Everyone on board went up to deck to see the sunset, now that the clouds and rain had passed. I went up to the captain's quarters to speak to Ted. The S.S. *Forager* had taken a rough beating from the storm, but according to Ted, there was no serious damage. A few lifeboats had been thrown off the ship, but since we were a small crew, it was not of any concern. Ted was alone in the quarters, observing the ship's sonar technology that was scanning the bottom of the ocean.

"So, this is how the search party is mapping the bottom of the ocean?" I asked, looking at the computer screen that had generated a 3D model of the mountainous ocean bottom below us.

"Yeah," he replied. "These parts of the oceans are so deep, and they've rarely been explored. If we find the airplane underwater, it is possible that it might be very difficult to retrieve it."

"Well," I said, "if we are lucky and our hunch is correct that the airplane might be at the coordinates we gave you, then there's also the chance it's not underwater. There could be land."

"That would be mind-blowing," Ted said. "I mean it would be the craziest story ever, mate. What is the best piece of evidence you found that leads you to believe it never crashed?"

"I have two pieces of evidence," I said. "The first was the fact that we saw one of the flight attendants who was listed in PA 619's manifest alive and well one year after it vanished. So, if he's alive, it is possible that the airplane never crashed. I have considered the fact that maybe he jumped out of the airplane or evacuated it somehow, but I highly doubt that happened. And the second clue is the fact that Royce Killington's assistant and now CEO of Phoenix Airlines, Natasha Wilkins, secretly had a flaperon cloned and manufactured after PA 619 took off on its final flight. That piece is what I believe allegedly washed up onshore. There's no doubt in my mind that it was planted there."

"That really baffles me," Ted said. "Everyone in the search party was really excited when it washed up onshore. The location matched what data analysts have said about the supposed final resting place of where the plane might have crashed, based on the amount of fuel it had. Not to mention, there were echoes of satellite pings analysts were able to uncover that show its projected diversion from the original flight path."

"I can only hope we are closer to solving this mystery," I said with fatigue. "I'm going to head to bed and get some rest. It was nice speaking to you."

August 23, 2017

The next few days at sea came and went with nothing much to write about. However, on the morning of the 23rd of August, Francesca and I arrived at the dining hall to find the breakfast buffet empty. Usually, a self-serve breakfast buffet was prepared for us to eat after 7:00 AM. I found a disgruntled Claude, Mark, and Craig sitting at the table, looking impatiently at the kitchen door.

"Is breakfast running late?" Francesca asked.

"I don't think any cooks are in the kitchen," Claude said, with irritation resonating in his voice. "I'm extremely famished."

Kingsley walked into the dining hall. He looked as though he had not slept. There were shadows under his eyes. He looked at us in surprise, and then to the breakfast bar.

"No food?" he yawned and stretched his muscular arms.

"The crew seems to have vanished," Craig chimed in.

"Sorry about that!" Ted yelled, running into the dining hall. "Our two cooks have fallen ill, to what appears to be food poisoning, ironically."

"What?" I said. "Was it from last night's dinner? I feel fine."

"Me too," Francesca added.

"I'm not sure," Ted said with frustration. "They have been extremely sick all night apparently. I went down to see them in their cabins. They're in so much pain, they don't want to leave their beds or walk too far from a restroom."

"That's unfortunate," Mark chimed in.

"We'll have to settle for canned goods," Ted said, over a heavy sigh from a disgruntled Claude.

For some reason, my team and I were fine, but the crew had begun to fall ill. There were ten crewmembers in addition to Ted, and by the following day, all of them were unable to leave their cabins due to some kind of illness. We were baffled. There was not even an on-staff medical doctor. Ted voiced his concern to us. He felt that it would probably be best to turn around or head to one of the nearest populated islands, so that the crew could receive medical attention. Their symptoms kept worsening. I found myself feeling slightly weak too. However, it was from the medications I was taking for my cancer. I was really good at hiding the fact that I was weak, but I looked pale and I was dropping weight. Francesca had begun to assume that I might have caught whatever the crew had. Regardless of the sick crew, we sailed on.

August 25, 2017

It had been exactly one week since we'd left Sydney. According to the ship's GPS, we were a few hours away from the coordinates we had input into the system that we'd stolen from the Zyphone satellite computer. Claude and I spent that morning arguing with Ted about continuing onto our destination.

"My crew is very ill," Ted said angrily. "We need to turn around. We should have done so two days ago!" Ted began to cough violently. He was holding onto his stomach as though it was about to pop out of his throat.

"Are you okay?" Claude asked him cautiously.

"No," Ted said, and I could see sweat pouring out of his forehead as if he was having some kind of hot flash. "I think I've caught what the rest of the crew has. We need to get to a hospital as soon as possible."

Ted suddenly passed out and hit his head against a table. Claude and I lifted his limp body and carried him to the infirmary, even though there was nobody there that could help him. I looked through the medicine cabinets in hopes of finding something that we could use to make him feel better. He was bleeding from his forehead, so I pulled out some ointment and bandages to cover his wound.

Craig came running into the infirmary out of breath. "D-d-ead." He panted. "They're all...dead."

"Who?" I exclaimed. "What?"

"Francesca and I went to check on the crewmembers' cabins on the deck below," Craig said through tears. "They're dead. Whatever they had has killed them. What if we are infected? There's some kind of illness. Maybe it's airborne."

"Calm yourself," Claude snapped. "The last thing we need to do is panic." The argument was lost, as panic seemed to have spread throughout my team already. We left Ted's unconscious body on the infirmary bed and walked to the bow of the ship, where we found Mark, Francesca, and Kingsley having a heated argument. When Kingsley caught sight of us, he spoke.

"We are now on a ghost ship," he said somberly. "The entire crew is dead."

"What the hell is going on?" I said in confusion. "Ted just passed out. He has whatever the rest of the crew had. This is definitely not food poisoning."

"Why were the crew the only ones affected?" Mark asked. "I feel perfectly fine."

"Me too," Francesca added. She reached for my hand and grabbed it. It was interesting the way she held it. It was in a careful manner, almost as though she knew I was fragile. It was not her usual tight squeeze.

"Does anyone here know how to maneuver a ship?" I asked. "We're going to have to turn around or find the nearest island. Let's head up to the captain's quarters and figure out a game plan."

We walked up to the top deck where the captain's quarters were. Claude reached for the ship's steering wheel and looked over at me. "I don't think anyone here is qualified to drive this ship."

"The French Polynesian islands are the closest inhabited land masses to where we are," Francesca said, looking at the digital map on the ship's navigation system. "They are hundreds of miles away though. It could take a few days. Maybe we should turn in that direction?"

"Why don't we just call for help?" Mark piped in. "We can send a distress signal to neighboring ships or islands. Maybe we can get the coast guard to send a helicopter over. We're pretty much stranded."

"I'll try to use the radio," Claude said, reaching for a walkie-talkie by the steering wheel. "Hello! Hello! Hello!" Claude yelled into the radio, but all he heard was static on the other end. He continued to aggressively click the call button, and yelled, "S.O.S." about ten times, to no avail.

The lights of the ship began to flicker. First it was slow and steady, and then it looked like strobe lights flashing until the power completely went out. It was midday, so we had sunlight. Had it been nightfall, we would have been left in pitch-black darkness.

"The power has gone out," Francesca cried.

"The radio is dead. We're screwed," Claude said angrily, and he slammed the walkie-talkie against the steering wheel, causing it to crack.

The engines of the ship began to give out as well. The silent rumbling and vibrations from below deck ceased. We were now officially on a ghost ship, floating in the middle of nowhere, far from any civilization…that we were aware of.

26

It was a weird feeling. We had no means of cooking a warm meal. There was no electricity or telecommunications. The entire crew minus Ted had died of some mysterious illness. I wanted to sit in the captain's quarters and start laughing, but I held it back for fear of causing my team concern. I knew I was dying too, but I was expected to live a few more months to a year. I think this was why I was not panicking as much. I did not have much time left, so perhaps it was a blessing from the heavens that I could potentially perish with Francesca and the rest of my team. It made me feel like an equal.

But then a scary feeling sunk in. We had come so far on this journey. The navigation system had gone out, but before it did, we had learned that we were only ten miles away from the exact location of the coordinates. I could not see anything in the distance except what appeared to be a vast and empty ocean.

Everyone was in panic mode. The sun would soon be setting in the horizon. We had some canned food that we could ration, but Claude calculated it would only last us three days. The refrigerated and perishable items were well on their way to spoiling, since the ships generators had failed. Kingsley had anchored the ship after the power went out so that we would not drift off too far, in case we found a way to call for help. Francesca and I sat on a bench near the stern of the ship, trying to figure out what our plan of action would be. I contemplated telling her about my cancer, as it seemed we were all doomed, but I decided against it. We were powerless in the middle of the ocean, far away from any hint of the modern world.

There was nothing but vast ocean and empty skies beyond the horizon.

"We can't even scan the bottom of the ocean," a disgruntled Claude said to me when I arrived at the captain's quarters alone later that evening. "To think, the plane could be buried below us, and we have no power on board. It felt like we were so close. I had a feeling this was exactly where we needed to be."

I looked up at the sky. It had turned purple and orange from the sunset. I could see the moon beginning to shine. "Do you think the satellite is up there right now, watching over us?" I asked.

"I didn't think about that," Claude said with worry. "What if they know we are here?"

"Then we can be saved?" I said hopefully, knowing that if The Omniscient Minds were watching us from the satellite, saving us would be the last thing on their minds. They had already marked Claude as a traitor for not joining them. I tapped on the radio, in hopes that it would start working by the force of it banging against the ship's control console. It was still dead silent. There was a sudden rushed knock at the door. Kingsley let himself in and closed it shut behind him.

"I have an idea," he whispered while holding up a compass. "It's nightfall. If we take a lifeboat and row ten miles east, we could end up at the exact coordinates we're chasing. By the time we arrive, it will be close to dawn and we'll have daylight. Would you all be interested in joining me?"

"What about the others?" I asked. "Should we bring Ted with us, since he is very ill? We may find land or something."

"He's dead weight," Kingsley said sharply. "The other men did not survive. He doesn't stand a chance. He'll be gone by morning. Do you want to tow around a dead body?"

"That's slightly insensitive," Claude exclaimed. "We are all one team. We need to stick together. I would feel terrible leaving Francesca, Mark, Craig, and Ted behind."

"I'm happy to go on my own then," Kingsley said. "There are several lifeboats, so if I don't make it back, you all still have a fighting chance to row yourselves somewhere. However, we are far away from civilization. I don't see any ships on the horizon or lights in the distance. The only twinkling of light is coming from the stars and the moon."

There was another sound at the door. Someone turned the knob and came in. It was Francesca. She had a concerned look on her face. She made eye contact with me and said, "Ted's not doing so well. His breathing is slowing down. What the hell could have caused him and the rest of the crew to become so violently ill? Why aren't any of us sick?"

"That's the million dollar question, isn't it?" Kingsley asked. He turned back to face Claude and me. "So, any of you want to join me on a lifeboat?"

"And go where?" Francesca intruded.

"It's a ten mile journey to where the coordinates are located," Kingsley said. "I want to see what's out there."

"If the plane crashed into the ocean, then it would be at the bottom of the sea," Francesca said. "We won't find anything."

"I thought we were all under the impression that it had not crashed because of my information about the flaperon," Kingsley interjected. "Remember? It was a spare identical piece that Natasha had put in a work order for. There must be something there, since those satellite images of the ocean in that area looked like it was modified to conceal what really lies there."

"If we stay on board," Claude said, "we only have food rationed for about three days. Either way, we are screwed. At least Kinsley's idea has the possibility of us finding something, someone, or even land."

August 26, 2017

It had been decided that we were all going to abandon the S.S. *Forager*. We embarked on two lifeboats. One held Kingsley, Claude, and Mark. The other had Francesca, Craig, me, and a very weak Ted bundled up in several blankets. We had brought all of the food from the ship, as well as the radios, in the off chance that they would start functioning again. The full moon gave some light over the dark, black water. It was winter in this part of the hemisphere, and at night it was very cold. We brought blankets and jackets to keep warm for our journey. We rowed our way through the calm ocean. Since any GPS technology had been depleted of power, we only had a compass to rely on to guide us in the right direction of the coordinates. We had no way of gauging what ten miles of travel would look or feel like. Our only hope was that we would see something interesting that would tell us we had found what we were looking for. Kingsley seemed confident in the direction he was taking us as he led our journey.

Hours and hours passed, and we did not see much ahead of us. It was so dark that if there was something in the distance, we would not be able to make it out until we were a few feet away, since the black sky and the endless ocean married together seamlessly. I was very thankful that the waters were calm. Our lifeboats were not that big, and a storm like the one we had experienced a few days before would have capsized us in an instant. Craig was shivering. I gave him an extra blanket to wrap himself with. He coughed, and fog escaped his mouth.

"Do you think Mallory is near?" he asked Francesca and me. "I want to say I feel her presence, but maybe that's just wishful thinking."

"I don't know what to expect," Francesca said sadly. "I don't see anything ahead. I don't even know how far we've traveled, or if we'll be able to find the ship again. To be honest, I'm quite turned around. I don't know what's north, south, west, or east."

"Kingsley seems to know the right direction," I said. "He has a compass and is taking us east. I imagine at sunrise, we'll be where we need to be."

"Or where we think we need to be," Francesca said with a hint of uncertainty in her tone. "I'm starting to think we got this all wrong. Maybe there is no reason why the satellite was hovering over this area the night PA 619 disappeared."

"It wasn't only that night," I said. "As of recent months, the satellite was orbiting over this location from space. There has to be some connection. I feel it in my bones. Or maybe that's just the cold night seeping into my skin." *Or maybe it's my body continuing to die from the cancer*, I thought morbidly.

Craig handled rowing the boat for the earlier part of the morning. I had fallen asleep for about two hours when I was awoken by the orange glow of the sunrise. I looked around and did a double take. There was land. It looked like a large island. I could only see trees, a few hills, and a very large empty beach.

"Kinglsey and I didn't want to wake anyone just yet," Craig said when he saw the look of surprise in my eyes.

"What?" Francesca yawned and rubbed her eyes in disbelief when she saw that there was an island a few hundred yards away. "Oh my God! There really is land here! TOM hid this place from the world!"

Kingsley smiled and winked at me. He had a smug I-told-you-so look on his face. Then he said, "Aren't you glad you decided to take a risk and set sail on these lifeboats?"

"It looks uninhabited," I said.

Claude and Mark had woken up too. Claude nearly yelled in joy. I could feel his excitement coursing through his veins. It seemed like ages ago that we were trying to find out sensitive information inside the corporate offices of Zyphone. And now, a few months later, we were on the verge of some kind of discovery because of that information. For a moment, I thought there could be a chance that the island was uninhabited. Then, Kingsley maneuvered us to a side of the island that looked much more flat, and we saw it for the first time.

"Holy crap!" Francesca clapped her hands to her mouth.

On one side of the island was a large, dark gray pavement with white stripes painted on it. There were two antennas on each side of the pavement with blinking red lights. It was the edge of a landing strip.

"Airplanes are meant to land on this island!" Claude squealed with excitement. "That's an airstrip!"

"My Mallory could be here!" Craig began to cry with joy.

"We need to be cautious," I spoke up. "TOM is a dangerous and powerful group. We can't just wash up onto this island and expect a friendly greeting."

"It looks abandoned though," Mark said. "What if nobody is home?"

"What if they already know we are here?" Francesca added. "We know that there's a Zyphone satellite watching over this island. We might have eyes on us already. I mean, isn't it strange that our ship's generator went out? What if they somehow managed to power us down because we came too close to the island?"

"I wouldn't put it past them," Claude agreed. "You might be right about that."

I could not shake off the foreboding feeling that we were being watched as we rowed both of the lifeboats onto the beach near the runway. Once we hit the sand, Craig and I jumped off and began to pull it onto the shore. Kingsley and Claude had done the same for their boat. Once all of us were on the sand, we cheered as quietly as possible, so our voices would not carry over the island.

"Do you think we should hide our lifeboats?" Mark suggested. "Just in case someone sees them?"

"I see some bushes over there!" Craig pointed to some shrubbery that was surrounding a few palm trees a few yards away. Kingsley and Claude lifted an unconscious Ted out of the lifeboat and laid him on the beach before they dragged their boat to the bushes. Craig and I did the same with the boat we had sailed on. Once our lifeboats were hidden from view, we walked back to the shore to Ted's side.

"His breathing is slowing down," Francesca said, kneeling over him and feeling his pale face.

"Let's hide his body," Kingsley said. "I don't think there's any hope for him to survive."

"We need to find someone on this island who can give him medical attention," Mark added.

"So you want to walk up to someone from TOM?" Kingsley said sarcastically. "They'll kill us instantly. Let's leave him hidden in one of the lifeboats."

I did not feel comfortable leaving Ted inside the lifeboat, but it was hidden out of view. I knew he would be safer there regardless. Carrying him around would slow us down, and it appeared as though he was in a deep sleep. Kingsley lifted Ted's limp body effortlessly and took him over to the shrubs. Francesca pulled out a video camera from her backpack and started filming the runway.

"What are you doing?" Craig asked.

"Evidence," she said with a grin. "These creeps are going down. If we find something big, the world will need to know the truth. It's possible that PA 619 landed here over a year ago."

Kingsley returned to our group and looked at Francesca apprehensively while she filmed the runway, but did not say anything.

"Let's follow the airstrip," Claude suggested.

"We should stay off the path," I suggested. "I don't want to be in plain sight."

"We could walk along the edge of the forest," Craig chimed in. There was a forest on the island. It was very green, which meant it rained consistently. I was hesitant to go near it because we were unsure of what kind of animal life was on the island. The forest appeared to be untouched by man. The only thing unnatural on the island that we had seen thus far was the runway. After careful deliberation, we walked towards the forest with Kingsley and Claude in the lead, since they both had guns that they had taken from the S.S. *Forager*.

We walked through the edge of the forest while not straying too deep into it. The only signs of wildlife we saw were a few birds skimming the treetops. The runway appeared to go on for miles, which helped confirm, in my mind at least, that a Boeing 787 could have landed on this island. It was hard to gauge how big the island was, but I guessed it might have been two to three miles wide. My stomach began to growl. We only had food rations for about three days. It was mainly freeze-dried fruit. If the island was empty, we would starve to death unless we could fish or hunt for something. The other option would be to steal from any human inhabitants on the island, but that would most likely mean they were members of The Omniscient Minds. I could not see how this mission would end with us escaping back to Australia alive. My only hope was that someone would realize our ship had gone off radar, and they would come looking for it. Even though it was ten miles away, it was still close enough for anyone flying over to find this island.

After an hour of hiking through the edge of the forest, we found the end of the runway. It led directly to an airplane hangar. My jaw dropped in awe. *It's inside there*, I thought. The hangar was large enough to hold a 787. It was tall and wide and painted white. Kingsley turned back to our group and began directing us with a plan.

"Let's have three of us stay behind and the other three head to the hangar," Kingsley suggested. "That way, if something happens, we have others in reserve who can come to our aid."

"Who goes and who stays?" I asked.

"Claude and I should go," Kingsley said. "And since you've been a big part of helping us find this place, you should too, Patrick."

It was decided. Claude, Kingsley, and I were going to walk over to the hangar to investigate. Francesca, Craig, and Mark were to stay behind and hide in the forest. Francesca gave me a kiss and a tight embrace as we said our goodbyes before heading out into the open. She handed me her video camera.

"Take video of anything and everything you see," she ordered me. Then she kissed me on the lips once more.

I let Kingsley and Claude lead the way to the hangar since they both had guns. I walked carefully behind them while scanning the area for any form of life, movement, or anything out of the ordinary. Truth be told, the entire island was anything but ordinary. None of us said anything on the walk over to the hangar. It was several hundred yards away from the forest, but it felt like several miles. I felt my heart beating fast. It was as if I could feel the presence of the airplane. Then I began to think about the passengers. Since we knew Joseph Conroy was alive, that meant there were 240 people left who had been on the airplane. Would we find them alive and well? It had been over a year since the airplane disappeared. If they were alive, how were they being kept alive, and in what conditions would we find them, if we did come across them? It was also possible that none of them were alive. This brought me great sadness. I had no doubt in my mind that we were about to find PA 619, but everything felt so surreal. I pinched myself a few times to make sure I was not dreaming.

"Almost there," Kingsley muttered quietly when we were about fifty feet away from the hangar's large door. Kingsley fidgeted with the jacket he was wearing and pulled out his gun. The hangar appeared much larger the closer we got to it. The size of the hangar could house a Boeing 787 easily. We approached with caution. It was eerily quiet on the island except for the sound of the breeze brushing against the trees in the distance. I looked over at the forest, and I could see Francesca, Craig, and Mark anxiously watching us as we approached the main door of the hangar. Kingsley reached for the handle, which had a large lock and bolt on it.

"Not surprised," he muttered. "It's locked."

"Maybe you can shoot it open?" I suggested.

"The bullet will ricochet," Kingsley said. "That would be a stupid idea. We need to find something to break it open somehow."

I turned on Francesca's camera and started filming the hangar. There were no markings or signs on it. I walked around the entire structure in hopes of finding another entrance; there was none. Claude cursed under his breath as he attempted to hit the lock with a branch he'd found nearby. More damage was done to the tree branch than to the lock. I continued to film in the back of the hangar. Behind it, there was more forest and a hill. I thought it would be a brilliant idea to hike to the top, as we could see more of the island. I walked back to the front and found Kingsley and Claude brainstorming ideas to break down the door.

"It's made of really strong metal," Claude said. "They must have shipped materials to this island to build it."

"Maybe we can climb to the top of the hill behind the hangar," I suggested. "We might be able to see if there's anything or anyone on this island. It's possible that the island is uninhabited right now. Maybe the only manmade things here are this runway and hangar. Perhaps the rest of the island is only trees and sand.

"Shhh!" Kingsley urged.

I immediately pulled up Francesca's camera and started recording instinctively. We could hear the sound of footsteps coming from behind the hangar, where I had been only a few minutes prior. Claude grabbed my arm and led me to the west side of the hangar to hide out of sight from the main entrance. Kingsley did not move. Once we were on the side of the building, I peered over the edge. Kingsley had his gun drawn and was facing the east side of the building where the noise had come from. After a few tense seconds, the source of the noise revealed itself. I had the camera pointed at a man in a blue jumpsuit. He had on round glasses and sported a long, silver beard. He looked like he was in his sixties.

"Oh my God!" Claude gasped quietly into my ear. "It's a member of TOM!"

There was a quick exchange of gunfire between Kingsley and the man.

I almost dropped the camera in shock. The sound echoed off the hangar. Kingsley fell onto the ground silently, hitting his head on the pavement. His body was lifeless on the pavement of the runway. The man in the jumpsuit looked over to where Claude and I were peering through, and he started to run at us with his gun drawn. I backed away quickly and started to run towards the forest. I heard another gunshot behind me and turned around.

"I got him!" Claude yelled. "Come back, Patrick!"

I stopped in my tracks and looked over. Claude had disappeared from view and walked over to the front of the hangar. I followed suit and found him kneeling over the lifeless body of the man in the blue jumpsuit. He was laying facedown in a pool of his own blood. I examined his jumpsuit. There were no patches or markings of any kind. It was just like the jumpsuit the men who had attacked me on the rooftop of Phoenix Airlines were wearing. I could hear rushed footsteps in the distance. Both Claude and I jumped to our feet in shock. It turned out to be Francesca, Craig, and Mark, running towards us with looks of fear on their faces.

"Are you okay?" Francesca cried.

"Yeah, we're fine," I told her as she rushed to me and hugged me. "One of the members of TOM came out of nowhere and shot Kingsley. Claude was able to take him down."

Craig and Mark examined the dead man, while Claude went to check on Kingsley. Claude returned with Kingsley's gun after a minute of examining his body. He was visibly upset about what happened to Kingsley, but he was also determined to power through, as we had come so far. He communicated this to me through the expression on his face. Mark found a set of keys in the pocket of the man in the blue jumpsuit. He pulled it out with a look of excitement that took our attention away from Kingsley's body.

"Something tells me we may need these," he said, holding up the keys for us to see. I reached for them and examined them carefully. There were three keys attached to a metal keychain that held them together. I felt my hands shake as I clenched them tightly in my fist.

"One of these three keys must open this hangar," I said. I started to cough slightly as I finally caught my breath from the tense few minutes I had just experienced. My adrenaline had subsided, and I felt lightheaded as I came to the realization of what I should do next.

"You should do the honors," Claude said. "After all, there should have been 242 people on that airplane. Not 241."

I looked over at Francesca, who had her arm around Craig. Craig looked like he was on the verge of tears. He was wringing his hands nervously and looking at me intently.

"Do it," he uttered almost inaudibly. Claude shook his head in agreement while holding one gun in his left hand and the other in his right.

"Okay," I said, taking a deep breath. I could not remember ever feeling this nervous, excited, and terrified at the same time. It was as if the last year of my life had been leading up to this moment. The prospect of finding the airplane was thrilling.

"Wait!" Francesca said. "Pass me my camera."

I handed Francesca her video camera, and she quickly began to record the moment. "I want to film you opening it," she said while following behind me. "I think we're about to make history."

I inched closer to the hangar and reached for the first key to try. It did not fit into the keyhole of the lock. Then I tried the second one. It went in, but it did not budge as I tried to turn it left and right. There was one key left. *This is it*, I thought. Everything we had been through had led up to this moment. I closed my eyes and recalled the memory of when I slipped onto the floor over spilled soda at the international terminal of LAX. I remembered the last time I saw Jim King in the conference room of Phoenix Airlines. It was as if so many memories of the last year decided to come racing into my mind at that point. I thought about the moment I had learned I had cancer and wondered if I would die before learning the truth about how PA 619 had disappeared and where it had ended up. I could feel the excited energy from my friends behind me. I could feel their gazes as I reached for the final key and inserted into the keyhole.

"Here goes," I said, turning the key. There was a click and the lock opened up, and I was able to pull it out of the bolt. "Can you guys help me? The door looks heavy. Let's open this up!"

Claude and Mark walked up behind me and helped me pull at the door. It was really heavy and did not budge. Craig walked up to examine the bolt and pointed at a red button I had not noticed before. He pressed it instinctively, and we heard the sound of a machine pulling a chain. The door began to slide open to the right via a mechanical pulley system.

All five of us gasped at the exact same time as what was hidden behind the door was revealed. There was only one object inside. It was the Boeing 787. Phoenix Airlines 619 was parked and in one piece, standing in all its silver metallic glory with the Phoenix bird logo staring me straight in the eyes. It looked as though it had been untouched for a long time. At long last, it had been found. This was its final resting place. It was not at the bottom of the ocean like the rest of the world was led to believe. Both its wings were intact, confirming that the flaperon that had been found did not belong to the actual airplane. Craig fell to his knees and began to cry. I felt a stream of tears pouring down my face as well. There were chills running up and down my arms. Claude looked speechless. His eyes were wide with shock and awe. Mark was grinning with excitement, and Francesca was going back and forth from filming our reactions to zooming in on the airplane. She ran into the hangar to get a closer shot. I started to follow her.

"I can't believe it's here!" I said as I walked up to the airplane and touched one of the tires. I felt that by touching it, it confirmed that this was all real, and I was not having some sort of dream or hallucination. The magnificent airplane was standing before us.

"We need the flight recorder," Francesca said. "The video footage and the recorder will be enough. We can take it to authorities back in Australia, and they can send a team back here to retrieve the airplane."

"The only problem is," Claude said, "even if we row back to the S.S. *Forager*, there is no power on the ship. We're stranded. More men in blue jumpsuits must inhabit this island. They'll be hostile. We'll need to see if they have a means of transportation we can steal."

"Hey, there's a ladder up against the wall!" Craig shouted. He ran to fetch it. Once he returned, he propped it up by the door near the cockpit. He ran up the ladder hastily and turned the handle of the airplane door. Surprisingly, it opened with ease.

"It's unlocked!" Craig said. He walked into the airplane. I followed behind him because I knew where to look for the black box. When I was on the airplane, I looked into the main cabin. Craig walked over to the seat his daughter had been assigned.

"Nothing," he said, after searching both her seat and the luggage compartment above it. "It looks like the plane has been stripped of luggage or any sign that passengers were ever on board. It looks clean and unused. Maybe they deplaned?"

I was relieved there were no dead bodies. I'd had a fear that we were about to encounter the decaying bodies of the passengers, but that was not the case. I took a peek into the cockpit and found that it was also empty. There was no sign of a struggle in the cockpit, or anywhere else on the plane, for that matter. I walked to the back of the plane; that was where the flight data recorder was located on that exact Phoenix Airlines model. The data recorders were inside a vault that was at the back of the airplane. The vaults were made of fireproof casing and were not common in other airplane models of other airline companies. There was a master code for the vault that worked for all the vaults across the Phoenix Airlines fleet. I would know, since I had helped design this model. I entered the code on the keypad of the vault. The door swung open, and I let out a groan. The black box had been taken out.

"Dammit," I said out loud.

Craig and I climbed back down the ladder and met back with the others.

"Someone took the black box out," I said. "They are stored in a fireproof safe at the tail of the airplane, but it's missing. We might have found the airplane, but we still don't have an answer as to what happened that night when it was diverted off course. We do know it was intentional, but now only half the mystery is solved. Why was it brought here?"

"We also need to know what happened to the passengers," Craig said. "And my Mallory."

I looked back at PA 619. It was the most famous airplane in the world, and also the greatest mystery in the history of aviation. Yet, it still held more mysteries. If only the cabin walls could talk and tell us the story of what happened on July 14, 2016.

"Well," I added, "we found the airplane. That's a big feat. I think our next plan should be to head up to the hill behind this hangar. I think that's where that man in the blue jumpsuit came from. We'll have to be very careful."

"Let's go then," Claude said with determination. He passed me Kingsley's gun, and then we all walked out of the hangar. Once we were outside, Francesca gasped.

"Where's Kingsley's body?"

Kingsley's body had been on the runway prior to us entering the hangar. It was now gone, and there was no trace of the blood on the pavement that would have resulted from an exit wound.

27

Everyone stood in stunned silence. I did not know what to make of the strange disappearance of Kingsley's body. Did someone take his body while we were exploring the interior of PA 619? Was Kingsley even dead? I looked around the hangar for a trace as to where his body might have disappeared. There was no blood. As I made my way to the back of the hangar, I found something to confirm that Kingsley might not have been killed. There was a set of footprints on the sand leading up the forest and hill before me. It was only one set, which meant he might have walked off alone. I did not understand why he had not entered the hangar instead. The missing airplane was in there. Francesca came running to my side, and Craig, Claude, and Mark joined us shortly after.

"I think he ran up the hill through the forest ahead," I told them. "There are footprints in the sand. They may belong to him."

"I don't understand," Claude said, scratching his head in frustration. "I saw him get shot in the stomach. There's no sign of blood either. How do you explain that?"

"He worked in security," Francesca said. "My journalistic instincts are telling me that he could have been wearing a bulletproof vest."

"No way!" Craig added. "Why would he pretend to be dead and then wander off while we were opening the hangar?"

"He's got it in for the Killingtons," Claude said. "That's why he offered to help me keep a watchful eye at Phoenix. He used to work with Jackson Killington ages ago. I think he wants to take matters into his own hands because of the Killington connection to TOM. I would not have let him run off without us. He'll be in danger. We may be greatly outnumbered on this island."

"So much for going in discreetly," Francesca groaned.

"Should we venture forward then?" Mark asked us. I nodded in agreement and put Kingsley's gun in my jacket pocket.

"Let's go," I said.

We made our way into the forest by following the tracks left behind. Once we got into the coverage of the trees, we were unable to find the footprints. My instinct was to head straight forward. The terrain was a bit rough. None of us were prepared for a hike. Mark was the only one wearing shoes that were ideal for the climb up the hill. I started to cough with every step up the incline of the hill. It was also humid, so most of us were sweating. My perspiration was causing my clothing to stick to me. I pulled out a bottle of water from my backpack to satisfy my thirst. Francesca was preoccupied filming parts of the forest, determined to get her story.

"I don't know how much further I can go," Claude was breathing heavily. "I'm much older than all of you."

"It looks like there is a flat surface a few yards away," I said, pointing at what appeared to be a nice break in the steep incline of the hill. "Why don't we take a break?" Everyone nodded in agreement. We got to a small plateau on the hill and were surprised to find a log cabin. There was classical music playing eerily inside.

"Oh my goodness," Francesca said, pointing her camera in the direction of the small cabin. "What if someone is in there? Do you hear that music?"

"Maybe Kingsley is," Claude said hopefully. He then proceeded to the cabin door with caution. He lifted his hand and clenched his fist, preparing to knock on the door.

"Wait!" I said as quietly as possible to Claude. "We can't just knock on the door. Let's peer into the window."

Claude and I walked over to the front-facing window. The music grew louder with every step we took closer to the cabin. The building looked empty inside. I gestured for the rest of the group to join us. Once they did, I opened the door with them by my side. It had been left unlocked. I walked inside to find an empty cabin that looked as though it had been recently inhabited. There was an old record player playing the classical music. There were dirty dishes left in the sink, as if someone had just finished a meal. There were no signs of life inside. It was a one-room cabin that was decorated as though we had gone back in time to the 60s. The kitchen, living room, and sleeping area were shared in the same open space. The furniture looked antique and dated. There was a wardrobe on one corner of the building. I walked over to it and opened it.

"Whoa!" I said loudly. I got chills up my arms. There were ten blue jumpsuits hanging inside and a pair of black shoes in the bottom of the wardrobe. "Maybe that guy Claude shot by the hangar lived here."

Claude walked over to stand beside me. "Well, I guess we don't have to worry about someone coming back home."

"What if," Francesca said, "someone else on the island realizes he's missing?"

"It appears as though only one person lived here," Craig said. "The bed is twin size, with only room for one adult to sleep comfortably. The couch is small too, but it doesn't look like it's used for sleeping."

I kept getting a foreboding feeling that we were being watched. It was paranoia at its best. Were there others like the man in the jumpsuit who tried to kill us? I was positive there had to be, but the question was, where were they?

"This eerie emptiness is giving me the creeps," Mark said. "The energy feels so strange here."

I decided to turn off the record player, because the cheerful melody was giving me chills and anxiety. Then, I began to ponder about where the electricity to run the record player was coming from. There was even a gas stove, so there had to be both gas and power being supplied to the empty cabin.

"I agree with what Mark said. This place is eerie," Craig added. "But I really hope my Mallory is here and safe on this island."

"The airplane was emptied out," I said. "Luggage was definitely removed. I was hoping I could find mine. My favorite gold watch was in my checked bag." I looked down at my wrist, which had been empty since the day I'd missed my flight. I'd never purchased another watch to replace it. Like most people nowadays, I used my smartphone to tell the time. My gold Rolex was very valuable, but nothing could put a price on learning the truth about what had happened. We had found the airplane. It had never crashed into the ocean as the media presumed. Someone had landed it on this island. Now the questions I needed answers to were who and why.

"Let's do some digging around," Francesca said. "Maybe we can find something that'll give us more information about this island."

I rummaged through a chest that was at the foot of the twin-sized bed. I found a set of what looked like schoolbooks and random fiction novels. There were a few spiral notebooks as well. Most of them had blank pages, but one of them appeared to be a log of some sort. The cover of it had the text "TOM Island Hangar Security" written in pen across the top. I opened it up and found a list of dates and names I did not recognize. It appeared to be a log of whoever was stationed to keep watch on the hangar at the foot of the hill we were on.

"This cabin must be for whoever is assigned to watch over the hangar," I said, passing Claude the notebook. He took it and examined it closely.

"The last log," Claude said, "has today's date. August 26. The name of the person stationed here was named Bill. There's no last name."

Francesca started to film Claude looking through the notebook. "I guess TOM assigns one person to stay here and keep watch on the hangar." She then walked over to the window and continued, "You can see the hangar clearly visible from this window. This Bill guy must have seen us walking to it."

"I don't like this place one bit," Craig complained.

"So, this place is called TOM Island," Claude deduced while examining the cover of the notebook I had handed to him. "At least we know, without a doubt, that TOM is the culprit in this Flight 619 fiasco."

"As if finding the airplane wasn't enough to confirm that," I joked with him. He gave me a serious stare, but said nothing more and continued to rummage through the chest for anything else. "There are schoolbooks here. Do you think there's a school on this island?"

"That is interesting," Francesca said, zooming her camera in on an algebra book that Claude was examining.

I continued to do a sweep of the cabin. I looked through the cabinets in the kitchen area, but found only pots, pans, cups, and utensils. There was an old-fashioned looking refrigerator. I opened it up and found the most generic looking packages inside. There was a tall white cartoon that had the word "Milk" in black printed text, and a few other white boxes with labels such as "Meat," "Chicken," "Vegetables," "Eggs," and "Yogurt." It was the strangest thing. They were prepackaged foods, with some products having expiration dates that did not expire for at least five more years. There was no way these foods were organic by any means. Craig reached for the "Chicken" carton and opened it up. There were slices of chicken breast that he began to pass around for us to eat. We each grabbed a slice and ate it. It was not until then that I realized how hungry I was. My stomach grumbled in gratitude.

"We can prolong our rations by eating some of their food," Craig said with urgency. "It doesn't taste bad at all. It's pretty good."

"It looks processed," Francesca said with disgust, but she obliged and ate it, knowing that we were limited on food options.

"Look at this painting!" Mark said, pointing to one side of the cabin. There was a small portrait hanging on the wall with a gold ornate frame. The painting was of a sun rising over the ocean with a human eye in the center of the sun. "What the heck is this?"

"It looks like something pagan," Francesca said. "Maybe it's the depiction of a sun god?"

"Are we suggesting that TOM is some kind of cult?" Craig added sarcastically.

"Close enough," Claude agreed. "They *are* pretty much a cult."

I clasped my hands over my mouth when I realized what I was looking at. "I've seen a painting like this before. However, the one I saw was much larger, and it was in Royce's office at the Phoenix Airlines headquarters."

"Oh, I've seen that painting too!" Mark chimed in. "It now hangs behind Natasha's desk in her new office."

"Well," Claude chimed in, "if that's not a connection to Phoenix, then I don't know what is. You should get footage of this, Francesca. If anything, it's evidence of Natasha's ties to this place."

"Already on it," Francesca said excitedly, walking up to the painting with her camera at the ready.

"What is this place?" I said out loud, more to myself than to any of my friends.

"Some kind of otherworldly place," Claude said. "Most of it seems untouched by the modern world."

The classical music began to play again, making us all jump. Craig had turned the record player back on. "I recognize this music. It's Beethoven. This is a beautiful piece. It's called 'Moonlight Sonata.' I used to play it on the piano when I was younger."

"Craig!" Francesca snapped. "You startled us. Turn that off. I don't want the noise to carry up the hill."

"Well, it was already playing when we got here," Craig said matter-of-factly.

Francesca rolled her eyes and walked over to the record player and unplugged it from the wall. She then turned to us and said, "Should we continue the hike up to the top of the hill?"

"Yeah," I replied. "Let's get going. The sun sets in a few hours. I don't want to hike up this hill in the dark."

We made our way outside and back into the humidity of the island's climate. I looked back down the hill at the hangar and empty runway. The bushes where we'd left Ted to rest were too far to make out. I hoped he was fine, but his condition had been very weak when we left him. I took hold of Francesca's hand, and we began our climb up the sloping hill through the forest.

"Are you okay?" Francesca whispered into my ear. "You look a bit ill."

The truth was, I had not taken my medication for the evening yet, so I was feeling sluggish from my condition. I gave her a tight squeeze and replied, "I'm fine. I'm very tired. This day has taken a toll on me. I've wanted closure on this mystery for so long, and we've already found PA 619. Now I want to know the why, and how it arrived on this island."

"Do you think we'll even find these answers?" Mark had been eavesdropping and chimed into our conversation. "Oh my God—watch out!"

Mark's sudden yell of warning echoed into the forest, causing some birds to flutter away. He was pointing at a green snake slithering on the ground ahead of us. Francesca immediately let go of my hand and ran back down the hill in the opposite direction to put several feet between her and the snake. Claude opened his backpack and pulled out a hatchet. He swung it violently at the snake and beheaded it. Blood gushed out of the decapitated body. Craig nearly threw up at the sight of the mutilation.

"Ugh," he said, grabbing his stomach.

"It's dead," Claude told a very frightened and pale-looking Francesca. "It doesn't look poisonous either. We may encounter more critters as we delve deeper into this forest. Let's keep an eye out. Good thing you spotted it, Mark."

Francesca reached for my hand again, and we began walking back up the hill. I pulled out my smartphone absentmindedly to check the time. It was 5:00 PM. The battery was at four percent, and the top part of the screen read "No Service." We were so disconnected from the modern world that I felt there would be no escaping the island. We were trapped. Francesca saw me glancing at my smartphone, and gave me a look that showed she had the same concern. I knew her so well that at times we only had to look at each other to communicate our feelings, without needing to utter the words we had been thinking.

"There's still no trace of footprints," Claude said. "Kingsley probably took another route. I do hope he's okay and doesn't try anything stupid. He's unarmed. We don't know what else The Omniscient Minds are hiding out here." Claude found a branch on the ground and picked it up to use as a cane. I could see the look of fatigue growing more evident on his face. Francesca looked over at Craig, who appeared to be deep in thought. She put her arm on his shoulder.

"I hope we find Mallory," she said.

"Me too," he replied.

"Maybe we'll even find Jim, Dylan, and Charles," I added with hope.

"Shh!" Claude said suddenly, making us all stop dead in our tracks. "I hear something in the distance." There was a sound of crunching leaves and branches. It sounded as if someone was walking in our direction. The sound was faint at first, but grew louder with every passing second. Claude grabbed my arm and whispered, "Hurry—let's hide behind those trees."

The five of us found a large tree to hide behind. We waited a few tense minutes for the source of the sound to reveal itself. Francesca let out an audible gasp when a man with dark brown skin appeared. He was wearing the familiar blue jumpsuit, like the man who had attacked us at the hangar. He had on a pair of large headphones connected to a very old-school looking Walkman cassette player. He was bouncing his head along to the beat, and then he started humming the tune, which echoed through the forest. The man was oblivious to us.

Claude whispered into my ear, "This guy might be next to take a lookout shift at the cabin. When he discovers his pal isn't there, it could raise alarm."

"What should we do?" I asked with panic.

"Silence him," Claude said, brandishing his gun at his side.

"We can't just kill this man!" Francesca said with a shrill cry. "He hasn't attacked us."

"His friend did not hesitate to try and kill us," Claude said matter-of-factly. He took the safety lock off his gun and began to approach the man from behind. He was completely unaware of Claude closing in on him with his gun held up and pointed to the back of his head.

I began to worry. I whispered loudly, "The gunshot will make a loud sound!" Claude ignored me and tiptoed stealthily toward the man, who could not hear Claude's footsteps over the crunching of leaves on the ground.

Francesca bent down beside me and picked up a large rock.

"What are you doing?" I asked her.

She gave me an inquisitive look and replied, "Let's knock him out. We shouldn't kill an innocent man!"

"We don't know if he's innocent," Craig said. "He's obviously a member of TOM."

Claude reached for the trigger almost at the exact same time as the man turned around. He had a look of horror and shock at the surprise appearance of Claude. Then his eyes quickly darted to the direction of Francesca, Craig, Mark, and me. They widened in horror at the sight of us. The man pulled out a radio walkie-talkie in an attempt to call for help.

"Drop the radio," Claude said. "Or I'll shoot." The man dropped the radio instantly and started shaking violently. Claude walked over to him and asked, "What is your name?"

"R-r-rick," he stuttered with anxiety. "Wh-who are you? I've never seen you—or any of them—ever. Did you come from the outside world?"

Francesca and I turned to give each other a curious look. She reached for her camera and began recording the man's exchange with Claude.

"Outside world?" Claude questioned Rick. "What do you mean by 'outside world?'"

"I…" Rick struggled for words. "I…well…the world outside this island. I've never been, but we've been informed about it."

"You've never been?" Claude sounded intrigued. "How have you never been off this island?"

"This is my home," Rick said. "I was born here. I work as Keeper of the Hangar. That is my job title. We rotate with fellow islanders. It is my job to make sure that the hangar remains sealed and safe."

"Are you part of The Omniscient Minds?" Claude continued his interrogation. The man scratched his short black hair and looked really nervous. He was eyeing Claude's clothing as though it looked foreign to him.

"No," he replied. "I'm just a worker. Our masters are part of that group. Only members of TOM can come and go as they please. For those of us born here, we must follow the duties assigned to us to keep order on the island when they are away."

I walked up to Claude, startling Rick by doing so. Francesca, Craig, and Mark followed suit and flanked my side. Rick was twitching nervously and squinting his eyes as if half expecting to be hit in the face.

"So, you're not part of TOM then?" he asked us. "None of you?"

"Um, no," I said. "Where are the members of TOM right now?"

Rick looked up at the sky then back to me. He waited a few seconds before replying nervously. "They are expected to arrive tonight via sky rider."

"What's a sky rider?" I asked.

"The machine with wings," he responded. "Wings like a bird, only much, much larger."

"Do you mean an airplane?" Mark stepped in.

"Oh," Rick said with embarrassment. "Yes, I think some of the masters call them that at times. The islanders call them sky riders. I've never been on one. We are not allowed. We've been told it requires training to travel by air."

Speaking to Rick felt like speaking to a Martian. It was evident that his knowledge of the world beyond this island was limited. He appeared harmless and more afraid of us than we were of him. I felt pity for him. I could not imagine being born on an island and never leaving it. Living on a small piece of land for your whole life seemed so unfathomable to me.

"Are you going to kill me?" Rick asked with tears pouring from his eyes. Claude gave him a look of sympathy and put his gun away after assessing he was not dangerous.

"No," Claude said. "But we need some help getting off the island. We also can't have the *masters* know that we are here. Can you keep a secret?"

"Secrets are against island law," Rick said. "I would be ousted from my home."

"We can help you," Francesca added. "We can help you leave this place."

"But this is my home," Rick said. "My family lives here too. I have nowhere else to go."

"If you help us," Claude said seriously, "we will give you a better life. The outside world offers so much more space. We need to know about the airpl—sky rider inside that hangar. How did it arrive here and what happened to the people on it?"

Rick took turns looking into each of our eyes, as if unsure whom to make eye contact with when he answered. He rested his eyes on me and said, "How do you know what is inside? Did you open the hangar?" I nodded yes, and he looked like he wanted to cry. "I'm going to be ousted. That sky rider is supposed to be kept hidden and locked away."

"Where are your masters?" Claude asked.

"They arrive tonight, as I stated before," Rick said. "You shouldn't be here. You must leave the island. If you promise not to hurt me or let them know you've opened the hangar, I can help you get off this island."

Claude looked at Francesca's video camera and shifted uncomfortably. "We can keep you safe," Claude said. "First, we need some help. One of our friends is down by the beach where the runway ends. He is very ill.

Do you have any kind of medication? He fell ill while on board our ship. We're not sure what he has, but several of our crewmembers got sick and died on board. Our ship's power went out about ten miles away. We'll need to travel back to our land somehow."

"Sick, you say?" Rick said. "You arrived on water rider? The masters also call it a 'ship.' The island is protected so that no vessels can come through. There's an electromagnetic pulse around the island that the masters set up. It shuts down electricity and power of anything coming within a certain distance. As for the illness, we do not have access to medications. The masters keep those locked away. We are only allowed treatments if our conditions are serious."

"Is there a boat, or water rider, if you will, that we can use to get off the island?" Mark asked.

"There are no water riders on the island," Rick said. "But we have a water sky rider. It's a sky rider that uses the ocean to land, rather than the runway by the hangar below the hill. That sky rider is on the opposite side of the island and locked away inside a smaller hangar."

"That's our ticket out!" I said excitedly, with hope that we might have found an escape route from the island.

"I have a question," Craig spoke up to Rick. "Do you know if a girl named Mallory Cooper is on this island? She would have been on that sky rider that landed here. I'm speaking about the one in the hangar at the bottom of the hill. There were 241 people on it. One of them was my daughter, Mallory. "

Rick looked at Craig with a nervous twitch. He shrugged and said, "I do not know any of their names, but they live on this island."

28

Craig put his hands together in the form of a prayer. He looked up to the sky and mouthed "Thank you." He began to cry silent tears of joy. I felt chills at Rick's words. They were *alive*. He'd confirmed it. Jim, Dylan, and Charles might not have been lost after all. Francesca was rummaging through her camera bag for a freshly charged battery and an extra memory card. She had a look of excitement. The energy from my friends was very strong and positive. The passengers of PA 619 were alive and living on this island. They had been imprisoned here for over a year. It was hard to believe Rick's words.

"So they are alive and well?" Craig asked happily.

"They are alive," Rick said. "They are well. They are healthy. They live separately from us islanders. They are housed underground on the other side of the hill."

"Can you take us to them?" I asked.

"It will put me in danger," Rick said. "We must go quietly. It is currently Feeding Time for my fellow islanders. They will be at the Dining Hall right now having dinner. Your people, the outsiders as we call them, never come out. They stay below in their bunker. The masters have made sure of it. They are spending today doing Schooling Time. They have a session once a week where they are to study in an educational environment. It will not be wise to disrupt their learning, but if this is what you wish, then I can take you there. I want no part in your plans, and you must promise me that you will never give my name away to the masters. My life and the life of my family unit depend on it. I have a wife and two children—a boy and a girl."

"We will make sure no harm comes to you," Claude assured Rick while pulling out his gun to show it to him. "I can protect you with this."

Rick looked at the gun nervously and replied, "Follow me up the hill."

By the time we arrived on top of the hill, most of my team was sore and out of breath. Rick looked unfazed by the steep climb. He appeared to be much more in shape than my group. There was still a lot of tree coverage on top of the hill. It had hidden the village we now found before our eyes.

"Wow," Francesca said excitedly, pulling out her camera.

"What is that?" Rick asked. "She keeps pulling out that object."

"Oh, it's…" I started, "to document memories."

Rick looked puzzled by my response, but appeared to lose interest in the camera. It was evident he had never seen one before. This island was so strange. However, the sight before us was even stranger. There were two rows of cabins. Each had a chimney where smoke was billowing. They were aligned in straight parallel rows, with a main dirt path in the middle of them.

"My people are eating in the Dining Hall at the end of this road," Rick informed us. "This is the Main Square—our town—our home. My house is the second one to the left."

"When the masters visit," Claude asked, "where do they stay?"

"In the castle," Rick said. "We are not allowed in the castle—ever."

"Where is this castle?" Mark asked. Rick gestured for us to follow him. We walked down the main path until we ended up at a log cabin building directly in front of us, the Dining Hall. There was a murmur of voices and the sound of plates and glasses clinking inside. Rick had us walk around the building. Behind the building was the edge of the hill. It sloped back down to more treetops and forest, but at the very bottom, near the beach, was a large gray building made out of concrete. It was a stone keep castle. It did not appear to be very large. There was a flag on top of one of the turrets that had the familiar sun with an eye rising over an ocean. A few feet away from the castle was a small hangar where the seaplane Rick had mentioned earlier was stored. I had never been to a stranger place in my life.

"I don't like this island one bit," Craig whispered to Francesca and me. Then he turned to Rick. "Where are the *outsiders*?"

"The bunker is just outside the entrance of the masters' castle," Rick said. "There is a stone surface sticking out of the sand on the beach. It has a door in it."

"I can just barely make it out," Francesca said. "But I see it down there. How do we open it? I assume it's locked, right?"

"Take this," Rick said, handing over a key to Francesca. "It will open the door. It is a master key. It will also unlock the hangar with the water sky rider."

"Thank you very much," I told him. "Will you come with us?"

"The masters arrive at some point tonight," Rick said. "I need to head back to my post to greet them. Please stay hidden and try to get out of here before sunset. They will be having dinner in the castle by nightfall."

"Can I ask for one more favor?" Claude asked. Rick nodded with hesitation. "As mentioned earlier, our friend Ted is hidden in shrubbery on the beach by the runway. If you can get him and keep him safe in your cabin, that would be greatly appreciated. Hide him from the masters."

"I'll do my best," Rick said. "I should be strong enough to carry one man. Please do not ever mention my help if you get caught."

"We won't," I assured him. "And we will find a way to help you all. I know you believe this place is home, but there is a far greater and vast world out there you are missing out on."

"I'll count on it, then," Rick said. "As long as it means safety for my family unit and me."

"It will," Claude said, reaching for Rick's hand and shaking it. Rick then set off through the Main Square and back down the hill. Claude and I peered around the corner of the building a few minutes later and saw several of the islanders walking back to their homes. All of the men, women, and children wore the exact same jumpsuits. There were no variations in the jumpsuit design by gender. There must have been about fifty islanders. None of them seemed to care to look back, so we had gone unnoticed as we stared in awe at them. It was like looking at an undiscovered species, except they were humans, and they had never seen the world beyond these oceans.

"All right," I said, after returning to the group with Francesca. "It's 6:05 PM. We may have about two or so hours of sunlight. It'll probably take us about twenty minutes to get to the castle. We should hurry down as fast as possible. It's not as steep on this side of the hill as the one we came up on. Ready?"

"Hell yes!" Craig said excitedly. "I can't wait to see my daughter."

The journey through the forest down the hill on the opposite side of the island was much quicker and easier than the one we had come up on. Other than a few mosquitos, we were not bothered by any kind of wildlife, and to Francesca's relief, there were no snakes. When we were a few feet from the edge of the forest, a strong pungent smell hit our noses. Craig immediately gagged and threw up. The rest of us held our noses in disgust.

"What the hell is that smell?" I cried.

"It smells like something died," Claude added.

There was a large hole that had been dug into the ground. The source of the smell was coming from what appeared to be a pit. Some of the dirt in the hole looked black and charred. When I got to the edge of it and looked down, I backed away instantly at the shock of what I'd seen. Francesca looked quickly out of curiosity and let out a cry of shock. There were pieces of bones and burnt bodies in the pit. It now looked more like a tomb that was the home to dozens of human bodies.

"Oh my God!" Craig cried. "Do you think it's the passengers?"

"There's less than 241 bodies," Claude said.

"It would be 240," I corrected him. "Remember, Joseph Conroy is alive."

"Right," Claude nodded.

"Who are these people?" Craig added.

"You mean," Mark said, "who *were* they?"

"Come on!" I demanded. "Let's get as far away from this smell as possible. It's disgusting."

Seeing that pit with dismembered and charred human remains did not feel like a good omen. We were racing against the sunlight before the "masters" were to land on the island. The stone keep castle before us looked hauntingly eerie with the red flag of the rising sun over the ocean waving lazily from one of the turrets. It felt like the eye in the middle of the sun on the flag was staring right at me, as a warning that we should not be there.

"There's the door to the bunker!" Francesca said, running over to it with her camera in hand.

We approached the stone foundation that stuck out of the sand about five inches. In the middle was a metal door with a handle. There was a keyhole and a lock on it. I pulled out the key that Rick had given us and inserted it into the lock. It turned with ease, and with a twist of the door handle, I was able to pull it open. There was a ladder that led down to a narrow entrance. Thankfully, flickering fluorescent lights made it possible for us to see all the way down.

"Who wants to go first?" I asked.

Craig seemed anxious to go, but I could tell he was nervous about the unknown that lay ahead. No one said anything, so I hoisted myself onto the ladder and began my descent. Claude followed shortly after, then Francesca, Mark, and Craig. Once I arrived at the ground of the bunker, there was a small concrete room with a brown door that led to another room. The rest of my team had arrived at my side, with Craig at the rear.

"I closed the door behind me," he said. "That way it doesn't stick out, in case any members of TOM show up. Oh, and don't worry—I double-checked. We're not locked in."

"Good thinking," I told him. I could see anticipation in Craig's eyes. We were close. I could feel it. He could feel it. He was anxiously playing with the zipper of his jacket, waiting for my direction.

"Okay then," I said, reaching for the door handle of the brown door. "Let's go through." I opened the door to find a long hallway that was lit by the same fluorescent lights as the entrance. Every step we took down the long hallway echoed off the walls.

"It looks like we are headed in the direction of the castle," Claude pointed out. "This bunker must actually be a basement."

"I think you're right," I replied.

My heart was racing. I kept thinking about what I wanted to ask Jim, Dylan, Charles, or any of the passengers, for that matter. The long walk felt like the final stretch of a yearlong stressful and tiring journey. Francesca was grabbing onto my hand behind me. I could feel her palms sweating nervously as we inched closer to the end of the hall, which had another door.

As soon as we arrived at the door, I turned the doorknob, and it opened into a much larger room. The ceiling was high above us. We were under the castle now. In that large room, there were several hundred empty beds spaced evenly across the entire room. At the foot of each bed was a tray with empty plates that had traces of food and empty cups. I looked over at Craig, and he looked horrified at the sight before us.

"What the hell," Craig said in shock. "What kind of conditions are they keeping them in? Where are they?"

"Do you hear that?" Francesca asked. "I hear music. Sounds like a classical symphony."

"It's "Für Elise" by Beethoven," Claude said, recognizing the tune.

We followed the source of the sound and maneuvered around the beds. It led us to the opposite side of the room. There was another door. Craig reached for it before I could and swung it open. We walked into an auditorium full of people. It reminded me of my university classroom back in Montana. There were over two hundred people seated and facing the front of the room, where there was a podium. Francesca let out of gasp. Craig was about to yell, but I put my hand over his mouth and my finger to my lips to signify silence to him. The music was playing through a speaker from the ceiling. It was oddly calming, but I could not help feeling that it was taunting us into an unnerving sense of false comfort.

"Is this what Rick meant by *Schooling*?" Mark asked out loud.

Every single person was wearing some sort of headset that covered his or her entire head and ears. The headsets, which looked almost like helmets, were black with a gold "Z" on the back of them. There was a sea of gold Zs staring back at us. Whatever it was, they could not see or hear us come in. It was the most bizarre and jarring thing to see, because up until entering this room, there was nothing on the island that had resembled anything modern or high tech. I should also note that each person in that room was dressed in the familiar blue jumpsuit that the local islanders were wearing.

"Virtual reality..." Claude said. "I can't believe it. They are wearing virtual reality headsets."

"Why do they have Zs on them?" Craig asked sadly. "Are they asleep?

Does it signify a state of sleep?"

"Z for Zyphone," I said, putting my thoughts together. "Robert Wong spoke about his company working on VR—virtual reality technology—last year, at our conference for the Forecaster system."

"This is so messed up," Francesca said, filming the eerie scene before her. "Are they being brainwashed?"

"Well, it looks like most of the passengers are here," Mark said. "Then who were the bodies in that pit outside?"

"I don't know," I responded. "Claude—help me find Jim, Dylan, and Charles. Craig—see if you can find Mallory." I did not need to tell Craig twice. He ran down the stairs of the auditorium and scanned the room for anyone that resembled Mallory.

"I don't see them," Claude said after a few minutes of scanning the room.

"Oh my God!" Craig cried loudly. We shushed him, but his voice did not seem to disturb any of the people. Craig then pointed at a young girl in the front row. "I think this is her! It looks like her hair!"

We all walked over to Craig's side. He reached for the headset and carefully pulled it off the girl. I recognized her face instantly from the photos on the news last year and from the photos Craig had showed me before. Her dirty blonde hair looked frizzy and unkempt. Her eyes looked unfocused and glazed. Craig broke down and hugged his daughter. It was a very powerful moment. Francesca started to cry as well. She put her camera in her bag and zipped it up. After about a minute or so, Mallory began to make moaning noises.

"I think she's coming around!" Craig cried, embracing his daughter. She started to drool onto his shoulder. Craig took off his jacket and used it to wipe her face. "Sweetie, it's Dad. Sweetie, can you hear me?"

She groaned again and then blinked her eyes a few times. It appeared as though she had gained consciousness, but she looked confused. She stared at her dad as if seeing him for the first time ever.

"Mallory, it's me, Francesca! Remember me? Remember your dad, Craig?"

Tears began to pour down Mallory's eyes. She returned the embrace and cried into his shoulder, "Dad! It's really you! Oh my God, I thought I'd never see you again! They've kept us here for God knows how long. Dad, those people are bad. They hijacked our airplane."

"Sweetheart," Craig was crying uncontrollably, but he was smiling. "I'm here. Nothing is going to happen to you, and nobody will harm you. What did they do?"

"It's all fuzzy right now," Mallory said, rubbing her head. "That helmet thing—that thing they made me wear—what all the other passengers are wearing—it's some kind of program that plays with our minds. It sort of hypnotizes us. Brainwashes us…"

I lifted Mallory's headset and put it over my head. The image before me was a 360 degree view of a beach and ocean. It looked much like the island we were on. There was classical music playing in the background. It was the same music playing over the speakers in the auditorium. I could hear the comforting sounds of the ocean and waves crashing onto the sandy beaches. I could hear the breeze and winds blowing through the trees. It was oddly relaxing. Then a man walked onto the beach wearing a white suit and black dress shoes. He was not dressed appropriately for being on a beach during a sunny day. I recognized this man from the cover of the biography written by Colin Shaw. It was Jackson Killington. He appeared to look older than the photo of him on the book cover. *Maybe he was still alive!* I thought. He folded his arms and stared right at me and began to speak in a smooth meditation-like voice.

"Hello there, my name is Jackson, headmaster of The Omniscient Minds and Keeper of The Presence. I'd like to welcome you to TOM Island. You will soon call this your new home. It is a vacation paradise, and you'll never want to leave this place. The good news is, you don't have to. You will find bliss and freedom from the modern and outside world here as you embark on this virtual reality project you've been selected to participate in. Relax and enjoy this feast for your eyes, mind, senses, and soul."

Jackson walked off screen, and then the beach scene faded to black. A few seconds later, an image of the sun rising over the ocean with a pupil in the center of it faded into the shot. The eye kept blinking, staring directly into my eyes. The music in the background grew louder. The piano grew intense, and I felt my mind slowly slip into a daze. Then I felt hands on my back. Someone was shaking me, but I could not open my mouth to yell at them to stop. Suddenly, I had to shield my eyes, as the headset I was wearing was yanked off my head. The colors of the world rushed back to my eyes. I squinted and found myself on the floor of the auditorium. I did not recall falling down. The headset was on the ground next to me. Mallory kicked the helmet and it rolled under a seat.

"Don't let this device control you," she said to me. "It's not a game. You don't want to wear it."

"Jackson Killington spoke to me," I said, wiping sweat off my forehead. "Well, a virtual reality version of him. He looks like he's aged since the last photos taken of him before he allegedly committed suicide. I think he might still be alive! He's the head of TOM."

"So, he must have faked his death after all!" Claude punched the air with anger. "I have a score to settle with that man."

"The Omniscient Minds are everywhere," I added. "You told me that once. This definitely isn't a surprise. Joseph Conroy is alive and well, and he was presumed to be missing along with all these passengers."

"Maybe," Claude said, rubbing his hands against his face in frustration. "And what about Jim, Dylan, and Charles? They aren't here." He was right. None of my three colleagues were in that room. They were the only ones unaccounted for.

"Maybe they are being kept somewhere else," I said hopefully.

"Should we wake up the rest of the passengers?" Craig asked. "We can take off these headset helmet contraptions that they're wearing."

"It may cause chaos," Francesca warned. "Let's leave them be for now. The masters will be landing at some point tonight."

"We should get out of here, then," Mark suggested. "Shall we make our way back out now?"

"We can't just leave these innocent people behind," Craig stammered.

"We have no choice," I said. "We need to be smart. Besides, they won't all fit in that seaplane. To be honest, I'm not sure if it will hold all of us."

"What about Ted and Kingsley?" Mark added. "Are we going to leave them behind?"

"We have to trust that Rick will be tending to Ted," I said. "He wasn't doing so well. It'll be a big risk to head back to that side of the hill, if that's where the members of TOM will be landing soon. And as for Kingsley—he should not have left us without a word. I'm not sure we can trust him either."

"Are you okay, darling?" Craig asked his daughter, who had taken a seat in the chair we'd found her in.

"My head hurts," she said, rubbing her temples. "There's so much information to process. I feel like I've lost several months of my life."

"She's a bit confused," Francesca said with sympathy. "Mallory, sweetie. We need to get out of here soon. Do you think you have the strength to come back out of this bunker?"

Mallory nodded. "I haven't seen daylight in so long. I haven't felt the air or smelled the ocean in ages. We've been locked away down here. There's so much to explain. There's so much to tell."

"There will be time for that," Claude said. "Right now, we need to go."

Craig reached for Mallory's arm and tried to pull her up to her feet, but she did not budge. She began to cry into the palms of her hands. She shook her head in protest and said to her father, "It's all coming back to me now."

"What is?" I asked.

"What do you mean?" Craig asked kindly. "Are you remembering something? Are the memories flooding back?"

"I…" she began, "I remember you dropped me off at the airport, and we hugged goodbye right before I got on the plane. I can still remember the smell of your cologne and the scent of the aftershave on your face. You had shaved that evening before taking me to LAX."

"That's right," Craig said. "You have a good memory."

"That's because it was one of the last ones I remember before being brought to this terrible place," Mallory cried.

"She's upset," Francesca said with sympathy. "Let's get her out of here. Let us all get the hell out of here."

"Dad," Mallory continued, ignoring Francesca's protest to escape, "those machines or whatever they put on our heads—they messed with our minds. My memory is coming and going. I am remembering some birthday parties I had with you and Mom. It feels like a bad signal on TV. It comes in clearly, then it gets all fuzzy. I think this machine messed me up, but right now, I can remember that night. The night *they* took the plane. Can I tell you all the story, in case I forget it later?"

"Yes!" both Claude and I said immediately. I pointed to Francesca's camera. She pulled it out and began to film Mallory as she prepared to tell her account of the night Flight 619 vanished from radar and ended up on the island.

I sat on the ground of the auditorium with excitement coursing through my veins. I'd never thought I would finally learn the truth of what had happened inside PA 619. I had theorized and hypothesized that all the passengers were dead, but here before me was Mallory Cooper, just as alive as her father and myself, along with most of the passengers who had been on board the airplane that night. I had always imagined that if the black boxes were found, it would tell the tale of that fateful morning on July 14. Instead, we hit the jackpot. Mallory was alive and well, and was going to share her account of the event. They say what goes up must come down… but what if it was never found? Or maybe someone did not want it to be found. The mystery was beginning to unravel.

"Go on, darling," Craig urged his daughter to speak.

"Okay." Mallory took a deep breath and began her story. "I waved goodbye to you at the LAX terminal. It was Gate 3, if I remember correctly, that evening on July 13. I pulled my carry-on luggage down the terminal's bridge to board the 787 Phoenix Airlines model. It was a magnificent plane. I was lucky enough to have a seat only five rows from the main entrance. I was seated by a window. The man next to me was on the phone with someone. He was urging someone to hurry up, because the flight was about to take off. His name was Jim. I eventually asked him, once we were airborne."

"That must have been my friend and colleague Jim King," I said excitedly. "He was talking to me, because I was running late." *Am I going to learn what happened to Jim?* I thought to myself. "My name is Patrick, by the way. I was supposed to be on that flight."

"And it was a good thing you were late," Mallory said seriously as she continued her account. "Jim was very upset and cursing under his breath. His two colleagues were seated behind us. Jim was sharing his frustration about your lateness with them. His two colleagues had a quick conversation, speaking vaguely about some back-up plans of continuing a meeting without you, Patrick.

"There were four flight attendants on that flight. Two worked the back half of the plane, and the other two worked the front half, where I was. One of our flight attendants up front was a red-headed woman named Christine. There was also another man, who was probably only a few years older than me, by the name of Joseph. They both pointed to the TV screen monitors in front of us so that we could watch the Phoenix safety video. I rarely ever paid attention to those safety videos, but as this was the longest flight I had ever been on, and the first time I was flying out of the country, I made sure to listen to every word. The most important part that would help me later on in that flight was the knowledge of where the emergency buttons for the oxygen masks were. The final announcement that the flight attendants made before takeoff was that the wireless system and seat phones were down due to maintenance issues. There was a disgruntled cackle of boos and frustration from the crowd because of that inconvenience. I groaned too, because that meant I could not use the Internet to pass the time on the flight.

"In no time, the plane was making its way down the runway and gathering speed as we rolled along the tarmac. The engines revved up and grew louder. Soon, L.A. was diminishing from the view of my window as we flew up into the air and over the clouds that night. It was pitch black above the clouds, as they blocked off all the sparkling lights from the city below. The plane took an unusual route in the direction of Hawaii, which was not common for an L.A. to Beijing flight, but the pilot confirmed it was due to weather. Flying always made me nervous, and I felt that a glass of wine would be the perfect cure, so I ordered one from the media hub in front of me.

"Christine, the flight attendant, brought me my glass of wine, and Jim took a glass of scotch once we had hit 35,000 feet. I raised my glass in silent cheers to him, and then we began a conversation. He told me he worked for Phoenix, which I found very fascinating. He said he was an engineer and was meeting with a company that built parts for the airlines' various working planes. I could tell something was bothering him. I gathered it was the fact that you had missed your plane, Patrick. It seemed a source of concern to him. He kept drinking his scotch until he eventually passed out and fell asleep.

"The lights in the cabin had dimmed. It was just after midnight, and most of the passengers had fallen asleep by then as well. I could see Christine and Joseph whispering by the cockpit. A few times, Joseph knocked on the door to speak to the pilots. I could not make out any word of what they were saying. They had serious looks on their faces. I was immediately curious. I closed my eyes just as Christine looked over to where I was, pretending to sleep. I'm not sure why I did not want her to know I was trying to eavesdrop, but something in my gut was telling me that their sudden lack of interest in the passengers was something to be concerned about.

"I heard footsteps coming from behind my seat. I opened one eye with a squint and saw the other two flight attendants. I could not see their nametags, but they were both men, and looked burly and strong. They were both over six feet tall.

"One of the burly men told Christine and Joseph that all of the passengers appeared to be asleep. They asked about waiting for some kind of orders, if I recall correctly.

"Christine mentioned that those two flight attendants were assigned to fly the airplane. At that instant I had both eyes open. My heart started to pound. *What was going on?* I kept asking myself. *Were those men about to hijack the airplane?*

"I comforted myself once the two men returned to the back of the plane. I figured I must have imagined them saying they were going to fly the plane. It appeared as though they were not, and they retreated to their section. Something told me that I needed to keep feigning sleep. The flight attendants in my section of the plane continued to whisper, but the hum of the plane's engines made their voices inaudible to the sleeping passengers and myself.

"Eventually I fell asleep, and it was not until maybe 4:00 or 5:00 in the morning that I awoke with a sudden jolt. Several people screamed at the sudden violent movement of the plane. The captain came on the speaker a minute after the nerve-wrecking shake to inform us that we needed to keep our seat belts fastened, as we were entering unexpected turbulence. I saw Joseph stand up and walk into the cockpit with the pilots. I found it strange that he stood up, because the other flight attendant, Christine, remained fastened in her seat. She had her hair in a ponytail, and I could see her forehead sweating as though she was nervous. I felt fear at that point. The plane began to vibrate like crazy again as we sped through the turbulence.

"Joseph then opened the door to the cockpit and stuck his head out to Christine. He gave her the thumbs-up and mouthed the sentence, 'It has been done.' I believe I was the only person who saw that. I had learned to read lips when I was in high school, because one of my closest friends was deaf. Having that ability helped me hear—or see, I should say—what nobody else on the plane could. Christine then unfastened her seat belt and pulled out a strange contraption from a cupboard. It looked like a vacuum cleaner. It had a long cylinder tank and a giant flexible plastic hose with a silver metal-looking nozzle. I had never seen anything like it, and I realized it was not a vacuum. The yellow-stenciled markings on the side had random letters and numbers, as if it were a model number. There was also a danger sign painted on one part of the cylinder tank.

"I knew something terrible was about to happen. My gut told me that Joseph had incapacitated the pilots somehow, and that the plane was now on autopilot. I looked out my window, and it appeared as if we were turning in a different direction; however, it could have been perceived as the plane attempting to fly away from the turbulence. The plane then made a sharp dip, and everyone screamed. At that exact moment, all the lights went out, except for the dimly-lit reddish ambient lighting that marked the floor below to allow for visibility of the walkway.

"I heard another sound that was not the plane's engines or the screaming and crying passengers. It sounded like air was being let out. The front of the airplane became foggy. Most people would have been unable to see what was happening because the lights were off, but I could make out Christine's silhouette. The side profile of her head looked strange, as if she was wearing a mask or helmet of some sort. She was spraying the cabin with whatever foggy and smoky substance was coming out of that machine she had pulled out. I instinctively pressed the button for my oxygen mask and put it over my face. Jim turned around to look at me. I think I heard him say 'What the hell is going on?' His words ended with a snore. He had fallen asleep almost instantly. I could see and feel the essence of the smoke filling up the cabin. I closed my eyes because the fog made them sting. I was breathing in fresh air, so I knew that whatever that substance was, it was not going to hurt me.

"I felt Jim's hot breath hitting my shoulder. He was alive and breathing. I came to the conclusion that the entire plane had been given a sleeping gas, or something of that nature. The flight attendants were behind what seemed like a hostage situation. The two burly male flight attendants from the rear of the plane walked by me again and entered the cockpit. They must have taken control of the autopilot at that point. Before they disappeared into the cockpit, I heard one of them say something along the lines of, 'The transponder is off. We cannot be tracked right now. It's as if we are invisible. Our presence will go unnoticed in the dark.'

"The next two or so hours felt like the longest of my life. It was dark and silent except for the sound of the humming engines and an occasional snore. It felt as if I was the only one who was on that airplane. Then, as if someone had lit a tiny flame in the distance, I began to see a faint orange light on the horizon. The sun was rising over the Pacific Ocean, and within the next hour, the sky went from black to purple to blue. The sunlight began to enter the few windows—mine included—that did not have their shades closed. The entire cabin looked hazy. I could see swirls of the haze lazily spinning through the still air of the cabin from the rays of sunlight that entered." Mallory took a moment of silence to think.

I felt chills creep up my arms and spine as Mallory shared her account of that day. Everyone in the group was deeply enthralled by it, with looks of deep fixation and interest. Francesca barely blinked as she continued to film Mallory speaking.

Then Mallory continued, "I knew that Christine and Joseph had now locked themselves in the cockpit," she went on. "I reached for my cell phone in my pocket and turned it on. Once it was powered on, I took it off airplane mode. It kept searching for a signal to no avail. I knew we were still very high up and it was pointless to try. I even double-checked to see if the Wi-Fi system was really down. It was.

"The door of the cockpit began to creak open. I knew that they would easily spot me once they came out, because my oxygen mask's cord was attached to the ceiling. With my survival instincts, I let go of my mask and it retracted back up. I took in a breath of air, and to my surprise, it felt clean, and I was not in danger of falling asleep. The potency of the gas must have subsided. I closed my eyes and pretended to be asleep. I could feel Christine and Joseph's gazes as they walked down the aisle to check and see if all the passengers were asleep. One of them shook me. It caught me by surprise, and I almost let out a gasp. Instead, I made it sound like a snore. My heart was racing so hard, I thought it was going to come up my throat and out of my mouth as vomit. Thankfully, whoever had shaken me to see if I was asleep was satisfied with my fake snore, and then checked Jim next to me. He also let out a small snore after he was shaken.

"A few minutes later, I heard a series of footsteps near the front of the plane. I squinted my eyes open and counted four people.

"Christine was informing the others that the gas had successfully put the entire plane to sleep. They all began to speak normally; they were whispering previously. Joseph revealed that he'd injected a serum into the pilots' necks to 'take them out.'

"At this point, I was so scared. I felt like I was going to throw up out of fear of being discovered awake. I began to realize that I was not going to see China. I was not going to finish college. I was not ever going to see you, Dad."

Mallory stopped speaking for a moment to wipe a tear out of her eye. She reached out and gave a hug to her father. They both had silent tears as they embraced. After about a minute, they broke apart.

"Everything is going to be okay," Craig assured her. "Continue with your story."

"Okay," Mallory said, and she continued to recount the events. "I kept my eyes closed and kept my body as still as possible. I made sure to regulate my breathing so that it looked like I was asleep. I could hear Christine's heels walking over to where I was. She stopped right at my aisle. I could feel my palms sweat from nerves.

"'Are you going to do it?' I remember her asking one of the other flight attendants. Joseph…I think. 'John won't be happy about this…'

"Joseph replied, saying he was going to do it. I heard him unzip what sounded like a bag. Instinctively and without thinking, I squinted my eyes to see what he was doing. He had a syringe that he was flicking with his finger. There was a label on it that read 'Keep out of reach of children. Highly toxic. For medical use only.' Joseph inserted the syringe into Jim's neck. His breathing began to speed up, yet his eyes remained closed. I could feel his body shaking as it reacted to what I assumed was some kind of fatal serum or poison. Jim's lifeless hand brushed against my leg. He was dead. The warmth slowly left his body."

At that moment, I lost it. To hear Mallory describe Jim's final moments really choked me up. I stifled my sobs into my jacket. Craig put his hand on my shoulder to comfort me. Francesca grabbed my arm and squeezed it with her free hand that was not holding her camera. Mallory avoided making eye contact with me and looked up at the ceiling.

"I can't believe he's dead," I cried. "I mean, I know that in my mind I had already considered him dead since the plane went missing, but to actually learn what happened…it's…it's closure, I suppose. But I had hoped that he was still alive, since we found most of the passengers in this bunker."

"So sorry, man," Craig said.

"He was targeted," I said angrily. "The same fate would have happened to me if I was on that plane."

"I agree," Mallory said. "Joseph then inserted his poisonous syringe into the two men behind me. They were Jim's friends. Their breathing stopped as well. My next fear was that everyone else was going to be pricked by that needle and meet the same fate, but I was never touched, nor were any of the other passengers. As my mind began to race as to why those three men were the only targets, the flight attendants revealed the answer.

"'It's for the sake of our futures,' Joseph told his other conspirators. He started to go on about how those three men he'd just killed were planning to create a technology so advanced that it would not only bring down the aviation industry, but also cause chaos among their ranks.

"'What about the fourth guy?' one of the burly flight attendants asked.

I remember him asking this question because I wanted to look around and see who they were talking about, but it was you, Patrick.

"Joseph replied to the attendant, who was named Michael. Apparently, they were under the impression that a 'Mr. Baldwin' was left in the dark about what those three men had been plotting. They seemed satisfied that Mr. Baldwin would not be a threat to them, since you didn't know about their plans for China since you missed the flight." Mallory said directly to me.

"The flight attendants began to plan out their takeover of the airplane. They mentioned having some coordinates given to them by...I think it was someone named Robert. The attendants confirmed amongst each other that the airplane's transponder was off and they were virtually invisible on the flight path. They said they only had communication with one special satellite, and it was guiding them to the final destination.

"They continued to speak openly and nonchalantly about their plans for the landing of the flight. They kept saying high-ranking members of 'The Presence' would be waiting for our arrival, and they would be pleased that Jim, Dylan, and Charles were taken out.

"The flight attendants looked very serious and determined. I felt more at ease knowing they were not terrorists, but it worried me to think that employees of Phoenix Airlines were a part of the hijack plan and plot to execute three men on board. The flight attendants continued their conversation, and mentioned that they were going to take possession of cell phones, laptops, and luggage from the passengers and properly secure them away from us. I wanted to cry when they mentioned we were going to be housed in an underground bunker. The flight attendants were not sure if we would be killed off or not; it was up to the discretion of some 'Agent Randolph Smith' person. I hoped in my mind that whoever Agent Smith was, he was going to spare my life, and I would be able to go back home to Los Angeles.

"The flight attendants made their way through the cabin, digging through sleeping passengers' pockets and carry-on luggage that was stored at their feet or in the overhead compartments. Christine was the attendant who put her hands through my pant pockets to obtain my cell phone. She pulled it out and gently placed my body back in a comfortable sleeping position. It felt like eternity as she dug for my phone. I worked so hard to keep my eyes closed without making it appear as if I was straining to keep them closed. I heard someone unfasten Jim's seat belt, and then I felt his body being pulled out of his seat by me. His lifeless and heavy body brushed against me for a few seconds as they pulled him out of his seat. The flight attendant Michael whispered to his colleague who was helping him to make sure Jim's laptop was taken to the front of the plane, as they were planning to hand it to Agent Smith.

"My eyes shot open upon hearing a man towards the back of the plane yell. Someone had woken up. There was a struggle coming from behind me. I carefully peered my head over my seat to see the four attendants trying to restrain the confused man.

"'What are you doing?' the man cried, just as Joseph injected his neck with the same syringe used on Jim and his friends. The man's body gave way, and he fell face-first onto the aisle floor.

"Joseph said he had no choice but to kill the passenger, as he could have been a threat to their plans. The others nodded in agreement, and began to drag the man's body toward the front of the plane where I was, so that they could hide it from view of the passengers. I was fighting the urge to cry. What these people were doing to us innocent passengers was illegal. I felt angry. A part of me wanted to find something heavy and fight off all four flight attendants, or whatever they were. But I knew that would be unwise. They could have easily overpowered me."

Mallory took some time to think for a moment. I used that opportunity to nudge Mark for the time, as he had a wristwatch. "It's 6:55," he said.

"We should probably head out of here now," I told the group. "They'll be landing soon. I don't want to run into them outside of their castle."

"What happened next?" Claude asked Mallory, completely ignoring my request for us to escape the bunker.

"They brought us here," she replied. "The passengers regained consciousness. There was chaos in the cabin of the plane once we landed on this island. People were relieved to be alive, but then they realized we had all been kidnapped. Two men met us outside. One of them was the Agent Smith guy that the flight attendants had been talking about. The other man was the same man who introduces the virtual reality Schooling Time in our headsets."

"Jackson Killington?" Claude asked in shock. "So he *is* alive? That means those text messages to 'J.K.' from Jim really were for Killington." Claude had directed the last part to me.

Francesca, Mark, and Craig looked at me with curiosity. They were unaware of our realization about the text message exchange between Jim and this allusive "J.K." that Claude and I had figured out the week before. I quickly explained to the group our theory about the text messages, and how we thought that Jim might have had a role with The Omniscient Minds in some way, shape, or form. I did not want to assume he was part of TOM, especially after hearing he was killed by their cold, bloody hands.

"I was not expecting that information," Francesca said. "Why didn't you tell me?"

"I did not want to start rumors or assumptions," I said truthfully. "But according to Mallory, Jim was murdered on the airplane. Why would a member of TOM kill one of their own?"

"He was working on the HyperTube," Claude said. "He could have fed TOM very important information. I'm not sure what to make of this. Was Jim on our side or *their* side?"

"We need to go," Craig said. "It's 7:00."

At those words, we shuffled up the stairs and out of the auditorium. I took one look back at the rest of the passengers. I wished I could have done something to help them, but they were probably safer in their virtual reality world than with us. TOM would not hesitate to kill them if we let them loose. The last thing I wanted was for them to end up in that pit by the forest. We'd spent so much time trying to find them. Our plan was to get back to Sydney and alert the authorities. Then they could send help over to the island.

We hastily escaped the bunker in less than two minutes, as we ran down the long hallway and climbed up the ladder as quickly as possible. Once I was out, I closed the door shut and pocketed the key that Rick had given me. The sun was beginning to set on the horizon. I could hear the sound of an airplane in the distance. It sounded like it was landing on the runway on the other side of the hill. Francesca gave me a worried look.

"Let's get to that hangar on the beach!" I ordered everyone. We sprinted down the side of the castle and onto the sandy beach.

"We're leaving tracks behind!" Claude said worriedly.

"There's no time to hide our footprints!" Francesca shouted. "Come on!" Francesca put her camera in her bag and zipped it up for safekeeping. The footage she'd shot was our ticket to shutting down TOM Island and saving the PA 619 survivors.

"Hurry!" Mark said when we got to the hangar. I fumbled for the key and hastily inserted it into the metal lock. It clicked open, and with the help of Mark and Claude, we pushed open the heavy door, which opened onto the water.

"Does anyone even know how to fly?" Mallory asked with concern.

A small seaplane with red stripes was parked inside the hangar. It looked like it could only seat six people, which was exactly the amount we needed, since Kingsley was now missing. I had no time to think about what had happened to him. Now the only concern was who would fly the plane. None of us appeared to have any flying experience.

Francesca raised her hand and put one of her fingers to her lips. "Shh!"

"What is it?" I whispered.

"Do you hear that?" she asked.

I listened intently trying to find the source of whatever sound she was talking about. Then I heard what sounded like the clinking of chains and heavy breathing.

"I hear it, but what is it?" I asked. I began to walk carefully around the seaplane, as the source of the sound was coming from inside the hangar. I put my hand back with my palm raised up, to signify to the group to stay behind. Francesca looked at me with worry, but she stood her ground. I crept around the plane and saw an elderly man huddled in the corner of the hangar. One of his legs had a metal cuff around his ankle, connected to a chain, which was attached to the hangar wall. There was a gallon-sized milk carton with water in it and an empty bowl next to him. The man had long silvery hair and an unkempt beard. It appeared as though he was being kept prisoner. He looked at us in horror and began to shiver. He had one hand over his eyes to shield them from the light that was coming from the open door. He must have been adjusting after being locked in darkness.

The others walked over by me and stared in horror at the man. Claude grabbed me by the shoulder to stop me from walking any closer to him. He whispered in my ear, "Do you recognize that man?"

The man held onto the wall and carefully lifted himself up onto his feet. He stared at Claude in shock. He'd recognized Claude, and Claude recognized him.

"C-Claude Bernstein?" he stuttered. "Is that you? Help me. They imprisoned me here. They turned against me. My s-s-son. They told me he's dead. Claude, help free me! I'm not on their side…anymore."

"Who is this man?" I whispered to Claude. Claude reached for his wallet from his back pocket and pulled out a twenty-dollar bill. He waved it in front of my face. My eyes widened with a dawning sense of apprehension.

"*Jackson Killington,*" I gasped.

30

Jackson Killington was standing before us, alive and breathing, but not looking so well. His clothes and face had dirt stains all over them. His hair looked as if it had not been washed in weeks, and his skin was ghostly white and dry. Claude walked over to Jackson to examine him closely.

"I thought you were dead," Claude said through gritted teeth. It sounded like it took a lot of energy for him to speak to Jackson. He continued in a very unfriendly tone, "The world thinks you blew yourself up. You made my life a living hell for not joining your cult-like group. *The Omniscient Minds...*"

"I faked my death to live on this island so that I could run our organization. You would have been a key player, Claude." Jackson said. "You're a brilliant man. You could have supported our cause."

"You stole the Forecaster idea from me!" Claude spat. "How dare you try to compliment my intellect! You're a disgrace and a thief! How the hell did you end up tethered down here? Aren't you the head honcho of TOM?"

"I was," Jackson said with remorse. "They turned on me."

"Who are *they*?" Claude demanded.

"The new regime," Jackson said, avoiding Claude's angry glare. "One of my members turned on me. His name is John. I trusted him."

"There's no time for chit-chat," I said urgently to Claude. "We need to get out of here. That airplane with TOM members landed. They're probably over the hill by now."

"Are you going to try to fly out of here?" Jackson asked.

I nodded. Jackson began to laugh, a kind of manic laughter. It was the type of laughter that I would presume someone insane would have, or at least someone who had lost their mind or dignity. It was disturbing, and it echoed throughout the hangar menacingly.

"There's a magnetic field around this island," Jackson said. "The plane will lose power once it hits the field, and then it will crash into the sea. The magnetic field was a creation of one of our late members."

"Ugh," Mark said. "The ship that brought us near this island lost power as we got close."

"Yes, that would explain it." Jackson said. "Also…I'm speaking the truth. TOM has turned against me. My loyalties do not lie with them anymore."

"Why haven't they killed you?" Claude asked in a cold tone. "You're chained up like a dog…"

Jackson answered, "Having me chained up like a dog, as you say, gives *them* great joy. It's torture. I know at some point they will burn me in that pit, like they do to anyone who betrays them. I'm sure you saw the pit near the forest. They burn members of TOM that break the rules and the islanders who fail to follow the duties that have been assigned to them. It's how order and discipline are restored here."

"Why did they turn against you?" Claude demanded.

"Power and revenge," Jackson said softly. "John was upset that I made plans to execute his son, who was on PA 619. I had realized his son was a double agent. He had been initiated into The Omniscient Minds, but was actually working against us to bring us down by working on an invention called the HyperTube."

"Wait a minute…what?" I asked in shock. "Was it Jim King?"

Jackson nodded. I could see sweat pouring down his forehead. "Jim was part of TOM. That's a fact, but his loyalty was not with us. He sided with you—Claude."

"I did not know he was a part of TOM, though," Claude said. "Patrick and I only recently put that together, after finding a text message exchange he had with you. We found a burner phone in the basement of his home. It appeared that you were both communicating in code."

"Which of you is Patrick?" Jackson asked suddenly.

"I am," I spoke up.

"The survivor!" Jackson said in surprise. "Yes, that's right. I recognize you from TV reports and newspaper headlines I've read. You were supposed to meet the same fate as Jim and his two colleagues, Dylan and Charles. I'm surprised you weren't taken out by some of my fellow members already. Some of whom have been hiding right under your nose."

I clenched my fists in anger at Jackson's statement. He spoke of the death of my friends as if it had been a business transaction.

Jackson continued, "But I never had a texting conversation with Jim. I'm not sure what you are talking about."

I pulled out my journal and showed Jackson the text message exchange that I had transcribed. He shook his head in confusion. "Yeah, that was not me," he said.

"You mean to say," I asked, "that you were not texting Jim about your son Royce by using the word 'sun' as a code?"

Jackson laughed his cackling and maniacal laugh again. He looked at me with a sinister grin and said, "Jim King was texting his father. His father is 'J.K.,' and the text simply appears as though his father was just asking about him—him being Jim. From that message, it appears Jim's father was plotting to overtake my leadership role and rule TOM. Jim's father had been trying to recruit him for years, and it looks like he had let Jim know about our society way before we recruited him."

"What?" Francesca said in a whisper to herself. She grabbed my clenched fists. Her hands were warm while mine felt cold.

"If Jim wasn't texting you, but was, in fact, texting his father, then who was he?" Claude asked raising one of his eyebrows with skepticism. Jackson closed his eyes for a few seconds, then opened them and stared at Claude intensely.

"It was John," Jackson said. "The man who brought me down from my role as headmaster of The Omniscient Minds and Keeper of The Presence. John King. He's Jim's father. That's who 'J.K.' is."

"I can't believe Jim's father is a member of TOM," I said in disbelief. "And he locked you down here because you orchestrated the hijacking of PA 619 and had his son killed, along with my two other colleagues, Dylan and Charles? Well, you deserve to be locked and chained down here, you scumbag!"

I had the urge to push him onto the ground, but I refrained. I was staring into the eyes of the man who was responsible for PA 619 vanishing without a trace. He was the reason my friends were dead. I could have been one of the victims. He had Mallory and the rest of the passengers locked in a bunker for over a year in captivity, and he was brainwashing them. The man whose book I'd read several months ago (which told the tale of his suicide) was standing before me. He was the reason others had been killed. He was a monster in my eyes. He had faked his own death to live on TOM Island and lead the rest of the members of his secret society. I had nothing but deep disdain for this man. I wanted to kill him with my bare hands.

"You might hate me," Jackson said, looking directly at me, "but John King's plans are far more sinister than my attempt to stop you and your engineer friends from building the HyperTube. Saving the aviation industry from the invention of the HyperTube is nothing compared to what John King has in store."

"Where is John King?" I asked.

"Last I heard," he said, "he had gone to the modern world to bring you here, Patrick. It looks like he succeeded. You were a pawn in his game."

"Huh?" I racked my mind, but I was confused. John King wanted to bring me to the island?

"He's bluffing," Francesca said. "He has to be."

"What are you talking about?" Claude asked. "Stop playing mind games. We're not one of your prisoners wearing your God forsaken virtual reality helmets."

"We need to get out of here," Craig cried, hugging his daughter. "What if TOM people find us here? We need to get on that airplane!"

"IT'S TOO LATE!"

A familiar voice yelled from behind us, making most of us jump in fright. We all turned around to see Kingsley at the entrance to the hangar. "They're already here. *We're* already here…"

Kingsley was holding a metal object that looked like a vacuum cleaner with an extension hose. I saw Mallory squirm at the sight of it. She whispered to her father, "That's the machine they used to put us under when they hijacked our flight!"

"Kingsley—*what*?" Claude gasped in shock. Claude was dumbfounded and looked like he was conflicted by the urge to cry and scream at the same time. Kingsley stared at him with a dark smile and a look of excitement written all over his face.

"*No...*" I said softly, but it happened way too fast. Kingsley put on a gas mask and then sprayed a gassy mist at us from the machine he was holding. My eyes stung a bit and became watery. I felt my body go numb. I lost balance because my legs began to feel like pudding, and they buckled under my weight. I fell to the ground, and then there was nothing but darkness...and *quiet*.

August 27, 2017

My head was pounding. When I opened my eyes, it took a few seconds for my vision to focus. There was the sound of classical piano music that filled the room. It was "Für Elise" by Beethoven. That same piece of music had been playing in the auditorium of the bunker where the PA 619 passengers were imprisoned. It gave me a sense of unease to hear it. The mood in the room was anything but cheerful. Kingsley was standing over me. I rolled over, as I was on my side, and tried to stand up, but I felt dizzy. I looked around the room. It was evident by the stone walls that I was inside the castle, in some kind of large chamber lit by torches fashioned on the walls. The rest of my friends were by my side. Behind me was the entrance to the chamber we were in. Francesca began to stir a few feet away from me. She awoke and nearly yelled in shock. Kingsley was standing alone in front of us. There was a golden chair behind him. It looked like a throne. On the wall above the chair was a giant familiar painting of the sun with the eye at the center of it, rising over an ocean. Kingsley was wearing a sleeveless shirt. His dragon tattoo was exposed—it intertwined down his arm. It made him look even more sinister.

"What do you want?" I asked in shock.

"He wanted you here," the familiar voice of Jackson Killington called from one corner of the room. I took notice of him. He was tethered to a chain on the wall at one corner of the chamber. "That's Jim's father, by the way. John King."

"Why, thank you for that introduction," Kingsley said sarcastically. "Allow me to reintroduce myself, Patrick. My name is John King. Kingsley is not my real name. Well, if you take out the S-L-E-Y at the end of it, you have 'King,' which is my surname. And yes, I am Jim's father."

Claude, Mark, Mallory, and Craig had also regained consciousness. Claude stood up on his feet abruptly. He was apparently more coherent than I had been when I woke up. He clenched his fists and raised them up to signify he was ready to punch Kingsley—or John, rather. John laughed at Claude.

"Foolish old man," he said to him with a taunting laugh. John was most likely close to Claude's age, which made his statement ironic. "Do you want to fight me? I wouldn't try anything rash."

"You're outnumbered," Claude spat. "Six to one. I think our odds are much better."

"Ha!" John laughed. He walked over to a table where a chessboard was set on top. He moved a few pieces and knocked a pawn over. He looked back over at us after playing his turn. "The Keeper of The Presence would like to call upon the Keepers of The Pact. Please enter!"

The door behind us opened. It was the entrance to the chamber. A few familiar people walked in. I was not shocked by their appearance, but I felt a tinge of anger and betrayal at the sight of them. Natasha Wilkins, Colin Shaw, Robert Wong, Joseph Conroy, and a man I had never met walked into the room. Then a sixth person walked in. It was Ted Holt, and he looked healthy. His appearance did surprise me. I heard Claude groan in resentment a few feet away from me. Was he a part of TOM as well? That was answered when John spoke next.

"These are some of my trusted disciples. They are some of the high-ranking members of The Omniscient Minds. I believe you may know most of them? I give you Natasha Wilkins..." John looked over at Jackson and gave him a menacing and taunting grin. Jackson's eyes glared at the sight of Natasha. She had been his assistant and right-hand woman at one point. She was a huge part of the Killington family. I saw the look of betrayal in Jackson's eyes. It was the same kind of betrayal I was feeling towards him for killing my friends and conspiring the hijacking of PA 619. I wanted to feel sympathy for him, but he was still an evil and heartless man.

"Natasha has worked for the Killingtons for decades," John continued. "She helped orchestrate Jackson's fake death so that he could live full-time here on TOM Island, and run the organization and its members, who span out all over the world. Jackson left behind his wealth for his son Royce to begin Phoenix Airlines and eventually create the Forecaster system, which Jackson so willingly stole from Claude Bernstein here." Claude shot an angry look at Jackson and then one to John, who was now taunting him with a sarcastic smile. "Royce was about to be inducted to join his father's ranks last December after the successful demonstration of the Forecaster. I kept a close eye on him while working for Phoenix Airlines as head of security. Jackson here was using me as a pawn to make sure his son was making all the right moves in this game of chess. But I had my own agenda. My plan was to take the king out. *Checkmate.*"

John reached for the king on the chessboard and knocked it off the table in the direction of Jackson. It bounced onto the concrete floor and landed a few feet from Jackson's foot. John continued.

"Royce, however, had an untimely death. It was accidental...or so he thought. Jackson was gutted by the loss of his son. I think Jackson blamed himself for his death, because Royce had recently learned his father was not really dead and he was asked to join TOM. Natasha was next in line to run Phoenix; she had done her time working for the Killingtons. She made the work order for the flaperon airplane part we used as a ploy to trick the world into thinking the plane did, in fact, crash into the ocean. Those were her orders from Jackson during his plan to take down the airplane and stop the engineers on board from ever creating the Hyper-Tube. I took my opportunity to fill her in on my plans, since we were both working at Phoenix, and convinced her to join me and plan to dethrone Jackson. Then you have Robert Wong, who helped with the building and funding of the Forecaster and our special satellite, the Peeping Tom. I convinced him and Colin Shaw to join my ranks. Colin here wasn't easy to persuade, because of his close ties to Jackson. They were the best of friends. He even wrote Jackson's biography to help convince the world that he had, in fact, killed himself. I promised Colin something that would change his mind. The same thing I promised all my Keepers of The Pact.

This gentleman here is Randolph Smith, head of the CIA."

John pointed to the man I had not recognized, but I knew his name from Mallory's account of the hijacking and from hearing Colin Shaw talk about him the night we'd infiltrated Zyphone Communications. John seemed pleased with the look of concern on all our faces. It was terrifying to think that a member of a United States government organization could be a part of a corrupt secret society.

"Randolph," John continued, "helps us with sensitive government information, as Colin's successor. He played a role in helping us make PA 619 look like an accident by feeding the FBI incorrect information and fooling the press and media. Now, you obviously know Ted as well. Ted Holt's role with TOM was to mislead the search party away from our island, because even with the transponder off on PA 619, the plane had been sending faint signals, or 'handshakes,' as the media called them, to other satellites, which helped analysts get an idea of where the plane could have potentially crashed. We created the illusion of a tragedy, when the truth is that the airplane has been locked away on this island for over a year. We created a façade of the greatest mystery in aviation history, but we also prevented the aviation industry from crumbling at the hands of Claude's and those engineers' new invention of the supposed HyperTube. Ted, like me, helped bring you to this island. He offered Patrick the opportunity to set sail on a search ship after meeting him in Los Angeles. He fed you a line that he was trying to convince Natasha to fund his expedition, when in reality, we were all plotting to bring you to this island. And you took my bait back in Claude's motel room a few months ago. I told you about Joseph to help you piece together the theory that if he was alive, then the plane might have never crashed. And while you set sail on your weeklong excursion here to the coordinates you stole from Zyphone Communications' satellite, Ted poisoned his entire crew and faked his own illness, so while you set off on foot to my castle, he would rally the islanders of TOM Island to help us with your *ousting*. You were able to open the door to our hangar and you saw…*it*. And that brings me back to our flight attendant pawn, Joseph Conroy, who helped coordinate the hijacking of PA 619 with three other attendants. He had help from a TOM member who works in aviation meteorology to coordinate a change in the flight path that would be more south in the Pacific than it would have normally flown. This helped us bring the plane closer to TOM Island by flying it near Hawaii. Joseph and crew killed the pilots on board and commandeered the plane after giving everyone the same sleeping gas you all experienced last night at my hands, from my little contraption we created here." John pointed to a corner of the room. The silver vacuum-looking machine that he'd used to put us under the night before was sitting up against the wall.

"Joseph," he continued, "kept an eye on Phoenix for me and started to tail you, Patrick. I wanted to bring you here because you missed the flight. Jackson wanted you dead, but you escaped unscathed...or did you?" John winked at me and gave me a strange stare. It was as if he knew something I did not know, or he was hinting at something both of us knew and no one else. I was confused, but then he said something that made my heart sink. "There's a lot more fresh air on this island than in Los Angeles, right, Patrick? It's better for your *lungs*."

He knows, I thought. *He knows I have lung cancer. But how? He is part of The Omniscient Minds—they tend to know everything.*

"A good set of lungs would enjoy the fresh air out here," John teased me. "But now you are all probably wondering why I wanted to dethrone Jackson and take his reign over TOM, am I right? The plan would have been for the Kings to rise to power as actual kings of TOM, but Jackson killed my son. That was not in the plan. Admittedly, I did not know my own son was acting as a double agent and working with Claude—even if Claude did not know he was a member of TOM. Even though I felt betrayed by the news, when Jackson came to me one evening and said he had intel of Jim and two other engineers' plans to go to China and meet with a corporation that would help them create the HyperTube system, I still loved my son. I asked Jackson to spare him, and he said he wouldn't have Jim killed. He would apprehend him and bring him to the island alive. Jackson lied and killed my son. I wanted my revenge. So, I convinced his trusted henchmen..." John pointed at Natasha, Colin, Joseph, Ted, Randolph, and Robert, "to join me. They would each get an equal portion of the Killington inheritance to do whatever they pleased with in the modern world outside of this island.

Once Royce died, Natasha was given the money, but only because one of our members of TOM works with the bank that the Killington trust had an account with. Money is powerful. Now they are very wealthy, and can run their operations and enjoy the riches of life free from worry, and I can take the reins of the organization. It gives me great happiness to know I've taken away the one thing that Jackson loved...*power*. He took my son away from me, and this is his punishment for that injustice. He lied to me. Lying to a member of TOM goes against the code of ethics of our secret organization. And now you are probably wondering why I wanted you to come to this island, huh?"

"Yes," I answered John, and looked him dead in the eyes with fierce intensity.

"That answer is both obvious and complicated," John said with a heavy sigh. "The obvious reason is because you stumbled upon sensitive information about our group. Claude was on the blacklist and was targeted to be silenced, but then he went missing. He took the alias of Wilbur Wright and went into hiding, but it wasn't hard to find him. I befriended him and pretended to become his ally. He thought I was acting as a double agent at Phoenix, but he was the pawn in *my* game. Claude—you did have one use for me for which I am eternally grateful. Do you remember the conversation we had the night before the Palm Springs demonstration of the Forecaster?"

Claude looked at John with horror, and then he turned to look Jackson in the eyes. Claude turned back to John with a sense of understanding and nodded, "Yes."

"I told him," John said, speaking directly to Jackson now, "that he should make sure to drive Royce home that night. He had a drug and alcohol problem. He would most likely be drunk and high by the end of the night if the event was successful—or even if it wasn't. Claude took him back to his estate and crushed his anti-depressant pills into a bottle of water. Then you fed him that water bottle, didn't you, Claude?"

"NO!" Jackson cried and fell to his knees. "NOOOO!"

"Ha ha ha!" John let out a satisfied and menacing laugh. "Claude physically killed your son, Jackson. But it was I who conspired and coerced him to do it. I told him what to do and how to do it. Can you see it now?

Twenty pills crushed into fine powder, slowly dissolving into a plastic water bottle. Royce took a huge gulp from it, and the liquid poured into his system, already full of vodka and cocaine. The news said his death was accidental. You were so heartbroken. You became distraught by the news and your depression became a distraction. One night, I used the sleeping gas on you, and you found yourself tethered to a wall inside the hangar like a dog. You took my son's life, and therefore, I took your son's life in return. An eye for an eye." John pointed at the painting on the wall with the eye on the center of the sun and laughed. He turned to Claude, "Your help was greatly appreciated, Claude. It will not go unforgotten. It's a shame, however, that you turned down your invitation to join the ranks of The Presence."

"You're an evil group," Claude spat. "You all are corrupt scum!" Claude ran straight for John. John looked surprised, but just as Claude was inches away from attacking John, his body seized up and he keeled over. Natasha had a Taser gun pointed at him. Claude was crying and cowering on the floor in pain. I started to walk towards him, but Natasha yelled, "I wouldn't move a muscle, Baldwin. And if any of you fools try anything stupid, we will Taser you too."

"Yes, don't be stupid," John said, and he pulled a large knife out of a belt holster I had not noticed before. The metal handle of the knife was fashioned in the shape of a dragon, similar to his tattoo. The blade was sharp, and shone menacingly against the firelight from the torches that lit the chamber. I looked at the blade in horror. I felt like it was about to be driven into my flesh. I had nowhere to run. This was the end.

"Jackson," John said, walking over to him while brandishing the knife like a sword before him, "the code of ethics say that any member of TOM or our islanders who break the law should be punished by the pit of fire outside these castle walls. However, as the new Keeper of The Presence, I'm going to make an exception for you. You're being sentenced to death for the wrongful murder of my son."

"J-J-John," Jackson pleaded. "We've been friends and colleagues for a very long time. We went to college together! Please. You already had Royce killed. Isn't that enough?"

"In the name of the Eye of the Sun," John said, pointing to the large painting on the wall again, "I sentence you to death for the murder of my *son*."

"But it was Joseph who injected him on the plane!" Jackson pleaded. "He physically killed Jim. Not me!"

"I understand that," John said, "but Joseph had no choice. He was bound to your orders as Keeper of The Presence. Joseph has made up for his deed by helping me bring Patrick and his friends to this place, after tracking them around Los Angeles. He's done a service for me that I am satisfied with. Therefore, he is not to be punished. He acted out an order from you that would have otherwise been punishable by the pit of fire. *You* gave the orders, and now you will die at my hands."

Joseph shifted uncomfortably and pushed his long-sleeved shirt up his arms. I noticed a gold watch on his wrist, which I had seen before, but not clearly. It was *my* Rolex watch. It had been packed in my suitcase when I'd checked in for my flight on PA 619. My father had given it to me. I'd thought I would never see it again. There was anger in the pit of my stomach. I wanted to cut off Joseph's arm at that very moment.

John raised the knife by the dragon-shaped hilt and said, "Eye of the Sun, the star of our world, in your name and by the names of all the Keepers of The Presence before me and before Jackson, give me the strength to ignite justice into Jackson's flesh. In the name of all of the members of TOM both past and present, may his death act as an example of betrayal within our own ranks. If we are to thrive for eternity in secret, we must abide by the laws our predecessors laid forth before us. Many of them are famous inventors, scientists, and political leaders who have helped shape the modern world. My fellow disciples and I are the next generation of worldwide influence and control. Jackson Killington, I sentence you to eternal sleep."

I heard both Francesca and Mallory squirm. They covered their eyes with their hands. Jackson backed himself against the stone wall and cried. He had nowhere to turn. John raised the knife and slashed Jackson's throat. His agonizing shriek filled the room and reverberated off the walls. It made the hair on the back of my neck stand. I closed my eyes for a second, but opened them as he choked loudly and gurgled. Fresh blood spilled out of the slit in his throat and down his front and onto the floor. He choked and coughed out blood before falling to his side. Jackson's body squirmed for a few seconds before it remained still. His lifeless eyes looked at me for the last time. John bent over and reached for Jackson's shirt and wiped his blade clean. He then put the knife back in his belt holster and stood up.

"The Killington bloodline has ended," John said happily, to cheers and applause from his disciples.

John walked over to me with his hands behind his back. I figured they were placed there so that he had easy access to his knife in case I tried to fight him, since I was not restrained like Jackson had been. John examined me and put his head near the right side of my face. I flinched slightly and stepped back. He put one arm on my shoulder and squeezed it firmly.

He whispered so that only I could hear, "You're dying of cancer. I know you are. Natasha has been poisoning you with radon for several months. Remember how traces of radon were found in the faucets at Phoenix Airlines? Well, Natasha was serving you water laced with radon. Do you recall the cucumber spa water she served you a few times? One time she gave it to you right before you were meeting with Royce. The other instance was during your Phoenix resignation meeting with her. Large traces of it were in your water, which you drank. See, we found a way to take you out and make it look like natural causes. I can see it in your eyes. Your face is pale and you look quite frail, to be honest. The problem is, your body has been fighting it off with medication and treatments. You've lived longer than anticipated. You will die eventually. We are everywhere. We know everything. Nothing gets past us. We are The Omniscient Minds, after all. I wanted you to come to this island so that we could silence you all here—off the grid. You and your friends know too much. I can't have you return to the modern world and risk exposing our secrets to the public."

So, that was why I had cancer. Natasha had slowly poisoned my body several months ago. She'd given me my death sentence way before I'd even thought she was any kind of threat. She had seemed so innocent and sweet that one day Royce had summoned me to his office. It was the day he'd given me a copy of his father's book. I remembered seeing the similar painting of the Eye of the Sun in his office. Now I knew what it meant and its connection to The Presence. It was some kind of pagan symbol to them. I tuned out the sound of the piano music playing on loop in the background over a set of speakers from the ceiling. I heard true quiet again. I was alone in that moment. John King, the father of one of my good friends, knew my biggest secret. Jim had died at the orders of Jackson Killington because he was trying to overthrow TOM by taking them down financially. He wanted to bring down Phoenix Airlines and put them out of business by inventing the HyperTube. Now, it seemed, the HyperTube would never see the light of day. I looked over at Francesca. She had tears streaming down her eyes, in apparent fear that John would pull out his knife and stab me. I was waiting for his blade to enter my flesh and help me to escape the slow death of my cancer. It would be quicker, and perhaps less painful.

But he did not stab me. He walked away from me and headed towards the golden throne. He sat on it and placed his arms on the armrests. He sat there, proudly living up to his last name, the image of a king. I heard footsteps approaching us from behind. Natasha, Colin, Randolph, Robert, Ted, and Joseph had their Taser guns pressed against our backs. There were six of them and six of us. Each of the members of TOM picked one of us to Taser. Robert picked me. I felt the electricity jolt up my body. I imagined the hair on top of my head standing up from the shock, but it was only my imagination. The impact of where the Taser hit my shoulder felt like a hundred bee stings happening at once. My nerves lost every sense of feeling, and my body could no longer support itself. I fell to the hard stone ground and smacked the left side of my face. I started to convulse and yell. I could hear Francesca and Mallory's high-pitched shrieks. I felt anger jolt through my veins, but the electricity was too intense, and had overtaken any kind of adrenaline my body attempted to produce. I wanted to save Francesca, but I was powerless. Claude, Mark, and Craig's voices shrieked in agony as well. This felt like the end. The pain overpowered me; I temporarily blacked out. All I remembered at that point was the vague feeling I was being carried or dragged for several minutes to another location. At one point, I opened my eyes and saw that a tall islander had lifted me over his shoulders. He was wearing a blue jumpsuit. Right before he carried me out of the castle, I saw a room to the side where there were piles upon piles of luggage stored. I vaguely saw my suitcase I'd checked in the night I was to board PA 619. *So that's where they took the passengers' belongings*, I thought, as my limp body was effortlessly carried outside of the castle. It was nighttime, and there was a path of torches that lit the way to a large fire in the distance. It was the pit we had passed on the outskirts of the forest. *We must have been passed out for almost an entire day in that chamber*, I thought, as I stared at the pit.

There were six chairs placed directly in front of the fiery pit that was burning brightly. I felt the warmth of it hit my face, and the stench of decaying bodies reached my nostrils like the crack of a whip. Surrounding the pit were dozens of men, women, and children, all wearing the familiar unisex blue jumpsuits. I saw Rick amongst them. He looked terrified at the sight of us. Perhaps he was afraid we would give him away for giving us access to the bunker and the seaplane's hangar. It seemed that the entire population of TOM Island locals were attending this cult-like ritual of our "ousting." The six men who carried Francesca, Craig, Claude, Mark, Mallory, and me placed us on each of the seats and tethered us with thick metal chains. They then placed a lock on each of us to keep us restrained. The chairs were on the edge of the fire. The heat was intense. I started to sweat instantly. I was wearing a jacket, and it became so uncomfortable that I wanted to rip it off, but I had no use of my arms or legs. Mallory was crying loudly a few chairs over. Claude and I were on the opposite ends of the row of chairs. I could see him staring at the fire intently, as if he had already accepted his fate. Francesca was in the chair next to me, crying silent tears. Her face was drenched with sweat.

A raised platform and podium had been placed on the opposite end of the pit in front of us. John was standing on top of it by himself. On the left side of it, Randolph, Robert, Joseph, Natasha, Colin, and Ted were huddled together, watching us intently. John raised his arms and said, "Which of you islanders gave these trespassers keys to the bunker and hangar?"

I could see Rick shaking nervously. He had one arm over his daughter and son. A red-haired woman next to him looked like she was fighting back tears. I presumed she was his wife. Rick was with his family unit.

"Well?" John demanded. "Okay then…you—*Mark*…"

John had pointed to Mark, who looked terrified. He was seated right next to Claude, and was sweating profusely and squirming from the uncomfortable heat before us. "Who gave you all the key?"

Mark stayed silent, completely unsure of what to answer. I could tell he did not want to give Rick away. The islander in the jumpsuit behind him placed his large hands over Mark's shoulders and started to wobble the chair back and forth in a threatening manner to get him to speak, or else he would be pushed into the fire.

"Please, no!" Mark cried hysterically.

"Speak now, or you will be pushed in," John demanded. "Which of my island people helped you gain access into the bunker?"

"I'll tell you!" Claude shouted, sounding very hoarse.

I looked over at Claude then to Rick. Rick looked horrified and deathly pale. Claude stared at John with malice. "Jim King gave me the key…"

John did not look pleased with that response. He was about to open his mouth to reply, when Claude shouted again. "Jim King came under my wing. We had a plan to take TOM down. I never wanted to join your *cult*. Jim was the key in helping me take down this organization. He might not have told me he was a member of TOM, but I knew Jim was passionate about our invention. Towards the end, I knew he'd become paranoid that he might have been discovered. I had a phone call with him a few weeks before, while he was at a show at the Hollywood Bowl with Patrick. His paranoia was warranted, since apparently, as I learned today, Jackson had found out he had double-crossed TOM. After all the work your organization did to hide PA 619 from the world, it still brought us here, to stare you straight in the eye and curse you for your sick agenda."

"PUSH HIM!" John ordered to the islander behind Claude, pointing at him with a deranged and angry stare. The man appeared to hesitate for a moment. John yelled again, "WHAT THE HELL ARE YOU WAITING FOR? PUSH HIM INTO THE FIRE!"

Claude Bernstein had been my professor almost two decades ago. It was around that time frame that Jackson Killington was working with him on his Forecaster invention idea, which he'd then stole. Claude had been a mentor of mine, and he'd pushed me hard in school and inspired me to one day teach. I had become a professor myself and made a vow to follow in his footsteps. It was strange, that in that moment, we were going to die together. By *fire*...

"Patrick, you have the ambitious fire inside you to burn forever. Never give up." That was a piece of wisdom Claude had once given me when I was younger. I had not forgotten it. How ironic it was to be restrained before a giant fire. I wanted to laugh at how ironic life was at that moment, but the heat was making it difficult for me to move my face. I yelled out my final words to Claude.

"You're a phoenix, Claude! You will be reborn from the ashes. You have the ambitious fire inside you to burn forever. Never...never give up!"

My throat was sore from shouting my words of honor to the man I called my mentor. He stared at me with pride and smiled. I could see his eyes swelling with tears.

"I killed three people in my life," Claude shouted. "This is my justice."

Three people? I thought. *I only knew he killed Royce and the islander he shot by the hangar yesterday. Who was the third?*

Claude's eyes opened wide in horror as the islander behind him kicked his chair over with his foot. Mallory and Mark shrieked in terror, as they were the closest to him. Claude and the chair fell into the fire, and his agonizing screams echoed into the dark night and over the ocean beyond. The screams cut off suddenly, and the flames silenced him as they licked his raw flesh into ash. I wanted to cry and scream, but I knew that Claude would have preferred to die than to ever join the ranks of The Omniscient Minds and become a part of The Presence.

Natasha walked up to the podium where John was standing. She had Francesca's camera bag over her shoulder. She handed it to John and gave a mischievous smirk to Francesca, who returned a dark, angry look.

"You've been filming my island," John said tauntingly, swinging the camera bag left and right like a pendulum before us. His arm was outstretched over the fire, in preparation to toss it into the pit. That footage was our ticket to exposing TOM to authorities, but as we were tied up to chairs in front of a fire awaiting our execution, it did not matter anymore. John set the camera bag down on the podium after teasing us. I found it strange that he had not thrown it into the pit right then and there, but I realized why. "This reporter was planning to make her big story," he taunted Francesca. "When it's your turn to burn, I'll throw the camera in with your body, so that your flesh and camera burn together."

His words were quite morbid. It was hard to imagine that this was Jim's father. Jim had never spoken of his father to me, and I had no idea what John King's history was. I recalled seeing a photograph of a younger John King wearing an army uniform in Jim's basement, but all I'd known was that he was estranged from Jim. I only knew a bit about his alias, Kingsley, who was head of security at Phoenix Airlines, and was almost unrecognizable from the photo I'd seen. Jim had never mentioned his father worked at our company. I saw Rick shuffle slightly. He bent over and whispered into his son's ear. His son nodded and quietly slipped away from the crowd of islanders. It was then that it occurred to me how disturbing it was for a child to see the execution of adults, but they seemed unfazed by it. I imagined it had been a common practice on the island.

Where did Rick's son go? I pondered, trying to stop thinking about how painful my death by fire was going to be. I grew up in Montana, where the winters were cold. I was not a fan of humidity or heat—both of which were being inflicted on me by the climate and the fire pit.

John raised his arms again and spoke. "Before I oust all of you to your fiery tombs, I'd like to share some wisdom of The Presence. I'm surprised that none of you asked how we began."

Of course I have thought about it, I said to myself, *but I'm a bit preoccupied with my impending death.* Even in the moment of true fear at the end of my life's timeline, I found sarcasm in the deepest parts of my personality. It did not matter who or what The Omniscient Minds were, since we would not live to tell the tale and expose them to the world beyond these oceans. However, my curiosity did get the best of me. It would be nice to learn why the hell these people did the disgusting and inhumane things they did to hide secrets while operating in stealth.

"The Omniscient Minds," John began, "came into existence during the

Industrial Revolution. During that era, income and manufacturing grew. Inventions, ideas, and new processes became a part of everyday human life. Humans built machines to help make our lives easier. Transportation methods such as the railways and steamboats grew in this era. So many important technological developments came from that revolution. The pioneers of that era were made up of some of the most brilliant minds in the world. Artists like Beethoven were among our ranks. Inventors and geniuses like Thomas Edison and Albert Einstein were early members of TOM. Amelia Earhart was a member as well, and she feigned her disappearance on her world flight in 1937 to work and live on TOM Island. Her airplane is actually on display in a chamber inside our castle over there. The most significant mystery in aviation history was her disappearance, followed by Flight 619. But both of those mysteries end here, and they will remain buried here forever.

"The most influential members of The Omniscient Minds, most recently the Killingtons, have shaped the history of the modern world we live in today. The founders of the biggest computer and operating systems of the world are part of our ranks. We possess influential political leaders and the heads of certain government agencies. Some of Hollywood's A-List actors and directors are in our ranks too. We are everywhere; we are unstoppable, because without our power, influence, and wealth, many of the operations of the world that civilians rely on would not exist. And now that I have been bumped up to headmaster and Keeper of The Presence, my colleagues in the American political system will help me use the Killington financial inheritance to fund and build a campaign for president of the United States of America in the next few years. It will be the first time that a U.S. president is a member of The Omniscient Minds. That is my ultimate goal. We need that political and leadership clout to continue to operate in stealth."

I could not believe my ears. TOM was much more powerful than I'd ever fathomed. That made them extremely dangerous. The thought of John King running for president made me sick to my stomach. He had no political experience, but because he was rich and powerful with deep-rooted connections, he had the privilege of running for the single most important position in the country, if not the world. And that was what Jackson Killington meant when he told us that John King had something more sinister in store with his rise to power. John craved to be the leader of the free world, with a drunken lust for power.

"Now," John said with intense passion, "let's finish off the ousting of our visitors. Alton, push that young man in!" John pointed at Mark.

Mark's eyes opened in horror, and he began to plead for mercy. The islander behind him, named Alton, put his hands on Mark's shoulders. A few seconds passed, and nothing happened. Mark stopped screaming to try and turn his head back to see why the man who was ordered to execute him was stalling.

"What are you waiting for, Alton?" John hissed. "Push him into the pit!" Alton looked at John and smiled, but he stood still, with his hands on Mark's shoulders. Mark was shaking uncontrollably in fear and the anticipation of being pushed over. He closed his eyes and mumbled something. It sounded like he was praying. I caught a few words he was saying: "love" and "Travis."

I saw Rick's son reappear behind the stage that John was standing on. He reached for Francesca's camera bag and grabbed it. Then he ran away, out of sight. Nobody noticed him except me, because everyone's attention was on Mark. What was the boy's motive for taking the camera? I heard a ringtone. The sound was coming from Robert Wong. He reached into his pocket and pulled out a satellite cell phone.

John looked over at him, visibly annoyed, and spat, "We are in the middle of a ritual! Can that call wait?"

Robert ignored John and listened intently to whoever was on the line with him. He looked horrified by whatever he was being told. He put a hand to his mouth, then looked up at the sky. I looked up as well, and saw a star that looked brighter than the rest of the stars in the sky. There was a full moon on that cloudless night. John also looked up in confusion.

The bright star seemed to be growing larger. *Strange*, I thought.

Robert spoke into his cell phone, "Are you sure? How did it happen? I can see it in the sky! No, don't alert NASA right now." Robert ended the call and ran to the stage to whisper something into John's ear.

"What?" John yelled loudly. "How can that be?" He looked back up at the sky and clasped his mouth with his hand in horror.

The bright star, which had been white in color previously, now looked red and orange, and it was growing larger and larger with every passing second. I could hear gasps from the crowd of islanders as many of them began to point at the sky. I caught the words of one elderly woman islander say, "Is that the Eye of the Sun? The time has come! It's Judgment Day!"

Several of the islanders began to scream and cry. A few of them ran off into the forest and up the hill back to the Town Square.

"Stop!" I heard Natasha yelling at some the islanders who had fled in fear.

The fiery light above was magnificent. It resembled a comet. The closer it got to Earth, the longer its orange-red tail of fire became. It was heading towards us.

Francesca turned over to look at me and said, "What the hell is that?"

"It's a phoenix," I said, without thinking about how ridiculous that statement was. "Claude has been reborn. He's coming back for us from the heavens." At that point, the heat of the fire had gone to my head, and I was already mentally drained from the anticipation of being executed; I was not in my right mind. I imagined I was hallucinating as the fiery comet plummeted toward us. The closer it came to the island, the more light it gave us. It was still very high, so we could hear no sound of it during its impending fall.

"What's going on?" Joseph asked Robert.

Robert ignored Joseph and ran full speed up the hill in the direction of Town Square. Joseph, Colin, Randolph, Ted, and Natasha stood transfixed at the sight of the fiery orb. John climbed down off the stage, said something to them, and pointed up the hill.

He then looked back at my friends and me and said, "It looks like you will still burn." And without a glance back, John and his TOM disciples ran up the hill in the direction of where Robert and some of the other islanders had fled. We were left dumbstruck. I felt the chains behind us loosen.

"We should head for the hills," Alton said. "The Eye of the Sun is coming."

"You're letting us go?" Mark said.

Before Alton could answer, Rick cut in. "We really have been held prisoners here. You were telling us the truth. I sent my son to free your people from the bunker. Perhaps the Eye of the Sun wanted to distract the masters from ousting you so that we can help you escape. We need to move before the fire hits us."

"Thank you," I said with gratitude, as I got up from the chair and onto my feet. Francesca ran over and hugged me tightly. We exchanged a passionate kiss.

"Let's go!" Craig said. "It's going to hit the beach!"

I heard yells in the distance. I looked around. All of the islanders were gone except for Rick and the six men who had carried us over to the chairs. I looked back at the castle and saw hundreds of people running out of the entrance.

"Oh my God!" Francesca said with delight and laughter. "It's the PA 619 passengers! There must have been a way up into the castle from the bunker's auditorium since it was technically right below it!"

The passengers were yelling in both fear and excitement. Some of them saw the comet plummeting toward the island and picked up their haste and ran. I noticed several of them were carrying pieces of luggage that must have belonged to them. Their luggage had been stored inside a room of the castle. For a moment, I thought about running in to get mine, but decided that the only valuable thing I had lost was my Rolex watch and Joseph was wearing it.

"EVERYONE!" I shouted. "Head up to the hills and into the town. There's something heading towards us!" I was pointing up at the sky. The passengers who had not noticed the comet previously had now seen it and were screaming in terror.

"Let's go!" I yelled to Francesca and the others.

We sprinted up the hill to put as much distance between the pit we were almost burned alive in and the fireball plummeting from the heavens. It was mass chaos. Hundreds of passengers and islanders were scrambling up the hill and through the forest. It took us about five minutes to get to the top of the hill and back into the town. Several of the islanders had taken refuge in the Dining Hall or in their cabins. We had a perfect view of the beach, castle, and hangar with the seaplane below. The sound of the comet had reached our ears. I could hear the sizzle of fire and whistling sound it made as it picked up speed. The entire island was lit by an orange glow. I could feel the warmth of it on my skin.

"Where do you think John and his goons disappeared to?" Francesca asked.

"They must be headed to their sky rider on the runway," Rick, who had followed us up the hill, chimed in. "But it doesn't matter, I tore apart its engines and slashed its tires."

"No way?" I said with amusement. "Thank you for that!"

"You promised to help my family unit and our people," Rick said with great pride. "We wanted to help you as well. I had my son Philip run to the castle to release your people from the bunker. My son and I have been in that castle many times, so he knew how to free them through the basement chamber door."

"You're amazing!" Mallory piped in. "Thank you!"

The sound of the comet grew louder and louder. I put my hands over my ears as the noise intensified. The screams and shouts from the islanders and passengers who were scurrying about Town Square ceased. Or perhaps the sound of the comet was so loud that it drowned out their voices. Everyone stopped in their tracks to look at the fireball. The light it was emitting was so bright, I had to squint and shield my eyes. I was never a religious person, but a part of me felt like this was Claude being reborn from the ashes of his death. He was like a phoenix. The phoenix was the symbol of the airline that had brought us to this island. It was apparent that the islanders had some kind of religion or cult-like belief that they were brainwashed with. The Eye of the Sun was like a God to them, from what I had deduced. They all believed that this was their God coming for them on Judgment Day. If I had been a religious person, I might have believed it too, but I was more preoccupied with trying to figure out what this comet was. I did not think it was a rock from space.

I did not scream. I stayed quiet and braced for the fireball's impact. I think everyone around me might have been screaming. Some people had run for cover into nearby buildings, but I just stood there transfixed, along with my friends and Rick. The fire lit up the entire island. It gave the illusion that it was daytime. The fireball made impact and hit the side of the stone castle. There was a loud explosion. We all braced ourselves and fell to the ground. The light from the explosion was so intense, I had to close my eyes. There was an intense wave of heat and the sound of stone crumbling. The explosion echoed across the ocean. The hangar had also fallen victim to the impact. It had been set ablaze by the tail of fire that fell onto the island. My heart sank, knowing that our only escape from the island was via that seaplane. Rick had damaged the airplane that the members of TOM had arrived on. We were now trapped.

Rick stood up and looked at the fire at the bottom of the hill. The castle had been destroyed. It felt almost poetic and even ironic. Rick said, "The Eye of the Sun knew the masters were evil. He chose to destroy their foundation."

Robert Wong walked up right beside me and it caught me by surprise. Francesca reached for a rock on the ground, in preparation to throw it at him.

"You might as well take me out," he said. "We're all trapped here. Our jet has been incapacitated. The castle is gone. Peeping Tom is destroyed. There's nothing we can do."

I looked at Robert in disbelief. He looked as though he had been defeated. His designer suit had been torn up and was full of dirt and leaves from his run through the forest. He looked like a man who had come to terms with his fate.

"The Peeping Tom is destroyed?" I asked.

"That's what crashed into the castle," he said. "Somehow, it fell out of orbit above us in space and crashed right onto the island."

"Serves you right!" Craig spat.

"I can't believe you all were a part of PA 619's disappearance," I said angrily to Robert. "Innocent lives were lost. The passengers have been separated from their families for over a year. Their families think they are dead."

Robert avoided eye contact with me. He turned his back to me and said, "You could have been a member of TOM, Patrick. You have the makings of one. The only thing is, you would have never chosen to join our ranks, because you have a heart, and our ideals do not match your morals. You are a good man. I am not. In the name of the Eye of the Sun, I pledge my failure."

Robert pulled out a gun from his jacket. I flinched and backed away with my arms outstretched to shield Francesca. Robert put the barrel of the gun to the temple of his head. We all looked away as he pulled the trigger. I opened my eyes after the ringing in my ears from the gunshot subsided. Robert was lying facedown on the ground in a pool of his own blood. Mallory started sobbing into Craig's shoulder.

Rick's son Philip came running out of one of the cabin homes. He had Francesca's camera bag and my backpack over his shoulder. He must have retrieved my backpack from inside the castle when he was freeing the passengers from the bunker. He rushed towards Rick and gave him a hug. Rick took my backpack from his son and handed it to me, and then he grabbed the camera bag and passed it along to Francesca.

"Now you can show your world—the modern world—the conditions of our people. We hope that they can welcome us with open arms," Rick told her.

"If we get off this island," Francesca said, "I will make it my duty to make sure each and every one of you is taken care of." Francesca turned to look at me and held her camera up in triumph. "We have our proof now." I smiled at her and winked.

I turned my attention to the castle ruins at the bottom of the hill, and watched as the flames lazily licked and burned hundreds of years of The Omniscient Minds' history into ash and charred stone. It was over. There was no way that they would ever return to power. *How did the satellite fall out of orbit? I pondered. It seemed almost too coincidental that it crashed when it did. The timing was impeccable. It had saved us from a death by a pit of fire. Maybe it was Claude watching over us?* My only concern now was getting off the island, but as fate would have it, the next morning brought us an interesting turn of events.

August 28, 2017

The sun had risen over the Pacific Ocean. Nobody had been able to get any rest in the excitement of the satellite's impact on the island. Rick had alerted us that we were needed at the runway. It took us some time to get down there, but when we arrived, the scene before us was powerful. Francesca pulled out her camera to document it. Most of the population of islanders had surrounded John, Natasha, Colin, Joseph, Randolph, and Ted. The islanders had apprehended them and tethered them to chairs, similar to what they had done to us at the fire pit. There were even a few of the PA 619 passengers in the crowd as well. John looked furious.

"The Eye of the Sun will not be pleased," he spat at the islanders. "Release us. We are your masters. We bring you food and supplies from the modern world. Without us, you will starve to death."

"Silence!" Rick ordered. "We've learned the truth. You've allowed us to live here because we were born on this island, but you deprived us of the *real* world out there. Patrick and his friends told us everything from how you kidnapped the passengers of the sky rider in the hangar behind me that I am Keeper of."

I looked over at the hangar and spoke to Rick. "Do you think that airplane can still fly?"

Francesca shook with excitement and jumped in, "Of course! We can use it to fly out of here!"

Rick looked at me and smiled, "Absolutely, Patrick. We have refueled it using fuel that the masters had brought in their smaller sky rider that no longer functions. The larger sky rider in the hangar is able to operate."

Mark and Craig shouted with excitement and were soon joined by a few of the PA 619 passengers in the crowd.

"Does anyone here know how to fly a Boeing 787?" I asked. "The pilots who originally flew it were murdered at the hands of these people." I pointed to John and the others he was tied up next to.

"I can fly," Joseph said squirming in the chair he was tied to. "I was the one who helped orchestrate its journey here in the first place."

I walked over behind Joseph and reached for his wrists. He had a look of relief in his eyes, as he thought I was about to untie him. I unsnapped my gold Rolex from his wrist and turned it over to see my initials engraved on the back of it. Then, I put it rightfully back on my wrist. "This belongs to me," I whispered slyly into his ear.

"The magnetic barriers that surround the island have been taken down," Rick informed me. "The controls were in the castle, but once it was destroyed by the object that fell from the sky, it powered down the magnetic fields. It will be safe to fly."

A man from the crowd walked up to me. He was wearing a blue jumpsuit, but I could tell he was not one of the islanders, since he was pale from lack of sun and imprisonment in the bunker.

"Hello," he said. "My name is Aaron Moss. Captain Aaron Moss. I'm a licensed commercial pilot. I was a passenger on board PA 619, flying to China for a vacation with my wife." Aaron pointed to a woman in the crowd, signifying she was his wife. She waved nervously at me. "I can fly PA 619 for you. Our best bet is to fly to the Sydney Airport." Several passengers cheered, cried, and hugged each other at Captain Moss' words.

"Great!" I said with excitement. "Then it's settled."

Rick put his arm on my shoulder and said, "Take the people from the bunker back in that sky rider. That's how they arrived here, and that's how they should escape. Will you promise to come back for us?"

"Absolutely," I assured him. "Keep these scumbags alive." I shot a dark look at John, Natasha, Joseph, Randolph, Colin, and Ted. "When we send rescue to get you, we'll want to make sure they are alive so they can be questioned by the authorities of the modern world."

"Mister! Mister!" came the sound of Rick's son running down the hill from Town Square. He had a metal object in one arm and was waving at me with the other. He passed me the object when he got to me. It was the flight data recorder from PA 619. "I found this in the ruins of the castle. The masters kept it guarded in a room and it looks undamaged. It belonged to the big sky rider."

"Thank you!" I told him giving him a pat on the back.

"This is amazing!" Francesca looked delighted. I could see ideas for her story churning in her eyes. This was one hell of an article in the making. What was the world going to think when PA 619 reappeared in the sky?

An hour later, all of the surviving original passengers of PA 619 boarded the airplane. The islanders had cleared the runway and locked their "masters" inside the hangar after Captain Moss had maneuvered PA 619 out of it and positioned it on the runway in preparation for takeoff. I looked at the magnificent silver airplane in awe. The red tail with the white Phoenix bird logo with its wings outstretched, to me, symbolized it being reborn to take to the skies from which it had vanished over a year ago. *Born to fly*, I thought, thinking about the tagline from the Phoenix Airlines commercials.

We said our goodbyes to the islanders and promised them we would send help to rescue them within the next few days. Francesca, Craig, Mallory, Mark, and I were the last ones to board Flight 619. Cheers and cries of joy from the original passengers greeted us. An elderly female passenger began to sing "Amazing Grace." A few more passengers joined in, and then the entire cabin was belting the song with pride. We took our seats at the front of the airplane. I gave a thumbs-up to Aaron, who had left the door to the cockpit open. He powered up the plane. It sputtered slightly and shook as the engines rumbled on after being shut down and unused for so long. The air conditioning came on and cooled the cabin.

"The transponder is on," Aaron yelled back to me. "We should be popping up on radar soon. The nearest air control tower is going to freak out—in fact, I'm sure the entire world is going to freak out when an airplane that was believed to have crashed a year ago reappears on radar."

"It'll make one hell of tale," I said to Francesca, followed by a kiss. I hesitated for a moment, because now that I knew we were going to survive and escape TOM Island, I knew that I would have to continue my journey alone with my final battle with cancer. I had made that decision months ago. The thought of it made me sad, but I distracted myself with the prospect of how her story would blow up as she told the tale of what really happened to PA 619. The families of these passengers were about to be in for the biggest reunions of their lives.

The captain's voice came over the speaker, "Ladies and gentlemen, we are about to takeoff. Please fasten your seatbelts and turn off all electronic devices and cell phones." Everyone laughed at his joke, because the passengers had been stripped of their phones when the plane was hijacked. "Prepare for takeoff."

I took off my seatbelt and walked into the cockpit. "Mind if I co-pilot with you?" I asked.

"Sure," Aaron answered. "You'll pretty much just sit there and do nothing."

"That's what I was expecting," I laughed.

There was a beeping sound, and a voice came in over the radio. It was still functioning properly.

"Hello? Hello? Hello?" came the excited voice of someone from air traffic control. "Is there anyone there?"

"Hello, this is Aaron Moss. I am a survivor of Phoenix Airlines Flight 619 and a pilot. We have commandeered the airplane after being imprisoned on an island for over a year. Most of the passengers are alive and well and are with us on board. Patrick Baldwin and a few of his friends have rescued us. He's seated right next me. Can you clear us to land at SYD?"

"Oh my God!" the person on the radio cried. There was a murmur of excited voices coming through. "I can't believe it! The plane never crashed?"

"Nope," Aaron said with glee. "We're coming home!"

"PA 619—you're clear for landing. We'll have emergency services on hand upon landing, as well as military personnel! Oh my God. This is a miracle! God speed!"

I looked out the window and saw the islanders waving us off. The plane picked up speed, and we flew into the air, leaving the island behind with hundreds of miles of ocean separating us from Australia. We ascended over the clouds, and PA 619 was officially back on radar, communicating its position with satellites in space. At long last, I had made my flight on PA 619. I laughed to myself thinking about how crazy it was to be sitting in the cockpit of a plane that was thought to have been lost forever and became the biggest mystery in aviation history. A few hours into our journey, two Royal Australian Air Force jets flew on each side of the airplane and escorted us on the rest of our journey back to Sydney.

Captain Moss spoke into the intercom to relay a final message before landing: "Ladies and gentlemen, as we start our descent, please make sure your seat backs and tray tables are in their full upright position. Make sure your seat belt is securely fastened and all carry-on luggage is stowed underneath the seat in front of you or in the overhead bins. Oh wait—we don't have luggage anymore!"

The entire cabin laughed, cheered, sang, and cried as we entered the Sydney airspace and touched down at the airport. We were greeted by thousands of strangers and the media upon our arrival. It was one of the most emotional moments of my life. There was not a single dry eye on board Flight 619. Francesca gave me a passionate kiss before we got off the airplane.

When we broke apart from our kiss, she said, "We have one hell of a story to share with the world."

"The survivors of Phoenix Airlines Flight 619 are almost home," I said. "You get to share their stories, Francesca."

Home, I thought, *is my cabin in Montana, where I can finally rest in true quiet.*

32

Two Years Later

Francesca Fields was sitting on a chair and looking into her compact make-up mirror. She could feel the warmth of the intense and strategically placed lighting above her. There were two large cameras on tripods in front of her. One was pointing at her and the chair she was seated on, and the other was directed at an empty chair next to her. She closed her compact and put it in her purse. She placed her purse behind the chair and out of the shot. She reached for a book that was on the table in front of her. On the cover was a photo of Patrick Baldwin deplaning Phoenix Airlines 619. A news outlet had taken the famous photo on August 28, 2017. It was the day PA 619 had resurfaced in the world and landed in Sydney. The title of the book was *A Bold Win for Baldwin*, by Francesca Fields.

A man with silver-white hair, piercing blue eyes, and a defined jawline walked onto the set and sat in the empty chair next to Francesca.

"Nice to meet you, Miss Fields," the man said while one of his make-up artists came to powder his face.

"Thanks for having me on your show, Mr. Harrington," she said politely.

"My pleasure," he said, "and call me Chris."

"We are going on live in thirty seconds," a female production assistant announced to everyone on the soundstage.

Francesca took a deep breath. She was not sure why she was nervous.

She had done many live TV interviews before. This one was different, however. Her previous interviews were about her survival from the clutches of The Omniscient Minds. This one was about the newly published novel she'd written about her late ex-boyfriend, Patrick Baldwin, and his journey to finding the once missing Phoenix Airlines 619. Francesca wrote it in honor to the man she had once loved. She could feel old emotions stirring up inside her. She stared at the cover with pride.

"Rolling! And we're live!" the production assistant yelled.

"Hello, America," Chris announced, staring at the camera that was pointing at him, "and welcome to *Live with Chris Harrington*. Today's special guest is former *L.A. Times* reporter and now *New York Times* best-selling author, Francesca Fields. Hello, Francesca! Thank you for joining us this morning."

"No, thank you for having me," Francesca said with a large smile.

"We're so pleased to have you. So, you're here to talk about your new novel, *A Bold Win for Baldwin*. It is common knowledge that you wrote this in honor of Patrick Baldwin, to share his story and your account of the dangerous journey you endured in the search for Phoenix Airlines 619. Patrick was your boyfriend back then, was he not?"

"He was," Francesca said, turning slightly red. "We had been dating for several months."

"Was it difficult to write about him?" Chris asked.

"You know, Chris, it was. I would say it was more cathartic, really. He and I took a big risk when we journeyed to the island where The Omniscient Minds hid the airliner. We had grown stronger as a couple, but upon our return, we were thrown into the national and international spotlight. We were instant celebrities. They called us heroes. Patrick was the true hero, but he did not want the attention or spotlight. He told me it was too much for him, and a week later, he broke up with me." Francesca wiped a tear from her eye with a tissue she had pulled out of her pocket. "It was the last time I ever saw him."

"Patrick passed away a few months later in the comfort of his cabin in his hometown in Montana, correct?" Chris asked.

"Correct. He died of lung cancer. It seemed like his condition came out of nowhere, but if I remember correctly, he was looking very ill in the last few months we were together. I was very heartbroken. There were so many things I wished I could have said or asked him."

"It seems as though he left you with great pain," Chris added.

"He did, but his story deserved to be told. I wanted to honor him regardless, because I loved him. I knew he loved me too. He just had to get away from the spotlight. See, I was writing for the L.A. Times back then, and I had brought back footage we'd shot on TOM Island. I wrote the biggest story of my life and used the footage to share with every major news outlet. Patrick did not want to be a part of this worldwide attention. It became too much for him."

"It was the story of a lifetime," Chris agreed. "What an incredible and remarkable journey. And to think, there was a group of powerful and influential people behind the hijacking of PA 619. John King, Natasha Wilkins, Ted Holt, Colin Shaw, Joseph Conroy, and Randolph Smith are currently in federal prison for life. Do you feel justice has been served?"

"I do. Many people felt they should have been given death sentences for what they did. They stole over a year of the passengers' lives, and even committed treason against our country."

"All the members of The Omniscient Minds, which was a secret society whose sole purpose was to control our world from their powerful positions, have been apprehended or tended to. Some of the members' names could not be released due to their prominent positions as public figures in society. However, the FBI and other authorities have dealt with them and punished them accordingly. One of the shocks of the uncovering of TOM was that Jackson Killington had also been a huge part of the group. He was believed to be dead. We learned that he had ordered his members to hijack PA 619 because three engineers and Patrick were supposed to be on that plane. They had their own secret, right?" Chris reached for a bottle of water and took a quick swig of it as the camera cut to Francesca.

"Yes, they were planning an invention called the HyperTube, which as you know, is now becoming a reality. Plans to build a line from L.A. to Las Vegas are underway for preliminary testing before expanding wider. It's being spearheaded by my friend and fellow survivor, Mark Crane."

"Mark Crane is finishing out the plans that Claude Bernstein had once envisioned," Chris said. "May he rest in peace. Claude was also rightfully credited as the original inventor of the Forecaster after it was revealed Jackson Killington stole his idea. The Forecaster was then carried out by his son Royce who, I must add, was unaware that the idea was stolen. Now, do you think the HyperTube will bring down the aviation industry? This was what Jackson Killington and the rest of TOM once feared."

"I don't think so," Francesca replied. "It'll be decades before the HyperTube expands globally enough for it to really make a dent, if it succeeds."

Chris smiled. "Well, there is one airline company that won't need to worry—Phoenix Airlines. They folded as a company after CEO Natasha Wilkins was arrested. Phoenix is now a distant memory. Let's go back to the book for a moment. There's a chapter in it where you talk about your volunteer work with the islanders from TOM Island. Can you tell our viewers about that and their current progress since being introduced and socialized in our *modern world*?"

"Absolutely," Francesca said. "A week after we returned PA 619 with the passengers who survived, the United States military sent out ships to rescue the islanders and bring them to America. They were taken to a base near San Diego, where they lived in a camp. I joined a group of volunteers that helped care for them and socialize them with our world. None of them had ever seen a TV or a computer. They had never been in a car. We had to have several counselors on hand to give them therapy treatments. And for the survivors of PA 619, well, many of them had to go through similar treatments. They'd lost a year of their lives and were being brainwashed by a virtual reality simulator. We have since learned that the technology used for that VR experience was a government patent weapon. Since some members of TOM were or had connections to the CIA, they were able to gain access to such equipment, and were using the passengers as test subjects for the weapon. It's not clear if TOM was going to use the passengers for something military related. Because these survivors went through such a traumatic ordeal, many of them are in medical treatment or are taking weekly therapy. Some are suffering from posttraumatic stress disorder. My friend Craig, who was also with us on TOM Island, has had to take his daughter to many therapists since her reintroduction into her home. She was a passenger of Flight 619. They are both doing well now, and they are working hard to put the past behind them."

"Robert Wong was also a part of TOM," Chris added. "He was the CEO of Zyphone Communications, which has since been bought out by another technology company. Can you tell us about how you and Patrick infiltrated the corporate offices to get information that was crucial to finding Flight 619?"

"Since the satellite was part of the U.S. government," Francesca said, "I've been asked not to comment about it. There's a short bit about it in my book, but government officials have asked that nothing further be discussed publicly. I'm sorry."

"Copy that. Well, moving along...there's one big mystery in this whole PA 619 story that was never solved," Chris addressed the camera. "Francesca and her friends were about to be executed in a pit of fire, but a satellite controlled by The Omniscient Minds crashed onto the island and destroyed a castle that the organization used as their headquarters. To this day, nobody at NASA or any aerospace engineers have been able to figure out how it fell out of orbit and crashed directly onto the castle. What are the odds? One in ten million?"

"Patrick believed that it was a sign from Claude," Francesca said. "He felt like Claude had returned as a ball of fire to save us. The islanders, on the other hand, had been brainwashed into thinking that there was some kind of powerful force in the universe called the Eye of the Sun. They believed it was the Eye of the Sun bringing down judgment on them on Judgment Day. I don't know what to believe, but I do know one thing...someone was watching over us that night."

"Well," Chris added, "thank you to Francesca Fields for coming on our show today. That's all the time we have. You can pick up her novel in bookstores today!"

"And...cut!" the production assistant yelled when the cameras stopped rolling.

"Thanks for having me, Chris," Francesca said. "I hope you enjoy your copy of the book."

"Thank you so much," he replied. "It's quite a thrilling tale. You're a very brave woman."

"Mr. Harrington!" Chris's make-up artist called for him. "You're needed on the stage next door."

"We'll keep in touch," Chris told Francesca before bidding her farewell and exiting the set of the show.

Albert and Georgia Baldwin lived a few miles away from their son Patrick's cabin in Missoula, Montana. Georgia's husband had Alzheimer's and was having a particularly bad day. She tucked him into his bed and kissed him on his forehead. She looked at him lovingly.

"I never thought we would outlive our children," she said sadly. "I miss Charlie and Patrick dearly. I miss *you* so much, Albert. You would have been proud of Patrick for saving those people from that island."

Georgia knelt down by the side of the bed and whispered a prayer for her husband. When she finished, she turned off the lamp on Albert's nightstand, where Patrick's Rolex watch was sitting. She then closed the door to their bedroom and walked downstairs to the living room, where a woman was waiting for her on her couch. She was wearing a fedora and drinking a cup of coffee.

"Bernadette, dear," Georgia said to her guest, "would you like more coffee?"

"I'm fine, Mrs. Baldwin," she replied. "Thank you for having me. It's really nice how close we live to each other."

"It really is, dear," Georgia said sweetly. "It's nice to finally meet in person and not just over the phone. So, you're Claude Bernstein's niece?"

"I am," Bernadette said. "And there's something I wanted to share with you about my uncle. This isn't easy to say, but I want to tell you now, because right before he went on that ship to that island with your son to find that airplane, he reconnected with me and told me his plan to take down that organization. He also shared some personal information with me."

Georgia's interest was piqued. She took a seat on a chair opposite of the couch that Bernadette was seated on and crossed her arms and listened.

"My uncle found a way to hack into the Zyphone Communication's satellite that crashed onto the island and essentially caused a distraction that saved your son from being executed. Unfortunately, my uncle was unable to escape that fate, but I think he welcomed the flames of that fire pit with open arms. Claude programmed the satellite to fall out of orbit and plummet to the coordinates of where the island was prior to boarding the ship, and even before he knew there was an island. He timed it for the duration of what he projected the journey to those coordinates at sea would be. He kept it a secret because he did not know who he could trust or if he was being watched. And it was a good thing he did, because his ally Kingsley ended up double-crossing him, as he was a member of that secret society. Claude saved your son and those people because he felt it would give him closure to something he had been dealing with.

"While it is now common knowledge that Claude was responsible for killing Royce Killington after being coerced by John King, and one of the TOM Island locals in self-defense, there is another death he was responsible for that he had kept a secret for a very long time. He told me before he went on that sea excursion. He never wanted Patrick to know, but now I think it's time you know the truth. My uncle was the man who killed your son Charlie. He made the mistake of getting behind the wheel after drinking one weekend, and your son was at the wrong place at the wrong time. It was a hit and run. Claude never forgave himself, and he made it his priority to take Patrick under his wing as a way of trying to find forgiveness for his sin. It was an accident, and Claude was so young back then, with hopes for a bright future. I'm very sorry, Mrs. Baldwin."

Georgia began to cry silently into her shawl. She looked at Bernadette straight in the eyes after a few minutes and said, "Things happen for a reason. Perhaps Charlie's death was meant to happen, so that decades later, the world would be saved from the control of that evil organization. Your uncle and my son played a role in exposing them to the world. Many lives were saved, and if Claude had been arrested, who knows what kind of world we would live in today. I forgive Claude, my dear, and I thank you for telling me this."

A few weeks later, after Francesca's book tour ended, she decided to take some time off and head to Patrick's hometown in Montana. Since he had broken off communication with her after their break-up, she had not learned of his death until months after it had happened. It haunted and hurt her to this day. It was a very lonely and empty kind of pain. It was a pain without closure. She felt compelled to travel to Montana to visit the cemetery where he was buried. Mark Crane was in town visiting his family at the same time. He had just met with Dean Brandon of his former university about taking a part-time teaching job and following in the steps of his late mentor, Patrick. He met Francesca at Patrick's tombstone. He was buried right next to his brother, Charlie.

Francesca and Mark embraced when they saw each other for the first time. "It's nice to see you somewhere other than on TV," Mark joked with Francesca. She laughed and smiled.

"It's nice to see you in person, too and not on some magazine article or news report," Francesca returned the humor. "It looks like your work on the HyperTube is coming along well."

"It is indeed," Mark said, looking longingly at Patrick's tombstone. "He would have been proud."

"Yeah, he would have," Francesca said. "And Claude too. Oh! Congrats on your engagement to Travis. I'm so excited for you two."

Mark blushed. "Thanks. He's wonderful, and he's been so supportive of me as I take on this HyperTube project."

"It's nice to see one relationship grew from our tangle with The Omniscient Minds and their greedy corporations," Francesca said, with tears of longing in her eyes.

"I'm sorry things ended without a resolution. I promised him I would never talk to anyone about his cancer," Mark told Francesca while putting his hand on her shoulder. "It seemed uncharacteristic of Patrick to just up and leave without telling you, but he had his reasons."

"I always felt that there was something more to his sudden departure from L.A.," Francesca said. "He came back to live here in private. And then he died of cancer. I understand why you didn't tell me, Mark. There's so much I wish I could have told him, though. I've longed for closure from our relationship. I really loved him."

"I don't know if this will be closure," Mark said while reaching into his pockets, "but I've met his parents, Albert and Georgia. They loaned me the keys to Patrick's cabin. If you feel comfortable, maybe we can go visit it. They gave me free rein to look around. It's been untouched since he passed away about a year and a half ago. Do you think it will help with closure?"

"Maybe," Francesca said hopefully. "Or it might be too difficult and emotional."

"We don't have to," Mark said.

"Let's go," Francesca said confidently.

Later that afternoon, Mark and Francesca arrived at Patrick's cabin in the woods. It started to drizzle as they stepped out of Mark's rental car. They ran to the front porch of the cabin and unlocked the door. Francesca shot a glance at two chairs rocking lazily from the breeze billowing through the porch before entering inside. The interior of the cabin looked as though it had not been touched in years. The air felt musty, and there was dust on the bookshelves and tables. Mark reached for a light switch, as it was pitch black inside.

"This place is giving me the chills," Mark said.

"It's as if I can feel his presence here," Francesca told Mark. "I know that sounds weird, but he did die here. It's this sense of energy that I can feel. It actually feels warm and inviting."

"It feels cold in here to me," Mark said, zipping up his jacket.

They spent the next hour digging through Patrick's old belongings. Francesca walked into his bedroom alone and found his bed. It had been made up. Francesca laid down on it and put her head against the pillow. She closed her eyes and remembered the day they had first met, in the courtyard of the Phoenix Airlines corporate offices. She opened her eyes and noticed another bookshelf up against one of the bedroom walls. She got up and walked over to it. There were several aeronautical books, and even the copy of Jackson Killington's biography, *Jackson Killington: The Man Who Made a Killing and a Ton of It.* Since Colin Shaw's arrest for his involvement with PA 619's hijacking and his membership with The Omniscient Minds, this book had gone out-of-print and taken out of bookstores across the country.

This was the copy that Royce Killington had given to Patrick a few years back. There was also a leather-bound book that looked familiar, perched on the bookshelf next to Jackson's book. Francesca reached for it, and her jaw dropped in awe. It was Patrick's journal that she had seen once before. The journal had his written accounts of his search for PA 619. The entries in the journal had spanned for over a year.

This would make an excellent novel, Francesca thought. *Maybe I could publish this.* She was about to call for Mark, who was sifting through a wardrobe closet in the living room, when a piece of paper fell out of the journal. It was a letter, and it was addressed to her.

"Oh my goodness," she whispered to herself as her heart began to race with excitement. She read the letter to herself. It was a letter that Patrick had meant to give her if they survived TOM Island, but for some reason, he'd failed to send it to her before he passed away.

August 14, 2017

Dear Francesca,

I know you will probably be angry with me. You might even hate me for doing this. By the time you read this letter, I will have gone my own way. The truth is, I love you. I love you more than anything in the world. You're my soulmate. We are destined for each other. PA 619 brought us together. I was diagnosed with lung cancer, and I found out the night I was feeling ill on our pizza date back in April. I could not bear it in my heart to have you deal with the decline of my health. The doctors said I had a few years left to live, but my tumor has progressed aggressively, and the treatments are way too invasive for it to be worth buying myself a few more months. I know it is not my choice to make for the both of us, but I do not want you to see me like this. I've chosen to live out the rest of my short life alone. I don't want you to see me in pain. I feel better knowing you are angry with me, and knowing you won't be wasting your time at my sick bed. I hope that you move on and find someone who will be there for you for a very long life. That is something I cannot give to you. I want to commit to you, but my time is limited. I know that when you read this, you will be sad and perhaps a bit of anger will surface.

That's perfectly fine. You have the right to be mad, but in my heart, I know I made the best choice for us. Seeing you hurt every day in my care would make my last days on Earth devastating. I will always love you. Thank you for making the last year of my life memorable. I love you dearly, Francesca Fields. To write my words down is to keep me immortal. Words will live on forever, even when I'm not around.

Love,
Patrick

Francesca sat on the edge of Patrick's bed in stunned silence. She folded the letter and put it in her purse. She had finally found the closure she'd never had. Patrick had left because he was hiding his diagnosis of cancer, and he had not wanted it to affect her. She felt angry that he had been selfish, making this choice without giving her an opportunity to make a choice for herself, but she understood Patrick well enough to know that this decision would have been extremely painful for him to make. She started to cry. Mark walked into the room and sat by her. He put his arm around her and gave her a tight embrace.

"There, there…" he consoled her. "I know it must be hard to be in this room."

"I found his journal," Francesca said, handing over the brown leather book to him. "It's very detailed. It's his account of his journey to solve the mystery of PA 619."

"Wow," Mark said in disbelief. He put the journal down on the bed and reached for one of Francesca's hands and squeezed it tightly. "Do you feel like this will bring you closure?"

"It already has," Francesca said.

Mark was looking straight into Francesca's eyes without blinking. They told a story that longed for a new chapter to be written, and now she could write it. Mark could feel the closure Francesca had received. A weight had been lifted off his shoulders, as the burden of keeping some of Patrick's secrets was over.

Francesca decided to keep the letter Patrick wrote to her a secret and not share it with Mark. She would take it with her to her grave, whenever that time came. In her mind, she could hear the last words of the letter Patrick had written to her being spoken as clearly as if he had been whispering into her ear:

To write my words down is to keep me immortal. Words will live on forever, even when I'm not around.

About the Author

Photography by Dexter Brown

A.J. MAYERS hails from the border town of Laredo, Texas. He spent his childhood dreaming of writing stories of spaceships and mysteries and turning them into books and movies. He graduated from the University of Texas at Austin in 2009 with a degree in Radio-TV-Film and moved to Hollywood, where he has worked in the entertainment industry. While writing books, he has juggled working full-time for MTV, Paramount Pictures, and most recently, Universal Pictures, in creative motion picture marketing. He's also a member of the board of directors for Boo2Bullying, an anti-bullying non-profit. He currently resides in Los Angeles, California, and is the father of a French bulldog named Dexter. He plans to write many more novels.

www.aj-mayers.com | www.finalboardingbook.com

 @AJMayersAuthor   @aj_mayers   @ajmayers